WHITE OAK FLATS

BOOKS BY RICHARD HOOD

Regret the Dark Hour
Carolina Blood
White Oak Flats

RICHARD HOOD

WHITE OAK FLATS

Down & Out Books
3959 Van Dyke Road, Suite 265
Lutz, FL 33558
DownAndOutBooks.com

The characters and events in this book are fictitious. Any similarity to real persons, living or dead, is coincidental and not intended by the author.

Cover design by Zach McCain

ISBN: 1-64396-224-8
ISBN-13: 978-1-64396-224-5

For Stoney...

OLD-TIME MOUNTAIN SONG

There's a place in Tennessee, just across the line,
No one ever goes up there, it's too rough a climb,
You won't find the name or place wrote on any map,
Folks down here 'round Shelton's Trace calls it
White Oak Flats.

Hazel Taylor was my wife, and I loved her so,
We was married on Shelton's Trace, fifteen years ago,
Now I lie here all alone, wonderin' on the past,
Wonderin' why she left our home to go to White Oak Flats.

I don't know how he looked at her, I don't know what he said,
I don't know what he could have done,
to turn poor Hazel's head,
Never in her darkest hour, could she imagine that,
She'd agree to go with him, up to White Oak Flats.

I can see the rocky trail up the mountain side,
I can see poor Hazel, now, lying by his side,
Folks down here still talks about how it come to pass,
Nothing but the silence now, up on White Oak Flats.

PROLOGUE

Andrew Kayer

There is a story about the bright wounds of youth and the dim regrets of age. It is about an extraordinary child fearing the old woman she may become and a dying old woman trying to understand the child she once was. It is a story, too, of one moment's decision to pick up and walk away. And it is about the flashes of violence and the long aching losses leading up to and away from that decision. And of the place, embraced and spurned, in youth and age, and a lifetime of justifying, questioning, measuring, reworking.

It is a story I found, and, like all true stories, as confused and uncertain as life itself. And yet, it is an arranged and composed tale handed to me by the old woman herself. A series of journal entries, but not left in order, as they were originally written. Rearranged, reordered, rebound, and passed on to me with hardly a word of introduction: "Here, take, read. This is my life."

And why me? To be brought into the life of a lonely woman who sits each day in the sun room of a Chicago nursing home, writing. Who has lived in Chicago for almost seventy years, but who seems to exist entirely apart, in a misty land of deep rocky hollows. Yes. I have to take a place within this narrative as well, because, like all listeners—readers—of stories, I have become both character and collaborator myself. And I don't know

1

whether I became agent or object of the story, whether I am finally the main character or whether I was a mere operative, a scene-shifter, who had to exist in order for the story to play its way out.

As I write this, I begin to feel her intonation, her inflections, speaking out of the words on the page, as if this were already her memoir we were reading. Because her voice speaks out of my own writing now, now that she has written her last sentence. Sentenced or reprieved herself. Or myself.

Because this is a story about guilt, too. Although the guilt seems difficult to place. It swells around and seeps into each character, a pool of complicity. Perhaps as much as anything else, this is a story about the spreading wake we throw out with every decision, every speech, every mere gesture. And about the fine and the evil people who inhabit each of us, tumbling and pushing and wrestling for advantage.

What am I hoping from passing this along? Well I don't know. I suppose I feel there is something to be learned from watching heroic people who fail. That is, after all, the soul of tragedy, isn't it? And this may be a tragedy. Mythic. Or it may be an enormous exercise in self-justification. Or neither. It may be merely a record of the everyday storms and stupidities of living. Or of trying to write what you live. Or of trying to attribute meaning, or of trying to pass it—something—along, out of a dark mountainous place inside us all, back and forth, among us all.

There are some things you need to know to make sense of the record I give to you. First, the majority of the narrative occurs as journal entries written by Hazel Taylor, born Hazel Tighrow, in 1905, in Maddy Creek, on Shelton's Trace, North Carolina. Who disappeared suddenly and without notice from that community in her twenty-second year. Who appeared to me, some seventy years later, in a nursing home in Chicago. And who, after precious little communication between us, began handing me packages of dense, evocative, writing. Narratives spread back and forth across a seventy-year gap, but focused, insistently, on that single night of her twenty-second year, when she turned back the covers, arose and walked out of her home, marriage, community, to escape the very self she was becoming.

In fact, there are two discontinuous journals involved. One is the journal kept by Hazel as a girl and young woman, a record that begins on the day of her mother's death, in 1917, and ends just after Hazel has made her disappearance, in 1927. The second journal was begun many years later, by the elderly Hazel, perhaps in anticipation of death, or in response to the kind of insistent call of memory that comes upon the very old. This latter record was begun in 1996, a few months prior to my meeting her, and it continued until the summer of 1998.

But I cannot present these writings as either complete or distinct narratives. This is because Hazel herself thinned the earlier journal, like a forester making a partial cut in a stand of cove hardwoods, and then edited and inter-leaved the more recent writings with what she kept from the earlier record. True to the beliefs Hazel had about how the story must be passed on, I have retained the pages in the order she constructed.

Meanwhile, true to Hazel's example, I have interspersed the other narratives: collected transcriptions of interviews I taped in a single visit to Shelton's Trace when, spurred by the vision of an intelligent and passionate young woman, I went in search of this place, and found the husband and one or two other survivors. Although these interviews were all made at the very end of my association with Hazel, they take a place—or places—in the overall volume very similar to Hazel's own commentary. And so I have put them where I thought they fit, according to Hazel's own rubric.

Finally, I have added my own voice, as sparingly as possible, in order to provide a context and perspective on the final period of Hazel's writing, and because she added some important words during our own conversations that serve as commentary of sorts to what she put on paper. These, too, I have arranged

3

as counterpoints to the journal entries, rather than as appendices or introductions to the entire record.

In presenting these pieces thus arranged, I hope to give you a fuller sense of the complexity of both Hazel and her story. This is important to me because I care so deeply for Hazel. More, in this America, where we struggle so hard to recreate values, communities, ideals that never existed in the first place, Hazel's story—of a real person with extraordinary sensibilities, from a very real, but vanished place—can tell us all something about ourselves as well as the people and places we have made and lost.

As for Hazel's place, like her journal, it has two distinct embodiments in this story. The second, current version is of little significance here except to mark the disappearance of the first. I speak here, of course, of a cultural, social disappearance, since the place maintains the same geology, and most of the same flora and fauna. Today, a major portion of the area is owned by the United States Department of Agriculture and makes up a relatively obscure section of the Pisgah National Forest. Whole belts of farmland, entire communities, have reverted to what we today call "the wild." Wandering near the land that Hazel and George once farmed in overalls and brogans, you will find no cultivated ground. Nor will you hear any banjos. You are far more likely to encounter a fleece-covered vacationer pitching a three-hundred-dollar tent than to see anyone whose ancestors grew up in these deep dark hollows, clearing and farming land that a more fastidious—or a weaker—person would shun. Today, swarms of wealthy Americans attempt to escape from the intolerable, aseptic prosperity they thought they wanted, and to which they have sacrificed time, sensibility, and most of their passionate, fleshly human contacts. They flee to the mountains in a grotesque reversal of Hazel's flight from them. And they find only themselves: identical middling-wealthy outfitter's models, squatting in scattered campsites all through these mountains, forlornly cooking freeze-dried delicacies over high tech, lightweight backpacker's stoves, and cursing each other for spoiling the quiet and the solitude.

Meanwhile, the dark, balsam-spattered mountains loom over them, eternal and patient. The wind roars through the last of the old hardwoods, with a sound it has made forever, a deep, rounded throb that can only be matched by the huge booming roar of the most abysmal sea, torturing itself with its own power. The bobcat, wary and smart, makes its groaning cough. The bear snuffs in her den.

The place Hazel knew was more populous than it is today, and yet much closer to the earth, the bobcat, and the wind.

Focal point of Hazel's story is one locale, stretched over the southernmost end of Lynco Ridge, a long, narrow serpent of a mountain that runs some twenty miles, northeast-to-southwest, from Southwest Virginia, though the point of East Tennessee, and across the sloping and bulging western boundary of North Carolina, and which provides the source for a fast mountain stream around which Hazel and her kith and kin gathered to live and to farm. The high, bald ridge-butt was known locally as White Oak Flats, though you can't find that name in registry or map. The same locals believed that the Flats were actually in Tennessee, "just across the line," but, in fact, the state line turns at this end of the ridge and runs due north-south, bisecting flats and ridge almost perfectly.

In truth, before the disappearance of Hazel Taylor, White Oak Flats couldn't be called a place, at all—not so much a reality in space as an idea, the endpoint of space or the headpoint of the unfamiliar, an indication of beyond. A measure of straying. Folks would gesture to it, verbally, as a general indication of the place where nobody goes. It served to enclose the usual, and to mark the outlandish: "I trailed that there bobcat clear up to White Oak Flats," or "You can look from here to White Oak Flats and you ain't a'going to find no damn bear."

The wide, slowly curved spur of the Flats narrows on its northern end and snakes away as a long, spiny ridge—unusual in itself in this country of close-packed knobs and coves. Coming along the narrow back of Lynco Ridge from the north, you would find the trail dropping to the west, to skirt the final extending crag. And then you would find the trail rising up, opening out, and giving way to a stretch of high bald plateau, enclosed by blackberry and hawthorn. The blunt, three-sided, south butt-end of the ridge leading down from the Flats is uniformly steep, and completely overgrown by scrub second growth—locust, sassafras, blackberry and laurel—wherever the rhododendron hells haven't yet completed what will one day be total conquest of these slopes. The sole means of access to White Oak Flats is either along the ridge from the north, or up a rocky, declivitous trail that half borders and half partakes of the rushing, perpetually frigid waters of what becomes a big, whitewatered mountain stream, known simply as "the Creek," that, lower down, will empty into the larger Laurel Creek. At the confluence of these two watercourses is the small, brushchoked island called Possy's Camp.

The presence of the Creek explains the presence of Shelton's Trace, a centuries-old community stretched along a series of natural granite terraces stepping the stream down through three narrow cataracts, known respectively as High Creek, "Maddy" Creek, and Low Creek. Three pools, or "beds," of water subsequent to each stretch of waterfall have deposited centuries of loam about them, just rich and substantial enough to support a series of tenuous farmsteads, where, eked out by hunting and a little fishing, the people of the community raised their generations of large, hard-working, thoroughly interbred families. Here they cleared, set out, suckered, cured and graded yearly patches of tobacco, meanwhile courting, marrying, breeding, fighting, and establishing fierce connections among three or four family lines: Sheltons, Taylors, Tighrows, Shorts, Blakenships.

This is the land of fiddle and banjo. Before the New Deal and the TVA, there was virtually no electricity or running water or regular medical care. Disease and death were never far away and hard, scrabbling work was the only answer to the insistent call of hunger and cold. Today, people look upon that time and that place as though it were an embodiment of simple, homespun peace. This stereotype is as far from the truth as it can be. And Hazel, whose life is neither simple nor peaceful, and who defies every image we have of the "mountain woman," may, in some extraordinary way, represent the enormous range of conflicts, tensions, abstractions, and real, gritty facts abiding in this dark time and place.

This sketch will, I hope, give you enough of a broad-stroke representation upon which Hazel can make her more detailed marks. Listen to her.

PART ONE

I.

JOURNAL OF HAZEL TAYLOR
May 10, 1996

I have to write about these things, because, long ago, I was involved in the killings, and the disappearances. And I have never determined who was perpetrator, who was victim...or at whom to point the accusing finger. So I suppose I have to start with me. I will try to write about this, and I will bring-out some writing I did back during the time. And perhaps I—or we—can come to some decisions.

But there is no real way to begin this, because there's no starting point to anything, no point where I have instantly become the *self* I believe myself to be today. Shuttered away in my past are those processes and progressions that have accumulated to become *today* and that we try in vain to pinpoint as turnings, or revelations, or what the poet calls them: *sudden rightnesses*. They aren't there. Nothing is sudden and certainly nothing is right, everything is only what it has become while it's on the way to becoming something else. No *I*, no *just now*, no *summing up*. Can't be done.

And still we sit and attempt the telling. I suppose that's the human thing, the attempt at telling, the pretense of moment, even when it's the very telling that exposes the illusion. *It wasn't like that at all*. However you try...

They used to put coal cinders on the asphalt road at the head of the holler, leading into town. I can see one as I remember it: a hard blueblack, glossy in semicircle, in oily purplish, its other half rough and misshapen, and unreflecting, like a glassy marble half covered in burnt caramel, except hard, hard as the marble. Actually, this, too, is impossible to describe, since I have to tell you about two things: the marble and the caramel, and the cinder isn't like that at all. It would not be what it was without the both: a blueblack glassysmooth sphere would no more remind me of a cinder than would a rough, lavalike whole. One thing, indescribable.

They would dump these cinders in the narrow road every now and again, and spread them out as a surface for folks to drive on. When they did that, the coal oil smell would suffuse the air. And without your knowing it, through the slow summer, the smell and the cinders themselves would gradually disappear, until, by autumn, you couldn't see any on the road. There were always a few along the side. You could always find a few. But only those out of all those piles of cinders dumped and distributed, inches thick, just a few months ago.

Whenever they first spread the cinders, you couldn't walk on the road. The sharp, hard edges would bruise and skin your bare feet. So you had to walk on the side, in the greens and sedge, where, once in awhile, you'd "tromp up a cinder," as Georgie said, and feel the deep bruise set into the bottom of your foot. But later those cinders had melted down, or spread out, or whatever miracle had slowly transformed them without your knowing it. And now you walked on the cool, smooth road again.

Or if there are important moments, they're not the ones we name in our tellings. More likely, they're moments of emptiness. I remember lying in the grass on the open side of Timb's Hill, after walking up the Creek from Badie's. And I cherish that lying in the grass. And luxuriating in that feel of tiredness and energy, another contrary, the sun warm in cool air, you know what I mean, fresh breeze on my face but my overalls hot where my thighs pressed them. You know what I mean. Some kids playing ball on a field on down below the curve of hill, the slow swing of bat and, later, the *chunk* of sound, and the high, thin voices that made my patch of grass on the hillside seem even stiller. Emptier.

There it is. And what part of me was that? What slow seeping of self was gathering up to make me what I have become? I will remember that moment for the rest of my life, but, in fact, it isn't a moment at all. It's a drawing out into elapse, the opposite of moment, indeterminate and dreamy. But there it is, and it must have some significance even if only because it blots out some other experience that no longer resides in memory, or anywhere.

Perhaps it's that link between the nothingness of the hillside and death. It may as well be, since this is a narrative about death, one death. Or several. Bear with me; I will begin soon.

It's just that it feels so important to try and know. How is it your life could became so linked up with one man, and then you look inside all the terrible violence and dismay and find…well, and find nothing at all. And then the other, coming along like my last link to something, after all. And what would he say? *Even when I never touched you, never had you in any way: not lover, not even friend, but some vague unrequited desire that I took to bed with me each night. I think it's important to tell you. Because if I betrayed anyone, it was you. Perhaps this is an apology for using you this way, disembodying you and rebuilding you in my own clouded, dirty, soot-stained soul. Perhaps.*

At times I try to picture you in your bodily self: the dripping of pancreatic juices and the chewed food descending, your interior smells and oozes. But it doesn't work, either because I have such an integrated picture of you that I can't dissect enough to enter into a part of you, or because you have become so attenuated as simply to have become the syllables of your name. As if the name itself is numinous the way our parents pathetically hope when they select, out of an impossibly paltry sequence of four or five letters, the word by which others will attempt to hold us. Sometimes I think that your name is, in fact, you. And then I realize that it's a totem—only my ritual reclamation of you as the embodiment or extrusion of everything I breathe, taste, smell—and so you disappear in the other direction again, so fully integral as to become everything. And so, nothing. You are not beautiful, you are beauty. And thus I eliminate you.

I've often enough told myself that I had to be crazy to do what I did, so maybe this is the sign and seal of my madness that I'm leaving behind me. A record of proof so that everyone can discount everything: *O it don't matter, she was plain crazy.* Does this make any sense at all? Or are you laughing, shaking your head and laughing, like Aunt Minny used to say, "What in the heavenly days?"

I could never explain to anyone all the reasons for going to that man. Perhaps I can explain them to you. Or at least to the you who resides in my own body. Because there is a self for each of us that no longer belongs to ourselves, but to those others who surround us in time and place. So there is a *you* that isn't available to yourself. It's that *you* that I carry with me, *my* version of *you*. It's a very real person, this self that is you, but that operates completely beyond your awareness or control. I can try, here, to bridge the gap: by telling the self, the *you*, residing within me, as I write to the *you* over there, dwelling within your own body, perhaps you can hear some echo of the interior conversations I've already had so many times with you.

Perhaps that's what the body is: the dwelling place of all these selves. A community made up of people passing and crossing and interacting, all bounded by this one place. It's these people who make the place, itself, since the embodied *me* is only the compendium of all these other selves, since they constitute my human experience, my interactions and stories, my self. It's something of a consolation to think of a version of *me* that has escaped my own group and is dwelling within yours, a real part of you so intimate that I can only quiver with an expectation forever delayed. I know

I'm there, in your body, ready to round a switchback or a corner and come into your awareness, perhaps a memory, perhaps a dream, a physical being within you. Even if only a looming question. What solace for a wounded soul!

I recall when Daddy sent me down to Lower Creek to fetch something, the morning after a big ice storm, when all the natural world was covered with a brilliant blanket of light. Everything was switched on by that clash of sunlight and ice, rayed in silvers and blues, so sharp you couldn't look anywhere for long, but had to wink and blink at the whole universe. The ice had bent down the rhododendrons over the trail so those on the right side had intertwined with those from the left and become the frame for a frozen curtain hanging across all the path. And each set of branches wound with another and the trail was just a succession of these thin walls of ice seven, eight, ten feet high, and the only way down the creek was to bust right on through them.

Every step shattered shards of sheer light.

JOURNAL OF HAZEL TAYLOR
July 30, 1920

I can't seem to shake that look from my mind. The way he kind of lowers at me and I can't tell whether to laugh or cry or run away. I shouldn't even be thinking about this at all so maybe this here writing is just a way to put it all aside, by finding some place to put him away on this sheet of paper, in this book. Like a story that's wrote down can't really be happening in the world itself, because if it is happening, a part of my life, how could it be a story that's wrote down. You see?

Maybe that's the reason why we write anything, to stand back and look at it someplace that isn't our own lives, because this life is too fast and too close even to feel anything, let alone understand, even the purest thing. Like death, and the things we write on tombstones, *here lies*, because *here* is in the words,

15

wrote down, someplace outside of our own lives and so we can breathe for a minute, looking at the dead folks over there. Because that's why we fear haints and ghosts, because they haven't been put into that tomb writing, they have no *over there* and so they stay right here and we can't get rid of them. Can we?

So I will try to write about Noah Kersin and maybe that way I can put him somewhere else. Because just like those haints, he needs a place outside myself and so this page can be his. Here lies Noah Kersin in this paper that isn't me and never will be me and he can be read about by whoever comes across him on this page, even if I'm finally gone far away across the world or in my grave even. He's on this page and you can look at him.

Kersin.

And what is he? He never was from around here and so he doesn't belong in any of our lives, rightly. But yet when he talks, you feel like he's known you a lot longer than anyone ever could. As though he's always able to know—not so much what you've done, as what you're going to be doing right now. Like as if he's never surprised at anything or anywhere he finds you, or he never even bothered to wonder about what you might be doing, since he knows already the one thing you're going to do, and there's no reason even to try to think farther than that, since everything you do will come to him before it does to you.

And the other thing is true, too. When he's around, you never seem to know what you're going to do. You feel stopped, somehow, by the man. Just his looking at you sets you to asking yourself about what you're fixing to do right now. It doesn't matter: you could be making the lye soap and just finished with the kettle and so you know you're going to do the dipping next, just like you've already done a thousand times, and here comes Noah round the tub and all at once you find yourself in a panic, inside, hollering at yourself: *What? What? Oughtn't I to be doing something? What? What?* It doesn't matter what you been doing up to then. There you are, standing there like a polled steer and your hands are dripping lye down your skirts just looking at Noah and wondering about your own self.

It's not just me. I've seen him do this to other people, too. The other day at Owen's forge when Molly was being shod. Owen had her fore leg up, scotched in between his knees the way he does and Molly and Owen kind of leaning on each other as if both of them are working together at getting one of them shod and the other one done with the shoeing. And Noah walks in and Owen has just driven the nail through, and Noah just begins to look at him, and slowly—ever so slowly—Owen lowers Molly's leg down and eases her back up to her own weight and very gradually he bends himself upright and puts his hammer hand on his hip, and never stops looking at Noah. But not deliberate. Confused, like he forgot what he was doing, forgot even that Molly was there, and looking at Noah as though the answer to what he, Owen, was up to might somehow come— had to somehow come—from that man's very look.

"Don't forget to clinch that there nail," Noah says.

JOURNAL OF HAZEL TAYLOR
October 12, 1923

I don't know. Maybe desire isn't wrong, maybe even lust. It's what you desire that matters. Sometimes folks get so tied up in wanting something that they don't pay attention to what they're after. *If I can only just have THAT, I'd be alright*, as if having whatever that is will redefine them, make them new, solve everything, everything. And so you spend all your time wanting until you don't exist, yourself, any more. It's just the wanting. So you become that thing and it becomes you.

And so its what you're after that matters. If you're after something that is less than yourself, then you're fixing to diminish yourself by that much—you're going to become that desire and you're going to be identified by that thing. So if it's a motorcar or a new outfit or new shoes, look what you've done. You've traded yourself for the thing that is so much less than yourself. And you've done this willfully. You've decided that you want to want this thing that's less than you.

And so maybe that's what sin is: the desire for the desire for something less than yourself. That's sure what happens to these fellows with the Jake leg: they get to drinking that stuff to the point where they get to wanting it—desiring it—and then that grows to the point of identifying everything they do—even when they're not drinking it—with the drinking. So they identify themselves by their desire for Jake gin and that's what they turn themselves into. Nothing but a drain for that alcohol. And they'll drag themselves along like haints, propped on canes if they have to, making their drop-toe stumble, *tip-thunk*, in the dirt on the way to get more.

Because desires always turn into needs, if they're real desires, because they are so tied up with who you are and what you do. And so if you desire something that is less than you are, and you start to look for it, spend your day wanting it, deciding it's all you need to be okay, then all of a sudden you do need it and so you don't desire it any more, you are it. And that's the end of desire and the truth of damnation.

And you can see this just in looking at how a person treats his neighbors. These Jake leggers don't even see you or bother even to remember that they don't know you anymore. They'll drag themselves right on over you if you're in the way of that Jamaican ginger. Or if you've got some, they'll do anything for you or to you. They can go into town with their fifty cents and buy two ounces, or they can wait for the man to bring it up the mountain and pay twice that because no one will take them, because you can see they have the Jake leg. And these folks might be the preacher or the lawyer just as much as the fellow with a wood hoe in his hands. And so they hate you. Because you're only real in that two-ounce bottle of ginger. You don't exist any more except as you relate to that gin, and so these fellows have made you into less than yourself and they're treating you that way because they have to. They need you to be less than you because they need you as background to that Jake. And so the whole world goes to hell with them.

And it doesn't have to be anything nearly so bad as Jamaican ginger. It can be a dress or a mule or a chaw, I suppose. It's the desire—the identifying of yourself with that thing that drags you down. It's not the dress nor the animal nor the tobacco, nor even the Jake that's at fault. It's in the desiring. Now you want to see Sadie because she might buy some eggs from you so you can get that dress and then everything will be okay. So if Sadie won't buy eggs, you hate her because she is keeping you from that dress you need so bad because that dress is the solution to your problems. That dress is you. And now that dress is Sadie. It's even them eggs.

Now if that's so, it's not the dress nor the desire even, but the direction of the needing—the quality of whatever you happen to tie yourself to. If you could find a thing *better* than yourself, and begin to desire that, you might go the other direction, by wanting to want it until you need it until you become it. And your neighbor rises too because you realize your neighbor is a link to that thing that is better than you and so you go to the neighbor in order to rise in this way. So desire is the way out, too. Desire the key to deliverance, rescue. Like touch: touch is greater than, better than just you, if it's really touching, and not pushing. And them eggs, too, for that matter. And that might be salvation.

JOURNAL OF HAZEL TAYLOR
May 11, 1996

It must have been the laurel itself that started everything. Because as far back as I recall, I found that I couldn't walk by it, leave it alone. And once you've picked a laurel blossom off the stem, you're already caught. Because the closer you look, the more you see. The small white blossom with the stains of pink, all set up in permutations of five: five segments, five stamens arching out of five blood-red points, and bending into the five tiny cups that complete the ridge of each section. The stamens are taut, like springs and when you've seen this, you see that you can release them, open them out from that taut arching, so full of longing, and watch them spring free.

And when the blossoms fall, they land upside down on the ground, for all the world like miniature five-sided porcelain cups. And when you've seen this, you can't keep from picking one up. Its shape is so solid, with its multiple fives supporting each other, but, all in all, so delicate and frail, like the most intricately designed Sevres, once it's lifted and turned and you see again down into the deep middle, the supple, taut arches, the smears of red.

That's how it started. And it got so, all year along, I'd watch for June, look for the laurel to come out. And find myself looking into them again. And every year, the laurel would come and I'd feel unease and disappointment: the color was wrong and the shape too angular. But then they'd open out and soften, and then they'd be my laurel, the beautiful, porcelain, five-sided wonder. From a distance, laurel is an anomalous fluff of whitepink in the dark mountain green, but even at a distance it has a delicacy that eludes the slattern rhododendron. Everybody talks about the rhododendron and about going to Roan Mountain to see rhododendron. But you believe me, once you've had a laurel cup in your palm, you've ceased to notice the slapdash old rhododendron. It's just a big sloppy plant. It's the fragile solidity of the laurel that you're after.

Laurel is an evergreen, but you'd never think to look at it in December that it would expose itself so tenderly next June. Its leaves are hard and deep, dark. But once you've had a season or two of laurel, you can see the blossom in its very absence, and so the hard green leaves whisper to you year-long of what they're hiding from you. *Wait and see. Wait and see. I'll show you, but only at the right time. It's down inside me, now, but wait and see—it will be yours to touch and hold.*

Looking at laurel must have started everything. Everything just waiting for the combination: Daddy's death, and Saint Dunstan, and Noah's return. Because I can't separate the memory of holding a cupped blossom from the longing to go. Looking into that blossom for more: more patterns, more puzzles, more intricate beauty, and thinking of all the laurel blooming and showing and draping itself along all these hollows and hills, swells and dips of mountain, and I'd feel that same aching, a blend of knowledge and fear and longing.

And now—isn't this strange?—I sit here in this cold, northern city, and I write this, where there will never again be laurel blossoms lying cupped in my path, because the urge they engendered led me so far away from these things I loved that they will never be among me again. No. And so now I walk along the gray street and a crumpled handful of waxy paper blows up against my leg and drops to the road with a *shushing* sound. It has a globular stain of grease and mustard on it. And I look at it, and think of Rosie, and Hastie, and I long for laurel.

JOURNAL OF HAZEL TAYLOR
October 15, 1997

So I left. In my twenty-second year of living completely within the mountain cove that I loved so. I sat up in bed that night and swung my legs over the side, onto the cold, bleached floor, and stood in one motion, already walking, already grieving, out of everything I was, to flee what I could not bear becoming.

It was dark night by the time I went. George was asleep, sleeping easy after all that work, and I tried to give him a last look that might somehow stay with him. I don't know. I thought maybe if I could just look at him right, as he slept there and as I was leaving, well maybe it would carry over somehow to when he woke up and found me gone and so maybe he would understand a little bit what was in my eyes. My mind. I looked at him that way, not thinking *I'll never see you again*, but *I will never stop seeing you, no matter how long or how far I go*. And I wanted him to know somehow that it wasn't really him I was leaving, walking away from. It was me—it was that version of me that I was destined to become the longer I stayed in this place. And though maybe I could have lived out the rest of my life with him, here on this mountain, it was her I couldn't stay around, not for even another night.

So I left. I looked at George, the way you will look across a room, from the table where you're standing, to the doorway where you're going to go, once you've extinguished the lamp. And you're looking to imprint that six feet of your own home into your mind so that you can step true, even in the pitch darkness. I looked at George, and I picked up my woolen shawl and my writing. I filled a flour sack with some things, a bit of money and some little things: a picture and a tortoise shell hair comb and such. My book, my pen. Rosie's pencil.

And that's all. I wrapped myself up in my shawl and left the room. In the parlor I picked up a lamp and the flint lighter. And out the door into the night.

There was a moon and the trail looked like a black piece of nothing on the far side of the lot. It was still as a dead man's breath all across the lot and into the dark shadow of the trail, grown in by briars and such. I didn't want to light the lamp unless I had to, and it was already awkward carrying the big sack of everything and the lamp too. So I stopped and stood, waiting to see if the light would get better after awhile in the dark.

When my eyes started to lighten up, I walked a ways along the trail, making out what I could and feeling the rest of the things with my feet. Your feet really can see, you know, when you're not able to use your eyes. If you try walking along a rough track in the dark, you'll find that you can tune your mind to what your feet are seeing, and you can walk surer than you could if you just tried to trust your eyes. And it's not *feeling* your way. Your feet really are looking, and you're seeing what they see. It's when you start to mistrust them and go with what your eyes are trying to do that you stumble or kick a stone and twist your ankle. Walking a mountain trail in the dark isn't easy: *it aint just a'going to the mill,* as George says. You're not in the same element as in the day and your daytime senses don't see the trail or the dark or any of the night things. And the world itself is shaped differently, it smells different, and it *moves* differently. And even time, the elapsed event: from the trail head upward, around switches, with the big looming black vegetation turning you around it and on up, not measured in seconds or minutes or in distances traveled, but in the rhythm of flexure and extension, knee and ankle, in the dark rising.

So I had the feel of the walking in the dark, as soon as the light stun faded. And I set the lamp down as careful as I could and left it there. "Well, that's that," I said, out loud. Because setting down that lamp was like a final leaving, like another closing of a door, maybe the last one. Or opening the first.

I still have that flint lighter. Most folks wouldn't even know what it is.

II.

ANDREW KAYER

And so, after holding these papers to myself for decades, I'm passing them along to you. Because there are only a few people— or perhaps only one?—who find their way into your life in such a way as to transform everything. I don't know. We all have close friends, and loved ones, and a surrounding of "important" people. But there are a rare few who take a shimmering place, deep in your life, and show you an entirely new kind of "self." And I know, now, that I am not that sort of transformative person. But, perhaps, I am wise enough, or open enough, or simply lucky enough, to be able to pass one such along.

And so, I give you Hazel.

I first heard Hazel Taylor whispering through a shimmering dazzle of sunshine. I had just swung through the maple door from the shadowy dining alcove and directly out into what everyone called the "conservatorium." This name, so ironically suited to a room in an Edgewater old folks' home, had been attached long ago to our institution's spartan glass-lined porch, in some unconvincing attempt at light-heartedness. But the designation had by now been in common use for so long that whatever humor might once have clung to it had entirely dissipated, and so we now grimly sent medications, messages, and ministrations to patients in "the conservatorium" without so much as an awareness that we had forgotten what a dourly fitting label we used.

What I never did get used to was the assault of sunlight that greeted me each of the several times a day that I swung through this door, on whatever errand took me from alcove to conservatorium, or back again. The change in intensity was so sudden, and the difference so great that, either direction, the comer or goer was blinded for a matter of seconds. Eventually, I saw whatever was in either room through a vibrating visual granulation, turning everything spotty-red. This was one of the regular assaults on one's reasonable expectations of normal physical comfort that made the experience of working in the Kinzski Nursing Home just slightly better than actually living there.

Six months prior to my meeting Hazel, I had wandered away from a graduate program in literature at the University of Chicago. Entered into with a combination of indifference and egomania, my studies had not thriven. I had convinced myself that I was a man of letters already beyond anyone's pedagogical reach, and I was utterly unaware that my behavior was an insult both to literary art and to the spirit of humanities. Meanwhile, I used my supposed dedication to poetry as an excuse to drink far too much, while I fooled more than a few young women into my bed, and generally led a life of righteous intellectual dissipation. After three sordid years of this sort, I hit the wall. At the age of twenty-five, I fumbled my way out of the University, took an apartment off Belmont Street, and got a job. Being thoroughly overeducated and totally unskilled, I had very little by way of choice of occupation. Finally, I found employment as an orderly in the nursing home.

To my amazement, I liked the work. The struggle against disgust that went along with cleaning up after sick, old patients, and the fatigue that came from eight hours on my feet became, in fact, a welcome respite from the ennui and disaffection of my student life. I found—again a surprise—that I liked serving people. And I began to develop an interest in the lives and thoughts of old people, of whom I had previously been positively afraid. I still spent my free hours on a steady regimen of alcohol, and I still sought release in impersonal adventures with females. I wonder what they must have thought—must think—of me. I certainly hadn't thought of them as anything but venues of pleasant sensation. The actual bodily touching, the event itself, seemed to dissolve from memory in the very moment of its own occurring. But now, during the workday, at least, I had found something requiring my presence, and the real contact with soil and sickness was a positive novelty.

At any rate, that day I wheeled through the door into the shattering light and rather groped than found my way toward Hazel.

She had been a resident for some time before I came to work there, and I had seen her occasionally, but I had not met her in my first several weeks of employment, in part because I had been assigned to the bedridden residents in my initial rotation, and in part because Hazel kept pretty much to herself. She didn't have family or visitors of any sort, but she struck me as more solitary than lonely. She didn't need a lot in the way of medical or physical support, and she didn't seem either to seek or willfully to shun social contact, the way some patients often swung from self-enforced isolation to frenzied converse. She was that rare sort of nursing home resident who seemed more guest than inmate, more visitor than patient. You walked by her in the way you would pass a hotel lodger: polite and solicitous, but not concerned—attentive rather than vigilant—caring to please rather than compelled to care.

In truth, I hadn't much noticed her. I discovered later that my inattention was more an effect of her independence of character, coupled with the striking mundanity of my own attitude, than any lack of salient characteristics on her part. She really was not an easy person to ignore, when once you managed to lift your gaze beyond your own occluded life and began to look around.

Or at least I say so in retrospect. I certainly care about her now, more than I have cared about almost anybody—certainly more than I bothered to care about anything at all on that day when I stumbled into the conservatorium, and heard, through the blare of sunlight, her whisper of warning.

"Beware the tray, Andrew."

Can you hear it? Sometime later, I asked her why she had whispered, where someone might be expected to speak up sharply.

"Did you want me to shout?" she asked.

"It isn't exactly usual to murmur 'watch out!'" I said.

"I know what it's like to feel a fool. I could see you were fixing to find out for yourself." The alliteration sounded unaffected, a natural cadence blending with the soft mountain tones that appeared to peek out from behind a curtain of cultured inflections. "I thought you might prefer a bit of privacy," she said, "at such a time." Her smile was open, honest, and instantly appealing, not because it drew you into her circle of light so much as it appeared to recognize a similar radiance you had always hoped to throw about yourself. She lent her own graciousness to your actions in a way that made you feel unaccountably better about yourself. I told her as much once, trying to explain why I found her so striking. She smiled that same smile and said, "I suppose that's what always passes for attraction, the ability to make another feel like the narrator, essential to the carrying on of the day itself. Don't you think?"

She talked this way, in these rolling, elliptical phrases, just the way, as I found out later, that she wrote. All of it in a quiet, limpid tone, that seemed, too, to acknowledge your own importance, as though she were letting you in on just how honored she felt to be conversing with someone of such confidential significance. What a person she was!

She was a handsome old woman, I suppose. Her broad forehead had remained remarkably smooth, with the exception of a single diagonal line, the result of some long ago accident, that almost exactly divided her brow into two triangles, framed by waving steel-grey hair. She had deep, narrow eyes, out of which peered irises of a remarkable pale grayblue. Around and below the eyes, in sharp contradistinction to the smoothness of her brow, her face was wrinkled in a complex web of fine lines divided irregularly by deep creases. She appeared more likely to have been raised on the broad and windy coast than in the deep and humid mountains.

She was "something over ninety," by her own report—it was written on her chart precisely this way, in what I later learned was her own hand—and her body betrayed an unusual degree of osteoporosis for someone still moving around on her own: the curved back and permanently tucked shoulders. This humping and twisting of her torso, combined with the inordinate slightness of her body, gave her the appearance of a moderately deformed child. Still, she got herself around quite ably, and took herself for a stroll around the home's rather featureless grounds each day.

Otherwise, she spent a good part of her day sitting by a small table and writing, grasping her old-fashioned fountain pen in a left hand that had been badly warped, the fingers terribly skewed, by arthritis. She invariably answered inquiries about her health with what I took to be an old mountain expression: "I seen better times, but I'm puttin' up with these," in a voice from somewhere out of her past, not her own anymore. And then she gathered you in with that smile.

When she was by herself, her mouth turned down in a characteristic frown. It wasn't a look of anger or sadness, so much as of abstraction, wondering. To me, in fact, the principal effect of the mouth's downward turning was to accentuate the beneficence of the smile, when it came, as it always seemed to when I invaded her awareness.

So that first day I blindly knocked over an empty cup on her neighbor's tray, clumsily righted it and stood looking down through the granular crimson toward her whispered warning. I responded formally, a little stiffly: "Thank you, ma'am. That's all right. And how're you getting by today?" to receive for the first time, the unvarying answer.

I was there to deliver medications. She had taken a turn recently and was now beginning the regimen of painkillers by which we would attempt—vainly, as it turned out—to usher her gently into her grave. "You know my name," I said.

"I do," she smiled. And I was caught on her line, and ready to be landed without even a fight.

You see, she was someone matchless and irreplaceable in my life before I had passed more than a few dozen words with her. I don't know why she chose me out, why she selected my bit of pond to throw out her line in hopes of dragging something worthwhile out of the boredom and mediocrity of what I pretended to be my "individuality." To find myself flopping and gasping at her feet.

I complained once about some insult to this individuality I so cultivated and she reproved me instantly. "You don't see, do you, that this struggle to maintain what you call 'individuality' is dooming you, this whole modern world, to destruction? Because nobody is an individual and such a pretense only assures you the very monotony you're so desperate to avoid. Individual, hah" she positively snorted. "Why would anyone want to be alone, having no one but some individual he already thinks he knows with whom to commune?"

"You're a bit out of my depth, Hazel," I said.

"No, Andrew, you're the one. You're sunk into a pool of self that will drown you, finally. And you think it's sustaining you. You—like most of the people you will run into at this supposed-to-be momentous turn of millennia—you so want to be unusual, when it's the very...the very *monomania* that signs and seals your classic indistinction. You need to come up out of that swamp and poke your nose above the surface."

"I don't understand a thing you're trying to tell me, Hazel."

She softened, at this. "No," she said. "I guess not. But you see, somewhere you've all been trained to think life ought to be *enjoyable,* and so you're always bored, as though *fun* was a real thing for which you could strive. But *fun* is the mark itself of the tedium—of the lonely, bored-and-boring *individual*, desperate to find something to do when there's nobody else there. Nobody but this tiresome undifferentiated self.

"No. I don't expect you could know any of this yet. It's not your fault," she said, and flashed me the smile as a blessed compensation for the scolding, or the lesson, or whatever it was. "You can't expect to know. But, Andrew, honey, an *enjoyable* life isn't worth living. You need to come out of there and find the rest of you. *Root, hog, or die*, to mix a metaphor."

"Whatever you say, Hazel," I said, trying to signal that, for me, anyway, this conversation was over.

"Alright, Andrew. I'm going to sleep. You go on home."

I realize, after looking this over, so many years later, that I've succeeded in making Hazel appear much more assured than she really was. In spite of her wisdom, and her apparent desire to share it with me, there was a deep core of uncertainty within her, as though she were constantly afraid she had been misunderstood. I think it was this suspicion of her own inarticulateness, rather than any confidence in her own sagacity that led her to speak in the repetitive, convoluted way she did. Never sure she'd said it right, she felt compelled to say it again.

All of this from a woman who had been raised so far back in the Southern Appalachians that *you could meet yourself going the other way*, as, she said, T.R. used to say. She certainly didn't fit the stereotype of the mountain woman. As I was to find out, that refusal to submit to type-casting was something of a willful decision and it was to be her life's work. Because she had disappeared from her own native place. It hadn't been enough to leave, to announce a departure, saying, "I'm sorry, folks, but this hollow can't hold me. I have too much to do with my life. And so I'm going to go away and seize my chances." Instead, she had to evaporate from the place, disappear as totally as if she were transubstantiated—one second, Hazel Taylor the young mountaineer's wife, and *poof!* She's gone. And she's another woman entirely, sitting in her room in an old folks' home in Chicago, seventy years (seventy years!) later, writing her endless explanations, or narrations, or pleas for understanding, or whatever they are.

And so, now, twenty years or so after THAT, here I am, giving this compendium to you, the one we might call, "dear reader."

And I discovered that she wasn't just destined, by whatever degree of intelligence, responsiveness, sensitivity—whatever it was that set her apart from the run of people in those remote hollows—to spend a lifetime shaping her mind and voice and gestures. It was more than that, worse than that. Because Hazel Taylor was one of those people doomed to make change occur wherever she was—or to whoever she touched. And so in working out her own history—and this was the sole motivation always, to be allowed the shaping of her own life—she transformed the lives around her, leaving a wake of longings and losses that she could only have prevented had she remained static. And this was something Hazel could not—or would not—do.

Finally, it was the wisdom she had to offer, and precisely the kind of wisdom I needed. It was a knowledge she had bought at a great cost, but that she tried to hand me as a gift. But as wise as Hazel was, she was filled, always, with wondering, wondering far beyond my own ability to follow, back into a life led so consciously that it must have seemed to her like multitudinous moments, each tightly folded into a complexity of possibilities explored, rejected, taken up, thrust upon her.

At what point her life turned from multifaceted exploration to intricate explanation, I couldn't say. Even when she began handing me pieces of writing out of eighty years of this combination of willfulness and doubt, I could never quite determine which piece of writing was the expression of a choice made, a path determined, and which was a commentary, an apology. I couldn't distinguish assertion from confession, voice from echo, argument from repentance.

It was as frustrating as it was rewarding—as though you were listening to a panel discussion, or reading the minutes of some weird, metaphysical committee meeting. I've never known anyone so able to carry on an extended, animated, discussion with her own self as Hazel was.

Perhaps that's what she had set out to show me from the start.

There are other voices, too. Those of George Taylor, T.R. Blankenship, and the others from Shelton's Trace, who make up the world from which Hazel disappeared. Because I found them. Drawn in by Hazel's journals—the youthful story and the elderly commentary—I found myself strangely involved with the Hazel I never could know in person, the young, vibrant Hazel, who broke all the stereotypes by being wise and lettered and sensitive and deeply disaffected from the place she nevertheless loved, in some core of her soul. The Hazel who, one night, vanished from home, husband, and her very self, and went away to make a life. And who, in vanishing, embedded herself forever in the place: inescapable, palpable, evoked in memory, discovered as presence, echoed in the very language of those mountains. And I was so taken in by this young woman that I had to enter into the narrative itself. To go back to that original place in search of that youthful, troubled person. And to find an entire planet of longing and regret. And so I went...down to the vast. Empty place in those deep, dark mountains, and I found a few of the people remaining, who could fill-in the story—or, at, least, could add their questions.

And now, after simply holding-it-to-myself, for many years, I am, at last, handing this volume to you, just as Hazel reached out a packet of writing to me, some twenty years ago. And, these many years after Hazel handed-over her version, this one, too, is carefully reordered and reworked so as to resemble more closely the utterly random confusion of event, memory, perspective, self. That much, anyway, I have learned.

III.

She would no more dream of going up to White Oak Flats than going to Jerusalem. Hazel was a good, strong woman, you know, but she weren't the least bit interested in climbing mountains nor going off on adventures. Not Hazel. She was always kindly inward. Dreamy like. Like everything she'd see outside made her start in to think. I've seen her to stand and stare at something—I don't know, a flower or a bird or just some little rock on the ground—like she was seeing way more than anyone else might see. Least more than I ever saw. She'd no more go clombering up to White Oak Flats than Jerusalem.

It ain't like she was useless, hanging about like these loafers and doing nothing all day but use up air. No. Hazel was dreamy-like, but she was always busy, too. She kept a good house and she cooked and raised the vegetables, and all the other truck. Chores, you know. She even added some things like most women don't. She kindly kept the place a mite better than most folks, not for show, or nothing. More like it was just kindly natural for Hazel to have a nicer place than most folks. Not like she took pride nor even cared, nor never even noticed herself that her place was more neatened-up than the other folks. No. Hazel was humble like. She always made you feel better than you was,

34

not worse, you know. No, it was like she needed to have things nicer around her or she couldn't be easy. Had to put one more touch into the place or she wouldn't fit it, somehow. Or like she made the place feel proud, stead of the other way round. You know?

Oh she was a good girl and I loved her so. And no matter what, day or night, everywhere I go, there's a piece of my mind that's always wondering why. Always startled, surprised like, as if it was that first night: *Wherever is Hazel?* And then wondering: *Why in the heavens would she leave our home and go to White Oak Flats? She would no more dream of it, no more than to go to Jerusalem.*

And there it is. You know. That's my whole life. Right there. I knowed Hazel Tighrow for twenty-some year just as sure as I knowed my own self. And I was married to Hazel Tighrow for three year. And I did love her so. And now I lie here all alone, musing on the past. Wondering why she left our home to go to White Oak Flats.

And I don't know.

I don't know how he looked at her. I don't know what he said. I don't know what he could have done, to turn poor Hazel's head. Never in her darkest hour could she imagine that she'd agree to go with him up to White Oak Flats.

White Oak Flats? You know? I say to myself must be twenty thirty times a day, I say "White Oak Flats?" Why nobody never goes to White Oak Flats, you know. It's kindly one of those places you just don't go. I lived here all my life and I ain't been there four times. Least of all not before Hazel went off. For awhile after she went, after they found her, found them bones, I might go up there right frequent. I guess I thought she might be coming back that way. I knew better, you know, but I guess I just kindly felt that way, you know? Like I might ought to been there in case Hazel was coming on back.

And there's nothing up there. It's just wide and open. Bald as a skinned rat. It looks like to be a great large pasture, but there ain't nothing there. There's a old apple tree right up in the middle of the clear, Lord knows how it got up there. You can see it ain't been tended. And you can see the long, deep grooves where the bears have dug it with their claws, a'climbing up to get them apples down in the Fall. You know? But there ain't nothing else. Once I come out of the scrub into the Flats and there was two deer yonder standing stock and staring at me. It like to scare me to death, you know. I mean, because I was up there a'looking for something, kindly feeling like I was expecting something or someone, but knowing for real that wouldn't nothing be there, you know. And then here's them deer standing still as a bench peg. It like to end my life right there.

That might be when I come back down and ceased to going up there no more. It done me no good at all. And I did love her so. And she would no more ever dream of going up there with him than Jerusalem.

And yet I can see the rocky trail up the mountainside, you know, with the pieces of white quartz a'glowing in the moonlight. I don't never even close my eyes, and I can see every step of the way up that awful mountain, the two of them. I can see her stumble a mite and him helping her along like I was there, right there, you know? And I can see poor Hazel now, lying by his side. And then I close my eyes, because I can't bear to see no more. That's all.

We was married right down here in Shelton's Trace, in nineteen and twenty four, right yonder at Hazel's ole home place. Nineteen years old, we both was. The church had got smashed all up in that big storm in April, so we was married right yonder at the house. In Maddy Crick, you see. Because Hazel's folks was kindly higher placed than we was, up here to Upper Crick. It didn't matter none. I always knew Hazel would be my wife. Times was right hard back then, you know, and was fixing to get a lot harder, but I could work more than two other fellers, I'd say. We had our little farm away up atop of Upper Crick, and Hazel, you know, she kept our place nicer than most, and I was proud of my tobacco. Folks would laugh at me for I was in the habit of grading my leaves finer than anybody. *George Taylor got more pegs on his bench than a burned pine*, and such. Well, I was proud and I knew my crop and so I'd separate seven, eight grades. Because I knew my crop and so just Long Red and Short Red, well, you know, that weren't enough middle grades for my crop. I'd have Bright, like everyone else, but then I'd have Bottom—or Yaller—and Top—or Brownie—Long Red, and Blood and Deep Short Red, plus the Lugs and Tips. So I had seven grades, right there, where everybody else had just the five. You know. Some years I'd even have a Purply Short Red, so I'd have eight, what with the ground Lugs, Bright, Yaller Long Red, Brownie Long Red, Blood Short Red, Purply Short Red, Deep Short Red, then Tips. Eight grades, flat out on the bench to everybody else's five. Folks believed that I figured to get more money with more grades, like I might impress fellers at the warehouse, but I never. It weren't money. I took pride in my crop was all.

Hazel, she liked that, the extra grades, and it was her named them, though she wanted "Madder Short Red," but I might not be able to recall that, or I might to get mixed up with Middle and Madder, so I kindly rewrote that name to Deep Short Red. Hazel didn't mind none. She said she'd just call hers Madder to herself, and I could call Deep Short Red right out, you know. And she liked packing them leaves in corn fodder to keep them in case, you know, when the weather might turn dry. She was funny, she'd wonder about things, like *Why does they call it "in case," when these leaves is limber, when they just says "dried out" if they gets brittle?* But not mooning-on, doing nothing, you know. She'd be working right on, packing down tobacco, or tying all them grades in hands, while she's wondering all them things all the while. She liked the tying in hands, too, and nobody could tie a hand of tobacco like Hazel. It was a treat to watch her, because she was so careful and just right. But she's quick, too, you know. She'll pick out leaves from a grade—long red—and even them just right, tap down them butt ends, and fold down that tie leaf, from the short red, always the same, and wrap it just right, neat as a clean shot. I can see her in the shed, now. She's wrapping that tie tight, from the tip end down and tucking that end in between the leaves, just perfect below the wrap. And she'll set that hand a 'tobacco down next to another and they'd be just the same as two knobs on a door. Just that perfect, you know. And she never said nothing about gum on her hands or nothing. And all the while wondering, *Who do you suppose ever figured out all this? I mean who found out that if you burned a bed and laid down a crop and set it out and suckered it and cut and sliced it and hung it upside down in the shed—that he must not have built yet—and rolled it up and smoked it or stuck it in your jaw or up your nostrils. I mean, who ever ciphered all that out? I mean I can see why they calls it "hands," because it's the perfect reflection of what you just done with your hands* and so on, meanwhile tying up another one, just as clean and pretty as a new skillet.

But I don't do it no more. The joy has done gone, just as sure as Hazel, and I couldn't care if I never saw the least tobacco plant ever again.

FIELD NOTES: INTERVIEW—T.R. BLANKENSHIP
May 7, 1998

I ain't been up this crick in a good long time. My lungs is plumb wore out and it's a mite of a chore just to climb from the car up the path to the door anymore. Used to be no road at all, up this far. Just kindly a path. You could get a wagon and team down it if you positively had to, I guess. Nowadays usually, George, he'll run on down to see me, save me the air, you know? George, he's in right good shape. I reckon he'll live about forever. But he'll be all by himself. They ain't none of them left up here no more. Nobody but me and George. And we're the last of a kind, I'd say. Ain't nothing like it was, nothing at all. But me and

George, we're kindly the same. Oh we're older'n hell now, and I reckon that'll grouch a feller up some. But we don't bother nobody. Just setting around here counting the damn stars. Get them all counted up, they'll let us drop dead, maybe. About time, most folks will say.

George, he's about the best old feller you'll ever meet. And now he's had a pretty rough row to hoe, ole George has. He's still dwelling on that Hazel of his who just upped and walked out on him, middle of the night. Without a trace. At least at first. Well and that was the setting seal on Georgie's whole damn life, right there.

No, it didn't bitter him. No, he's just as sweet a ole boy as you'll meet anywhere. Didn't make him mean nor make him to drink or nothing. Just saddened him up. He's the saddest feller I ever knowed in my life. There are heaps of folks back here that had tough times, had things happen to them they didn't want, didn't deserve. It weren't easy to live down this way back in them days, I'll say that. And some folks suffered right bad. But I never seen anyone sad the way George is. Has been since Hazel left. Nineteen twenty-seven. They was both twenty-two years old. So it's been a hell of a long damn time to feel bad, I'd say. I told my wife once, "You run out on me I ain't going to grieve for more than a week. Then I'm fixing to find me a better one." Well she says, "T.R., if you can find any woman, good bad or indifferent, will put up with you even for that one week you're in mourning, you better take her." I says, "Honey bunch, I reckon that's a point of fact."

But it ain't really no laughing matter. And poor old Hazel, she didn't turn out having much of a life, dying so young. I don't care if she run off nor if she got tied up with that no good Noah, nor nothing. I don't care. I said it when it done happened and I'll say it again: that Hazel was a fine young woman. A good wife to George and that's the truth. Whatever happened she didn't want it to happen, I tell you right now. He either drug her up there or fooled her somehow into going there. He'd done fooled her before, so I reckon he might have done it twice. Most folks down here, round Shelton's Trace, I believe they thought she'd just done run off with that rat. But I don't care. I won't believe it of poor Hazel. And whatever she done, she paid the price for it, didn't she? Dead on a mountainside at twenty-two. Hell. It's a goddam shame, young nice woman like that. And the two of them was just matched, you know. Couldn't see no other woman for George nor any man for Hazel but George. Well, it's as sad a story as you are likely to find down here.

They was some good times down here when we was kids, for all that. Rosie and Hazie and George and me, we was always running together. Didn't get in no trouble or nothing, just kids, you know, running around these hills. About the worst thing we used to do, I remember how we used to sneak in and heat up a stick of cane in the fire under the syrup, when it was cooking you know? Making molasses? And that cane'll get heated up and you smack it on the ground, WHAM, it'll go off, make a sound like a goddam gunshot. Scare the pants off the folks it would, every time. Things like that. Sneak a handful of corn meal when it's coming warm right out of the burr mill. Grandaddy, he run a burr mill and a hammer mill both, and we'd go down there and eat us some of that warm meal ever chance we'd get. Grandaddy would holler, "That ain't none of your meal." But we'd eat her anyways. Didn't never do nobody no harm, just kids having some fun. Plenty of troubles and cares coming round the bend, you may as well have a mite of fun when you're a kid, because it ain't going to be no farmer in the dell in a little while.

And after Rosie was gone and Hazel run off, well that left me and George kindly the last of us. And now we're the last of the whole goddam shooting match. All the old folks is gone. And the young 'uns don't care.

So we both is just a setting here counting the damn stars.

FIELD NOTES: INTERVIEW—GEORGE TAYLOR
May 8, 1998

I roved about all day, searching for Hazel, asking everybody I lit
on if they'd seen her. I weren't thinking of all the talk would get
started up out of all that. I was just looking for Hazel. You
know. And run back on up to the place every now and again to
see if she'd showed back up there, and asking myself right
along, *Now, where in the world,* like that, just over and over
again, *Now where in the world.* It got so I made so many trips
up and down that crick that folks would start asking me, you
know, instead of the other way round, *You find Hazel yet? You
seen Hazel anywhere yet?*

So folks naturally started to looking around themselves, and
some started to climb on up the crick to our place, just naturally.
You know. One or two at a time, just wandering up to our
place to see what might be happening, or to wait and see what
might happen when Hazel and me met up at last. I don't think
they meant no harm by it. It's just natural for folks to come on
up if there's something new in the air, you know. But it shames
me to this day to remember myself a'looking and asking and
climbing up and down that crick while everybody watched me.
And ever time I'd come back to see if Hazel had showed up,
there'd be a few more of them standing around, you know. And
they'd sing right out *Did you find her? She ain't showed up here
yet, neither.* And it got to be like the whole thing was on show,
you know, like me and Hazel weren't really folks no more but
just part of some show. And it got to be like I was the whole
show myself, and I got to watching myself sweating up and
down that crick all day, like it weren't me clambering around at
all, but I was up there with the rest of them watching this feller
run about looking for his wife. You know? And that shame
sticks with you, so that even now I don't want to see folks and
every time I come upon somebody, I see it all over again, and I
start to watching myself up and down that crick and I feel

ashamed. So I don't go around folks much. Maybe they still want to watch me a'looking for Hazel.

So near the whole crick was up to the house by and by, and folks commenced to talking about where else to look or maybe she'd just stepped over to somebody's place who ain't got up here yet, you know. And Tom Blankenship ups and says "Noah Kersin left town last night, too, come to think on it." And somebody says, "What'd you say?" And he says, "Kersin done left town, too." And the whole crowd got right quiet and folks started to looking down and kicking the dirt, you know?

And I didn't reckon nothing, nothing at all. Everybody in the crick thinking the same thing and I weren't even on the same row with them. Oh, I knew something was odd about the whole thing, but I guess I just weren't thinking. You know. So I has to up and ask.

"What?" I says, to everybody. "What's wrong?" I says, looking round at everybody. But they was gazing at their feet yet, kicking the dirt. Nobody wanted to say nothing to me. But I kept on.

"What's that Tom said? He done said something," I asked, and I was starting to feel right sick. But I still didn't think nothing. Nothing at all. "Well what'd he say?" I calls out a mite too loud.

"I believe Tom Blankenship says he's got to scoot back on down to his crop, before it gets to missing him," says Jimmy Taylor, staring straight and hard at Tom. And Jimmy walked on over to me, glaring at Tom yet, you know, and he didn't look at me, but he puts his arm round my shoulder.

"Don't git swelled-up, Jim Taylor. Didn't mean nothing," Tom said. "Just sayin…"

"That's right, Tom. Most times, if you're fixing to talk, you're fixing to say nothing," said Jimmy. "Now you come on in the house, George," he says, touching my nigh arm. But he still ain't looking my way. "Let's get away from all these folks don't got nothing better to do than stand out in the sun. Let's get in the house, yonder and I'll fetch you some water. You're plumb wore out."

"I ain't catching-on to something,'" I said. "Something ain't..."

You got to say old Jimmy tried his best to plug me up and get me out of there. But right about then it begun to come to me, what they was all kicking the dirt about. It kindly floated up into my thinking, you know, like a fish up into the slow water floats on up to snatch at a fly or something. It floats on up into my mind, just like that fish. So I let out.

"You all ain't saying...You all don't mean Noah Kersin..." I hollers, dragging myself on Jimmy's arm and he trying to hang on to me and pull me on up the other way to the house.

"They don't mean the least thing, George," Jimmy says. Then he swung his lief arm out at them all, still hugging on to me with the other and trying to turn me up the hill. "Maybe you folks might figure maybe you done helped enough for one day?" he says. And folks begun to turn on down and kindly shuffle down the trail, one or two at a time, you know. Just slow and quiet, until we was standing there on our own, me and Jimmy. He still was hugging on to me and I was still watching that fish rise up in my mind, fixing to snap up that dragon fly.

"Noah Kersin ain't..." I says. Then it was me floating up, covered all over with scales and them fat white lips yawing wide. And I swallowed the whole idea in a seething surge. And all I wanted was to sink back into the dark pond.

"Don't you worry none about Noah Kersin. Never done nobody no good to be studying Noah Kersin. Let's get on into the house," Jimmy said.

"No," I said, and I shook off his hand and curled out from under his arm. "Just leave me be, Jimmy. I need to set."

He looked at me for the first time. "You alright, George?" he said. "You okay?"

"Just leave me be," I says. "I done lost all I got to lose." And I climbed on up to the house and into the dark.

I lost all I got to lose.

IV.

ANDREW KAYER

It was roughly three weeks after our initial meeting that Hazel first gave me a piece of her journal. To this day, I can't understand what precipitated the event. We hadn't been talking about thoughts or feelings or identities, for once. I guess we were talking about the past. We were talking about cooking. Or about food. Preservation, I guess. It was autumn and I'd brought her an apple on her tray. I liked to bring Hazel one extra little thing whenever I brought her tray. It had become a bit of a game, a part of the ritual greeting that was growing up to be a tradition between us.

By now I was anticipating her typical response and she was tickled that I shortstopped her, tried to mimic her. I'd burst into the conservatorium where Hazel would be sitting in the, thankfully dimmer, fall light, writing.

"Pretty rough times, today, Hazel," I'd say. "But I'm puttin' up with them."

This brought a laugh. That little, high-pitched laugh that almost sounded a touch crazy, as though a part of her that had been concealed had leapt up for only a second, and rushed out in that warble of a laugh. That was it: it was because the laugh was at once quiet and uncontrolled, more bubble than laugh, that made it seem strange. And it was as though she spoke something while she was laughing. But you could never make it out.

"What have you brought for me on this puttin' up day?" she'd say, and I'd whisk away her napkin with a mock heroic aplomb to reveal whatever trivial prize she'd won.

"Oh my heavenly days!" she'd exclaim in awed astonishment at my largess. "You should not have gone to such lengths! I'm simply swept away!"

That day it was an apple. Hazel always talked about cold days as "getting down in the fall," and so this day it was "away down in the fall." And I flourished forth a deep, wine-red apple.

She picked it up, and globed it in her hand. She slid her pale eyes upward from the apple to me.

"You know how we used to put up apples back home?" she said.

"And that," I said, "Is the primest apple in the kingdom."

"Yes, it's a fine one. Now listen to me. We'd peel and slice up a layer of apples into a big ten-gallon crock and we'd put a saucer of sulfur right on top of the slices. And we'd light the sulfur and let it burn."

"You're pulling my leg," I said.

"No. We did this. Sliced a layer and burned sulfur on them. Then another layer of peeled apple slices, and another burning saucer of sulfur. Then, next day, another layer, and so on, until the crock was filled. And they were put up for the winter." She was still weighing the cupped apple, still laying those pale eyes on mine. "I can smell that today, right here in this room, just from talking about it." I saw her eyes water for a moment, and I thought *she's feeling that smoke.* Then I shook this off. I saw her shake it off, too.

"God, Hazel. What did they taste like?"

She bubbled a laugh. A blessing. "Tasted like apples you'd burned a plate of sulfur on," she said. "No, I'd say they tasted right good. They had a flavor you'd never get today out of any apple you ever ate. I used to wonder who ever imagined that you could put up apples that way. I mean, where did this practice come from? It's not the sort of thing you'd try out, you know? *Let's just burn a mite of sulfur on them, maybe they'll get through the winter?* No.

"And not like hominy, where it could have happened by accident. You know hominy is corn that's soaked in lye until the husk drops off. Softens the kernel. And you have to rinse it down to get the lye out of it. Because that lye will kill you. And I used to wonder about this, too. *Who in the world ever thought to soak corn in lye for something good to eat?* But I do imagine that was an accident. You can see some poor mountain family down to their last sack of dried corn, when the child dumps the kettle of lye out onto the corn. Or the child decides she'll be like Momma and soak the dried corn for tomorrow. And the folks find their last corn floating in that soap lye, all swollen up. And it's a terrible year, dead winter and nothing to eat. You can't throw that corn away, and you're afraid to give it to whatever animals you have left alive. So you fish out those kernels, and you scrub them off good, and you cook it up anyway. And you dip it out with a little grease or a little butter, if you've got any, and that's supper.

"But you're scared to death that it'll kill you. After all, it soaked overnight in your lye kettle. But you don't have any choice; it's eat this stuff or don't eat. So you do. And it's good! It tastes fine, tastes really good! *Now who in the heavenly days would've thought that?* you say. And you dip out a little more, and sop up the juice with your biscuit.

"And as soon as you tell your neighbors about it, it ceases to be an accident and becomes a food. It's hominy. And the lye has imparted a flavor that is indescribable, and so you get to wanting hominy for supper. You won't get it, today, in this store-bought hominy. But the farm-style, well that could only come this way. There's nothing in the world like farm-style hominy."

She looked at me. Those pale, narrow eyes.

"But the apples," I said.

"The apples," she said. "No one could have accidentally sliced a layer of apples out and burned a saucer of sulfur on them. And no one would just try it, to see if it might work, the way George once tried curing a few sticks of tobacco in the springhouse, to see if they'd cure slower in a cold fall. Like this one," she said. "Now that wasn't as crazy an idea as people thought," she said. She shifted her eyes to the window. Turned her head for a moment, and looked long and deep, out the window.

"I've got something I want you to read," she said, her eyes still in the distance.

"But the apples," I said, and drew her back to me. I felt like a child who was demanding that the attention continue. "The apples?"

"The apples," she said, a touch perplexed. "Well, let's see. The apples would have been neither accident nor trial, experiment," she said. "So the apples were decided by some sort of pre-determined process, some sense that *it's just what you're sup-posed to do with a apple.* And so it wouldn't have been a surprise when the sulfur worked. *Them's good apples.*" She wasn't laughing. Wasn't making fun. She was trying to tell it.

"The apples were drawn from a formula," she said. "Do you see?"

"No, Hazel," I said. "As per usual, I don't see."

"Genesis. Apples and the devil," she said. And now she was looking straight into me, again. "Do you see?"

"So you suppose they burned sulfur on the apples not to prepare them for winter but to…"

"Prepare them, yes," she said. "Get them ready for the grim, cold death of the years. The apples that come along in the autumn to tell us the end is coming. The apple that means seduction and death. Eve's apple," she said. She wasn't laughing.

"Well, I guess it worked," I said, smiling a little to test whether she would smile back.

She did. "Worked like a charm," she said.

"But red is a Christmas color, too," I said. "Can't be all Satan and death, then, can it? Red is a Christmas color."

"It is," she said.

So she gave me the first excerpt from her journal that day, without explanation, as though she had thought of it in the middle of that talk about putting up apples, and the apple discussion itself was all the background I needed to know. When I look back on that day I realize what a momentous occasion it must have been for her. What a striking and terrible risk she was taking.

"Would you read this?" she asked, and handed me a narrow sheaf of papers, gathered into a cotton sack.

"What is it?" I asked.

"Just something I wrote," she said. "Would you take it and read it? And bring it back."

"You've been writing?" I asked. "That's great! When did you decide to start writing? What is it about?"

"Don't patronize me, Andrew. Just read it," she said.

"Oh I'd love to read anything you've written," I said. I meant it. I was curious, eager. And pleased that she'd asked me, that she'd opened herself to me to this extent. "I'd love to read it."

"Bring it back," she said. "The sack, too."

V.

JOURNAL OF HAZEL TAYLOR
June 8, 1922

Mr. Dunstan came by again, today. I can't get used to calling him by his first name. He said, last month, "Hazel, this may be bad news, but you reach a point where you're not a little girl anymore and you can't hide behind other folks' titles. That's especially so since I'm not your schoolteacher any more. I'm just a peddler who comes through here once in awhile and who *wants* everybody to call him by his first name. When you're selling Watkin's products and all such, folks likes to buy from folks they feel comfortable with. So if I made everybody call me 'Mr. Dunstan,' I wouldn't sell a dern thing. You don't buy spice nor vanilla from a man who makes you call him Mr. Dunstan.

"So I want you to stop being my school child and start looking toward being a grownup. In these parts, there's women your age—what are you, seventeen?—who are already married and bearing children, some of them even younger. Fourteen. So you don't need to go off and get married, but you do need to talk like an adult. And I want you to call me 'Saint.' That's my name, and you need to have the courage to break through the adult-and-child divide and learn to call me by name."

But I have a terrible time with this. And I think he's right about courage, it taking courage: because it's hard to just come into a world in where we talk as Hazel and Saint, after all those years of Hazie and Mr. Dunstan. It might have been easier if he'd been around for the past year. But with him gone, that seems to have put ourselves, the two of us, on the back of the stove. So it couldn't grow naturally. And so when he returned, it was "Look! It's Mr. Dunstan," who may have been "Saint" to other seventeen year old women, but was Mr. Dunstan to me. Because I hadn't had time to be seventeen around him. I was still twelve. Do you see? I still saw him as if he was still inside the schoolroom, the oiled floor and the skidded, wood benches. His black frock coat and his arm in the air, pointing at the slate. Teaching.

And it does take courage to make a to-and-fro, over-and-back understanding between two people who have already been okay in the old way, don't it? *Can't we just go on as we are? I like being Hazie and Mr. Dunstan. I don't know this "Hazel" of yours; and this "Saint" of mine doesn't even come off my lips right. I don't know how these two will get along. I like the Hazie you showed me, and you liked the Mr. Dunstan I held out to you. So why leap out into the cold water of these new people?*

Besides, childhood doesn't become adulthood in just one moment, or with some specific gesture, like waving a wand, and it's "Hazel" and "Saint." It's like the coal cinders on the road. You can't see them transform themselves from the hard, awkward, oily-rainbowed cinders into the smooth, cool, bluegray roadway. It's something that assuredly occurs, but it doesn't occur as a moment. It's more of a mystical process: the compulsion to blossom in a laurel bud, or the transformation to ice on a bear pond.

Maybe it's the accumulation of all these selves that others bring to you, to show you. When Mr. Dunstan starts to call me "Hazel," and Badie stops handing me penny candy. They are transforming me—the me that resides in each of them. And perhaps I begin to recognize that me and it begins to transform the selves that I hold, inside. So that, like the cinders, I begin slowly to merge these new selves into my own city of people, and then I discover that the road is smooth, Hazie is Hazel, I am adult.

So it's a collaboration, this building of who you are. And maybe the only ones you have to be careful about are the ones who construct a version of you that they just won't change. Because if it doesn't change, it's a *what* instead of a *who*. Like the dead. So the collaboration never ends. We keep trying to construct truer versions of each other. Or at least we should.

So hanging on to "Mr. Dunstan" and "Hazie," and insisting that we had them summed-up, worked out, would be to destroy them as people, who always move and change and wonder and wish. It would be to make them less than they are, because you don't want to be any more than you were.

Okay. There remains the moment of dumping the cinders in the first place. And maybe that has to be a deliberate—or at least conscious—agreement to try out these selves. Maybe I had to decide to look: to deliberately see myself growing the buds that would become breasts. Unless I had made the decision, I wouldn't have seen the swell of my surface, or felt the urge inside. So perhaps I must decide to build this Saint Dunstan in my own self, and to speak it out in a frightening word. Not "Saint," but Saint.

This time, true to his promise, he brought me a copy of *Wuthering Heights,* by Bronte, and another Thomas Hardy novel, *Tess of the D'Urbervilles.* He said both of these books made him think of me. This made me uncomfortable, in a strange way. I don't recognize the feeling, precisely, but it makes me want to shrink away, somehow. To retreat into the warm cave of "Hazie," where people don't ever tell you that they're thinking about you, characterizing you. Especially not like these fulsome characters in great literature.

Does he have a right to assemble a version of me that is so serious, so exigent? How free are we to invent selves for each other? Is the shaping of identity a struggle among a whole circle of people, tugging and pushing, and forcing yourself on you? Do I have a right to resist? Can I critique the characters that others make of me?

Or am I being coy, rejecting Dunstan's—Saint's—comparison of myself to some character I know nothing about? Am I growing jealous of myself? Or is Saint renovating our selves in ways I don't wish? And how do I have a say in making up a process I don't understand? It's impossible for this all to be just something that's *happening* to me.

Because they aren't books until you read them. Before that, they're just weight, a stack of inked paper between boards. Nothing at all like a book. You make the book when you read it. I read "yesterday afternoon set in misty and cold," and I see a wide field on a hill, with a twisted black tree just off the top center, defining the curve of the slope, and a wash of graywhite over everything, and the smell of wet earth and rain. And the feel of chill midday. So reading these seven words, I have brushed in an entire scene, all of my own making. So I suppose novels are like people. There's a *Wuthering Heights* that is mine alone. One that no author has access to, control over. This must be the great suspense of writing, just as it's the great fearful thrill of meeting people. They build a you out of a few words: clothes, face, body, gestures, speech, just as I painted that curving hillside out of seven.

So is there a me created by the novel? Does my book read me as well? Is the act of my reading the act of Bronte's writing?

I wonder how I look in Saint's mind? Today, he sees a thin, curving girl—woman—leaning against the fence. Her body is a slightly arched vertical, without too much in the way of hip or breast, often awkward, but with enough of grace to beckon in the appropriate directions. He sees that I am pretty—maybe a little plain in my face, but perhaps my face is deep, meaningful.

Bah! This isn't how he sees me at all. I'm making myself up. Fool!

So, perhaps more productive: how do I see him? Saint Dunstan is a nice man. Passionate small eyes, kind of animal: like a bear, maybe. He knows a lot, but he seems forever dissatisfied with what he does and how he does things. As though he doesn't feel worthy of all that knowledge. That may be what makes him a teacher. He has the air, teaching, of passing on knowledge into better hands, as though he's glad you came along to take this off his hands and use it better than he ever could. Something like that.

Some folks think he's arrogant, because he talks passionately and storms around. But deep inside there's a core of nearly crippling humbleness. He may be the most frustrating person I've ever met, because he will never be satisfied with himself. But that frustration drives you to learn from him, to acknowledge the need hidden behind his encouragement, his praise. He feels so good when he can show you a book, hand you another volume for you to discover. He's not trying to control your brain. No. He's starving for validation, and you are his medium of redemption.

He so wants you to be magnificent.

JOURNAL OF HAZEL TAYLOR
July 12, 1923

Saint came by and we went on up to the Flats. It's getting to be a regular routine. Whenever he comes to the Creek, he looks me up. He's always got books for me, and he likes to sit and talk about them. He has what I would call an extreme passion for literature, as though the books were truer, more real, than anything else in his life.

Not to say that I don't have a similar passion. But, to me, books point outward, where, for Saint, I think they point in. He sees a book as a healing wash, for bathing some wounded part of his interior soul. His books are always about him, in a sense. For me, books are about what I'm not: places and other people and possibilities that I haven't achieved. They make me want to get up and leave these mountains, where no one knows other places or people or chances. Here, I will grow to be another mountain woman, working in the patch, and putting up beans, and putting out children. By the time I'm thirty, I will be indistinguishable. I will have ceased to be all these many selves and will have become static and whole: monotonous.

With books, I look out beyond my own future, and I feel numinous and multiple again, because I'm looking out there, instead of in here. Out there, I know I am extraordinarily graced and capacious. Am I being haughty?

At any rate, we went up to the Flats again. It's a hard walk, up there, and it almost feels illicit, as though we're running away. But being up there is a reward for the difficulty of getting up there. For some reason, I never tell anyone else where I'm going, or where I've been. But we just go up because it's quiet and open—not like these coves, where there is hardly any sky—and we sit under the strange, tangly apple tree and read poetry or talk. No one ever comes up there, so it feels like a new place, all ours. Saint says people used to live up here and the apple tree is the only vestige of their time on this mountain.

"It's awful to imagine how isolated they must have been up here," I said. "Imagine: no roads at all, and that climb, just to get down to a grown-over creek, and then on down the creek to where the road doesn't exist yet." I shuddered a bit. "It's awful."

"I don't know," Saint said. "It might have been splendid. A little, lonely paradise, where time means nothing, and only the turn of the seasons to bother with—the planting and harvesting. No cash crop or any of that horror. No tobacco, at any rate, except rabbit tobacco, for your own amusement, eh? It could've been paradise. Why do we come up here?"

"Paradise was a garden of earthly delights," I said. "This is a windswept mountain top. I wonder how many generations of people grew up and died here, are buried here, without a mark in their lives or their deaths. It's nice here, it's my special place. Our special place. I like it here, but I like it because I know the way out." I sat still a moment. "That's why I don't like the Creek."

"How's that?" Saint said.

"I don't know the way out," I said.

"I bet they went in and out of here by going down the ridge, away from the Creek, eh? It's not so steep, and it's a bit more like a natural route than what we hike."

"That would take them down to Camp Ten?"

"That direction," he said, "But Camp Ten wasn't there yet. It came out of the logging. Probably the cutting is what drove these folks down into the hollows with the rest of us. Camp Ten is called that because it was a loggers' camp, originally."

"I wonder what became of Camp Nine, and so on," I said.

"Well, Camp Ten was a big one. They had a narrow-gauge railroad, with mules or oxen that pulled the log carts from there and ran them down the ridge to the bottom. Might have had a little pony steam engine, eventually. They pretty well logged every inch of this country, except in the deep coves, like you all come from.

"Anyway, Camp Ten was the terminus of that line. Above there, they dragged out the timber on cables. So I imagine a sutler set up shop there, and the workers probably lived out of tents or little cabins—they were loggers, after all—and a community grew up around the site. The camp's long gone, but it left its descendants in the folks that live over there. It started out as a rough tough place, and it still is."

"Everybody's afraid of Camp Ten. I wonder why a place has to become so violent and bad."

"Oh, I don't know how violent it is. It's just folks like us. Except they got up there working those logging operations and they forgot how to farm. They were laborers, and they probably even got to scorning farming after a generation or two. But the logging gave out and there they were. At first, they had been just fifty brawny boys who'd traded suckering tobacco for working to a whistle, and who probably made a little whiskey, enough to get drunk and fight each other every Saturday night. But the logging was a boom, a gold mine, and so that little outpost of a camp grew into a dwelling place: with families and stores and dogs and cats. It seems sometimes that people will build up a place like that just in time for it to go bust.

"And that's about what it did. Or rather, it didn't so much go bust as it ran out of trees. And left these families sitting in their little cabins without a means to live. They knew how to cut trees down, but they'd already done that a little too well, and they'd pretty much forgotten how to farm. And once you start working for pay, you need money forever more. So they were just about fated and determined to become moonshiners and rounders. It's just their way of getting by. But even nasty people have to have some places where they can go and be quiet once in awhile. And I reckon folks that make white liquor for a living don't have time to drink too much of it themselves. So I suppose Camp Ten isn't all that bad. Just folks, like I said."

I don't know. I certainly love to listen to Saint tell about these places and tell me his view of how things happen. But I'm not entirely convinced that Camp Ten is a peaceful village of folks like us. We've been frightened of the place for too long not to have some reason for it, I believe. Sometimes I think calling people "just like us" is a way to stop yourself having to learn about them. If they're "just like us" then there's no reason to get to know them, or wonder about them, or think about what makes them so different. They are different: we don't run moonshine and bootleg liquor and carry guns and all that. And they don't set out tobacco or farm or worry about their stock and all that.

"Have you been there much?" I asked him.

"Oh yes," he said. "I sell things there. They need things, too, you know. You know, Hazel, you need to think of it this way: they're poorer than you, they have to scramble around to get what they can, they're always having to watch out for the law. And if the law does come and takes one of them away, and busts up a few stills, well that's like a bad crop and a death, over here. It hits you all over, doesn't it? But even so, they'll give me a ride up the mountain from town, and back down, on the day they're taking a load of corn to town. Wednesday or Thursday, usually. Put me up in the meanwhile. So I don't have to use the wagon or wear the team.

"And so I've found when I go over there that these Camp Ten folks aren't mean nor wicked. They're scared and they're timid. They're afraid of what you can do to them. Because they know that you're in a better situation than they are. And then one of your boys who thinks he's such a tough rounder goes over there and winds up getting his skull cracked. And he staggers back over the mountain and comes down the creek and tells you how he went to Camp Ten and got attacked. And from over here, you can't see that he was the attacker, he was the invader. They had to protect themselves from him, you see?"

"I suppose it's the same thing with the Indians," I said. Whenever we come up here, we always lean back, both of us resting against the rough, scarred support of the apple tree. We're shoulder to shoulder, but our bodies stretch out at right angles, moving apart in a vee shape. So we don't look at each other. Just hear the voices, while each of us will select a blade of grass or a leaf off a thorn runner and slowly take it apart, breaking it up into pieces as we talk. Then find another blade to pull apart. Why do people always do that? Or draw up a long stem of sedge, pulling and easing the stem out of the clasping leaves, as though you're pulling it out of its own self, so that the end is white and naked and tender. And put it in your mouth. Everyone does that.

"The Indians? Yes. Very good. Same thing," he said.

Every conversation is like a lesson, an unraveling, pulling

apart ideas, like we pull apart the grasses and runners around us. He is so eager, so excited to hear me say something he'd not thought in quite that way. He likes to see me extend his ideas instead of just telling him what he has told me. Like the Walt Whitman he is always reciting to me:

I am a teacher of athletes,
He that by me spreads a wider breast than mine proves the
width of my own,
He most honors my style who learns under it to destroy the
teacher.

And I see what he means, of course. But he shouldn't participate so eagerly in his own destruction, should he? Sometimes he hands me ideas, like he did today with that switch in attackers, and then he'll act forever more as though the original idea was mine. It wasn't, and I don't want it.

"So you're saying that the folks at Camp Ten are just afraid of us. So even when they shoot at us, like they did at Camber that once, they're not attacking us. Right?"

"They're defending themselves," he said. "They're afraid of you."

"Leastways they're afraid of Camber with a nose full. I would be too."

JOURNAL OF HAZEL TAYLOR
May 13, 1996

I look back upon these priceless afternoons sitting on the Flats with Saint Dunstan, and, in retrospect, I wonder how we possibly could have done this—a young girl alone on a mountain with this older man. Where did I have the time, amid all the chores and housework, to get away? And how, in a community notoriously suspicious of its own sexual mores could such a relationship—no matter how innocent—have been borne? Is it possible that no one really knew about these walks, these solitary conversations? Was I really so much more inconsequential than I would have thought? Well, I suppose the knowledge would have been a relief to me, who felt watched and controlled, enough so that I took the trouble not to tell anyone where we were going.

And Saint? He was old enough to understand the nasty turn everyone would have put on these meetings, had they known. Was he really so innocent that he simply trusted his own good intentions to protect us from the harmful intimations of gossip, or concern, or whatever it would have been?

Because I still insist that these meetings were just what they had seemed to me at the time—happy, fond conversations between two people who enjoyed thinking and talking. Nothing more. Certainly nothing less.

And is it his fault that all of this may have lulled me into believing that all men meant well? Or at least that an innocently phrased invitation to private converse must in fact lead to innocent converse? Because I believe my trust of Noah Kersin must have stemmed in part from my experiences of White Oak Flats with Saint. And so is Saint to blame for this? Or would it have been better had my Daddy, or the town gossips, or whoever might have spied and judged and falsely condemned Saint and me for our joyous meetings, would it have been better had they acted according to small-minded dirty suppositions, before the ugly resolution could have taken advantage of my own experience of trust and innocence? I don't know. Would I have walked-out with Noah Kersin that day had I not walked out before—without consequence—with Saint Dunstan?

My mamma died in a bad season. Just as Saint had said, it hits you twice. Momma got sick and took to her final bed, in July of my twelfth year, 1917, and a week later we had a bad storm and the hail took the tobacco crop. The next year, a man came around the creek selling hail insurance to all the farmers. All but Daddy.

"I reckon I can't buy no insurance," he told the man. "I done lost my crop to hail last year and so now I can't afford to buy your insurance. Right now, it just feels like your insurance is a way of making me pay for a crop I done already lost once. Ain't that a thing?" he said. "I don't reckon you'd sell me that insurance against this year's crop, would you? No, you couldn't do that, because then you'd be the farmer and I'd be the insurance man."

And Mamma died the same week as the hail. I was twelve years old, and I scrawled in my copybook, *Mamma is dying, hail took the crop*, and that was the beginning of my writing, that lasted ten years until I left, and now has bubbled back up again, as I move along toward dying.

I was in the room when she passed away, but I didn't see it. I had been brought in with my brothers and Daddy, to see her. She was still alive, still seeing something out of bright, red-rimmed eyes. She didn't see us, or at least we didn't see her seeing us. But it was clear that her fevered eyes were looking, searching after something.

I was told to take her hand, and I held the hot, dry, hard palm in mine. Her skin felt like tanned leather, and her index finger tapped reflexively, fast, against the curved back of my hand. The burning eyes sought mine, and moved on.

And that was that. I was ushered back a step or two and people began to move forward, toward her, and I was shuttled inexorably backward and sideways, into the far corner of the room, blocked from any view except the indistinguishable overalled backs, the worn, whitened heels of brogans. I couldn't even see the high knobs of the headboard that Daddy had brought up the creek from Badie's, hand-carrying the whole bed in three different trips, and roping it together the same day they were wed.

So I was in a little isolated alcove of my own. It was like being backstage at a play, hearing muffled voices and a cough or two from the audience, but beginning to close yourself away from all of that and exploring the ropes and weights and pulleys of your separate place, not so much behind the play as beyond it. I heard a fly rattle against the pane of the back window, just next to me, and I watched its uncertain, stumbling buzz. Then I turned down and saw Mamma's scrap box, and I began lifting out patches and looking at them. I could recognize some of them as scraps from a red shirt I'd worn two years ago, or one of my brothers' fancy blue slacks. A piece of bedsheet, or a scrap of yellow linen.

I sat down in front of the box, and spread my legs and began arranging the patches on the floor into some kind of pattern. I laid out a square of pieces, then began revising it: switching a yellow piece with a blue, moving the red patch upward, turning the square into a diamond, or making the letter T, *Tighrow*. This was not play, or fidgeting. It was serious, deliberate. I have no idea what my purpose was, but my arranging and rearranging was definite, calculated, critiqued, and rearranged again. Mamma's scraps moved about in orders by a twelve-year-old daughter, while everyone stood silent, backs to me, watching her die.

The fly stumbled down the pane once more, and I wondered what Mamma was hearing. And that was it. The room cleared out, I was ushered up to kiss her dead cheek, and that was that. I remember looking back, as Daddy hugged me out of the room. I was looking at the scraps of cloth, not at Mamma.

I liked the way the colors looked against the bleached, scrubbed wooden floor. Leaves floating on a pond.

VI.

ANDREW KAYER

So she was—is—a runaway.

I read Hazel's packet at home in my little apartment, and felt the full power of the disjunction between my own history and hers, and my own place—this third floor studio on Chicago's North Side, with the rumble and honk of traffic rolling outside and the snatched shout of a voice or a laugh, or five notes of a song sliding by on a car radio. And Hazel's journal speaking out of some deep hollow in the mountains, so soundless, here, that only her voice filters out. *But, of course, some of this was written right here in Chicago,* I tell myself. *She's lived here most of her life.*

But it wasn't true, really. Hazel had never had an air of residing here. As I've said, she seemed more like a guest, passing through, from some other locale entirely. And now, with this writing, she appeared even more distanced, as though the voice on the older papers—some of which seemed to be as fragile as tissues, or as her thin, translucent skin—had captured and retrieved the later Hazel, and drawn her on back to that deep mountain cove. It's as if the Hazel who sat in the conservatorium and wrote was merely some sort of speaker system, or transceiver, for the voice that speaks across the decades of time, from some impossible place in those mountains.

Or more than this, even. Because this was no mountain gal I was reading. Instead, here was a graceful, sophisticated voice, rising up from these pages. Impossible to be speaking out of the hand of a seventeen-year-old, *no matter how rapidly experience might grow-them-up in those hills.* And how could I have been prepared for any of this, since, to me, the mountainous backdrop meant that the voice must be crude, primitive, unlettered? And, instead, here was a young, self-taught genius, some improbable Bronte-sister from the furthest of our backwoods, writing so feelingly and sensitively that she put my own intelligence and training to shame.

And why did she give me these sheaves of loose paper, tied together with a short length of red yarn through a hole punched in the upper left corner of each? *She has arranged them carefully*, I thought. *Not chronologically, but in some chimerical thematic way. The meanings are elliptical, like her speech.*

"Of course they're in order," she said, insisted, in response to my questions. "I put them in order before I gave them to you." We were sitting together by her writing table, with a hard rain beating irregularly against the glass, the wind throwing it in sidearm handfuls, with a sound like cloth being shred in a series of short tears: *rrrip—riprip—rrrip.*

"Some people would say you took them out of order," I said.

"You mean out of sequence," she said. She reached down and pulled another group of pages out of her bag. "Here," she said. "Switch out the ones you've read and put these in the sack. And then look at this."

I did as I was told, fumbled the yarn-strung group of pages out of the cotton sack and replaced it with a new, identically gathered batch. Hazel was holding up a stained and faded photograph.

"What do you see?" she asked.

I saw a young woman in a rather shapeless light frock, more like a shift than a dress, and I recognized her immediately—by her smile and her eyes—as the young Hazel. She appeared to be about twenty, maybe younger. She seemed at once strikingly pretty and strikingly plain, in part because, in spite of the smile, she seemed disconnected from anything outside of herself, as though the pale narrow eyes were directed inward upon some secret scene. Or perhaps they were gazing long, far beyond the immediate view. It gave the face an expression of absence, a sort of autism that was a personality in itself. But there was a distinct sense of the body, lean and graceful, where the shapelessness of the shift betrayed itself in a delicate swell of breasts and curving flanks. She was what we would call "willowy," and she looked a good bit taller than today's hunched and bent Hazel. She didn't seem to be posing so much as barely noticing the camera and whoever stood behind it, so the overall impression was of lassitude, a kind of benevolent, fluid lounging. She appeared to be standing on bare ground, next to the corner of a roughly planked outbuilding. The land rose rapidly behind her, in a tangle of indistinct growth.

"It's you," I said.

"Better look again," she said, smiling. "Past tense," she said.

"Okay: it was you," I said.

"But it's here," she said. "Now. Present tense. What of that?"

"Yes," I said. "Of course. It's a picture of you. It was taken many years ago, and here it is, today." I put an inordinate emphasis on the "was," and "is." Mildly sarcastic.

"But she isn't here today, is she?"

"You're here," I said. "And she's you, only many years ago. She's the you you were," I said.

"She is the me I was?" she asked. This time the mocking, emphatic "is" and "was" were hers. "Certainly not the past recaptured. More the past transformed. Because, you see, she's changed by the very fact that we're looking, together, here, at her. If you had come across this photo somewhere else, before you had met me—in some dusty antique shop—you would look at it as an entirely different object. But you look at it now out of your knowledge of me. And that changes the young woman in the picture, doesn't it? And so it's not anything like a window into the past. In fact, it becomes a new image, developed out of the occurrences of the present, each time it's looked at. If I told you, now, that it was a picture of my twin sister, that would change the photo again, wouldn't it?"

"Do you have a twin sister?" I said. I was joking, trying to lighten-up this conversation a little. Hazel was hard at it: teaching. She ignored the non-question.

"A photo, like any memory you have, is about absence. Parted lovers gaze at each other's pictures precisely because they are parted. You don't look at your lover's picture when your lover is sitting there. So a photograph is about the past, yes. But it's about the present, as well. Photographs change like everything else.

"There are songs that will do that. There was one Saturday night when George played with his string band at a place over the way, toward town. I used to go along with him to these dances, now and again. I liked the music and seeing other people, getting a step or two beyond the creek. This place was a kind of dance hall: you turned across and ran down to a little handmade bridge that spanned the creek and then you curved back and down to this place. It was a long, low shed of a building. You could hardly see it as you rode up to it, and then there it was, a pasty white wall with a dirty-yellow handpainted sign: *The Country Club*, and I remember George just peering at that sign and saying, 'You'uns got to be kidding me.'

"It was a pretty rough place, and I liked it for that, too. Strange, isn't it, that I would be drawn to that sort of hard, savory place? There was plenty of white liquor being passed around all night, and a feeling of barely suppressed violence, as though the men were reluctant to lay down their rage even for the time necessary to greet a woman, dance with her. 'I don't mind the drinking,' Dawny said—he was the fiddler—'Long as they ain't no jar-pitching.' George always said that you could stay safe in a place like that if you listened to the talk. 'First time you hear somebody say *What you looking at?* that's when you best find a table to crawl under.' The women seemed to know that they were the focal point of both the violence and its temporary suspension: they seemed to move in a kind of hushed alertness, always glancing over, like a cat walking along a wall will always be looking sideways to make sure that wall isn't a trap.

"Anyway, the night went on, and some old farm boy in incredibly dirty overalls asked the band to play *Liza Up a 'Simmon Tree*. That's a nice, quick little dance tune. I always liked it, the way it turns in the second part gives it a dark edge, even though it's a bouncy song. Well I suppose that tobacco farmer understood the dark edge because he stood there right in front of the band as they played it. We had expected him to grab up a partner and dance, or just start to dance himself, the way they will. But he just stood there, in that dark, musty shed, with folks now dancing and clogging around him. And he began to weep. And he stood there, with his arms hanging straight down at his sides, in those stained and greasy overalls, and he wept, through the entire song, through all the dancing and drinking and uproar. Wept, through all of that swingy, running fiddle tune, made for buck dancing and carrying on. And when the song was over, he pulled a blue bandanna out of his hip pocket—still facing straight-on to the band—and slowly and deliberately wiped his wet face. Then he turned and shambled out the door into the night.

"So you see? If you have writing from the past, you need to see it as it is, in the present. Chronology isn't real, because time is a hopscotching of memory, here and there, back and forth. And it's all ordered by a present that is never quite here, always, in its turn, organized by memory, as past. Why would I give you pages in the order they were written? And if you were to pass these on to someone else, you would say something like, 'These are papers that Hazel Taylor gave me once.' But your reader would already be experiencing the story 'out of order,' as you say. Because I wrote them before I gave them to you. My handing them to you should come at the end of your friend's reading, not the beginning. Do you see?"

"No," I said.

She settled back into her chair. "I disappeared, once. Walked away from my place, without anyone knowing the why or where of my going."

"Yes," I said. "I read that."

"Without knowing it myself," she said. "Because it's only now, now that I'm almost dead, that I can gather up the evidence of my disappearance and try to decide why and where I went. To write an explanation. Not just to me."

"Yes," I said. "I see that. But why are you giving these to me? You don't owe me any explanation."

"Don't you want to read them?" she asked.

"Of course I do. Hazel, don't play games with me."

"Oh, this is no game," she said. "I knew a man once—he is a part of this story, who was a teacher. Passing things, knowledge, information on was just about everything to him. This passing of his deepest knowing to me was always a very touching gesture. You see? *Touching*, because it is always so deeply intimate. Am I embarrassing you?"

"You're confusing me," I said. The rain smattered the windows in a particularly hard handful. And again.

"It's the wind," Hazel said. "Not the rain; the rain is only there to show you the shape of the wind. At night in the mountains the wind will get to roaring in huge, rolling waves, and you can hear its shape. As though it's a ravening animal, nuzzling at the curves and notches of the mountain. You hear it come round the turn of a big knob and start to whistle as it runs down along a ravine. Then it's silent a moment as it climbs the next big slope and then it booms over the top. You can watch it come around and across and along into these mountains as it wends its own way to you. It shapes the mountains, you see. It's there to show you the curve and contour of your own place, right down to the whine in the eaves of your own house, rising and falling, from a hum to a shriek. When I was a little girl I would listen to that wind and tell myself, *It's looking for me. It's rolling across them high knobs and down into these coves just hunting for me.* And I would curl down into the warm cave of my own body-heat, under the quilts, and tell myself that I was a rabbit, curled into my burrow, and the wind couldn't find me as long as I stayed here. But by and by it would ease up and get quiet, and I would want it back, so I would lay my naked arm out over the top of the bedclothes, trying to entice that wind back out, to start hunting me again, so I could hear its roaring and booming.

"There's something else," she said. She reached her hand out and placed it on my forearm. I felt its clawed crookedness. It was like being brushed by a tree limb.

"Yes," I said.

"I believe I've killed someone. At least one. No. Three."

VII.

July 6, 1917

Mamma is dying, hail took the crop.

July 10, 1917

I miss my Mamma. I feel empty when I walk around the house and I think I will see her. I told Daddy and he said it's because she is still here. He said we feel sad because we love her and she loves us, so being sad is good. He says love is joy but always sadness too.

July 18, 1917

We will have a hard winter since the hail took most of the crop. Daddy says we'll get by. We are all so sad. Georgie came today and said he would walk with me down to the road. So I went. We didn't talk about Mamma or anything else. I cried by the riverside, though. Georgie didn't say anything. Then he said I should listen to the water. I did and I felt better.

JOURNAL OF HAZEL TAYLOR
July 19, 1917

I'm worried about being the only girl in a house full of boys. My brothers are always working outside and now I work in the house. I used to do a lot more work outside, but now I have to stay in more and tend to things Momma used to do. I don't think anyone will sing to me anymore. I told Mamma I would teach her to read and she said we could write down her songs and I could always remember them, even when she is gone. Now I know what she meant, but she is gone and I can't remember the words to write them down. I will try to remember some of them and write them down. Then maybe I will remember more later. The stories are so strange and they sound so far away:

> Lady Margaret sitting in her high hall chair
> Combing back her long yellow hair,
> She saw Sweet William and his new maid bride
> Riding up the road so near.

I thought I would know more than this.

JOURNAL OF HAZEL TAYLOR
July 20, 1917

> Black Jack Davy came riding by,
> A'whistling so gaily,
> He made the hills around him ring,
> And he won the heart of a lady,
> He won the heart of a lady.

How old are you my pretty little miss,
How old are you my honey,
She answered him with a silly smile,
I'll be sixteen next Sunday,
Be sixteen next Sunday.

Come go with me my pretty little miss,
Come go with me my honey,
I'll take you across the deep blue sea,
Where you never shall want for money,
You never shall want for money.

She took off her high heel shoes,
All made of Spanish leather,
She put on those low heel shoes,
And they both rode off together,
Both rode off together.

Last night I lay on a warm featherbed,
Beside my husband and baby,
Tonight I lay on the hard, cold ground,
By the side of Black Jack Davy,
Beside of Black Jack Davy.

Well, I remembered one. I think this is all the words, but I
might have missed one. It's a good song, but it don't tell as long
a story as most of them. Mamma used to say that the lady is
sorry she went away. She said we know that because the lady
talks about how cold the ground is. I don't know. I think she
thinks it's an adventure and she wants to be outdoors next to
Black Jack Davy. I sure would.

Georgie just came by and I sang it to him. He says he knows it.
He says he bets he could play it on the banjo. I bet he could too.
He said he wants me to call him "Black Jack Davy" for awhile,

but I think that's silly. He isn't anything like Black Jack Davy. He can't even whistle.

JOURNAL OF HAZEL TAYLOR
August 19, 1917

Oh my heavens, this is a terrible day. Little T.R. and Rosie and I were playing up in her barn and she jumped out onto a pitch fork. I don't know how it happened, I was lying down on my stomach, drawing pictures on a paper with Rosie's red pencil. And then she gave a laugh and jumped off the ledge and the pitch fork was right below her and she landed on it. It stuck in her back and she couldn't even scream nor cry. She just lay there and whimpered. Little T.R. cried and run off. So I run to the house and got Mrs. Blankenship and she hollered for Big T.R., who was out at the smokehouse. I was so scared.

Big T.R. kept saying, "Easy now, Honey. It'll be all right." I could tell he was scared too. He turned Rosie over, while Mrs. Blankenship hung on to the handle of the fork, and he ripped her dress open and looked at her back. She looked so small.

"Well, we're going to have to pull it out," he said. And he just reached down and hooked his fingers into the heel of the fork, and gave a hard pull. Rosie screamed, then, and then she lay still. There wasn't any blood except a little watery stuff with some blood in it. But her back was all black except where the fork had gone in, where it was greenish-white. It was terrible.

They took her into the house and sent me to fetch Gran' Cawdle. I thought I was too shaky to run, but I did, and got over Timb's Hill to her place as fast as I could. Gran' Cawdle was out with the chickens and it took a minute to find her. And she's slow, so it seemed to take forever before she gathered up her bag and came on out. And then we had to walk on back across the hill. I was so worried that we were taking too long, but there weren't anything to do but to keep walking.

We finally got there and Gran' Cawdle went in. They kept me outside because they said I "shouldn't see this." But I saw her fall and saw Big T.R. yank that fork away, so I was bound to look. I wandered on in to see Rosie.

Gran' was leaning over the bed and Mrs. Blankenship was holding a lamp while Gran' put some sort of salt paste on Rosie's back. Rosie didn't make a sound. I couldn't see anything but a bit of her back and her shoulder. She looked like gray dough.

Gran' Cawdle put a piece of linen over the salt paste, and handed something to Mrs. Blankenship. Then Big T.R. came up behind me.

"What you doing here, Hazie?" he said. "You scoot now."

"Is Rosie all right?" I said.

"Lord knows, Hazie," he said. "Time tells everything."

So I come home and told Daddy, and I cried some, and he said I should get busy and sarcle the garden and sweep up the porch and such. I didn't know why he was making me work at such a time. But bye and bye I got less scared and so that was why Daddy made me get busy. Then I came in here and wrote this.

I just noticed that I'm writing this with Rosie's pencil.

JOURNAL OF HAZEL TAYLOR
September 10, 1917

It's getting down toward time for school to start. They're putting linseed on the floors right now, and I'm setting out front on one of the benches that's stacked around out in the yard. Mine is under the big chestnut tree, in the cool, and I can hear their voices booming from inside the vacant room. I like that smell when the year starts; it's so strong that the whole world smells like linseed oil. You can smell it at night on your clothes after setting in the room all day.

George is working in there with Mr. Dunstan, putting the oil down. I wish they would let girls do it, too. I go over and watch now and again, and it's a pleasure to see the room all bare of benches and the oil poured out onto the floors. The yaller curl of oil has shining bubbles set into it like little planets, all aglow with their own summers. Then the wave of linseed out in front of the big brooms as they work it around on the floor. It's thick enough that you can see layers, one wave lopping over another and then gradually merging together. When they finish, the floor has a shine with a dark underneath, like the surface of a puddle in the evening.

I wonder why they don't sing while they're swopping the oil onto the floor. If it was girls, women, doing the job, well they'd be singing, sure. I don't remember ever a time when Mamma weren't singing while she worked. And then she'd sing when she got done with the work. But a different kind of song. I guess I don't sing when I work. I talk to folks. Or to my own self. And when I get done with the working, well, I guess I read. And you just can't read and sing at the same time, can you?

JOURNAL OF HAZEL TAYLOR
October 28, 1917

We spent the day getting ready to cut the tobacco. Daddy says it's going to freeze early so we'd best get what we can out of this crop now. The leaves are still pretty green, just starting to yellow, but we can't take the chance of waiting. We got the sticks out of the barn and Johnson said, "We won't need so many this year. Most of it's tore all up." Daddy said, "We'll get by."

I helped Junior build the frame on the sled. I like the smell of the wood and I pretend we're building a cathedral. I don't do much, just hand things to Junior and hold up the side sticks while he hammers on the runners. I helped him to find the right limbs with the curves just right on them. We got good hickory limbs and he says it's a good sled.

I like the cutting because it's a long job. In the morning you can look way ahead and see that big field and we haven't even cut the least stick. Then you get to work and all you see is this plant, then that plant. And then you kindly become part of the job, so you can tell how much is left by how tired you are. And after a few hours, you look back and you think *we was way on over yonder this morning and now we're here.* And then you look at the next plants.

Daddy built a frame for holding the stick and I held the other end. Daddy and Junior and Johnson cut and Billy brought the plants over to slide down the stick. The sticks get heavy when all five plants are on them, and there's gum all over. I asked Daddy why tobacco plants are so gummy, and he says, "Where else would you want them to put all that gum?" He says "They couldn't put it on the taters or you'd starve to death a'trying to peel the durn things." Everybody laughed, but it just got me to thinking.

Daddy has a new long-handled snath so he doesn't have to bend over so far and his knee doesn't hurt, he says. It looks right strange, and they all laugh about *Daddy's scything tobacco.* "You got to bend down to ratch the plant anyway, Daddy," says Junior. "So what in the world's the use?" Now and then he trades with Junior or Johnson so they can get straightened up.

Johnson let me try to cut a plant. He had to hold me up to start because the top was so high. I did a good job, Daddy says. I didn't split any leaves. I almost split the stalk down too far, but I didn't. When I pulled the knife to cut the plant, I couldn't do it, so Johnson cut the plant for me. Anyway, I'm learning.

I asked Johnson why folks from Tennessee are called *volunteers.* "Because they ain't got sense enough to come in out of the rain," he said. I asked him what they calls folks from North Carolina and he said, "Folks." I don't think he wanted to talk to me so much.

Big T.R. came by to see if we needed help, and we put him on the sled, so the boys didn't have to clamber up and down, and he set the sticks on the runners when Billy and I handed them up. "Don't you bruise them leaves," T.R. hollered at us all day.

Nobody talks much, except me.

JOURNAL OF HAZEL TAYLOR
October 29, 1917

We're finished and I'm too tired to write. My arms hurt like the dickens. It feels kind of good, even though it hurts. I think that's because you can stretch out and feel tired and that feels good. And you have that whole field of tobacco in your arms and legs and feet. I never got all the gum off, and I lie here and pick at it, even though it hurts, too. I wonder why people do things like that.

JOURNAL OF HAZEL TAYLOR
November 11, 1917

Mr. Dunstan says poems are for saying a lot in a very few words. He says the things we feel the most deeply about are the things we can't name. And so poems try to find ways to name those things by holding them up next to other things that we do have names for. How the way I feel when I see Little T.R. Blankenship feels like eating a good mess of green beans. I said this, and everybody laughed, but I didn't mean it to be funny.

Rosie is bad off.

JOURNAL OF HAZEL TAYLOR
November 16, 1917

It's hard to write tonight, with my thumb all bruised and hurt, but I might just as well try to write because I know the throbbing is going to keep me from sleeping much. Daddy has us cracking walnuts every night now, and I took a good whack with the hammer tonight. Daddy says it's bound to happen, if you crack enough walnuts. He says *you smack yourself a little bit with the hammer about every ten nuts, just to get practiced up. Then, when you're right good at it, you drop that hammer right squat on your thumb and it still hurts like tarnation no matter how many times you done rehearsed it.* I wish I could be as funny about things as Daddy is. He's got a way of saying things, just quiet and straight ahead like, that makes them even funnier.

We went out Saturday morning and gathered up piles of nuts, up the holler beyond High Creek, where the big old trees are. It's a mite steep up that way, but if you get them all rolling down the same way, you can pile them up at the bottom of a rise. T.R. and Georgie helped us, me and Junior, and it was funny watching them knock the black, rotted skins off with the stick, all the while singing "I'm Going to Eat at the Welcome Table," and smacking them walnuts in time.

We lugged them down here and spread them out in the sun. I was all over black stain and goo, and Georgie couldn't keep from wiping his face, so he was *streaked and smeared like a sinner on Sunday*, T.R. says. We got them back up by Sunday, so we've been cracking them ever since, nights before bed.

It's nice to hear singing in the house again, because everybody sings while they're cracking the walnuts. George sang a funny song about Jonah and the Whale. Daddy says George sure knows a load of songs for a kid. I can't sing and crack the nuts, because I can't pay attention to holding them so I can hit them right on top. If I try to sing, the nut slips over and I smash the shell. So Daddy says he cannot afford to hear me sing more than one song a night. He says God put the point on the bottom of a walnut just so we'd have to hold them up to crack them, where our thumbs are bound to get in the way and get hit. He says *that's how God done figured out tribulation for us folks that don't live near no whales.*

Cracking walnuts is hard work, and it takes a long time to get even a pound of them, but Daddy says we need some cash money extra hard this year because of the bad crop, and so we're at it extra this Fall. Sure hurts plenty.

JOURNAL OF HAZEL TAYLOR
January 8, 1918

I went to see Gran' Cawdle today, when I got out of school. I wanted to ask her about Rosie. She scares me a mite, because she's old and talks different. But the same things that scare me are the things that make me want to get to know her. I think if it's not a little scary, maybe it ain't worth doing. And I didn't used to be able to understand anything she said, but now I can follow her pretty much without really knowing how it is I understand her. Like finding your way along a new trail. You can't even spot the trail where it switches back maybe the first time or two. But then, without even knowing it, you can just walk on up that trail without looking at it. You just seem to have come to understand it.

So I went on over there. I remember Mamma would always bring something with her when she went to see Gran,' so I searched around for something. I went hunting the fence rows to get some guinea eggs, until I recalled that she raises chickens and probably has a plenty of eggs. So I went around back to the smokehouse and sawed off a big slab of ham for her. I know she doesn't raise pigs, and these hams are as good as anybody's.

On the way across the hill I tried to remember Lady Margaret and I just kept getting stopped at the end of the first verse. I tried Omie Wise, but I didn't even get that much. It's sad, because those songs are a part of my life and my knowing of Mamma. She sang them all the time, and she feathered them out, making her voice like a fiddle bow. She said she learned to sing the old time way from her own mamma and someday I'd show my girls how to sing them. But it won't be.

I'm glad to have learned how to read. I'd a heap rather read than anything. But I think maybe Mamma had a gift in not knowing how. Because she had all those songs, like a huge collection of books in her mind. And she had Omie Wise and the House Carpenter and Fair Ellender and all of them passing back and forth inside her mind. And it was as if she opened up different doors and let them out. Because each one had a different story and a different feeling and she sang each one in its own way. And each of them was a different part of her, too, mixing in with the way she used her hands patting down lard biscuits or wrapping a towel around a slice of cold ham. Slicing up fruit and putting them on the screens. And setting them out to dry on top of the smokehouse, you'd see those screens and that was Mamma. Or dipping out of the cedar bucket. And if you can read, you lose that, somehow. I guess I wouldn't trade. But I wish I could remember.

I did get some of the eerie part, where Margaret comes and stands at the foot of Sweet William's bed, like some sort of spirit. And she asks him these questions:

How do you like your snow white pillow,
And how do you like your sheet?
And how do you like that fair little maid,
Lying in your arms asleep?

And William answers just the same way. I think it's even eerier because they use the same words. Like haints.

Very well do I like my snow white pillow,
Very well do I like my sheet,
Much better do I like that pale white vision,
Standing at my bed feet.

Daddy came in once when Mamma was singing this and said, "I believe he's referring to Lady Margaret, her own self." It was funny the way he said it.

Look at this! I've gotten away from Gran' Cawdle and on to these strange old songs and here it's plain late and I must sleep.

Same thing happened on Timb's Hill today. I was going to watch for arrowheads on the way to Gran's, and then I got to thinking about Mamma's songs and forgot about where I was. Just like I was a haint, too.

I'd best go to sleep. I'll write more tomorrow. I'm getting to like writing this almost like reading books.

JOURNAL OF HAZEL TAYLOR
January 9, 1918

Gran' Cawdle told me yesterday that I could bring her ginseng next year and she'd pay me a good price for it. Daddy was happy to hear that, but he said he thought "Gran' Cawdle mints her money out of the full moon." Which I think means that she doesn't really have any money to buy with. Or maybe not: I've heard the same thing said about folks who make corn liquor, that they're "minting money out of the full moon." I don't know.

Gran' lives out off by herself, away yonder past Short's place, in a little cabin tucked into the cove. She's the shortest grownup I know, and she looks like an old twisted ironwood. Big T.R. says some folks think she's a witch, but he says that's just because she knows a lot more than they ever will. Everyone calls her "Gran,'" as though she's always been an old woman, but, of course, she was a girl my age, once. I wonder what it was caused her to stay out yonder away from everyone. She tells me lots of things about roots and yarbs and such, but she won't say anything about growing up out here. Even to a direct question, she is very dodgy. I asked her yesterday if there was some reason she chose to live alone, away out in the woods.

"I mean, when you were little, you didn't live all by yourself. You lived with your family, in Shelton's Trace?"

"Mmmm," she said. She was pouring water over muslin cloths, for making poultices. "Gotter sparge'm good. Raah me, pottered poultice ain't fer healing you'uns'"

"But Gran,' I was just wondering why you decided to live out here. Away in this cove, I mean."

She stopped and turned. She moved her hand out at an angle from her waist, and the water drooled off onto the floor. She stared me a look that wasn't anger or sadness, but wasn't anything else.

"Lore," she said. And again, "Lore. Cunnin.'" She stared hard at me for a second and then went back to sparging her cloths.

I believe I know what she means.

She says Rosie is very sick and the fork hurt her really bad inside. She said a poultice won't do for a hurt that deep. "E'en er's a callet 'r two'd sail you'uns 'un.

Rosie, that'uns needing tonic, but ever batch I purrelate, she'll hove it yanders. Can't be holpen, poor littluns. She's a'pottering-up inside, if she'uns a'hoving toot all."

So I'm very worried about Rosie. They won't let me see her anymore, but little T.R. says she's all yaller and he says the room doesn't smell good. "Like a old dead whistle pig," he says. But that's just his way of talking. And now Gran' says she's throwing up everything they give her, so she isn't getting enough medicine or water, and she's getting *pottered*, dried up, inside.

It's hard to believe she's still lying in that room. What does she see? What is she thinking, right now?

JOURNAL OF HAZEL TAYLOR
March 6, 1918

Rosie has died! Rosie, my friend and I can't find any way to put any of this in writing.

* * *

JOURNAL OF HAZEL TAYLOR
March 6, 1923

I am writing with Rosie's pencil, which I have always kept near me, because T.R. came by earlier today and told me that this is the fifth anniversary of Rosie's death. I find it hard to believe she's been gone so long. And I looked back at my journal and I see that I never wrote her anything. So I am going to try again to write about these things. I think I need to put this down. At her funeral, Daddy said *her grave won't seem so lonesome when she has her name on it.* So this can be a place to put her name in my life. Rosie. Rosie.

She was shorter than me, but a year older although she always seemed younger. It seemed as though a time came without our awareness, and she just stopped getting any older. So even though she had a birthday each year, she seemed not to have noticed: like a dogwood will only get so big and never any bigger. The way she ran around and jumped and laughed all the time. She never worried about acting silly and this made her seem to stay still while we moved on by her, the rest of us, growing a little more serious and a little more controlled each year. None of us would have been killed by that pitchfork, because none of us would have jumped out of that loft. I guess Rosie just kept her trust in the world a little too long.

And then she was stilled forever. She will remain the little girl, while all of us move further and further beyond her. It is horrible. At the funeral the choir sang the usual song that they mean for comfort, but this time it only increased my fear and sadness. It's what should really be written on Rosie's grave, a message, a reply from that world, or nature, or God, who betrayed her trust when she hopped the sill of that loft and dropped laughing into nothing:

I have heard of a land, on the far away strand,
'Tis the beautiful home of the soul,

Built by Jesus on high, where we never shall die,
'Tis the land where we'll never grow old.

Never grow old, never grow old,
In the land where we'll never grow old.
Never grow old, never grow old,
'Tis the land where we'll never grow old.

I don't think I have ever heard that song in peace again.

I've been sad all day long, because she is gone, and the sense of her is not. So I expect to see her coming up the creek, skipping a little bit, like an eight-year old. The expectation creates a kind of reality, as if the path itself had absorbed her absence and now exudes her, like a fragrance, whenever I walk along it. And it feels as though she has been summarized in every detail of the place itself. She isn't gone; she is absence, not erasure. Her absence regenerates everything around me, everything a sum of her, like Saint said once, when he was still our teacher, "One is the most powerful number in the universe because all other numbers contain it." And after school, I asked him "What about Zero?"

And he looked at me, a little surprised, and said, "What do you think, Hazie?"

And I said, "Maybe Zero is God, because no numbers can contain it."

VIII.

I came out one afternoon, after the wash, to look for ginseng up the mountain. The laurel was coming out all over, and I can still feel it nodding all around me, opening itself through all these mountains. The day was warm and bright and I hunted through the thickets of laurel like walking in a floating of snowfall. I stayed at it, hunching over and working up the mountain through the maze, back and forth over the creek. You can smell the fresh, cold water up here as the creek narrows down and splits up. You can follow any of these fingers up to a spring and drink pure, cold air.

And suddenly I was there. On a wide, open meadow at the very top of the trail I remember thinking, *This must be White Oak Flats...And here I am.* I think I may have immediately taken it on, named it as a special place, because nobody had been up there in a long time, and nobody was likely to come. *Folks always talk about this place like it's the other side of the world. So I can climb up here when I want some time to read or write.*

The meadow was surrounded by laurels, like a flowered crown on a huge, curving forehead. I sat at the very highest part of the head, under the wrinkled, old apple tree. I looked over its long, vertical grooves, judged they were from the bears. *And it splits*

84

at about eye level and turns back, crouching over itself. It's not like an oak, that expresses the power of time in its strength and growth. Instead, the apple tree shows its age in its sadness and loneliness. And somehow I find that more attractive, more welcoming. It sits here all by itself, like Gran' Cawdle's shack, a piece of human effort beyond any further human connection. Until you sit here. And you can feel the tree breathe against the nubs of your back.

Something about this memory tells me why I so longed to leave these mountains, as though the meadow, the laurel, the tree were signs to some doorway, within myself. *Take us, take us into your body and draw us away. Wound yourself on our skin and break through into your own self.* It's as though I gathered in the only urge left to this place: the urge not to be. I don't know. Even as I sit here, an old woman, I feel it: I feel as though it would be easier to walk to Asheville than to go back home and watch myself curl back on myself, like that tree.

Perhaps leaving was the only way.

I believe people have been trying to get out of these mountains since they first set foot in them. Because most of the first white settlers were runaways. They came from indentured service or from the prison colony in Georgia. Well maybe they remained runaways even after they thought that they had stopped running. Maybe that's what a runaway is. Someone who can't, won't, stop breaking out, can't help but look for another place because wherever he, no, she, is has become an unbearable ground on which to grow. As though there's someone she finds herself becoming who is so completely linked with this place that she's got to run from her own becoming. She discovers that the things she looks at every morning, the way she uses her hands—even, maybe especially, the things she's growing to love—are turning her into a woman she can't bear to remain with. Since this becoming is the place, itself. And so the runaway from Georgia who has fled her prisoner-self has headed off for these mountains because this is a place where no one owns anybody. So she comes here. And she loves these coves and hollows where she no longer has to see, be, the indentured servant, all bound down to a servitude she had once sought so eagerly, because it released her from whatever unbearable place she'd run away from in England or Ireland. And finds herself holding this place, this life that belongs to her, in amorous embrace, loving it so deeply in her body that she can caress, lay a hand on, nothing else. Until she awakes at some point and finds out of that very love that she has grown some new self that she can't bear to stay around.

Or maybe it's not her, actually. Maybe she hasn't had time to live that many lives. So it becomes her daughter or her granddaughter, who has been born out of that loving for this place, born out of a love for these mountains so strong that it has driven her grandmam to face Lord knows what terrors and struggles to get from that indenture on that tidewater farm to this implausible place. And she has drawn in from her mother's own breast that passion to be away from somewhere, and so has taken it into herself and finds herself so linked to this place that she suddenly knows she can't stay. Because she can't grow herself in a place where she's already emerged fully developed. Already a mountain woman the moment she emerges from that loving womb, loving the place herself, and fated to become a woman, like they say, already done cured, tied an' tagged. And there's no prospect of becoming anyone but the woman she is already prefigured to be. And so she begins to feel that longing, that same incipient urge that her mother or grandmother or great-great ancestor felt out of some hovel in the slums of London or some blasted heath on a hillside in Ireland, loving perhaps the very smell of peat smoke in the air, the burr and lilt of the voices—their own voices—or even the noise and smell and crush of those city slums, the roll of barrels on cobbled streets, the grit beneath their nails. Loving it so much that they know they have to get away. In order, you see, just to become. Not some predetermined "Irish woman" or "slum girl" or servant.

And now it's the granddaughter looking out across a tumbling, bone-cold stream at the dark forest, and hearing the deep winds roaring through the coves and hollows, feeling the looming

*mountains that have covered her and made her and will haunt
her forever, and knowing that she can't be this woman, this
"mountain gal," any longer.*

*These mountains have been losing people for three hundred
years. Even the Cherokees, who found they could become the
people they wanted to be in this very place, and so maybe felt
that they had ceased their struggling flight. Who had come here
out of some distant urging to flee, and had wandered away
from some long ago steppe or icefield or tundra in some incon-
ceivably deep longing. And had crossed an impossible span into
these mountains and had thought that here, at last, they could
remain and build the people they could stand to be.*

*And even they couldn't stay. But instead, found themselves
sent off their final place, driven west by some new power that
already possessed things these Indians never thought existed, and
discovered it had to have these mountains, too. And so, exiled
and remote, they live out their lives on arid plains a thousand
miles from here, where they confront plagues of grasshoppers
and sit in fabricated houses made of yellow mud, in dry cracked
heat, now constantly dreaming of a flight backward to a mountainous land that isn't even there anymore. And those Cherokee
who stayed—you see them around all over these parts of the
mountains—they're the worst off of all. You can see it in their
eyes, a frenetic longing to get out, to go where they won't have to
see themselves turning into the pariahs they have become in their
own place.*

JOURNAL OF HAZEL TAYLOR
June 26, 1997

I so wanted to come here. It wasn't just the getting away, escaping
that woman I was bound to be if I remained, although certainly
that was the main part. But here, I knew, were schools and libraries and museums, where I could feed the thrice-starved self who
fostered and raised the dreams in the first place. I came here like

Miranda, never having seen such things, but knowing, intimating somewhere deep in those interior conversations we call *intuition*, that I would find my mainland here, among these houses of ideas.

When I first arrived here, I would walk from my little apartment up to the library—it was a mile or so—and I would talk to myself about all I saw going on: *here's a fellow in the market buying a soda pop and some pudding. The pudding he is taking home to his daughter, who stayed out of school with a bad throat, today. Daddy's hoping it isn't the influenza or the typhoid fever. Yes, look, he's bought a penny candy, too! Now here's an old woman getting off the streetcar. She's come to visit her son who is living in those new houses down the block, and making quite a name for himself at the insurance company. She's worried that she's losing him* meanwhile thinking about books and writing, the scratch of the nib, the ritual of blotting, the miracle coolness of paper.

At the library, I'd sit and try to read, but I'd invariably find myself looking around. I could never quite get to reading in a place like that. There was always a poor man or two huddled over with a book open in front of him, trying to get warm after a night out on the street, and hoping the open book would stay the imperious hand of the "watcher," who, like "watchers" everywhere, knew you were there, floating warily in one of these pools of lamplight ranged down the long reading tables. You were there to be found and yanked out of there. And he (the watcher) could feel that almost sensual exhilaration that you know all watchers feel at the absolute certainty that you would be caught, fished out, and exposed. Because it was the exposure that produced the most delightful thrill. The strident command, sounding even louder in this room made for whispers, the readers' heads popping up out of their aloneness, to witness this surge of power. The grasping and thrusting out, the rapturous holding forth of the wriggling catch, held naked and desperately embarrassed in front of the entire respectable world, so the watcher can show everyone how shameful it can get, and make them all sit a little straighter, read a little more decorously. The watcher, who loves to be seen.

So it's always the watchers who disturb the decorum, actually. After all, the poor man huddled into that pool of light wants quiet and loneliness above all, prays for quiet invisibility. He has tucked himself behind the open book, hoping—with that hopeless foreknowledge of failure—to snatch a few more minutes of warmth before the watcher hooks him back onto the street. And he wants peace and quiet, above all. Really, he'd be an excellent reader if it weren't for all the watchers creating their secret little disturbances, to fire their secret little lusts. All good readers are huddled behind their books, all curled up into quiet loneliness. But no one can read knowing the watchers are there. No one.

And so that was the end with the libraries. I couldn't bear playing the part of audience necessary to the watchers' shows, who needed their power witnessed. Perhaps it was the watchers themselves that kept me from reading. Perhaps I knew they were looking for runaways, too, and that I was circling just below their nets, myself.

I never read quite as much as I did back home, though there are some lovely places for reading. I discovered a thirst for fountains, public fountains in the middle of plazas or squares, with the people and birds strutting by, tracing intersecting paths, each leading to some hidden destination. I'd love to sit there with a book and become the still center of the strutting, bustling movement, until, by centering it, I could sink away from it, and mingle with the words on my page, as they grew larger and larger. And then, once in awhile, to break the trance, to look up and see the people and the birds, like a seal breaking the surface and grabbing a breath, and then down, down, the process of submerging into the immeasurable depths of the page, again, the absorbed walkers falling away into another place.

I discovered that fountains were the place to read in this city. And I found that a beautiful fountain attains its splendor in its ability to make air palpable. It's not the water; that's merely a frame to the twisting tumble of air, smoothed by the hand of the water. Just as the wind shapes water—the wave curled in the hand of the air.

But all around me the city burgeons with people, buying and selling, buying and selling. In the mountains, most of us, perforce, thought of needs as food, and clothing, and such inescapable demands upon time and wealth. And so we saw wants as something beyond. I think we knew that wants were frivolous, mostly, and that the joy in wanting lay in the partaking of the inanity of the item—whatever it was—as an object of personal desire. Most mountain people have this much of health, sanity, about them. And I expected this to be universal, except in the case of addicts and others sick in their hearts.

I found this not to be true, and I still wonder at it. Here, the mythology is that *we create products to satisfy needs*, but all you need to do is look around this city for a week or so and you'll discover that business doesn't do this at all. And it's not even that they create things to satisfy "wants." No. Because wants are satisfied by their own senselessness, their own awareness of the ludicrosity of wanting something in the first place. No. What has happened here is that products have been designed, produced, in order to create the needs. And that's the terrible thing about it. That's the devil about it.

Today, everyone appears to need a computer, let's say. Now even ten years ago—certainly twenty, no one needed a computer. And everyone got along about as well as they get along now. Except now they need just a little more money because they need to pay for that computer. Or, perhaps better, how about these cell phones? Five years ago, nobody needed a cell phone. Now you can watch as people go from wanting one to needing one. And it's not just a conceit, not a turn of phrase. It really is a need. You really do need a computer, now. And you will need a cell phone.

Now people will do just about anything to get their real needs taken care of. If you have no food, or no shelter, no clothes for your kids, you will sacrifice yourself and others to get those things. But even then, you know that survival is at stake. You have taken those needs into yourself. They aren't abstracted at all: you need to see that child's swelling belly taken care of. What you really desire, here, is life, health, breath, self and other. Love.

But what of these present-day products, these things that appear one day and inexorably become *needs* the next? If you really need a computer, then you will take extravagant steps to obtain one. You will become less generous with your time and wealth, because you need to pay for that computer. Or that cell phone. Or that CD player. And the difference is that these needs aren't backed up by desires like health, breath, love. These new ones are raw needs, existing only for themselves. So instead of taking these needs into yourself, you squeeze yourself into the needs. You become a person who discovers needs. And these needs are always less than yourself, less than your neighbors. There's nothing behind them but having.

This is what I see here. Crowds of people struggling against one another—against themselves—to obtain, consume, collect, control things. They've forgotten about making things and have taken to getting things. And it's not their fault: they need these things. They need them. And what will happen, when all the effort to produce—all the talent and the money and the steaming factories—are turned toward producing these things, *satisfying these needs*? What happens to food, and clothing, and health, and love?

Now mountain folks—at least back when I was home—they don't have this sickness, most of them. But it struck me the other day that we fulfilled our needs in the mountains by raising tobacco and making whiskey. And whoever discovered that you could turn harmless desires into desperate needs must have learned that lesson from tobacco and whiskey. So maybe we're not so innocent of this stain after all.

But all this is musing, pure speculation. Oh I'm an expert on the mountains. I looked at everything, studied and dreamed on everything, each and every day of my life on the Creek. I can tell you about the mountains down to the last laurel cup. But they're the mountains of the nineteen-twenties. I could explain everything there is to know and see, and you might go there and look around and say, "Why that Hazel's crazy. These mountains aren't anything like she said. She must have lost her memory. Or she's been *a'hatcheting on me*," as George says.

I heard, or read, a story somewhere about a young fellow whose parents had emigrated from Poland to this city. He grew up all his life with the dream of returning to the land his parents spoke about, to partake directly of the place he had seen and touched so many times, for so many years, in his dreams. He loved the stories of the music and the dancing, the village saint's festivals, the smell of earth, of place. He dreamed them so well that he became a Pole, in his mind. He nourished and cherished the language, insisting that the family speak Polish around the house, even when the younger siblings rebelled in scorn. As a child he lied to his friends about being born in Poland, and he set his life's course on getting there to live. So he saved his money and he pawned his gold watch and chain, and he traveled to his beloved Poland.

And it just wasn't there. He asked people his own age about the dancing and the festivals and they laughed and stared. He spoke to them in their own language and they laughed at the odd colloquialisms, the quaint inflections. He sang a song for them— one he had heard his parents sing again and again, their eyes full of home. And these people, these "Poles," gaped and laughed, and asked him about basketball and rock music, and called him a "motherfucker," and walked away to get a hamburger.

So he returned to America, to his parent's neighborhood, and he began to haunt the places where the older folks were: the church clubs and the Polish-American club, in an old brick building on South Halsted, near the old stockyards. And he talked to them of Poland, sang with them of Poland and of longing and of going home. And at night he dreamed of the colorful festivals and the dancing and the buxom happy girl whose waist he encircled on a cobbled lane beside a medieval church.

Five years later, they closed the Polish-American club. The membership had pretty well died out and no one wanted to maintain a big hollow building, with an echoing gymnasium that had served as ballroom for uncounted weddings, but now served only as a reminder that no one was there. And the bar had kept a few old customers who hunched and drank with rheumy eyes and discussed weather. The boy who had dreamed of Poland sat there with them and talked about the snow.

IX.

JOURNAL OF HAZEL TAYLOR
October 15, 1920

What a strange, bright day!

I went on down to Badie's store right after school today. I won a ticket for spelling and that gave me enough for a fountain pen, which I'd been hoping for for so long it got to seem like the hope was just going to become a part of me. As though folks would say, *There goes Hazel Tighrow, the girl that's hoping for that there fountain pen.*

Well, I got it, the ticket, and it was no mean shakes, either, because I had to spell *sacrificial*. I did it fine, and when I got to the last part, the *c-i-a-l*, I heard T.R. give a little whistle and say, "I'll be damned." And Mr. Dunstan was extremely pleased. I could tell that.

Badie's was full up with the usual old fellows around the stove, spitting on the iron, even though it was a nice sunny fall day. As long as I live I will never get so I'm not bothered by that spitting. Well it sounds awful, like some small animal dying and it smells terrible, to me. T.R. says he likes the smell. Well I imagine so.

And walking into the store with them watching you come in, I don't like that either. There's times they'll just watch you every step you take as you walk in and up to the counter. When I was a little girl, I'd laugh and talk with those same men and one would buy me a stick of candy and it was just good fun. But now they're still as the grave, just watching me walk by them. And I'll get up to the counter and then one'll just let go with the tobacco juice and *spass* that hot iron will say. And then one will say, "I reckon," or some such thing, answering something someone else said fifteen minutes before. Well, they're old men and they've worked hard, as Daddy says, *And if they want to set and spit they've earned the right, ain't they?* But it's no fun to have them staring.

And so today I went in and there they were and I underwent the usual inspection. But there was a younger man sitting with them. He had a leather satchel opened up and a great large book propped on his knee. He was a wholesaler of some sort, like you see now and again, selling stock to Badie and maybe buying hides and ginseng and such that we all have sold to Badie. But this one was a younger man, and I've got to say he was one of the prettiest boys I've ever seen. Nice looking. Now I didn't see him much that minute because I was trying to get on without attracting any more notice than I already had.

So I walked on up to the counter and Badie wasn't there. And so I just had to stand there and bide and pretend not to be all flustered. And then one of the old men spit, *spass*, and said, "I reckon one or two more ice cream seasons and it'll be cherry picking time."

Now he expected he could say such a thing and I wouldn't know what he was talking about. But I do have two grown brothers I've had to listen to and I knew exactly what he meant. And I couldn't do a thing but only stand there and shut my eyes and squeeze my fists and wait on Badie.

But the next thing I knew I felt a touch on my elbow, very soft. And it was the young man. And he said, "Pardon me, miss, but I wanted to offer my apology for what that man just said. A young pretty gal like yourself shouldn't have to endure such talk."

Well, I couldn't believe my ears! And the next you know, he was going to the back to fetch Badie. I heard him calling her and saying, "There's a young lady that needs your assistance." A young lady.

And Badie came out. She wasn't any too happy about it, but there she was. "Here's your order," she says, snappish, to the man, and gives him a list. Then she saw it was me and she softened up a bit.

"Well. Afternoon, Hazie. What can I fetch you today?" She turned and looked hard at the young man and said, "Anything amiss in that order?"

"No," he said. "No, it's just fine, honey." Well you could see Badie didn't much like that *honey*. But I thought it sounded kind of sweet.

"Then don't you let us hold you up none," she said.

"No no," he said, and hustled back over to the stove. He grabbed up the satchel and thrust that big book down into it. Snapped it shut and went straight out the door. *With alacrity*, Mr. Dunstan would say. He hollered "My pleasure," just as he pushed the door to.

So I gave Badie my tickets and she rummaged around and found the box and put my tickets in a drawer and gave me my fountain pen. It's a beautiful amber color and very important looking. I thanked her very kindly.

"Now you run straight on home, Hazel Tighrow," she said, looking at me straight on. I wondered why she said such a thing. Until I got outside and saw the man standing and waiting for me. Well I must say that was a surprise.

But he has the softest manners and a great deal of sophistication, I think. He bowed to me—bowed—and said, "We wasn't properly introduced, miss. My name is Noah Kersin, at your service." And he put out a hand that was clean and smooth, and the nails were perfectly even.

I took his hand and said, "I'm Hazel Tighrow," and that was about the whole of it. I hope I didn't make a great fool of myself.

I was just about struck dumb by the attention of such a hand-some gentleman. And he must be close to twenty!

"So pleased to meet you," he says. "And here's hoping I get to see you again sometime."

Well what do you think of that?

But that's not all. I started up for home and I was just getting up to the falls at Maddy and here he comes, running up to me from down yonder.

"Miss Hazel Tighrow," he says. And bows again. He was about out of breath but still he said everything with a kind of style. "I went back into the store and they told me you'd won a fountain pen for your intelligence. And I wanted to congratulate you and offer you a token." And he handed me a bottle of ink and a blotter pad. Can you imagine?

So here I am, writing with my new fountain pen and the ink given me today by that pretty young man. Can you just imagine??!!

And now I've got to go get up water for washing tomorrow. And it's getting dark.

JOURNAL OF HAZEL TAYLOR
November 19, 1920

Noah came by in the afternoon, after I got finished up at school. He always appears to know just when I'm going to be turning round the switchback and up to the house, because he'll step out and take me by the arm, just graceful and debonair as can be. Imagine one of the boys around here doing any such thing. And he understands that I don't want to hear about who won the ball game or who smoked some rabbit tobacco. He talks about the cities he's been to and the places he knows I'd love to see. Today he talked about London, of all places. I was just thinking of London. Because of *Bleak House*. But then I guess I talked to Noah about that yesterday, too. Told him about the novel, and chancery. He said he "admired" me. Admired me!

"Hazel, I saw a poster about Jolly Ole London on a window in Asheville, and I wish I could bring that picture right to your door," he said, today.

"What was it a picture of?" I asked.

"I told you, it was Jolly Ole London," he said. "It looked like a place that's just waiting on a young, pretty gal like you."

"But what was the picture? What part of Jolly Ole London did it show?"

"Oh, lights and palaces and all that thing. I seen some books about English ways in town once, and I talked to some fellows that was there in the war. They say it is quite sophisticated, yessir Mr. Boone," he said. He gave my arm a squeeze. He seems to know just when to do that, to make me feel as though I've seen all those places, been to all those towns, too. Imagine riding a car on one of those busy streets up to the opera or the theater, on the arm of a refined man. Or coming out and talking about the play. Let's say it's been *King Lear*, and now you're discussing whether the actors had done a good job, brought the characters out. *Oh, Noah, I didn't like her characterization of Cordelia at all. Yes, it was a bit over-played, I thought. But Lear, Lear was magnificent. Yes, wasn't he?*

Or going to a café for an absinthe. Well, I'm being really silly, now, because I don't even know what an absinthe is. But then, I suppose, that's how you find out.

"Have you ever been to the theater, Noah?" I asked.

"The theater. Oh yes, I've been. I went to a play in Washington D. C.," he said.

"What did you see?" I asked. But it didn't matter, somehow. Just to be with a man who had even been to Washington and gone to a theater, and who knows how to take a woman by the arm and how to talk about things. And who doesn't get all covered in tobacco gum every day.

"Oh singing and dancing, jokes and all. But you know what's

swell, Hazel?" he said, and squeezed my arm again. Sometimes he holds a little too hard, or kind of pushes his elbow in under my arm, as though he's gotten carried away a bit. But it doesn't matter. He's alive and eager and I'm no little Eva, after all. I just kind of rearrange my arm at his side and we can walk on. "What's swell is to go to a dance and to spin round together, all close and electrical. You know what I mean?"

"I've been to dances, Noah. I've never been to the theater." I laughed a little bit, and he pulled me closer, so that I had to stop walking.

"Say, Hazel. Why don't you and me meet up somewhere that ain't so public? You don't seem like any of these schoolgirls, anyways. You seem a great deal older, to me," he said. "Not a hayseed like these other folks. So we're both too old to be walking home from school, don't you think?" He said this in such a funny way that I laughed. But I felt a little scared, too. Nervous. Unsure and wanting to get away, to break through something, and be out the other side.

I need to think about all this. Why is it nice, but frightening, too? Why do I find myself feeling good when he has me by the arm, but feeling fearful, too? Why don't I like it when he holds on too much, pulls me over to him? It's like getting ready to swing a grapevine out over a deep pool and knowing the feeling of dropping in your belly even before you start to swing. And when you do swing out, it isn't even the outside—the ravine and the pool far below and the rough, twisting burn of the vine on your hands—but something far down inside you, like a cold burning, an ache, so far deep in your belly that you didn't really know you had a place that deep. And if it keeps up you won't like it at all in just a minute. But you let go and that deep burning rushes up your body and out the top of your head, and you hit the water. And it feels like that plunge into the water has swept you back out of the fear and the discomfort and into a memory of just how much you liked that swing and drop. And you climb out on the bank, and now you feel all outside: the water slaking off your body and the breeze on your skin and the gritty dirt on your feet. But there's an empty place now, deep inside. Where you hadn't known there was a place. Because it's been stirred. And now that you know it's there, you can feel that it's been emptied. And so you do it again, because your deep body never gets used to that ache, and so you need to make that plunging release again, because you need to let it rush up out of you and it can't unless it fills you until you're just about unable to bear it at all.

I don't know.

Anyway, Noah was asking me to meet him somewhere. "I think we're grown up enough to stop acting like school kids," he said. "We ought to be able to have a spot where we might converse as adults, don't you figure?"

"I don't know, Noah," I said.

"Well, let's just give her a try," he said. "If you don't like it, we'll go back to school kids."

That made me laugh again. I can tell I'm thrilled. But scared, somehow, again. I do wish he wouldn't pull on my arm that way.

JOURNAL OF HAZEL TAYLOR
August 17, 1927

I keep telling myself, *This train is taking you to Chicago. Chicago*, and trying to put myself into a state of expectation and excitement, but it doesn't work. This train is taking me away from home, and from Hastie, too, and my mind keeps jerking back to that final scene and the rattling train seems to stop, suspended, swaying back and forth, but going nowhere. Except to that little room up the stairs. And I don't want to see it again and again and again. *This train is taking you to Chicago.* But it isn't: it's holding me still and making me look.

So I told myself, now, to write about another past, to drop back further, before the leaving, and that might help erase the more recent past. Get this train moving again.

And I want to write about Noah Kersin and about love and betrayal. I don't know why. But I think I can write this.

And I've a strict need to get this down as it really happened, from his own words. I recall running on home and across the lot toward the shed. I can hear the chickens hollering as I run through them. And I stood just out of sight, inside the open door of the shed, shaking, so I could hardly stand. I was wrapping my arms around my body, trying to hold it together tight enough to smother the trembling when my Daddy came through the door. He gave a start when he saw me and I could see his eyes trying to recompose the inside of the shed, to accommodate my presence. So we were both of us, for a moment, trying to recover, reaching back for the familiar self that had been startled or shaken away from us, as though we were set loose off the ground itself, with nothing but the pure thrill of the unexpected, the unprepared-for, a whole new world struggling to burst forth and shatter all the old dimensions and diameters. And now we were a step beyond—that new place, these new people, gathering up and trying to organize themselves so they can get along with the first new steps, the tentative fumblings and stammerings, of two brand-new people trying to feel their way into a new place, a new intercourse between them. And the old familiar self we'd looked for by reflex was no longer anywhere in that shed, but was fleeing out of sight as Daddy said his first words, breathless, like he'd been running, or was trying to stop himself from running.

"What in the world you doing here, Hazie?" he said.

"Daddy," I said. And then "Daddy," again. "I was looking for a place to be alone and think." He was looking at me like he'd never seen me before.

"Well I guess you didn't find that, now, did you?" he said. "I believe if I was a girl a'looking for some place to set without having to fret about prowling farmers, or Daddys, or whatever have you, I believe the shed might be about the last place I'd be selecting. Unless I was in too much a hurry to be too particular, and I had to duck into the first dark space that happened to come up, shed or not."

He turned and reached up for the bow saw hanging by the door. Then he spoke over his shoulder, without looking at me. "You in some kind of trouble, Hazie?"

"Daddy, I might be troubled but I ain't in trouble."

And that was the truth, because I was just excited and confused. He turned, now, and he did look straight at me, his mild blue eyes, kind of permanently narrowed against the sun and the wind and all the hard times, and surrounded by his deep wrinkled skin, as dark and burnished as burlwood. But his eyes were a clear, pale blue, a little watery, without the slightest touch of rancor or impatience or bitterness with the life he'd been called on to lead. His eyes were not what you'd call *penetrating* but were the opposite. They appeared to draw you in, to afford you a place deep in their bluest of waters. Just a pale gaze that spoke love and acceptance, and that condemns my restlessness and discontent outright, even today, every time I see him again in memory.

So now he set that soft profundity at me, without any trace of lightness or flippancy. "What you got to be troubled about?" he said.

"I don't know, Daddy," I said.

"Don't know or can't say?" he asked.

I looked downwards. It wasn't embarrassment, yet. I had awhile yet to be free of the hot shame. That would come soon enough, but now I believe I was merely being thoughtful, trying to answer him as truthfully as I could. Because we were two different people, now, and I was looking for a way to speak to him on this new plane.

"I haven't fixed on a name for it yet, Daddy," I said. "I don't know what to call it, myself. So how am I to tell you? Just kindly troubled, I suppose."

"Or at least ain't fixing to say." He spoke quietly, still without any trace of frivolity, sedate, unsmiling, bemused, perhaps—not grave. Serious. Then he curved his dark, weathered face into the trace of a smile. "I suppose that's the reason you was setting out to get by yourself. So you could work up a name for it?"

"I reckon so," I said.

"Well, now, Hazie. You let me know when you get it worked out. I'd bet a brass nail to a Barlow knife, you'll find a word fer it. Seems you're always a'hunting words, and I ain't known you to miss a one you ever took aim at. You'll get her," he said.

"It don't matter, Daddy," I said. "It ain't much, anyway." I was beginning to feel the imposition of his presence in this new place, in this, the most solitary emotion I'd yet felt. Do you understand? Because up until that day, every thing I'd done, or felt, every gesture I'd used, to every purpose, had been guided and mediated by my folks. Until then, I had perforce viewed myself and my total range of experience through the larger lens of the visualizations, already polished and focused, of my mother and father.

But now that had changed. I had come, completely unprepared, upon an entirely personal experience. It was nameless, and provisional, speculative. But it was mine, alone. There was no lens or focus through which I could peer at this new thing. And, as vertiginous as all of this felt, I found I didn't want the supports he was trying to offer me just then. I found that I desired this blind groping for a meaning or a context or a taxonomy in which to fit all of this. I was awash in my own experience, now, and something in me wanted the furious, vain effort to sail a straight line, the boat swamped even before it begins to move into the deeper parts. I wanted this. Up to now the longing and searching and appetite had just been directed at a fairy story, something else than here, but nothing definite, a wallow in indistinct wanting. But now, now all of that was gone and there was something real before me. So real that it began to shimmer.

Daddy turned and left, and the wood door banged to, bounced lightly, and settled, the way it had tapped its "*Slap!*

Dun-dun" rhythm a thousand other times. This time, though, I found myself drawing a quick, sharp intake of my breath. Not fear or surprise, but a kind of preparatory inhalation, like a man will take just before he hefts the axe to throw the first split into the trunk. And, exhaling, I breathed his name into the close air of the crib. *Noah Kersin.*

JOURNAL OF HAZEL TAYLOR
June 30, 1921

So much is happening that I can't begin to keep up. Right now I seem to be in between two important events in my life and my mind is whirling. Time has sped up so much that I seem not to have the still moments to think anymore. It doesn't quite seem like the right arrangement: just when you need the time to think things out, all the ticks of the clock come so fast you can't dwell-up in between two of them and *kindly ponder*, as Georgie says. It's in between those ticks of time that you can sort and rename things, put things that have happened into the right spot in your memory and clear a space for the things that are fixing to happen. And I'm totally inexperienced when it comes to going through things with those spaces slipping out of my hands like a wet fish. At this moment, the moment when you think you've caught it: you've unhooked the poor thing and you're weighing it in your curved hands, feeling its strange, drooped, horizontal body. And you think it's yours. Then it's gone, and all you have is a flash of tussling memory tingling in your wet hands where that fish has writhen right out of your world.

So now I have the absolute detonation of last night's kiss to work out, and today's walk to Possy's Camp, all the way down the Creek, to think about, and no time. Of course, I imagine that one reason for all this swift fleeing of minutes is my own excitement. I am excited! And frightened! Who would have thought even a year ago that I'd be walking out with a handsome, older, city man? Who has traveled and dined and waltzed? Of course I can't think!

All right. I have to relax and write calmly—

Noah wants to call me Hazie, but I won't let him. First, it sounds like a grown up speaking to a little girl, and that surely is not what either of us is interested in. Second, it doesn't sound right when he says it. Hazie is a name from back here. It sounds like back here, with the savor of the Creek in it, and Noah isn't from here. Folks here have a much softer resonance in their voices. Even Mr. Dunstan, who isn't from around here, precisely— he grew up in the coal country—has that hushed elasticity in his speech. So here it sounds kind of like *Highzeh*, sort of windy-like. But in Noah's mouth, it sounds like a sneer, almost as though he's making fun of me: *Hay-zee*. And, strangely enough, that makes me see myself as nothing but a mountain girl, with bare feet and a shift, where the mountain way of saying it makes me feel as though I can be who I want to be, and maybe become someone beyond these hills and farms

And even as much as I like him (and I LIKE him!), I feel a little jealous of the name, Hazie. It belongs to my Daddy and my teacher and Georgie. Folks that I can't ever remember not having around. It's an emblem of love, but a different love than I could find in a handsome, sophisticated man. I certainly don't like Noah because he reminds me of my past. Or of Georgie. It makes me laugh just to think of putting them in the same room.

And that's just what happened last night. Georgie and little Shelton and a fiddler from down creek were playing for the dance. And I've never even thought about it as a real dance. Not the sort of event where you meet anyone you don't know, or where the dancing takes on any more complicated possibilities than *fun*. Then Noah Kersin walked into that schoolroom and everything changed utterly. Suddenly a dance meant a great deal more than it ever had before. It didn't matter that the string band was playing a silly song like *My Brother Jim Got Shot*. You would think that nothing serious could possibly transpire with that going on. *Well my wife got a mouth big enough for both,* good heavens, what could be more likely to turn the whole thing into a foolish embarrassment but that? Here's that little Shelton singing about a mouse ran down his wife's throat and all that nonsense. And everyone laughing when he puts the cat and the hunk of cheese on her chin even though they've heard this silly song a thousand times: *Jury said it wasn't me, my brother Jim got shot.*

And right into the middle of this, the door opens and Noah Kersin walks in, in serge slacks and a waistcoat. And the place was transformed. It didn't matter an ort what the string band was playing, or who was clomping around on the floor. All at once, a dance wasn't just an old dance anymore. It was a swirling, eddying wonder, with me and Noah at its center. Oh my.

I don't remember hearing music or feeling the rumble of the floor as the brogans clomped around it. Except for those looks from T.R. and Georgie, I don't remember seeing anyone. Except Noah. He stood alone by the door for awhile, as though he were surveying the room. Thankfully, the band finished *Brother Jim* and started a regular dance tune. And after a while, he walked straight over and crooked out his arm for me. He leaned close and said, "This orchestra ain't the sort of music fitting for a fine lady like yourself. How about we take some air?" Can you imagine? And waltzed me out the front door before I knew what was happening.

We passed by T.R. on the way through the door and he waggled a finger at me, as though to scold me, or warn me. I'm still angry about that: who does he think he is? He wouldn't understand the allure of Noah Kersin, or any other man who didn't have a stream of tobacco juice running down his chin, for that matter. Oh, he's George's good friend and I suppose he may have been trying to warn me about that. Well, it didn't work, did it? And so I've injured Georgie's feelings and perhaps I've lost him forever. But I have to move on, don't I?

Noah escorted me across the schoolyard—it's more likely

that he dragged me, I was so awkward and giddy—and pulled me up under the big chestnut and gave me a kiss on the mouth that I didn't even feel, I was so surprised and anxious. I just kind of gasped, "Noah."

"That wasn't quite enough, was it?" he said. And kissed me again, hard, full, and soft. I certainly felt this one. "Let's walk out a teeny," he said, and I followed him out the gate and down toward the creek in a kind of daze.

He didn't kiss me again, and I found myself gradually getting over the shock and amazement and beginning to wish he would do it again. But he didn't. We sat on a big rock by the creek and he draped his arm around my shoulder. I must say I was nervous about the way his large hand hung down over my front. But he just sat like that, easy and comfortable. Once in awhile his hand would jounce and brush me a bit, but I know it was just an accident. Besides, this was the closeness I've thought about and wanted. And he was, after all, a perfect gentleman. So I can't feel badly about any of it.

Sitting there, he asked me if I'd like to slice up some ham and bread and walk down to Possy's Camp with him today. He wants to be alone with me where nobody can bother us because he has so much he wants to say to me and he needs a special place where we can be covered from peering eyes for awhile. His voice was very measured as he asked me, as though he was afraid that I would misunderstand or would refuse. But I didn't think a minute about it. I'm going with him in a matter of hours, now. I'm extremely anxious about what he wants to tell me. I think I can guess some of it. But I don't think I can stand to hear everything all at once. It would just overwhelm me.

At any rate, I'm going with him. I've already got the food up and dressed as nicely as I can for a hike down the creek and out to the island. I haven't waded that big stream in years. Well, this time I'll have a strong arm to lean on.

And last night appears to me to have been a wondrous, nervous joy.

Except George. This sours the evening a little, because I wouldn't want to hurt him for anything. George is as much a part of me as my long hair and I want him to be pleased with me, not angry and hurt. But I told Noah it was time we got back to the schoolhouse, and so we strolled on back up the hill and into the yard. And George was standing there, all alone, as though he'd been looking for me. And I could see he was ashamed of being seen, himself. And he was angry. His face was turned up as though he might either start to cry or lash out and hit Noah. I felt a hot surge of indignity run through my body and now, when I think of this moment, I don't have a word for my emotions. I suppose I feel some guilt and sadness at George's pain. But I am angry too.

George wants to hold me back, to make me remain a little girl in bare feet that he can walk around with no more seriousness than that silly song. And I have grown up. I am frustrated and impatient with a life surrounded by people who don't read and don't think and can talk about nothing but whether the leaves are in case. Oh yes, I love this place, and I love Georgie, and I love the sluice of the creek and even the ache of climbing around these hills. But they are forcing me to stop at that. Everyone—even T.R.—thinks he knows who I ought to become, what my life ought to be like. And I can't live that life.

Mr. Dunstan talked to me the other day and said, "Once you discover a passion for reading, you're ruined for chores and gatherings both. You've got too much to do." He was joking, but there's a core of truth to what he says. This place wants me for chores and gatherings. It needs to know and predict and to see me carry on, just like Mamma and her Mamma. And when I forgot the words to Mamma's songs I forgot how to accept her life. I can't help that.

Noah Kersin has been elsewhere, is from elsewhere. His eyes have places in them that I want to see. And I believe he wants to take me somewhere.

X.

Hazel Tighrow MY
Haze Tighrow Hazel Tighrow

MY SELF

Because, you see, I had never met anyone even remotely like him. He was active and bright and responsive—he was older—and he knew so many things. This is the child speaking, of course, who never had the opportunity to distinguish *slick* from *sophisticated*, who couldn't know that *worldly* is often a cover for *worthless*. Of course, but I was perfectly set up, who was yearning and seeking and looking beyond the creek with every glance—perfectly prepared—for a man like Noah Kersin.

Oh yes, it was me. I can't find a way to look at any of this without seeing that it was me, some version of me, not yet grown, but impatient, too impatient. Ready, even eager, for anything, for everything. And so it's difficult to record any of this because I find myself writing about a ridiculous little girl, asking myself, *who could have been so foolish?* And recalling that I began asking these questions—*why couldn't I see this?*—the very day that I caught up with what I had been stalking all along. That very day, lying hurt and humiliated, still feeling the burning hurt. And already, while my body was still feeling the deplorable outrage, still repudiating the atrocious invasion, my mind had already begun scolding, trading the shame and outrage for disgust and guilt: *How could you have let this happen? What did you think was going to happen? Why couldn't you just have left it all alone?*

And I can still hear that voice, reprimanding, admonishing. But who is speaking? And who is *you*? What is this phenomenon of these voices all about? I wake up in the morning, and I hear myself telling someone *You'd better not miss that train, today.* And who am I talking to? Or who am I listening to? Are these interior conversations the places where we can look for the "better angels of our being?" Or are they the sign and proof of our futility: the endless bickering that we continually engage our own selves in, demanding of ourselves behaviors and solutions that we know already we are doomed not to answer? *How could you ever have gone there with him? Why, Hazie, why?*

I don't know. Who is talking? Who listening? Perhaps these could be the tones and accents of prayer, these interior conversations, if only we would let them. If we knew enough to let the voices lead us from inside ourselves outward, through some secret opening carrying us up beyond the terrible, bound, feeling of being only one self. But too often they pin us down, pointing our own selves out as isolated fools desperate to force our puny oneness into some elucidation that will leave me satisfied with the pretense that there is one of me. Do you see? A voice that shows us, proof positive, that we are numerous, various. But we are so afraid to recognize, to engage these multiplicities, that we turn our own dialogues into feuds. Rather than see that we are offering to walk with each other out of this trap, we turn on each other, dragging ourselves back into our own prisons, our "selves."

And so I lay there, torn and shamed, and scolded myself. When I could have held and comforted this hurt girl who had been drawn in by her own longings, only to find those pent cravings fleeing in burning, amazed grief. Because it was only longing, only desire. I had no crime yet, ready for expiation. I came to Possy's Camp with the breathless excitement of a child, and I left with the frenzied despair of a woman. And the learning, the experience of the worldly, wasn't worth the price I had to pay.

Perhaps the worst of it lies in the recognition that the shame and disgust didn't dampen the longing, at all. Even as I picked my torn self off the wet ground, even as I waded into the swirl of icy water, another voice was calling this all a mistake. *You've figured it wrong, Hazel. He proves that. There is nothing here. Nothing has changed. It's just going to be a great deal harder than you had thought. That's it. At least he's showed you that. You were a child. You thought it would be like a Christmas gift, that it would just be there for you to open and take out. But it isn't. It's going to be more like a crucifixion: more forfeit than gift.*

The laurel—the blossoming must be a hard thing. It must be a throbbing, thrusting thing forced out through itself, taut and aching. Those cupped blossoms holding themselves open to a sudden world, a yearning exposure of beauty so new that the very air bruises and wounds it. The blossom bursts free because it has to, it must. But it's work, and the freedom can be harsh and rough. Because it has to come out and be. It can't hold back. The yearning pulses it forward, swelling through itself. And out into the wide, brutal world.

So I picked and swayed myself across the stream, that Noah had said would hide us, when it showed me more than I had ever wanted. Picked and swayed, waving my arms against the draw of the current, like some antic bird, afraid to lift off. I recall grabbing at a branch on the bank and jerking back, sudden, even before I recognized the sharp sting of the thorn. And that brought tears, as though this was a final outrage. I had reached to the branch for help and it had stung me, propelled me back. And I stood in the shallow swirl and wept, my legs and feet beginning to ache with the cold water.

Sometimes I still feel like that wounded girl, standing between island and shore, holding my sad hand cradled against my breast, and dropping tears into a stream that rushes them away, out of sight, before I can take some hidden solace in feeling them drop off and land. As if the violence and violation of my entire body was of no matter, but as though the scratch of a thorn on my finger was the worst of the pain and outrage I had suffered, that day or ever.

JOURNAL OF HAZEL TAYLOR
July 6, 1921

Shame is too terrible, I think, and so we put it somewhere deep down, where it burns itself into guilt. But he had said sandwiches and he had something to say to me. That was what *he* said. And we got there and waded out, and I was laughing and holding his hand and he was shouting. "Don't get the sack wet," and laughing, too.

It seemed so right and so perfect, I don't even know when it started to be wrong. Maybe that's where my crime is, because I should have known when it was wrong. I should have known. But I just went on. Until it suddenly was wrong, and had been wrong for too long already, so he wouldn't listen to me. I should have known, but it started so good, and so much of what I had wanted that I never thought he we. I don't know.

And as soon as I discovered that it had already gone wrong I realized that he had already started grabbing and pulling and he pushed me over and he was on top of me. And before all the pain, his wet lips on my breast, where he had torn my clothes. Then just nothing just me somewhere above these two figures watching them: her struggling legs and the fists on his back, her struggling hair, but I can't see her body. It is under his pushing pounding burning. A smear of wet mud on her forehead.

And after, I wept and he laughed and called me a foolish little gal, and tried to kiss me, saying, "I'll wipe you off," but I pushed him away, this time. His hand. And I rolled over and tried to cover myself. I was burning and I was bleeding. I stopped crying.

"You shouldn't be so upset, Hazie," he said. "It's the way it happens. I can tell you liked it a little. And it ain't the easiest the first time. You'll feel fine and next time you'll really have a good time." He crooked his arm around my neck and tried to pull me to him. When I struggled, he let me go. He laughed.

"All right, honey baby. All right. I guess you ain't as grown up as you thought you were." He stood up and arranged himself and thrashed into the stream, leaving me there.

And now I still feel like I'm there, lying in the leaves and scrub on Possy's Camp, trying to bring the two of us back together: the girl up in the air, watching, and the hurt, torn girl on the ground, trying ineffectually to brush the harsh debris off her back and buttocks. And I feel all wrong. I feel like I've been caught by my own body, like the fox, vixen, who believes she has found a miracle: a succulent morsel of meat just waiting for her, right there. And she feels the juices begin flowing in her mouth, behind her needle-teeth, and the expectation in her narrow belly. And she laps for that impossible, beautiful food and begins to feel its flavor emanate and then the metal trap springs. And she stands there, stunned by the explosion, shivering, her entire world whirling out of control, while she vomits the morsel and then looks, bewildered, at the steel teeth that have broken her leg and are now gnawing at the light, thin bone.

And where was she wrong? Her hunger? Her belief that maybe this once there would be food that didn't need to be hunted and fought and killed, but was merely there, hers, to be savored in a bright intake of flesh and juice and peace? Her eagerness to have such a thing? She doesn't know. She knows she's at fault, or at least that she's made a terrible mistake. But she can only stand there in the current and eddies of shock. She has learned only that trying to pull away from the grasping teeth is more painful than letting her body go with the weight, the intention of the trap.

Or is it the world that has betrayed my trust, the way it did Rosie when her free, joyous, perfectly irreproachable leap turned her young body into a festering, fatal wound? Does the world, nature, God fool us into desiring brightness and joy only to push us along toward catastrophe after catastrophe, until we are sufficiently stunned and demoralized to welcome death? Because then we will thank God for letting us die?

JOURNAL OF HAZEL TAYLOR
November 6, 1997

It wasn't until much later and further that I realized who the ultimate victim in all of this was to be. Because he hadn't longed or wished for me, or for any communion of selves, or even for a moment of warm embracing. Not even that, the intimations of the other's delicious shuddering release. None of that.

Oh, he wanted, sure enough. He had plotted and planned to take me there and to cover us with the churning stream while he did away with my girlhood. But he didn't even know that he got even less than I did. Because he didn't know any of that—the communion, or the quivering of the other's release, or even the selves, themselves—didn't know any of that existed. He thought he had gotten what he needed. Because he wanted to want his own power, only, solitary and alone, and so my destruction was just a part of that inexorable down-pulling desire, putting him beyond any intimacy anywhere in the world. He had driven himself to define his sex as control, authority, sway—and so he was forever to be victim, lost and disowned from his own possibilities. He wanted to want to wield his sex. So he couldn't know that sexes should meet in a whisper. And so he would never know how to speak in that whisper. And he would never hear the sibilant answer.

PART TWO

I.

FIELD NOTES—INTERVIEW—T.R. BLANKENSHIP
May 9, 1998

"White Oak Flats? It's up on the top of Lynco Ridge, way up yonder. Everybody talks about it, but don't nobody hardly go up there. It's too rough a climb. Once in a great while somebody might come around, like yourself, asking about Hazel Taylor, and somebody will take them on up there. They always come back down cursing the hike and the blackberry briars, and the slipping in the crick, and what not.

"Lynco" came from a big man that mined coal out of the Virginia end of that ridge, away up toward Norton. They say he had him a little girl name Lynn and so he called that coal operation LYNCO for her. And that kindly stuck to the whole ridge. Lynco Ridge. I guess that's as good a name as any. Better than some.

I don't know how White Oak Flats got called as it is. You won't find that name or place wrote on any map. Ain't no oaks up on the Flat at all. It's bald as a banjo skin. I guess there is oaks up around it and it's flat so they might just have called it White Oak Flats because that's what it already is. Ain't nothing else to say about it, much.

Me, I ain't been up there in forty years. I'm too old to go scrambling around up that way now, and I already done seen all

I wanted to see the one time I went up with the newspaper fellow, after Hazel made such a stir back in twenty-nine. Twenty-seven. Twenty-nine, I guess it was, two years later, about the same time of year, I reckon, when them bones got found.

That was the same year as the big storm over to Rye Cove, and it seems like the news boys got ahold of these mountains and tried to write up everything that went on. Everything on the darker side, if you know what I'm saying. Mysterious like. Deaths and disappearances was just their line, so to speak. I guess after that Rye Cove cyclone with the big schoolhouse turned into smoking splinters and all them poor kids and that teacher. Well that made the papers clear up to New York and gone. Some of them fellows just stayed around and snuffed up anything they could find that had what they called "mountain flavor" to it. Said the folks wanted to read about "mountain flavor." Hell. I lived in these mountains all my life and I ain't never found much flavor to speak of. Unless it was hard work. I guess you can taste the sweat running into your mouth when you're out suckering tobacco in the summer. Well, that's flavor. I guess so. And you like to never get the gum off your hands. Setting there at night over a bucket of kerosene rubbing your damn arms raw as a skinned rabbit. More like tearing it off than washing. Made you wish you hadn't a hair on you the way that gum gets on your arms and your head. Time you get it all off you're a hair or two shorter, by God. And it don't matter how many times you done it, it never is a thing you get used to, that tobacco gum.

Jimmy Shelton got into a fistfight with old Camber once coming right off the patch from suckering, all gummed up like that. Camber had a way about him that could make you madder than Durham's bull, and he said something to Jimmy, I don't think we ever did know what. But Jimmy just went at him, and Camber throwed him down in the mud like the he'd been kicked by a mule. And he said, "Hell, Jim Shelton. I don't mind beating you down, if that's what you're after, but please-Lordy-please, keep that god damn tobacco gum off of me." And Jimmy come up out of that slew with a coat or two of mud plastered over the gum and he looked all smashed-up an' furry, like a bear with the mange, or what have you, and he didn't say nothing. He just took himself off, looking at the ground and not saying a damn thing, and disappeared into the shed. And all the while, Camber just a'standing there alone, saying, "Goddam tobacco gum" over and again. And that was that, as the man says.

We all thought that was right funny, you know. But then Camber got to dogging him round, and folks got wore out on that right fast. It's one thing to whoop up on a ole feller, and even to give him a ride whilst yer whooping on him. But it ain't no good just dogging on him forever. Hell, ain't nobody ain't been whooped now or then. No damn body.

But I never went up to the Flats much after that hike with the reporter. After Hazel left, I reckon a few folks went to looking up yonder, and some might say, *I done searched all the way to White Oak Flats.* But I doubt they meant they actually went and looked all the way up there. It was just a way of speaking round here: folks would say, *I looked all the way to White Oak Flats,* just to kindly say, *I looked everywhere,* you know. It don't mean you actually went right on up there. Hell, nobody ever did go up there. And so ain't a single soul thought Hazel might be gone to White Oak Flats.

And I never quite been easy with it, since they found them bones. I mean what in the world was Hazel Taylor, Hazel Taylor of all the people in the world, doing running on up to White Oak Flats? Hazel Taylor!

But there it was. I seen it myself, when that reporter talked me into fetching him up there. He was all afire to see it whenever they took them bones out of there. "I'll *pay* you," he said, "I'll *pay* you, right *hand-somely.*" Just like that.

Well now I reckon I know what it is to get *paid right hand-somely.* It means to get drug clear up to White Oak Flats to see something you never wanted to see in a million years. And then drug all the way back down and fetch him a drink of water. That's the first damn thing he says to me after I drug him back town that mountain. "Damn them briars!" he says. "Fetch me a drink a water." I reckon that's what getting' paid *right handsomely* means—you get to fetch him a drank a water. Because that's the last I saw of him, I'll tell you, him or any of his god damn pay, was when I handed him that there glass of water. I just done blinked and he was gone like Hazel. He done slaked that thirst right quick.

Folks thought that was damn funny and they'd ask me, "did that feller get around to paying you yet, T.R.? I believe you was fixing to get *paid* right *hand-somely.*"

It didn't bother me none, the folks making fun. Hell, it was funny, the way he got me to fetch him a drink a water and all, and then he's gone like Hazel.

After a while that got to be part of the way folks talked around here. Like you'd say, "Junior, my kids is down sick, might you be able to come around and help me fetch in my crop? I'll see you gets *paid hand-somely.*" Like that. Folks took to saying that all the time, just for a joke. Still do. It's right funny how them things gets started, ain't it?

There's another one. I just said it, without thinking,' I said, *gone like Hazel.* That's another one: *gone like Hazel.* Folks says that all the time around here, even now. *Gone like Hazel.* Well, there you go.

So I climbed on up there with him to see them bones. It is a bit confused about who kicked up them bones first. It was one of them Shelton twins and folks is always getting them snarled together. I never could tell one from the other. Odge Shelton, I believe, though some says it was Camber. Might have been Camber. I believe it was Odge. He's the one got killed not much later, I think. Or was he already dead by then? If he was, then it must've been Camber. Camber, you know, he got picked up by the law, fooling around over there to Camp Ten with them moonshine boys. Did a heap of time for it, too. It was a big crime, they said he done, messing with that moonshine, and they sent him up to Kentucky for quite a spell.

You know he come back acting right proud of having been up there. Got to going round telling everybody about how he "done a stretch" and how he "been up on a federal rap." Hell. I don't say I wouldn't be changed-up a mite, neither, but I can't see how I'd get to strutting too much about any "stretch" that I had to work every day for anybody I never even seen, raising his crop, or busting up his rocks, or whatever the hell it was they made him do. I'd feel like the governor or the president or somebody done kindly stole all that hard work right out of me. No. It wouldn't never make me proud to have done that. But I weren't going to tell Camber none of that. He's a big 'un and meaner than a wild boar.

Whichever it was, Camber or I think it was Odge, unless he was dead, he said he was tracking a bobcat way up in that cove and he just stumbled on them bones. He saw right off they was human bones, he said. I bet it like to turn his hair. And about two years since Hazel done gone. Think of that!

Well that news done went through the whole crick like buster through the buckwheat. Everybody talking about what are them bones doing away up that cove? Oh yes, and that scrap of clothing? Well didn't that put a damn tin hat on it? So folks run all the way up that cove to see, and right off, they find a couple more bones. And Camber, or Odge, he climbs right up above the spring, almost to the top—Lord only knows how he got up that slope—and he fetches down them other clothes. And I believe that's when folks started saying, *by God, it's Hazel Taylor.*

And it sure enough was. They fetched that shawl of hers on up to George and says, "You seen that before, George?" And he didn't hardly look at it before he says, "I reckon that's Hazel's shawl."

George, he never hurt a damn flea. He was just the nicest old boy.

You never saw him running wild or drinking or fighting anybody. He's just as nice as cobbler. I don't know. It does seem like the worst things is always happening to nice folks like George. Like Claude Tighrow, when his wife got bad. She just got bad-headed, you know. Crazy like.

Well, she was older, you know. But it took her right funny. She lost a grandchild and it took her right bad. She took to mooning around the place, you know, and not talking to no-body and then she took to weeping and carrying-on. Tearing up her damn clothes and yanking out her hair? Well Jesus. That ain't no good, is it?

And Claude was a right nice feller, just like George. Smart, like George, nice and easy and good hearted, you know? Wouldn't do nothing to nobody. And here he's got a damn cross like that to bear, with his wife howling around and tearing-up her own head and all that. It was an awful thing to see. Now there's a feller that didn't deserve none of that. Just like George.

Claude, he took and had somebody fix him up a shuck doll, life size. And he dressed it all up in that granddaughter's things and he gave it to Nelle. Nelle, that's his wife. And that done it. She settled right down and took care of that doll just like it was a real child. You could go on up there any time and there she'd be, just setting on the porch rocking that damn shuck doll to sleep. Humming, "What'll We Do With the Baby-O," or some damn thing. Calm and quiet as a mud cat.

So I guess Claude took care of that, after all. But he never deserved any of it in the first place, he was such a good regular kind of feller. And she about run him to ground. Just like George.

Now you look at Camber Shelton. There's a feller ain't worth a can full of tobacco juice. Just mean. And his brother, Odge, just as calm and regular an old boy as you could hope for. And Odge gets himself killed, up in Asheville, for no reason that I could ever make out. While Camber, that you wouldn't give a nickel for him living past twenty, he lives on to a peaceful old age. He might be alive to this day, for all I know. It ain't right, is it?

Folks liked Hazel fine, too, now. Weren't nothing wrong with Hazel. She was quiet, like. And some folks would talk like she's a bit strange. But she never. Oh, when she was a younger gal, they'd make fun of her on account of how she's reading all the damn time. You never saw nobody for reading like Hazel. But I couldn't say she's strange. I wouldn't say that. She's just quiet, just dreamy like.

And she was a good worker and everybody thought she'd made a good wife to George and all. Kept a right nice house. She and George, they had a nice little chink-and-daub house up there to High Crick. And she'd work right alongside George in the tobacco, right along. Went down to the warehouse with him. And helped him in grading and tying and all. Like any good wife.

They was crazy about tobacco farming, I'd say that. They'd not ask anybody to help in the getting-in, nor the grading. Now they didn't have no kids and they didn't have too much close kin, not the way most folks does around. And I couldn't even imagine trying to raise a patch of tobacco without no kids to help or nothing. But they done it. Oh they'd accept a hand now and then—I helped George to burn out a bed one winter, or I brought out some arsenic of lead to him, that kind of thing—and they weren't being high toned about it or nothing. Not like they thought they was better than folks. No, no. Nothing like that. They was just crazy about tobacco, far as I could tell.

They did it, most of it, all by themselves, the two of them. Now setting out, you're going to need four folks for that, you and your woman, and two kids, anyway. But not them. They'd do it all themselves. George and Hazel, they'd pull the plants and get them into bushel baskets, then they'd do the setting twice over. First trip, George has the basket and drops the plants and Hazel comes along and scoops and sets them. Then they'd come back round again, and George with the bucket and the dipper, a'sploshing water in them holes, then here comes Hazel, covering and firming-up the plant. Now anybody else would have the kids doing half of that and would get it all took care of in one swath. But they'd do her twice.

Now I'm telling you, that wouldn't make me fall in love with no tobacco farming, having to do everything twice over. And you don't grade no crop in a week, even if you got the whole damn crick working for you. But there's them two, working-away and Hazel just talking about this and that like she's at a goddam church dinner. And let's say it starts to dry out, some, going to go out of case, well, then you're going to have to sparge and repack the whole damn thing. Hell. You think you might enjoy that? Hell. But they just seemed to love it better than a bowl of dry beans. Just crazy about tobacco.

Now that's the only argument I ever saw those two have, was down to the warehouse. It was a bad year, I recall, the tobacco was curing too damn fast and everybody was getting-in with spotty leaves, specially them that was up the crick or on the hills. Let's say long red back then might run eight, nine cents a pound. That year everybody's getting' five, six. Now that's bad.

So here's George and Hazel got their crop all laid out— George, he'd grade about thirty different grades, I couldn't never figure out why, but he couldn't just have long red, but had to have "curly long" and "yaller long" and "dead injun long," or some damn thing. Don't ask me. I had enough to just grade the damn stuff and get it off the goddam wagon and into them baskets and weighed and tagged and logged-in record to the goddam office. But it didn't bother anybody, them grades of George's. It might have, for sure, if he was high-toned about it, folks just figured it didn't hurt nobody if George wants to lay out a hundred damn grades. Didn't matter t' me. And Hazel could tie off a hand of tobacco as pretty as a new calf. Yes she could. And they didn't never try to lay out no loaded hands or nothing. I don't know anybody that wouldn't try to load a hand or two now and then. Hell, especially in a bad year. I had my crop turned-out in Greeneville once, because they said I was loading lugs in with the reds. Hell, I might have done something like that by accident, once. Wouldn't go back there to Greeneville again, though, cause they'll look me over extra hard. But not George and Hazel. They were just like that. Straight and honest. And all the owners and even the buyers knew it.

So anyways, there they was, with all them goddam grades laid out and it ain't a good year, and here comes the auctioneer and the buyers and they give a price and scratch it on the tags, you know. And then here comes Hazel—Hazel, now, not George—and she looks at that price and she just turns the tag. Refuses the damn price. Didn't ask George or nothing, just turned the damn tag. Hazel.

Well George didn't like that anymore than a cat. He says "what you meaning to do, Hazel?" he says. "I'm turning the tag," she says. "We can't take six for that," she says. "It ain't pre-determined that we've got to take six cents," she says. Something of that sort. Like it ain't so much the price that she's turning down but the play-acting. The pretending to be wondering what they'll get for a crop when already everybody knows it's going to be six cents, because their crop will be better than most, but worse than usual for them. So it'll be six, and all the auctioning and scratching on tags and all is just play acting.

And Hazel, she couldn't stand that, seems. Like she couldn't bear to look at that tag already wrote down with what they knew damn well it was going to say all along. So she done turned the tag, which means, "I refuse the offer." And not too many people ever turned the tags.

Well, so they got into a fight about it. I mean, I don't mean they had a real fight, you know. Hell, neither of them would say "goddam you" if they was rapping at the gates of hell. But they got riled, you might say. Got to badgering.

And the funny thing about it all was that it wasn't at all what anybody would think. You'd think George was hot-up because Hazel took his place, and turned that tag like she's the damn farmer, and who the hell is George. But that wasn't it. No. Not at all. It was George had some green spots on his leaves and he was so goddam crazy about his crop he was ashamed to ask any price at all for it, and here's Hazel turning that tag and refusing a price that's higher than most is getting all season. Well, you could watch them, there, waving their hands around and arguing. Hazel's saying,' "Just because it's wrote on a tag, it don't just have to be." And George: "Hazel, I'm ashamed to take six with all them spots on there. We done missed the weather and cured too fast. Let's just get shut of the whole thing." Words to that effect.

Well, I reckon Hazel won that one, because next thing you know, here's George pulling his crop out and now they have to get it reloaded, reweighed, and go through the whole damn process again. Now you don't just turn your tag for nothing, especially when you got a pretty damn good price for a fair-to-middling crop, you know? But there they done it and go back through again, and, this time, damned if they haven't got five-and-a-half wrote on the tag, and Hazel, she just looks over to George and smiles. "I reckon you're right," she says. And gives him a little kiss.

"Well sweet Jesus," I says.

FIELD NOTES: INTERVIEW—SHELTON BLANKENSHIP
May 12, 1998

Well, now, Uncle T.R., he's a Blankenship through and through, ain't he? I reckon you'd have a hard time keeping-up with these names, hereabouts, what with Shelton's and Taylors, Tighrows and Blankenships all snarled around. I suppose folks has been back this way so long they got themselves all mixed-in together. They'll laugh about it, you know. There's a tune called "I'm My Own Grandpaw," actually got some airplay for awhile about a fella who'd worked-out how all his relations and connections added up to he was his own grandpaw. It's a hoot.

You know, nowadays, on stage, you got to be right careful what you say, for fear you'll offend somebody. You even got to watch some tunes. We was up in Chicago one time, playing to the folk festival, and some women got worked-up about "Banks of the Ohio," or one of them murder tunes. Said we was encouraging violence against women. Well, I says, we wasn't encouraging nothing. Just playing the tune, you know. And that's a tune is as old as the hills. I tell them, I learned that tune from my Ma, and she weren't a'tryin' to encourage no violence against women.

But folks back here, I don't know, they seem to get a kick out of all them jokes about hillbillies and rednecks and whatever. They'll run right for the T.V. to watch "Hee Haw," with all them folks dressed up to be hill folks and Junior Samples, you know, sounding dumber than a car door, they love that sort of thing. I ain't saying it's right and I ain't saying it's wrong. Most folks to-day'll get all wrought up if you don't call them by the right name. But mountain folks, hell, you'll call them hillbillies or rednecks or hayseeds or covites—that's what the uptown folks down here calls us, "covites"—and we'll just say, "Yes, I believe that's right. I ain't nothing but a goddam hillbilly." And laugh.

I mean I reckon them women was right, if you think about it. Them murder tunes, well the old boy'll go for a walk with his girl, and then, for no reason in the world, he'll pick up a stick and whoop up on her, or stab her, and drag her around, pitch her in the goddam river. Yessir. They ain't pretty. And I don't know about encouraging anything, but they sure do explain all about beating up a gal. I reckon I wouldn't want to be setting out in the crowd and to have my husband up on stage singing "Knoxville Girl" and all the time looking right at me. So I reckon they got a point. But you don't holler at the song. Or the singer, for all that. They ain't the problem. Problem is folks will beat up on a woman. And think it's just fine. Putting her in her place, I reckon is what they'll say.

But them songs is telling the tale, and you got to tell it if you are going to do anything about it. It's the being quiet about it that's going to make it happen. And they ain't nothing in them songs about thinking it's all right to be doing that. There is a good old tune called "The Wind and the Rain," where the fella kills the girl and pitches her in the river. And she gets fished out by a miller, with a long fishing line. And he fixes her up into a fiddle: makes pegs out of her fingers and a bow out of her hair. Sometimes you'll hear it where he makes the whole damn fiddle out of her breastbone. Breastbone does look something like a fiddle, when you think of it. But the only tune that fiddle will play is "The Wind and the Rain."

It's a strange and eerie tune. You see, it's about itself: how this here tune tells the story of the death of this woman who is now a fiddle that will only play the tune about her death? So it's like she's shouting out her woes and making her own accusations—look what these men done to me. Like that. That's a hell of a tune.

But names, now. I'm a Shelton and a Blankenship and my name shows it. And they's a Taylor Blankenship, a cousin of mine, he's Blankenship and Taylor. But, like as not, I'm some Taylor, too. It'll get you right busy trying to work out the who and the what of how everybody's related up here. It's best to just give it up and figure you're just talking to everybody's cousin whenever you're talking to anybody. Safer, too.

Because folks will get worked up about that. They might laugh at themselves, but they'll get mad up about what you said or done to second cousin Delbert. At least, some will. Some of these folks are just as quiet and kind as doves. But there's a few will smack you right over the head like a possum.

Old Camber Shelton, now, he was a mean one. And, think of it, he was a possum hunter. He liked to do that better than most anything. I'd go with him sometimes, back then. I was just a little bit of a thing, tagging around them big boys. Me and Odge—that's Camber's twin brother—we'd go with him now and again. Now Odge was just a sweet old boy. Wouldn't hurt a gnat. And looked just like Camber. Now you think names is tough to keep straight, you toss in a few pairs of identical twins and you got a hell of a mess. But they wasn't nothing identical about Odge and Camber, once you got past the looks. Camber was a hell-raiser of the first damn note. And he sure did like catching possums.

We went up there with him one time, got the board and the stick and all and wrestled it up the hill behind their place. That board must have weighed thirty pounds. Flatten a god damn possum right into next week. Cam had augered a little hole about a third of the way down, to fit the prop stick into, and then notched his ground stick around the prop. He took some time doing it, but it worked, I'll tell you that. Them possums would go for the meatskin that he'd strung onto the end of that ground stick. And dragging on it, they'd pull the stick, that's notched around the prop. And WHAM, down comes that thirty-pound chunk of oak right on that old possum's head. That'll kill him deader than a ham. Well, you'd get a half dollar for the hide, down to Badie's, so I reckon it weren't all just for fun.

Anyway, we went up there with him that time, propped that trap up on yonder's side of Timb's Hill, down at the bottom, by the spring. Put her in under a blackberry bush, tucked back in a mite. I remember them briars snooking through my shirt. Camber said that's where the big ones will be. Hell, I never seen a possum anywhere near a blackberry bush on a goddam hillside. But what Camber said, well, you did. So we propped her in there and tied on the meatskin, just like regular.

Come back next morning to see what we caught. Me and Odge and Camber. We come round the bend there, and Cam says, "Great God we got a goddam bobcat!" He got right excited about that, and we could see something stretched out on the ground about that size, with the oak board on its head. So I got excited, too.

"That ain't no bobcat," says Odge. "Least I never seen a bobcat wearing a gingham dress."

"Hell," says Cam. "Thought we had a goddam bobcat. What the hell is it, then?"

We kindly stood back, afraid of what we might have caught, like it was a lion or something.

"I believe it's Santhamum Short," says Odge. "I think them's Hughie's brogans."

I saw them big rough shoes on the feet. They was stretched out, poking out from under that bush. There was a basket tipped up next to her arm. You couldn't see her head, because it had that oak board on top of it.

"You think she's dead?" I said. "She ain't moving a bit."

"Hell no, she ain't dead," says Camber, a bit irritated. "That there deadfall wouldn't kill no regular human being. She's just knocked out a mite. Look there: see that hand a'twitching? She's fine."

"Well, oughten't we to help her up, anyway?" says Odge.

But Camber was already on his way up the hill. Odge shouted his name, but he just kept on going. So we left Mrs. Short stretched-out there under that board and ran to catch up with Camber. Odge started to say something, but Camber shut him right up.

"Sonofabitch," Camber says. "Now I'm going to have to carve me a whole new possum trap."

We heard later that Santhamum Short was laid up a week or two, what with the lump on her head and the chest cold she caught from lying out there under that board for a whole day. Camber, he said he was going to sue her for costing him his trap, plus a half a dollar for the possum he didn't catch. Well, Hughy Short said, what did he expect when he goes and lays out a perfectly good meatskin that anybody poking by is going to want?

Odge had a bad death. They found his body, all carved up, in a alleyway in Asheville. We always figured he'd got mistaken for Camber and that's what got him killed. Well, Camber was a bad sort, and he got worse as time went on. Odge, he got killed around nineteen and twenty-eight, I reckon. We knew a little something about it, too.

Because we was sitting with him on the porch of one of them hash houses that sets up around the warehouses at tobacco auction time. Me and Odge and Camber. I was in off the road for the first bit, and I'd done helped them get their crop into town. So we took it in and was waiting our turn and we decided to go on down and get some banana pie. Odge was a big one for banana pie. He said it was the whole reason for him to farm tobacco, was to get into town ever fall and get him a slice of pie. So there we was up on that porch, and I was kindly gazing around and I seen a man standing across the street, just looking us over. He was a thin, dark fella, all dressed in a tailor-made suit and a John Stetson, just like the song says, both hands tucked down into his pockets.

"What the hell's he looking at?" I said, just joking. you know.

All of a sudden like, Camber says, "Damn," and he jumps up and dives through the front door of the place.

"Well I'll be," says Odge. Then that man starts across the street, all the time looking at that empty doorway where Camber had run through. He sidles on up to the steps and mounts up two or three of them. Gnawing on a toothpick.

"You," he says, still keeping' his eye on that front door.

"You talking to me, mister?" I says. He come on up the rest of the stairs and stood over us. Gnawing away on that toothpick. He was dangerous looking. Like a gangster or something. I reckon he was holding on to a pistol all the while he was talking to us.

"You Camber Shelton?" he asks Odge. He talked like a city boy. "No, I imagine not. I imagine that was him run through that door a minute ago. Wasn't it?" Well, he looked as if he'd just as soon kill you as sing you Liza Jane.

"Who should we say was inquiring?" I says. He just looked at me.

"You should say it was Tony Serlin," he says. "If you ever

get the chance." Then he pulled that toothpick out of his mouth and mashed it down into Odge's banana pie. And stood for a second to offer Odge a opportunity to do something about it.

Then he turned and sidled on down the steps and across the road and out of sight.

And that was that. Camber, he never said a thing about it, and we done forgot about it by the time we was laying out the tobacco in the warehouse and all. But two weeks later and Odge was dead. And I reckon that's the feller that done it.

II.

Hazel Taylor
Hazel Taylor—HTT

Hazel Tighrow Taylor
Mrs. George M. Taylor

Mrs. Hazel Tighrow Taylor

H George Morgan Taylor—Hazel Tighrow Taylor
T
T

It doesn't seem possible that I will be George's wife. Or even stranger, that he will be my husband. George? I've known George all my life. Well, I certainly love him, I won't try to deny that. But I guess I've always felt more like he was a brother or a dear close friend. I never felt romantically about him at all. And yet, I flushed all warm when he asked me. And when he kept on, after I'd said no, emphatically, no, well, that alone made him seem closer to a lover. I suppose we've done most everything together up to now, we might as well do that!

Listen to me. This is a serious thing and you're tying yourself to a man forever. *That ain't just putting the cows out*, as Daddy says. Then why can't I seem to believe it? Why does it seem so impermanent, like a play, or a movie show, and we'll all get into costume and act out our roles and maybe even act two and three, but we'll all know when it's time to ring the curtain down and go back to normal?

And if this is forever, what does that mean? Am I now forever a Hazel Taylor that will be his wife in just the way every woman up in these mountains becomes a wife, almost semi-consciously, stepping into a pre-cut form, to become worn and tired, a farmer and brooder, birthing fifteen children, or, if you're lucky, like my mother, only live long enough to bear six? And watching half of them die before you finally split apart inside, your heart as broken as your sex, and die?

I can't bear that. And I can't bear to give such a woman to George. He deserves a whole life as much as I do. But he will give in to this place. I know he will. He has these mountains in his eyes, and he won't ever get away. And will he, then, pull me down with him, into a life where thinking is a liability, reading a waste of kerosene, loving a positive physical danger?

And am I doing this just to redeem some token handed me by Noah Kersin? I think George is trying to offer me something of an escape from the self that was drawn from me, or perpetrated upon me, that day, at Possy's Camp. I think he wants to wrap me away from that pain. He has always tried to do something like that: when Mamma died, and he told me to listen to the stream, or Rosie and the snubbed pencil I no longer will use but always have. Bless George. But he doesn't understand that the pain is something I can stand. What I fear is the lack, the emptiness, the calloused hand that no longer even feels the hot wearing friction of the knife handle, no longer even notices the stick of the gum, or the twisting distortion of her fingers themselves.

But no: it is love, surely. That much is true. I love George and he loves me and we certainly know the best and the worst of each other. He knows I'm a reader and a thinker, and, although he won't ever take up with me on that, he will suffor my dreaming and my ambling around. And it's not the work I fear. I welcome working alongside George. There's a deep beauty in two people working the earth together, bending and pulling and turning, like a dance or a well-matched team. I would work my heart out for him.

And George has a kind of thoughtfulness himself. His music is that, and I know he feels the weight and the curve of the instrument as a sentient thing, much the way I love the heft and cool surface of a book, or the timid, insubstantial realness of the laurel cup in my palm. George is no clod, but a fine, feeling man in his own right.

And so I will marry and I will attempt to find a way among these traps and sinkholes already prepared for me. And I will become the woman I need to be. And if I can't? Well, I don't know…

FIELD NOTES: INTERVIEW—SHELTON BLANKENSHIP
May 13, 1998

Me, I was just a kid whenever George and Hazel was married. I reckon it's hard to imagine an old coot like me was a kid at any time, but I sure enough was. But I remember that wedding. Like it was yesterday. I played the banjo at that wedding and I believe that was my first time ever to perform on the five-string in public. Oh, George and Howdy or Cousin Dawny, they'd get me up to do a number on the five-string every once in awhile, you know. Folks always likes to hear a youngster pick. I don't know but I suspect it's part because they think it's just amazing that a little fella can pick out anything at all. But it's also because they are tickled to see that the music is getting along, that here's someone coming along who's going to play the old style, you know, keep the tradition. Folks is right jealous of that tradition, even today. You don't want to get too far off the mountain when you're picking bluegrass or especially any of the old time tunes. There's some old boys'll get right mad about it. You go to a bluegrass festival and there's one of these young bands wants to try to play something a little uptown, and there's fellas out in the crowd'll just shout right out, "play the goddam music," or some such thing. Folks that's been drinking a mite. I seen a man wanted to fight a young kid who didn't know how to play Dear Old Dixie. "How'd you like to *ride* that banjo home?" he hollers at the kid. Well, there ain't no point in that.

But I played the five-string at the wedding, all the way through the party, because, of course, George weren't available, being as how he was the one getting wed. And it was a right nice wedding, far as I recall. I remember Hazel looked right pretty, I'll say. After the wedding, at the party, there was some fella there that had got into some liquor, and he said if he'd known Hazel looked like that under them shifts and all that hair a tumbling around all the time that was tied back and swirled for the wedding, well, he said, "Old George wouldn't of got near her, because I'd be kicking in that stall, my own self." Well I was just a kid, but I still felt mean hearing that sort of talk at somebody's wedding anyway, and old Saint Dunstan, the old schoolteacher, he was there, he went right after that man. Madder than hell he was when he heard that kind of talk. Well, I don't blame him. He says something about how folks that don't know how to behave appropriately ain't got no cause...that sort of thing. And, of course, they just laughed at him, told him to save his speeches for the schoolroom. But he weren't schoolteacher any more, anyway. He was some sort of a peddler, went around to these little one-horse towns and up the coves, you know, selling whatever: Watkins products and such. Trading more often than he ever sold a damn thing. He'd go back down the mountain with more stuff in his pack than he'd hefted up here in the first place. But there to the weddin, he was mad as hell, and them old boys laughing at him, and one of them upped with something about did Saint ever get a look under that shift when he was teaching Hazel, and another of them says he'd sure as hell like to show her *his* hornbook, and, by God, that done it. Old Saint, now he weren't a big man and he was most peaceable, you know. But I reckon maybe he had a snort or two himself. It weren't like him, but he was worked up that day and that's certain. So he throwed a glass of that wedding punch right on that tough young drunk that had started the talk, and they all went for Saint, and there was a heap of commotion for awhile, everybody trying to hold them moonshine boys back and hollering *settle down now, boys*, that sort of thing. It didn't last long and everything was back to normal. Hazel and George, they never knowed a thing about it.

But when things got rearranged, I looked around and Dunstan, he was gone. Just plumb up in smoke. Well, the thing took him that way, I reckon.

But Hazel, she was looking around for him later. And she did look good enough to break your goddam heart in that muslin dress that she'd made her own self. Pretty as a spotted pup. "Where's Saint?" she says. "I wanted to see him especially today," she says to me. "You seen him?" Well, I weren't going to tell her nothing about that mix up or that somebody was saying them low down things about her at her own wedding. That just makes me sick to think of, even today. What's wrong with them boys?

So she went on looking for him. But she never spied him that day.

FIELD NOTES: INTERVIEW—GEORGE TAYLOR
May 10, 1998

Well now, I believe I just always figured I'd marry Hazel. It weren't like I chose her, or she chose me. We was just together all the time when we was kids, you know. And after that mess with Noah Kersin, well, I just naturally found my way back beside her. She weren't any too happy about it at first. Tried to get me to just quit her. But there was never any doubt in my mind, Hazel's the one for me. Me for her.

Oh I knew something bad happened with that Noah Kersin. It was bound to. Everybody knew that. That Noah Kersin was a slick talker and he was flashy, you know? Nobody round here liked him much. But Hazel, she was always thinking big thoughts, you know. And weren't nobody round here could keep up with her. I know I couldn't. So I reckon Noah Kersin sounded like he might just be the sort of feller to understand her, to talk her talk, you know? I think that was it: she found him to be smart and educated and everything. And she was so longing for all them sorts of things and she thought he might just have them. I suppose it's right hard to see a muskrat when you're wanting so hard to see a mink. Everything looks so bad when you ain't found nothing. Until that muskrat turns up. Then you been longing so hard for that there mink that you're ready to convince yourself that you're looking at one. When it's just really a muskrat.

So sure enough, something done happened. It don't matter what, though you don't have to set on a stump to figure it out. I never bothered to puzzle into it none. Hazel, she tried a couple times, later, to tell me about it, but I shushed her. It don't matter. Just don't matter.

So we was married. We was both of us nineteen, which is getting late around these parts. Lots of gals, anyway, gets married when they're fifteen or so. Hazel, she might have married that Kersin feller, so it's a darn good thing, after all. Funny how that can be. She hung back some, not wanting me to find out, you know, about how she might not be, you know, not be a virgin, you know. But tell the honest truth, I wouldn't have known anyhow. Still don't. And who cares about all that when you got somebody and you know she's going to be with you forever. You don't go checking her for scale worms. You know?

It might be a real thing and it might not, but it ain't worth even trying to kill the leaf just to get to the scale. You ain't thinking straight. You got to wrap around all of it and take it all, or you ain't never going to have none of it. That there Noah Kersin business was a part of Hazel, too. And so if I was wanting Hazel, herself, then I was going to have to have that Kersin part of her just as much as the rest. Besides, there ain't all that much about me that'd make anybody too glad to get tied up with. You do what happens, and you love what you love. That's all.

I never did believe that she left with him. Not even that he took her, drug her up there and throwed her off that cliff. I still can't get my mind around any of that. It ain't just that I don't want to, though that's what folks is always telling each other. It ain't. If it were that, I would have stopped at the first Noah Kersin business, wouldn't I? You know.

It's just that none of it makes no sense. Hazel, she never would have dreamed of going up to that place with nobody. There ain't a chance in the world and they could find all the bones they wanted to and a book or two with her name on it and I still wouldn't credit it none. No. I don't think Noah Kersin had a thing to do with it, this time. I think he tried. Sure enough, he tried. But I don't believe he got nowhere with Hazel this time. She weren't no sixteen year old girl no more to get fooled by a slick man.

No, Hazel gave that feller the air, sure as can be. So he left in disgrace. That's why nobody knew where he went to. If he'd got Hazel to go with him, believe me, he'd have pranced out of here with her on his arm for everybody to look at. But since he didn't get nowhere with Hazel, well, he just slunk out of here. You know? But it was just a matter of accident that Hazel left the same night as he done. The one didn't have nothing to do with the other. Except how she done turned him away like I said.

Well, now. Still you got the bones and them clothes. And you know what? I don't never take a second to wonder how she got killed. No. It's terrible, but I don't. Much as I mourn her. I don't. Because I'm forever worrying about why Hazel done went away, with him or without him. That takes up all my time, I reckon, and I ain't got nothing left for worrying about the killing.

III.

So they found them bones up on the ridge, and brought them on back down here, and put them on the ground down front of Badie's, and moved them around to see would they fit, or was they shin bones or what was they. And most everybody come by, everybody but George, and had a look, and Odge told how he found them, seven or eight times. And Badie rang down to the town and got the sheriff up here next day. And he looked at them a while, and moved them around some, and come back up on to the gallery where we was all squatting and says, "Well, now."

And they showed him the clothes and told him that George'd said they was Hazel's. And told him that Hazel had disappeared that night two years ago and that Noah Kersin, the son of a bitch, had done come back to town a few weeks before, then left town the same night as Hazel done, as well. And how they figured Noah had done talked Hazel into meeting with him that night because for some reason he was fixing to get rid of her. It'd be just like Noah Kersin to steal somebody's wife, wear her out and get tired of her, and toss her over a goddam mountain.

Only thing was nobody could figure out why Hazel would have gone with him in the first place. I mean, Hazel just weren't the sort to be snoogling about with no low down wholesale distributor or whatever he called himself just for the hell of it.

"Well, let's see," says the sheriff.

And then somebody remembers how Hazel and Kersin had done had something like a romance back a few years before he left town the first time. And how they was seen walking around together, and dancing together about a year or so before Hazel married George. And how Kersin took off that time too, like a singed hare, without bothering to say goodbye or pass the time or nothing.

"You reckon he'd set a crop out?" says Cousin Tommy.

"Shet up," says Jim Taylor. He's George's cousin. "You don't know nothing about Hazel Taylor nor Noah Kersin, neither. Nobody don't know nothing about no romance nor nothing else. When did any of you ever see Noah Kersin when he wasn't nosing around one woman or another? So I'd just suggest that everybody just shut up about things they don't know nothing about." You see, he was kindly protecting George, and putting in a word or two for Hazel's reputation as well.

Well, Tommy gets mad and says "Goddamit, Jim Taylor, you seen Hazel a'walking out with that feller sure as everybody else did. Now what do you suppose is going on, when he leaves town like his damn shirt tail done caught fire, then comes back years later, then runs off the same night as the girl that made him run off in the first place? I figure he done thought he'd set a crop out that first time, so he scooted. Then I guess he heard from somebody how Hazel ain't got no young'uns and is living up on High Creek, and is looking just fine. So back he comes…"

"Shut up," says Jim.

"…Hazel and when she sees him, well the ole fires of love gets to burning in her heart, and she takes up with him kindly on the quiet."

"Goddam it, Tom," says Jim.

"And this time he does get one set out, and he's afraid, with her married and all, that he's in a peck more trouble than he thought he was in in the first goddam place. So he tells her, 'Honey bunch...'"

Well that done it. Jim gets up and starts after Tommy, and the sheriff, he makes a grasp at Jim when he's passing by and snatches him up by the snood of his overalls and starts hollering at everybody to just get the hell out the way and stop trying to solve everybody's business but their own, and settle down Jim, now, will you set-tle down?

And that's just about all there was to her. The sheriff, he took them bones and them clothes on back into town with him, and we never heard nothing about them one way or the other. If it weren't for Tommy Blankenship flapping his gums about Hazel done this and Noah done that to anybody that would listen and meanwhile looking out for Jim Taylor so he wouldn't get his ears tore off his head, why nobody'd know them bones had ever been there in the first place.

They was gone like Hazel. Yes sir.

FIELD NOTES: INTERVIEW—T.R. BLANKENSHIP
May 11, 1999

George was a fine musician, best around these parts, and he taught my nephew Shelton how to play the guitar and the five-string both. Shelton, he's back home this week and you might could talk to him, some. He went out on the road with the music a long time ago. He was always picking the banjo and he talked some about it and he figured that there weren't nothing much for him to do up this way except to farm a little tobacco, like everybody does. And he says, "T.R., if I got a talent that can get me the hell out of here, so I don't never have tobacco gum on my hands no more, nor have to roust up at rooster crow in the morning nor have to ever again stick a god damn hog, now wouldn't you just say I ought to give her a try?"

Well, now, he was right, and he been at it ever since. He's a good picker and that's half of it. But the other half, that's big too. Because a lot of them gets out there and gets to making some money. Now down here, we never makes much in the way of actual cash money. Tobacco money is all the cash crop we got. Everything else, well we raises it or hunts it or kindly borrows it. So you get these boys down the mountain and give them a little loose cash and they don't know what to do with it. You see? They never had money just running-round loose in their pockets before. So they goes to drinking and poker and playing around with women just to have something to spend the god damn money on. And they'll get to taken them there-and-backs when they're on the road, and, before you know it, they're so hopped up and boozed out and run round that they ain't worth last year's crop. And now the music, the one thing they brought out of here, that they was thinking they could always turn to and rely on, well they ain't no good at that no more, because there ain't nothing left of them but the scraps. They ain't pickers no more, they ain't mountain boys no more. They're bums, just like everybody else.

So I reckon Shelton was lucky. Or damn level-headed, for a Blankenship. I'll tell you one thing, I know better than to get too far down this mountain myself.

George, he might have had a career as a musician. He could pick as good as any of them, and he was even solider than Shelton when it come to keeping your head tied on tight. But, you know, there is some folks you just look them in the eyes and you see that they ain't never going to be away from these mountains. They got that mountainous look in the eyes, I reckon. Because you can tell. And George, he's got that look. Hell, I don't know what. Me, I'm staying here just because I'm too god damn lazy to go over there, but George, he's got these mountains in himself, through and through.

And he was crazy for Hazel, too. He weren't too damn active about it, and he nearly lost her for all that. But he was always lurking around, kindly waiting on Hazel to make up her mind to what he already figured was going to happen. Like a young feller's got to sow them wild oats—now ain't that peculiar? Hazel weren't no wild one, not in the least. But it was as if George saw that she had to get something shook out of her, and when she finished with the shaking well, he was going to be standing nearby with his hat in his hands.

So he weren't a'fixing to go on no road, not with Hazel dreaming around where any feller with a shine on his shoes and a slick story was likely to snap her right up.

Hazel's most the smartest woman I ever seen, but I tell you, I'd a heap rather have a droudy old thing with a bit of common sense. She's about the only one on this whole god damn mountain that might not see through that Noah Kersin. Leastways not after he come back to give her a chance to see what a snake he was a second time. To run off with that miserable feller and his god damn order book and leave George here like a goddam ring pigeon. You ever seen one of them doves when its mate gets shot? Hell, it'll fly right down there and set next to that dead bird. And it'll just look at it, stunned like, and you can see it's trying to work out what's happened. And you can see it don't know what to do about the least thing, except just stand there and stare at that dead bird that ain't never going to come back. And it don't even know that it's got a broke heart, but you can see in its eyes that it's just exactly that. A broke heart.

You might be doing it a favor if you just took and shot it, too. And it was just the end of George, when Hazel done went off.

Kill himself? Hell, no, I don't reckon George'd do nothing like that. I don't believe he'd ever even have thought about any such thing as that. Of course you'll say, "I wish I was dead," and what not, but folks around here, no, they don't take to that sort of thing. George, he's a right steady feller. He don't go flying off crazy. No. He wouldn't ever have even thought such a thing.

Now Hughie Short, he done tried to kill himself. That's so. So I suppose it's been tried around here at least that once. But he was just stump crazy anyhow. He and his wife they lived away up on the side of the hill, over there near Grandma Cawdle that used to do the herb-healing and birthing around here. That's all federal land, now, don't nobody live on it. Them Shorts was damn scared of Grandma because they thought she'd witched them there when they birthed that young Enow with the funny ears. Old Hughie come running down the crick hollering——neither one of them could talk right, so it was always like trying to jawbone with somebody that had got a god damn bull frog crammed into their mouth somehow and was wrestling to get it out. Couldn't hardly unerstand a thing neither one of them said. Which was usually just fine.

So Hughie come wailing down the creek hollering, "Tat tamned wee-hitch done stradged my boy's heers out, she done twitched them out ant he loogs lak a goat! My bavy loogs lak a god damn goat!"

My Mamma was right nice to them two old idiots. Hell, they didn't have the least thing in the house, didn't even have a door on the hinges and them kids all stropping around naked as a god damn day-old shoat. Mamma would send them up a quilt or a feather pillow or something nice ever now and then. One of them kids had the god damn lepalepsy or some awful thing and he'd pitch a fit every time he got the least bit excited. All the other kids would just drool and daze like somebody had hit them over the head with a rock. Mamma always said we shouldn't get to laughing at them the way we did, that we ought to feel sad for them and to thank the Lord we didn't have the kinds of problems some folks had. Well, Daddy would say, "Boys, she's right there. I reckon I fall down on my knees seventeen eighteen times a day and thank God and everybody else you can name that I ain't Hughie Short. Or no kin to him neither."

I reckon that's why Hughie tried to kill himself: he done found out he weren't only just kin; he was Hughie Short, his own self.

Anyway, it was way down into the winter and my Daddy

and me was burning-out the tobacco bed and here come San-thamum Short—that's Hughie's wife—running down over the hill bellowing "He gont ter till he shelf! You got ter come hep me! He gont ter chill he telf!" She was about besides herself and carrying on. It was tough enough to figure out what any of them was saying when they was just passing the time. But get them het up, and Lord you couldn't make out a god damn thing without you went to studying it.

So it took Daddy a few minutes to cipher-out what the hell she was hollering about, that Hughie was going to kill himself. But once he finally got that, we lit out over the hill toward their place just as fast as we could, to try to save old Hughie from killing his god damn self. And Santhamum running right along-side, screaming "My Hyoo-hee gont ter chill he shelf! Till he telf! Oh Hyoo-hee!" Well, you never saw any such a thing.

We got there right quick and Santhamum is a waving and shouting, "Hyoo-hee down in ta barn!" until we ciphered her out again, and we all headed for the barn, which was about half stove in from a storm that probably come through there fifteen years before and none of them so much as lift a finger to prop her up even. And there's Hughie, a'standing up on one of the god damn cross beams that has a rope tied to it and the other end wrapped around his neck. He's got his eyes squeezed shut and he's looking up to the heavens, like. Them kids is all lined up like toads on a driftlog, just as moon-faced as ever. And the dogs is all bellering because we all run in there so fast they didn't get time to sort us out. And then we notice that Enow is there, because he starts in to foofin' and pitches one of his fits.

And Santhamum grabs Daddy by the overall bib and points up at Hughie and says, "Ter he tis! See Hyoo-hee? Right ter?" And then she looks up at Hughie and hollers, "All right, now, yoo sonner ta bits! Go ahead! Till yer damn shelf! Tey can't pin it on me! I god a witner!"

Old Hughie, he opens up his eyes and kindly peers down at Santhamum a second. Then he just screws them eyes shut again and recommences to looking at the heavens. Santhamum, she's still tugging on Daddy's sleeve, and the dogs still moiling, and Enow just flopping around on the ground, making these gargly noises. And Hughie kindly snarls out, "Somebody'd art to mind der own bidnits."

"Run home and fetch my shotgun," Daddy says to me, when all of a sudden, Hughie starts to sagging down. I mean he's standing on that crossbeam yet, with the halter wrapped round him and what not. But the whole damn thing, crossbeam and Hughie and rope and all is kindly easing downward. Hughie's eyes snap open and he looks sick, and the next thing you know we hears a loud KEERACK! and then there just ain't nothing there. I mean the whole goddamn barn is gone and we're standing in a pile of lumber, gazing at the sky.

It took us close to an hour to wrestle all them folks out of that barn, or what was left of it. Hughie was laying near the top, with that rope still wrapped around his neck and his feet a setting on that cross beam yet. He wouldn't let nobody touch him, so we just dug around him to get the other folks out. Hazie said later about how we ought to call Hughie "Roderick Usher," and Daddy said he didn't know nothing about that, but he knowed at least Hughie wasn't going to have to worry about repairing that barn no more.

FIELD NOTES: INTERVIEW—SHELTON BLANKENSHIP
May 12, 1999

George? Well, I guess I've known George since the day I was born. He was my teacher, you know. Showed me all there was to know about picking this music. Made me up a little banjo from a cheese box and an old hide. Piece of lath planed down. Strung her up from an old screen. I couldn't much more than walk and he gave me that. I played on it every day for a few years, until I grew into something a little more real. And then

George found me a way to wrestle-up the cash to order one out of the catalog. Put me to work cutting locust fence posts and setting them until I'd got paid enough to afford that banjo.

I don't know what it was made him take a shine to me that way. I think I recall first seeing that banjo of his, though I might be wrong: I couldn't have been more than a few years old. It was in the open case, and I do recall going up to it on my hands and knees, and it was just a big round shiny curve of metal and that wide white head, you know. It looked important to me, like it was bigger and brighter than anything I'd yet seen. Had some sort of importance just in the way it sat there, with them wires strung tight across it. Probably somebody told me right sharp to watch out and not mess with that thing, and probably George said it was all right, I wouldn't hurt it none. So I had that idea kindly dropped into my mind and that's why it made such an impression on me. I don't know. It's hard to explain. But it had a manner about it.

So I played all my life. He showed me the chords and the right hand. Back home, we played with two fingers, picking the tune out and filling in whatever way you could. It's a pretty way of playing. Got a more delicate feel to it than this here bluegrass three-finger stuff. Of course, that's where there's any money to be had in it, is in the bluegrass. So you have to play that style, if you want to make a dollar. And it's a good style. There's plenty of hot pickers out there these days can really show you some things on that three-finger style. But tell the truth, I prefer that old way. And George could play that prettier than a speckled calf. I tell you.

He taught me to chord on the guitar, too, and had me playing rhythm with them before I was big enough to see over a dead cat. I'd play all the dances and such and they were right nice to me. Old George would work with a fiddler from down the crick, name of Howdy Grimm, now he could play a fiddle, or later with Dawny Shelton. We'd do all the old tunes, Soldier's Joy and Forked Deer and like that, things folks like to dance to. Sycamore

151

Shoals. And they'd get me up and I'd sing some sort of novelty tune, like "Cat's Got the Measles and the Dog's Got the Whooping Cough," or some silly tune or other. Folks got a charge out of that.

Old George was as good a feller as you will ever meet anywhere up in these hills. A good, quiet, steady feller.

And played as good a five-string as you'd ever hear. And he never made no sort of thing out of it. He let that banjo do the bragging. That's the way it is with the real fine pickers, anyway, ain't it? You'll ask him if he plays the banjo and he'll say, "Oh I pick it a little now and then." That's how you know that old boy will unlatch that case and whoop down on that banjo like you never heard. Then he'll finish the tune and your eyes is bugging out, and he'll say, "I never could get that tune right. I reckon I'll get it someday." Something like that, you know?

I played with George for years, before I got that job playing in town, on the radio, and went on the road. And I got to say I took more pleasure in picking down there on the crick with George than I ever got out of working on the road. He was just as good as anyone at picking that banjo. There are some tunes I never could hear nobody else play after I'd done them with George for years, you know. "Barlow Knife," or "Sycamore Shoals," well there was some of them tunes that you just couldn't listen to nobody but George play them.

Hazel played some too. She got to be a fine banjo picker, herself. But she gave it up. I never could understand why. I used to could hear her play around their place, some evenings. And she could really play. Nice tunes, like "Hollow Poplar," that ain't any easy thing to pick out on a banjo. But then she just up and quit. I don't know.

We was up to the school playing at a dance one time and George he talked Hazel into coming up and taking his banjo and playing one of her tunes. And she come up, you know, bashful and quiet, like Hazel always was. And she played "Fisher's Hornpipe" along with me, and I tell you it was a pleasure.

She played that tune right down to the ground, now I'm here to tell you. And most folks around Shelton's Trace, they didn't have no idea that she could play the least note on the thing, you know? And they was right impressed by that. Well they should have been. I mean it was good, and you just didn't hear a woman that could pick a banjo like that. Somehow it just wasn't something women did much, you know. Now I heard Maybelle Carter pick a banjo now and again, after I got onto the road, and she could pick a banjo as good as a man, too. But Hazel was the first anybody around here might have heard. And I'm telling you, she could play.

So folks was right excited to hear her. And everybody told her how good they thought she was and how they'd never imagined a woman could pick like that, and got to treating her a little extra special now that they'd heard her play that banjo. And got to talking about the woman banjo picker, Hazel Taylor, you know?

And she just quit. Just as soon as folks heard her and got to talking about how good she was, well she just ups and quits. I never could figure it out.

So I been playing music as long as I've known George Taylor, and that's about as long as I can recall doing anything. My daddy played a bit of fiddle and I just grew up listening to him and then George took-hold and got me picking. I guess it just come natural to me that I could play an instrument, same as some folks can whistle right pretty, or some can track a bobcat. I can pick a tune. And so when I found out I might get paid to play one, well that sounded fine to me. It sure beat hell out of suckering tobacco or working in a mill or any other kind of work folks had to do around here. And we didn't have no land to speak of, and my older brothers was already farming what bit we had. So I took-up playing music as a profession. And I been playing ever since, all up and down the road.

It ain't hard work, but it's a hard enough life in its own way. It's a lot of long lonely drives without much happening in between one little town and another, and a feller can get to drinking or pick up on troubles here and there that he can't get out of. There's a lot of them should have just stayed home on the patch and not got mixed up with any of it. But I guess I could handle it fine. I never was one to tear up things and get drunk or gamble or what have you. I'm pretty level-headed when it comes down to it. So I was just suited for the music, didn't need no liquor nor nothing else besides the music itself, you know.

George, he could have done the same as I done. Sure could play as good as any of them. But I guess he had Hazel, and they had that little place, and he appeared to like working a crop as good as anybody liked anything. So I guess he didn't need to get on the road.

But I guess he hadn't figured on Hazel needing to. Because she up and gone. Quit him for no reason, just like she give up that banjo when everybody took to saying how good she could pick it, better than any woman you ever heard. And George, he just gave up after that. Still played the five-string a bit. Still does. And still just as good an old style picker as you'll hear in any of these mountains. But he ain't got no fire no more. Plays sad like. And he don't go around folks. You'd not see him playing for no gathering anymore. You just might hear him picking on the porch at home, all by himself, quiet and mournful like.

Folks that think a banjo can't be sad and mournful don't know much about banjos. Or never heard George Taylor playing one, all alone out there on that porch.

FIELD NOTES: INTERVIEW—T.R. BLANKENSHIP
May 10, 1998

George busted his leg right after the wedding so Hazel had to mind the farm and tend to him and everything else.

We were coming down the mountain, Sauver's Knob, up there above Short Fork, with a thumping big hive of honey. We had the hive branch slung across both our shoulders, between us, and we was coming down the mountain just regular and usual. Hazel was right up behind us, toting the smoker that George had got out of the catalog. It did a right smart of smoking-out bees, I'd say. And that day we found the biggest hive I ever seen, I believe that's so.

That's a right pretty stretch yonder alongside the crown of that knob. Sauver's stands out nearly by itself on that north slope and it's clear along there. So you can see all along that range of mountains all the way to Bethlehem, seems like. And I don't believe I ever come along there without drawing a breath and gazing across. It ain't every day you get a view like that.

Nowadays, what with these here highway overlooks and everything, I believe folks think these mountains is just one beautiful view after another. All you got to do is drive up and spool-down your winder and see the whole damn show. But that ain't the real way of these mountains. No sir. Most time you can't take three steps and turn around to see where you just was. Too damn many rocks and bushes and trees and cricks all tumbling up around you. You want some kind of fancy view, well you got to clamber on up one of these hollows, where you can't see nothing but the rocks you all is fixing to pick your way across the stream on, and so you ain't looking around anyhow, never mind you're down in the damn hollow where you wouldn't have a view if you were standing on grandpa's head.

You know when it comes down to it, I believe them folks that cut them roads, well they thought that mountains was full of them *grand panoramas,* like they say. So they made viewpoints all along because that had to be what a mountain road was all about. But, you know, those views never was there, one minute before they made them. So they just must have reckoned that if these mountains didn't suit the way they believed mountains ought to be, why they'd just make them be that way once and for all. Now ain't that just the way?

So, like I was saying, the real mountains, you want a *grand panorama,* why you got to work for one. You got to get all the way up that hollow picking your way up the rocks and across the goddamn stream a hundred and fifty times and maybe thrash yourself through all the shrub and laurel thickets at the top and then if you're mighty lucky you come out on a clear stretch and you can see something. That's the way it is. Mountains is dark and deep. Ain't bright and clear. Not too damn much, I'd say.

So it's a treat to find a view like that one out north from Sauver's Knob. Yes sir. And like I says, I always grab a look when I'm going through there. And I reckon George likely does the same thing. You know goddam well Hazel does. So, one thing or another, I figure George done gets his feet scrambled a mite. And he commences to topple. I was down in front of him, toting the lead end of that hive, so I didn't actually see a thing. I felt that hive branch slewing-around on my shoulder and *KER-AATCHT* I hear that branch snap loud as hell.

Except that branch didn't snap. It was George's leg bone, just as sure. Sounded just like a damn branch snapping. And down he went like he'd done been mauled. Right over the edge of the trail. So I turned to look, and I saw the top of his head right about foot-level, you know, like there weren't no rest of him no more. First thing I thought was he'd been bit by one of them bees, somehow, and he'd jumped off the goddam mountain. Still thought the clackering I'd heard was him smashing that branch. But I'd say it weren't. It was all George busting his leg. And just by taking a step on the trail while he was admiring the view, or because he was waiting to listen to Hazel admiring it. And how in the thunder he broke his goddam leg—both them two bottom bones—just taking a little walk on Sauver's Knob, where he'd done been a million times before.

But there he lay, proof positive, straight out on that steep slope, and saying, "AAARN! AARN!" and me and Hazel just gaping there, peering down at him, like we just seen one of them Mars men stepping off the space station or what have you.

And he says, "AARN! AAAARN! I think it's broke," he

says. "I done heard it bust."

And I says, "You're goddam right it's broke. Sounded like a tree limb. How in the hell you bust your leg just walking along the trail? I know my cousin Davey, now he…"

And he says, "Let me get on up." And he grabs a root and commences to scrabble around a mite, and he says, "AAAARN! AARN!" again, and then lays still.

And I says, "Cousin Davey McCrary, he walked plumb off a scaffolding five or so year back. Busted his leg. Course, he was right drunk at the time, and…"

And Hazel says, "Shut up, T.R. Can't you help drag him up the mountain?"

So me and Hazel, we hooked his armpits and hefted him up to the trail, with him sayin "AHREN," a little weaker than before.

And Hazel, she took right over. She got him stretched out and still, and her cradling that broke leg like a Mamma. She set me to hatchet-off three sticks of wood from the hive branch. She took them sticks and her handkerchief and wrapped him right up in a splint, neat as a popgun, and sent me on down the trail to fetch a horse and get him down off of there.

Johnny Cantle lived over that way, on down the knob and across the fork. He had him a few of them little horses you used to see around these parts, here and there, one place or another. I believe somebody brought in a breeding pair about two hundred years ago and they done got mated up and down these hills until they was quite a barrel of them.

You don't see them horses around any further. They was tough little goddam critters, all over brown, no bigger than a fox and half mountain goat. Folks back in there would make saddles out of three pieces of piney wood and put a rope halter on them. No bit, no shoes, no bridle nor stirrups. Just all horse. You could take one of them ponies and strap two hundred pounds of dead weight on her and she'd walk it right up the top of any goddam mountain you pointed at. Downhill, why they'd pick their way among the loose rocks and such, real delicate, like they was walking on busted glass. But going up, why they'd stop and scrunch themselves up and wait, just like a goddam cat. Then, SWOOM! They'd clamber and crattle up the steepest set of rocks you ever saw. And riding one of them was just like setting in Grandma's rockin' chair.

Only thing was, them ponies would take you right up or down stretches that'd set your hair straight on end. Wilt your damn pecker to look over the ears of one of them critters at the rockety drop she was a'fixing to take you down, where if you was onfoot, why you'd be grabbing roots, and your feet sliding, and looking for footholds and what not.

So I went down to Cantle's and got-up one of Johnny's mountain goats and we threw on one of them wood saddles that was like riding an ironing board, and up I went. It's a damn steep ride with two good legs, and going up, like I was, was a hell of a lot easier than coming down, like we was fixing to have George do. Going up, well you're looking straight at that mountainside, about two inches in front of your horse's nose. But going down, you're looking across, and all you see is air, with the next piece of solid mountain about twenty feet below you, where if you or the horse falls, either one of you, you're going to bust your goddam head like a squash, right on them rocks. Feels like you and that pony is fixing to jump off the barn roof, ever step she takes.

Well, we got on up there, and Hazel, she got George up on a rock next to that pony and she helped him to sling his bad leg over and hop on and we worked him down that trail. Every time that pony would head down a steep patch—and they was a few made you feel like you was eighteen foot tall—old George'd get to saying, "AAARN! AAARN!" again, and working his ass around on that saddle. And Hazel would just coo at him, and he'd shut right up and listen to her. Now it ain't just any woman can settle a man with a just-broke leg riding a half-grown horse with a wood saddle and no stirrups about two hours straight down a mountain. But all she had to do is say a word: didn't matter none whether it was *grandpa's knickers* or *chess pie*, and that done the trick. I got to say she did look right lovely setting there holding him and keeping his courage up. And helping him along. I'd say.

So George was laid up that first month, and Hazel doing the cultivating and suckering and the wash and everything else there was to do on that place of theirs. Didn't seem fair, a young bride and all. But she done it. She was a right capable woman, Hazel. It don't matter how pretty she talked.

JOURNAL OF HAZEL TAYLOR
May 10, 1997

So we got along, and I got to relaxing and really feeling right about being married to George and working with him, living the life. It was sweet and comfortable with him in the house and the work was hard and tiring. It feels good in your body to work that hard. Somehow the hotter and gummier and more tiring the work was, the better you felt at the end of the day. So George's broken leg, within a month of moving up there, was not a burden to me so much as an opportunity. With him laid up, the place became my responsibility. And I would feel free and tough and a part of the place. Alone out in the field all day, and have you ever noticed how concentrated your thoughts can become when you're in the middle of a hard job? Driving fence posts or something, and you get to thinking deep and long about things, so that your body is stretching and flexing and working and your mind is curled down so far inside of you that it can operate without anything distracting it at all. You can't do that if you're working with someone else, because you're talking and looking at each other and so there's no space to burrow down there, inside. But alone, you're further away than you've ever been, while your hands are setting that post and then the next. And the next.

So it was all right. More than that: it was good. It was a life I could live, and I told myself so, reconciled to stay and struggle against the fates that would try to coarsen me and empty me of everything but the work. The fence posts. I loved George and I loved our place and the pitch of the slope flowing off the big mountain. I would have stayed. I believe I would have.

And then George got better and was up and around. And I had to accommodate myself to the new rhythm of the work, with him alongside. But it was fine. The deep, quiet thinking was gone, but the exchange seemed a fair one. For now I had George and I could talk with him and wonder about things, thinking aloud, almost. And he listened, not just polite or solicitous, but as though he would rather hear what I had to say than anything in the world. So the distance from deep inside to out in the air became very slight, and I could just let my mind go on while we worked. And, sometimes, we would stop, right in the middle of a job, and touch each other, wrap our arms about each other. And I will never relinquish the feel of his shoulders and back with the damp, sweated shirt that seemed to make the touch even closer, the soft, pale cotton like a part of him, curved over the muscle and bone and warm, wet. Or my own shirt, smoothed under his hand as he showed me how I was shaped, curved to his beautiful hand. And I would talk out my thinking and he would just say my name, every once in awhile, just speak it out. And not *Hazie* anymore. No. *Hazel. Hazel.*

But it was wrong, and I believe I found out: how the young, vibrant women I'd seen became the shapeless, toiling wretches they were just a few years later. Because the work, the marriage, everything seems at first a fulfillment and vindication of their alive, sensual bodies, minds. The movement and the sweat and the curving hands all a part of a new connection to the place. And to the man. So they don't see it, don't suspect the inexorable coming. But the work goes on, and the routine of the hard labor, and they don't even realize that the thinking has begun to get in the way. And one day they lose a sensation and the next day another, and each gap, each deficit is not a loss they can recognize, because it is awareness itself they are losing. So it doesn't matter to them. It doesn't matter.

One morning in that second fall, while I was in the smokehouse, I heard rifle shots outside. Gunshots are so difficult to place up there, because the mountains pitch the sound around, drawing the percussion itself into a stretch of noise, a *skeeyooo* sound that appears to belong to the flanks of the hills themselves. And I came out of the barn and George was up the hill, shooting crows. And I went on up to him and watched for awhile, rubbing my wet hands on my hips. Shooting crows is no easy thing, but George was a steady hand and eye and he brought down quite a few of them.

"You want to fetch them birds?" George said, in the act of aiming another shot. He let the barrel down and bent to pick up a canvas sack. I took it from him, gave him a smile.

"Yes sir. Yes sir," I said in joking deference. And I jumped to the job, running and hopping through the sedges and brush, like a gun dog, and finding the stilled bodies, tossing them into the canvas sack. Blood beads up and pearls on the feathers of a bird, because of the oils I suppose, and so each of these little bodies bore a rounded droplet or two of shining blood, so red against the black of their feathers. And I scampered around the field, gathering crows.

I looked back at George just as he fired off a round, and I heard the *fudfudfud,* the dropping bird, as it fell directly at my feet. And it wasn't dead. It flailed and scrambled, turning horrible silly little circles around itself, a crumpled beating of instinct, reflex gone frantic.

"Stop it," I said. And reached down both hands to scoop up the wounded flapping. With one hand, I broke its neck and tossed it into the bag. Wiped my hands against my overalls. And went on.

The next day was bright and cold and I was in the garden,

gathering beans for canning, when I heard a flight of crows pass over. And I stopped and straightened and watched them fly. And something passed through me. I felt it the way you'll feel an echo of tender flesh beneath the callous on your hand or the ball of your foot. And this was grace: a last flutter of sensation somewhere in my depths. And then I shuddered, as though this timid sensibility were a wave of cold wind flowing across damp flesh. And I said, aloud, "You sure knew how to kill that bird."

And I saw that I had been caught. I saw it, and that was grace. Vouchsafed this tiny glimpse of what I had already lost, I could see the future Hazel Taylor lurking in the fields and slopes all around me. I could recognize numbness seeping around me, into me. And I realized that nothing—nothing—felt as it had even a few months ago. And I said, aloud again, "Dear God. Dear God. I've got to get away."

IV.

JOURNAL OF HAZEL TAYLOR
September 20, 1926

There's a certain s

JOURNAL OF HAZEL TAYLOR
May 14, 1997

That single line is all I had written when George came in to tell me that my father was found lying dead in his own barn lot, a trace chain in his hand.

So I stopped writing, of course, and I didn't put anything down again in my journal for a good long while. A month or so.

I don't know why I should have stopped at this time. There is an ironic symmetry to the silence, since my mother's death had elicited—or at least marked the emergence of—the first entry. Perhaps, this time, a hiatus was a tribute of sorts, a memorial moment of silence, in honor of my father's own ability with language. Because if I had learned anything in my life about language as a shape, a modeling of personality and moment, I learned it from listening to my father. Our very sense of self, as people and as a family, grew out of his talk, his gift for spontaneous metaphor—*it's wetter than a duck at sundown*—his sense of the expressive possibilities of a laconic, self-abrogating style. His was a kind of humor grounded in a deep, personal humility, and, at the same time, a reminder, selecting himself as chief example, that we are all fools together—*They ain't no place on this here farm for any boss man a'strutting around and laying down rules. And that there is rule number one.*

My father was not alone in this gift, but a master among many skilled talkers on the Creek. Mountain people are adept at using, inventing, language to mark their experiences—T.R. announcing that he's going to try to *snurf up* some pawpaws, or his daddy, Big T.R., telling him he's got to *croff* a load of straw out of the barn for repacking the bed shucks. It's a deep knowledge of how language and sound pool to make meaning. And I think it's why our enduring mountain culture isn't found in the permanence of painting or craft, but in evanescent speech and improvisational music. Mountain folk have never been much good at producing or ornamenting lasting things. They never bothered much with setting anything down, in paint or in print. Mountain crafts are really quite crude, compared to the fineness and fluidity of their music and speech. Perhaps quilts are exceptional—and who ever did any quilting without either talking or singing? So we make improvisations by shaping the mountain air to our lives, and this floating, vibrating nothing creates a sort of tradition that changes with each utterance, and that will last forever.

So it was part tribute. But at least as important, I couldn't bring myself to write any reactions because, along with the scalding grief and loss—mostly for him and the hard, useless life he had had to live—there was, above it all, a distinct sense of release. An exhilaration, almost, that could certainly not be shared, expressed, even among my own selves, or written down, even for my own eyes.

I felt as though I had somehow been freed from an obligation, or, better, as though an indenture had been served and I was now, by very dint of the years of service, able, even expected, to cast off that woman and take up another. At any rate, his death opened a perspective of possibility that I had not allowed myself to see during his lifetime, and that now urged me into the spaces of its own landscape. So, whether I would admit it or not, and regardless of my refusal to write it out, it was release. Freedom.

Emily Dickinson has a poem about "a certain slant of light," and when I came upon this poem a few years ago, I thought of the interrupted phrase in my journal, cut short by the words of death: *there's a certain s...*and then, nothing. The death not only arrested the flow of writing, expression, it turned back on itself and obliterated the original thought. I have no idea what I was writing about on that afternoon when George clomped into the room in spattered brogans and overalls, an undignified messenger for such profound news." Hazel," he said, and put his hand on my upper arm, a gesture of comforting intended to still the writing as well. "Hazel, they found your father out front of his shed a hour ago. Hazel, he's done passed on."

I remember looking upward into George's eyes and thinking *Daddy works too hard. One day he'll just give out.*

"He's just tired," I said, ridiculously, still looking straight into George's eyes as though he might be keeping something from me or playing some trick. "Isn't he just tired?"

"Oh, Hazel, I'm right sorry to be the one that's got to tell you. I so wish it weren't so."

And somehow, that did it. I drank the meaning of his words, his voice and touch, and the simple *wish it weren't so.* And I found myself weeping in his arms, crying tears of black sorrow and of bright release.

I took up writing again after Saint's last visit to the Creek. I had seen him, talked to him, at Daddy's funeral and his final visit was the logical closing episode of the earlier talk. Because he had something to say, and I knew it, felt it, as we walked back toward the house from the gravesite. Something looming, spreading and covering the moment and its people and places, leaving only Saint and myself uncovered and upstage, where you can all watch our foolishness and stupidity.

Perhaps this sense of tone derived from the storm that blew through that morning as we gathered in front of the old home place to head for the graveyard. It came up so suddenly, just as the pine coffin was carried out the door. A cold, powerful downdraft, sweeping off the mountain with a sound like a tremendous rolling. And then, before we had time even to notice that it was all taking place, a sharp, plosive sound near at hand, the big tree limb dropping as though seen on a screen, in slow motion, from some impossible angle, so that it seemed an act of conscious will, not as though the wind was wrenching off the limb but as though the tree itself had furiously expelled one of its members in some paroxysm of self-disgust.

At the precise instant that we turned and saw the limb already in mid-descent, the rain struck with a sound as though some monstrous hunter had torn out the viscera of his enormous kill, spilling a streaming torrent of sky-entrail upon us. We walked to the gravesite as though through a fuming cauldron of blood and flesh.

At the grave, the pallbearers stood stock, and I can see even today the rain hitting the raw white coffin lid and rebounding in thousands of bright, frenzied, silvery bubbles, like water jumping off a hot skillet.

And all of us grouped around that jeweled dance rising from Daddy's coffin, as the rain tumbled over us, smearing mountain and creek and house into undifferentiated and indifferent grays. So that there was nothing, nobody, in the entire world except we dozen or so sodden, dripping mourners arrayed in stark solitude around a bubbling, leaping pine box. While the heavens were slain and gutted.

The entire affair of the funeral took a bare twenty minutes, the walk to churchyard and, the rain having given out, the lowering: a shining, immaculately rinsed coffin, smelling of woods and sky, consigned to a Verdun of mud, quagmire and trench.

As the coffin was lowered, two great clods dislodged from the side of the hole and dropped with a startling hollowness onto the coffin lid, throwing out a pattern of red debris on the white, blank skin of the pine. I reached reflexively and held tightly to the forearm of the man standing silently beside me. But it wasn't George. It was Saint Dunstan.

It's odd, when I think of that funeral, I don't remember George at all. Of course, he was there. But it's as though he has been written out of the scene and is standing backstage, somewhere, waiting to re-enter when he hears his cue. But for now, just standing by the curtain tackle, sipping a coffee, listening to the actors on stage as they deliver lines he already knows by heart.

Saint reached across himself and put his hand over mine as we watched my brothers—already strangers from another life, some other family—fill the grave, the spade's light *baatch* as it bit the mound of wet clay, and the heavy *thubb* of its load dropping into the hole.

And we returned along the rocky pathway that skirts the hillside, while the others—presumably with George—disappeared down the lane.

"He was a good man, your daddy," Saint said, after we'd gone a ways in silence.

"He worked hard," I said. "And died of it."

"Yes," said Saint.

"And left nothing. Had nothing all his life, worked hard all his life, left nothing of his life. A hard storm and a muddy grave."

Saint stopped. I walked on a pace beyond him, then stopped, too, and turned back to where he was waiting for me. A fresh breeze was blowing and the clouds were breaking up and shredding, snaggling themselves on the mountainsides. I turned to find him and he reached out and touched my elbow.

"Hazel," he said, sounding muted, almost weary. "Look at yourself." He released my elbow and brought his hand to my cheek. I do believe these are the first times he ever willfully touched me in any sort of gesture intended to convey emotion. "And you say that he left nothing?"

And I began to weep, tearing up great clots of grief. And he wrapped his arms around me while I wept into his wet, warm shirt, and he rubbed my back, soothing, and saying my name again and again.

And that was that. Until he came back and declared himself.

JOURNAL OF HAZEL TAYLOR
October 23, 1926

What am I to do? I don't know if I'm about to laugh at the absurdity, snarl at the outrage, what? Shrink in disgust or bow in gratitude? Resent the man's audacity, admire his honesty, pity his hopelessness? I don't know.

Saint has stopped by to say farewell and to declare his love. These both come as rather a shock. The first, he says, is an "economic necessity." The second, well, he feels that I "have a right to know."

Those gas-fired flatirons that he sold all over these mountains last year have changed, it seems. Once the means to overwhelming success, they appear to have become only the medium of his ruin. I can tell you this because I bought one of those irons, like everyone else, and it went bust pretty quickly, itself.

Oh it's a fine idea to fire up a flatiron with coal oil. And it worked beautifully at first. The iron stayed hot, just right, as you pressed the clothes or the linens, and it was a good sight lighter and easier all around than an iron on the hearth. And you could do your ironing anywhere you wanted, because you didn't need a hearth at all. George thought I was crazy to iron outdoors, but I liked it. I can think freer outside and no chore is a chore if you can think while you're doing it. In a hot, smoky room, with that heavy flatiron, you're working and sweating and there's no space left for anything but the job. So all you can be is a drudge. But outdoors, with a light-handed iron, you've got room to dwell and dream, while the least part of you runs that iron.

But it didn't work for long. Those little jets all around the outside, where the flame springs up, gradually got clogged. Or, on a few, the valve to the "compressor pump" got stuck. Mostly, it was the clogging that ruined the venture. The holes are too tiny to clean out with a common pin or anything else. So you used that iron for just as long as you could, and then it turned itself into worthless junk. But that wasn't the worst of it. No. The worst was going back into that hot room with that heavy flatiron after you'd learned about the pleasures of ironing outdoors. Oh yes, the worst was going back.

So I believe folks felt cheated by having to go back to something they'd been doing all along. All of a sudden they couldn't bear it, and, since the means of escape, the tunnel out, had collapsed, they blamed the man who had first shown them the shovel.

There were women who vowed never to trade with Saint again. *He done took me for one ride, but I ain't going to get on board again, I'd say not.* He tried to pay folks back some money, even. But the worst of it was he had done so well with that first stock of irons that he immediately put his assets, including his proceeds from the first order, into a double or triple order of the things. So not only did he have fifty women wanting their money back, he had a brand new stock of one hundred and fifty gas-fired irons that no one wanted to buy.

So he has come to tell me that he is out of business and that he won't be coming around again. He brought me a big stack of books and a new dictionary, because he knew I had worn out the first one. Then he told me he loved me.

No. He didn't say that, precisely. And he was careful not to agree to walk up to the Flats with me, where any such declaration would have carried a much more profound weight of threat, or at least of secrecy. In fact, there really is nothing particularly illicit about any of this, my marriage—which marks him a few years late—even my age—which marks him twenty years late—notwithstanding. No. The marriage is an irrelevance, and not because of the implausibility of Saint's avowals. Marriage does not require fidelity as a first-condition, the way the moralists would have us believe. Because love shapes its way as it goes, never able to conform to any standing prescription. It is always a tension and a contradiction between the two bodies who make up the union itself. Because there are so many of us, in each of us, that the creation of personal fidelity is something like a village meeting: some of us aren't the least bit interested, and so we don't even show up. Others have definite feelings on the subject; and there are many with a range of conflicting views. Each claims to speak for the will of the entire self. And so, out of this Klootz convention, as the author says, we forge a tentative understanding about how we hope we will behave. That's what it all comes to.

But then Saint is not asking anything of me. He's certainly not engaged in an attempted seduction, or in any sort of persuasion. It is rather more to the contrary: he was informing me of a condition that he had discovered within himself and had been unable to treat. His declaration was born out of at least as much *confession* as *avowal* and was perhaps more *warning* than either. Like a drunkard, in a moment of sobriety, will warn you not to leave your liquor sitting out. Not that he is going to harm you in any way beyond the loss of your liquor, but that he will make you unwitting accomplice in the further corruption of his own self. I don't know. I don't have this right yet. I'm saying it all wrong.

Which is what he said, himself, sitting with me under the chestnut in our old schoolyard, where he had wanted to go, as though the location would emphasize the enormous inaptness of the situation: a man twice my age, my teacher as well, asking me to try and understand, comprehend his message, and then, at the last, suggesting that I ignore what he was feeling in his deepest core. All of this would be odd enough if he had merely

selected me to be confidant to some secret affair he had em-
barked upon with a young married woman in Asheville.

But he's talking about me, all about me, and how beautiful
and desirable he finds me. Me. Saint.

Can you see? Here I am, both sole confidant to and object of
a passion that neither of us wishes to claim, which neither of us,
apparently, wants to do anything about, one way or the other.

"I'm sorry, Hazel. I'm saying this all wrong." he said, "But
you need to understand. I can't *not* respond to you. That much,
at least, is out of my control. But I must tell you that I *do* respond and that, as far as I can see, I *will* respond. Because if I
didn't tell you, as clearly as I could, it would be only a sordid,
disreputable inclination, brought up in stealth and feeding on
itself, alone, like an addiction, some dirty habit. And it is much
more than that, Hazel."

"I see," I said, looking at his round, lined face. I have no idea
how I felt. Taken advantage of, compromised. *What am I supposed to say? What is there that can be said at all? Where is this
coming from, this "love," so unwelcome? This is ridiculous.
No: this is sad. No, no: this is an assault, to be fended off. No.
Of course not. This is Saint.*

"And to know that I would never try to complicate your
life," he said, as though he were totally unaware that he had
just done exactly that. "And, more, that this is a pledge: I will
be always eager to see you, to talk with you, and, more im-
portantly, to help you, in any way I can. I want you never to be
hesitant about calling on me for any sort of help whatever.
Don't worry about imposing upon my feelings, using me for this
or that. I know that being useful is all that is left for me. And I
will remain true to this pledge, always."

"Courtly love?" I said, and tested a smile. I wanted to break
this tension—Saint had been leaning forward uncomfortably,
one hand beating on his thigh at each word he said. Meanwhile,
I was offering a touch of sarcasm to the conversation. I think he
is being a little over-dramatic in all of this.

"Well," he said, answering my smile to show that he caught both the token of friendship and the note of derision. "Certainly not at all courtly."

And I realize, now, that this was as close as he came to saying the word *love*.

FIELD NOTES: INTERVIEW—T.R. BLANKENSHIP
May 13, 1998

Old Dunstan was a pretty good old feller, but he weren't much at selling, far as I could see. Didn't stay at it more than a few years. I'd say he should have stuck to teaching school.

Not that I was any kind of shakes in that school. I never had any care for sitting on a bench while somebody took and pumped me up with a bunch of things I weren't too interested-in in the first place. And was flat contrary to when I could see you were fixing to make me listen for an hour or two of you talking about them. So I ain't no expert on schoolteaching. But I set there a few times as a boy, so I seen Saint do both the selling and the teaching And he was a right smart better teacher than he ever was a peddler.

I believe he cared a lot about his teaching He sure enough would get pleased if one of them kids did a good job of something, got the spelling right or figured out one and one is two, or any damn thing like that. Hazel, she could outshine anybody at most any school matters, and old Saint, he'd just beam at her like a grandma at the christening. So he took a right smart of concern in being a teacher. Even after he done quit to take up the peddling, he'd bring up a stack of books to Hazel every time he came through. Hazel, she'd get talking about some goddam book she's reading and go off rambling about it. Hell, I couldn't never follow what she'd be saying, but you could see she loved it all so goddam much that you'd get interested. anyway. It's a treat to see anybody get so much pleasure out of a little thing like a book.

George, he'd just get goggle-eyed when she'd start up on something like that, some book, or how bright was the god damn moon or ain't it amazing that who-jigger done invented the ice cream cone or whatever damn thing she'd get on. He'd just stop and watch her go on about it and you could see he'd rather listen to Hazel read a goddam feed sack than anything in the world. He weren't one to talk about such things. But he told me once that he believed Hazel's voice was the prettiest sound he'd ever heard. Even more, he said, when she'd laugh. He said she sounded like bubbling water. I said she sounded like Hazel Tighrow to me. but that just got him mad and shut him right up. So he didn't never mention it again. But you could tell he loved to hear that woman talk.

Well, Saint, he took up peddling, I guess, because he couldn't make a go of teaching. These teachers they ain't got no time to farm or nothing and so they pretty much need to have cash to live on every day. Well now, it's got to get hard on a feller to need that kind of money, and it might could have soured him on the teaching. Only reason I could see for him to quit. And then he done lost his star pupil, because she done quit schooling, all of a sudden, about the time of that business with Noah Kersin. So all Saint had to work on was a bunch of bowl-eared hillbillies that couldn't read the inside of your hat.

George and me, we had quit away back before that, so he done already lost his worst students, I guess, and I reckon he thought things would be just clover, what with Hazel in there lapping-up Romeo and Juliet or whatever else he had them poor kids to read. So I imagine when she quit it was quite a bring-me-down for him. And like I said, he wasn't making no goddam money and he couldn't have farmed if the whole world was to-bacco. So he went to peddling

I guess he didn't do too bad until he got into them fancy irons. He figured he'd hit the jackpot with them irons. And everybody around here that had a damn nickel in their sock wanted to buy one. You ran them with coal oil and you'd work them without ever having to spell them on the fire. Pump them up with a dern piston, so that coal oil would spray out them little spigots, like a feller spitting between his teeth. Hell, they're damn lucky one of them didn't blow up in their hand. Anybody that would try to iron their clothes with a goddam coal oil fire burning in your hand, well they ought to be locked up tight.

Hazel's dad, he was about the only person on this crick who didn't buy one. He said if he got a yen to burn his house down, he'd just buy the coal oil and save on paying for the flatiron, too. Well, he had some sense about him. He passed on right around that time I believe.

Anyways, old Saint Dunstan just went belly up. Had to quit peddling, at least in these parts. I never saw him again. I believe somebody said he'd died a right smart time ago. Back in the forties, maybe. Heart got him, or something did. Who knows? He should have stuck to teaching.

V.

JOURNAL OF HAZEL TAYLOR
February 24, 1927

Noah Kersin has returned! Oh, this is terrible. Terrible. I hardly can hold this pen in my hand. The blotter shakes and smudges as I lay it on paper. I am so distracted. What to think? Where to go? How is it that such a thing can come to me at this stage, when I have begun to shake off the old shame and to build enough courage for thinking and acting independent of the woman who creeps up on me with each day, the woman who wields my own future in her hands like an axe, the woman I am *supposed to* become? Oh! Is he here to remind me that degradation is, has been, will be, my lot? That I am born to be overpowered, not only by his crude hands, but by George's loving, by the beautiful looming place itself, overborne, pounded into shape, hewn by that terrible woman's axe, that Hazel Taylor awaiting me around every turn of the clock? And was that Hazel Taylor, that *to-be*, that *must-be* born on that day at Possy's Camp, born by his plunging obliviousness? And did he know this all the time, and so he has only come back to bear witness to his own return? Or to collect his reward—a subdued Hazel Taylor who he need not even try to overpower anymore because he can draw his seamy fill of satisfaction from seeing her every day, not dragging behind her the remembrance of his past conquest, but looking before her in anticipation of that woman who wields the axe that he tempered and whetted and placed in her hand? Oh, I am distracted!

I was standing over the wash kettle in the midst of the smoking steam that covers you so completely in this weather, so that it's as though you are working inside a gauzy tent, turning and sweeping the slick paddle for all the world like a witch at her seething cauldron. And I was feeling spooky-like anyway, the way you can get in the shrouding steam, when you lose sight of all the familiar stable things, the unmoving mountains and tree trunks and your own solid bulk, all swirled away in soapy, smoky mist, so that it feels as though someone could creep up on you from the very inside of your self. I was ready to be set upon by the terrors. And just as he has always seemed to know precisely where and when to take the most advantage of his own entrances, Noah sank himself into the fog, like a viscous clump of some strange, foreign material, dropped into the water and floating idly, sluggishly down, only to hit the first jutting object on the rocky bottom and to spread glutinously along and over until the entire outcrop and all around it has become the sticky sludge, itself, no longer the outside extent of the water but, now, the center of this new, massive heap. Yes, Noah Kersin dropped into the steam of the washing and suffused his own sticky self-ness into the entire scene, so much so that he became paddle and kettle and soap-scum and the bubbling hot reek of the clothes themselves, even the slick soapy sweaty skin of my own hands on the paddle.

"Well look who this is," he boomed, as though he was greeting some old school chum, not the vanquished souvenir of his own grasping power. "Hazie, I believe you're a picture of beauty, even with your arms in the suds. Why I believe you'd look right pretty in a coal mine, Hazie."

How can you even be affronted by such shameless aggressiveness as this?

I dropped the paddle and moved back out of the cloud, trying to leave him within, rubbed out by the intervening haze, or hoping at least that stepping into the clear I could think straight. The bright air was cold against my sodden skin, and the sudden chill made me feel exposed, vulnerable to his very gaze. So I moved back to the kettle. I preferred sharing the gray dimness to standing on such unambiguous display before his hidden eyes.

He put his hands on me, touching my arm near the shoulder, as soon as I was within grasping distance. I ought not to be surprised or even offended by his forwardness. I had already seen that he was an expert at possession, possessing. And, in fact, his touch was a blessing, for it shattered me into speech and outrage.

"Let go of me, Noah. Who do you think you are, walking in here and grabbing at me? You leave me alone, now." I could feel the shock beginning to give way to anger and repudiation. "Go on."

"Now, Hazie…"

"How dare you?" I said. "How dare you call me by any name, most particularly by a name I cherish? I don't want you around me and I don't want you to touch me and I won't have you intrude upon my life. Haven't you had enough of what you call 'fun' with me?" This last was a mistake, and I found myself flinching as I said it.

"Hazel," he said. "I couldn't never have enough of you. They say you're married to George Taylor. Well I swan." He laughed a greasy snicker. "It don't matter, though. I've come back just to see you."

"Well, you've seen all you're going to see, Noah Kersin," I said. "Now leave me alone." I pulled my arm away and moved around the kettle, grabbing at the paddle and holding it between us, as though it were some sort of protective screen.

All of this has the flavor of a dream. You see, it was all acted out within that swirling, smelling pall of woodsmoke and steam, my entire body drenched from the humid fog, so that I must have looked like some sort of castaway, grasping to a piece of flotsam. And here, where drowning had seemed all I had to fear, I now faced the open jowls and teeth of some rising predator who already knew I was pinned to this paddle for sheer survival's sake, and so he could take plenty of time with me.

"Oh, Hazel," he said, trying to soften his voice. "Let me try to say this right. I didn't intend to come barging in like this. I don't want to hurt you or make you mad."

"It's a little late to worry about hurting me, don't you think, Noah Kersin?" I said.

"Just let me say my say, Hazel," he said. "In fact, I came to offer my apology and to ask for your forgiveness. I know I did you wrong, before, and I want to make that up to you. I have no other interest but to find some way to take the edge off the harm I did to you back then. Honest to Pete, Hazel."

He looked a significant degree older. His eyes were strained and narrow, as though he'd spent a great deal of time in the weather. But he was nattily dressed, as usual, and his mouth was as supple and fluent as it had always been. I am not to be taken in twice, fool that I may have been the first time.

"Noah, the only thing you could do for me would be to leave me entirely alone." I twisted my wet hands on the slick, burred wood of the wash paddle. "So, if you're that eager to please me, why don't you just take yourself off, away from here, right now?"

"As you say, Hazel." He swept an exaggerated bow and stepped out of the fuming fog. I watched his blurred form disappear down the trail. I was chilled and nervous.

"Noah Kersin," I breathed into the wet air.

So he is here, and I think I know better, now, than to expect that he will be true to his word. But I don't know what to do, when my greatest wish and my own surest protection lies in doing nothing, but in living along with George as though he weren't here, or anywhere else, for that matter. But how can I live a life ignorant of Noah Kersin's presence when the man himself weighs on me each day? I find myself watching around each bend of the trail for his form, or waiting for the knock on the door that will disturb George, and our life, so much more than either of us deserves. Oh, this is terrible. I have lived out the rest of this day with a deep burning in the pit of my body, which he already tried to sear forever, that once.

And now I wonder whether or not to tell George about this. George, who has never feared the first part of the story, because I left it, instead, to sink slowly beneath the surges of affection and passion we have ridden on these few years. We have collaborated so thoroughly that it has become as though the terrible beginning never occurred. And so my silence, my never having spoken of it to George, has been validated, the frightful original lapse redeemed by the very silence that has kept it hidden.

But now it has returned, in person. And so I don't know whether telling George that *Noah Kersin has returned* will be to enlist him in alliance against the man or to draw up the neglected memory and to drop it, writhing and gasping, horribly alive, between our two separate selves.

FIELD NOTES: INTERVIEW—GEORGE TAYLOR
May 10, 1998

Yes sir, she told me he was back, Noah Kersin, and she asked me what she ought to do. I don't know but what the world is just made that way: just when you figure everything is going to keep on about the same, peaceful and nice for a while, so you get to relaxing, and putting your feet up so to speak, well that's the time you're going to get scrambled all up. You know? So all at once you don't know if you're up or down and there ain't nothing you can count on no more.

So here I am, setting by the fire and picking a little on the five-string, just easy and quiet, and Hazel, she's been sitting there listening, not saying a thing. And then I finished a tune and Hazel, she looks over my way and she says, "George. Noah

Kersin has come back." And then she just looks at me.

And you know I felt like somebody had dropped me out of a hole in the bottom of the ground and I was just falling, steady and fast. And Hazel and the house and the fields and just everything just let go and went to breaking apart into chunks and just crumbling. And so there was nothing to catch hold of no more. Not Hazel, nor our farm nor even these here mountains, you know?

"Noah Kersin," I said. It was all I could say, and I felt like I had a mouthful of tobacco gum. "Noah Kersin."

"He come up yesterday when I was doing the wash," she said. I'm sorry. I can't never repeat nothing exactly the words Hazel used. It never will sound a bit like what she actually said. She'd say it just exactly right, you know, and she had a voice that burbled, like a dove's does. So it was partly what she said, the words she used, and partly how she said it, you know, the sound of her voice. Nobody could ever sound like Hazel, anyway. So I ain't going to pretend that I'm using her words, even.

"He come up and said he wanted to apologize, you know, for anything he might have done that we might yet be feeling wronged about," she said. "But I don't believe I'd trust a man like Noah Kersin."

"No," I said.

"No," she said. We just sat and looked at each other.

So you see? How could she have told me he was back and told me right from the first when he took to coming up and speaking to her and told me right out what he said and that she didn't trust him, anyways? And then run off with him no more than a few weeks later? You know? Hazel?

And so we sat there with just the fire snapping on the hearth and the criddling of Hazel's rocker. Nothing else. Just looking at one and the other, Hazel and me. It seemed as though the whole world had just busted right up, and nothing to do but sit and watch everything go away. And scared. I could see my scariness shining out of Hazel's eyes, and I knew she was looking at the same thing across at me. Just setting in the room, waiting for the world to end. And then of a sudden, my right hand give a jump, for no reason, the way sometimes will happen, you know, and hit the thumb string of my banjo and BRONG!! it let out a yell like a pup that's been tromped on. And we both give a start and like to jump out of our skins. And Hazel up with one of them burbling laughs of hers, and that got me tickled, too, and we just sat there and laughed at ourselves until all the crumbling and falling apart had just worked itself back together, you know.

And it was just me and Hazel again. I loved it when she'd reach over and tap the banjo head a little, just tap-tap, like you'd pat a man on the back to say, "everything's all set now."

I surely did love to hear her laugh. I surely did.

But I saw him my own self a day or two later and I felt that same ole sinking come back. It's like being all by yourself, coming steep down the mountain, and without no warning you trod up an acorn, not thinking a thing about what you're doing. And you roll on that thing and hit the ground so sudden, flat on your back. And yet that ain't the full of it, neither. Because just when you think you've got done falling, that you're a lying still on your back, you find out you're still sliding, feet first, all the while, down the slope.

It has forever bothered me the way I could let a man like that put me to such shame. But it was true: I'd see that Noah and I'd feel like I couldn't do nothing at all. Just the sight of him would shut me up and seem to paralyze me, you know?

Tell the truth, I was afraid of him. Yes sir. It's a fact. I wasn't feeling confused or uncertain or het up. I was downright scared. Scared half to death. And you know, the funny part is, I wasn't scared of what he was going to do to me, the way you'd think if somebody tells you he's scared of somebody. No. It wasn't what he was fixing to do to me. It was what I might do to him. That was the thing. I was downright terrified of finding myself doing something I never would have felt was possible for me to actually

181

do to nobody. And tell the truth, I think I might have had more hate inside of me for that than for the other, you know? More just seething' inside at him because he could make me likely to do something I wouldn't ever have thought I'd ever see myself doing. You know. Made me ashamed of myself. And I reckon that made me more coward yet, you know?

And there he was, right on the trail, heading up the crick toward our place. I was on my way down to Badie's to pick up some Cloverine salve and I come round the switch and there he was. He looked about the same to me, spite of the years. Had on a brand new suit and some kind of shiny shoes on his feet.

"Well, now, if it ain't George Taylor," he says, like he was pretty glad to see me. And he sticks out his hand like he couldn't think of nothing he'd rather do than to shake mine.

And like I said, I was just plumb paralyzed. I couldn't think of nothing, and I stuck out my hand, and all the while some voice inside me saying, *What are you doing, George Taylor? You tell that dern feller you won't let him up to your home no more. Tell him stay away from Hazel, he done hurt her enough for a couple of lifetimes.*

And I never done a thing. Just stood there like an iron pump, my hand stuck out to him and him just a'working it up and down. Not a darn thing.

And I wonder if I deserved to lose a woman like Hazel if I was enough of a coward that I couldn't even say nothing to a feller that is likely headed straight up that creek to go and visit my own wife. Or I wonder what Hazel would have done if I'd just reached up and knocked him down? Run him right out of the country. Would that have done it? Kept her here with me, instead of turning her back and going off with somebody had sand enough to keep her?

If I loved her so, why is it I let her go so easy? Just standing there watching him gaiter on up that crick in them fancy clothes, and that voice inside me saying, *you ain't no part of a man. You ought to be ashamed.* And nothing but a burning swallow dropping down my throat and into the pits of my belly. Well, I paid for it ain't I? I done lost her, ain't I?

VI.

JOURNAL OF HAZEL TAYLOR
January 10, 1999

Noah Kersin had realized that he couldn't fish the same hole, as they say back home. He was brash and he was blinded by his own opinion of himself, but he was certainly not stupid. And then, if I've learned one thing, it's just how clever people can be when they're set on having something that will destroy them. It's a stock plot with alcoholics, who can connive and concoct and convince everyone around that everything is perfectly healthy, when, in fact, their entire world is diseased. They're hiding bottles and sneaking drinks and calling hangovers the croup. Or like the morning the preacher's wife turned up with the Jake leg, too. She said she'd gotten the rheumatic fever. And even then, they've become so infatuated with their own consumption that they find ways to validate their own behavior and transfor the stain of their own greed onto someone or something else. And so they cast down their own neighbors and kin into the abyss of their own long-ings. And the entire world falls a notch lower.

Watch those who have inherited wealth or position sufficient to guarantee comfort, or those who have been handed multiple opportunities as a "birthright," those whose income is assured, not by their own labor or worth, but by position. These are the very people most likely to insist upon the sanctity of their own property, most likely to point to the failings of the poor. Isn't that odd? As though the mere proximity or genetic tie to wealth conferred moral deserving. When it is in fact this moral reordering of the world totally according to the centrality of one's own addictions that is the mark of the decadence of that self, and the abrogation of world, entire.

Worse yet, though, the self-deluded predator like Noah Kersin, whose obsession with physical control, conquest, in fact had long ago overrun and defeated his own best self. So that the very ability he could bring to bear upon his current scheme of seduction succeeded in driving him inexorably further into isolation. He never could see that a desire to overpower disguises the ultimate weakness. Because at the very moment that he thought he was marshalling his forces for the campaign, his own troops were deserting him, refusing him, going over to the other side. Because the first ones he had to conquer existed within himself. And the next, the ones that finally made him insane, were the ones he could never reach: all the Noah Kersins residing within the minds and bodies of the women (or was there only one, only this one? No; I doubt it. He would not be able to resist a continual, multimorphic corruption). Because each time he tried to slay one of those selves, he created another, and so he became that frenzied, horrified sorcerer's apprentice who despises the very success by which he has willfully drowned himself.

So he was clever. He came to me with apology and remorse, but, in a way remarkably similar to a nobler version I had just heard from Saint, he simultaneously excused himself by placing the responsibility upon me. I had swept him away. I had so enchanted him that he was helpless in the hands of his own desire, which redoubled each time he attempted to hew it down.

This does sound a great deal like Saint already had, a few weeks earlier. But here it was strategy, connivance: *You made me love you and so I am not the one at fault. The violence of my assault was, in fact, a measure of the vehemence of the passion you instilled. Even so, I am generous enough to wish to*

make up for the harm you think I have done. And so, I fervent-
ly wish to serve you, to give you pleasure, to follow your com-
mands. So come away with me, that I might surrender myself to
you.

Once, when I was quite a little girl, we heard news of an entire
large family killed in a house fire just over the way in Hace's
Springs. I believe this event marked my first encounter with the
concept of death, the hushed, excited conversation and the refer-
ences to *them poor kids.* My reactions were hazy enough—none of
the terror that comes at a later age, when you realize that each
familiar death is a presentiment of your own. Still, the occasion
marked a distinct emotional moment in my life, the initial
sounding of an unfamiliar tune, trying the shape and flow in
your mouth, *"death."* I would ask certain indistinct, unanswer-
able questions of my mother, and then retreat to some private
place—springhouse or laurel bush—to try the name again:
"death."

At any rate, I recall a visiting preacher who came to our
church at this time, shortly after the fire. He preached a long
and passionate sermon about sin and the horrors visited upon
the sinner, and he selected the terrible burning of those children
as his text. I was no more than five years old, and I was afraid
of him, but I also believed that he knew. He knew what I had
been thinking, wondering, doing, and he was eager to bear witness of me.

Even today I see his thin, ardent, heavily-browed face through
the tremulous fear of childhood. That vision of bobbing brows,
snapping mouth, thrusting fist mingles with the gently insistent
tugging of my mother, gathering me to her in the pew, placing
me on the lee side of his storming words. The curve of her hand
and arm, creating a shelter shaped exactly to my body, recreated
me as a sheltered being, and shaped his words as objects helpless
against this impermeable barrier, the grains and stones striking
and shattering and bounding harmlessly off my shell made of
mother.

And this man, this preacher, spoke of the "cleansing fire" visited upon a family "wallowing in the trough of sin." And he began to pant and gasp and stutter in his passion as he discerned the "wonderful and terrible hand of God at work." And he grew breathless and drenched, and, in a shuddering verbal paroxysm, he praised "God's searing breath blistering and boiling the bare skin of these wicked children, while the black smoke from their flesh covered the iniquitous dwelling." Then I see his eyes laugh, and a terrible, wet, smile twists his lips.

That was plenty for my Mamma. "Let's go," she whispered, and she stood, straight and quick and nudged me along the pew's length to the aisle. We walked out, our feet clapping too loudly on the puncheon floor, the preacher, temporarily spent, mouthing the words by which he would arouse himself to another ecstatic release.

We weren't alone in leaving that day. Several people had heard enough even before Mamma summoned the physical strength to match her spiritual anger. Later that day, the preacher was confronted by several church members and elders, who expressed outrage at his sermon. Daddy said the preacher was completely, contemptuously self-possessed.

"I reckon my sermons is too strong for folks who can't handle them," he had said. He leaned back and, Daddy said, "wafted" a gold watch out of his waistcoat pocket. "Snapped her open and looked at her like he was admiring himself in a mirror." Snapped it shut and said, "They's only a few can handle the truths I can tell."

Do you see? Do you see that Noah Kersin believed, deeply assured himself, that he was offering me a matchless treasure? That, earlier, I had been too young or too foolish—unable to "handle it." And so he had been patient and tender with me. Biding my time, not his, until I might be ready to understand the value of his offer.

Yes. He even outlined and annotated his own delusive descriptions. "Hazel," he said, at our second or third encounter after his return. "You're your own worst enemy, don't you know that?

187

You got to throw your fear away and grab at what you can. What you deserve. You can't throw your life away on some half-wit tobacca farmer. Not when I'm willing to help you. Help you, Hazel. And not to expect nothing in return. Nothing in the least. I done you wrong once, I guess, and all I want— honest, Hazel—all I want is to have the chance to give you something you want. Do you right. I didn't give you no choice that one time, I know. And I was wrong, Hazel. So I came back because I want to give you that choice now. Now, Hazel."

I do believe that the creative perverseness of his logic inspired me, exhilarated me in a strange way, so that I felt something— some growing within me, gradually swelling and pressing against its own boundary, spreading itself from inside out, wanting to burst and open into some new light. Isn't that strange? To think that the transparent, inflexive lust of this Noah Kersin could trigger the urge that would drive me through and outward?

Because I believe Daddy's death had opened one part of the way. Until Daddy died and loosed some tenacious blood link, I could not have burst through. But now, with both parents gone, I had moved into the full recognition of my future. The young Hazel who might by some miracle avoid her own adulthood, had now stepped fully into that place that demanded either total escape, or no release at all.

And then Saint's declaration and pledge, followed hard on by Noah's reappearance and his own perverse version of the same pledge *let me help you, Hazel*. These seemed to afford scope for thinking, planning, using.

And was I wrong? I took them both at their word. They asked me to let them help, and I did. Was this wrong? Should I have denied their request? Should I have spurned Saint's wish? For, after all, he had said, "use me." *It is all I have left to ask.* And if he was true, true to me, to himself, who was I not to grant his wish? So I used him.

And Kersin. If his offer to help was mere lure, mere self-serving strategy, what wrong did I commit in turning that offer back to my own benefit? In protecting myself by using him to my ends, rather than the other: remaining victim to the predatory choices of the man who had assaulted and betrayed me already?

No. I had been requested, even cajoled, by each to afford him the opportunity to be of service. I would accede as fully as I could. In wishing, either way, to hold me, each would become medium of my escape.

I don't see in any of this the efflorescence of this alternative Hazel, the runaway. Never did I write *I am thinking of leaving, disappearing, forever, from the predetermined mundanity of my own begotten self, who already dogs my every step, awaiting me every morning when I arise.* Neither did I weigh the pros and cons, consider the moral burden, measure up the losses and the opportunities, even to myself, in my thoughts. I only found myself thinking, *I could do it this way,* or *I'd never get away with doing that,* always thinking of some concrete tactic.

So that the first writing I found myself engaged in involved constructing details for carrying out a plan I didn't realize I had even made.

JOURNAL OF HAZEL TAYLOR
June 1, 1927

1. Leave, carry everything. Little as possible: two changes, journals
2. Money?? Prhps Saint D.
3. Saint, destination. PROBLEM: How to keep it secret? Answr: he'll do it. Trustworthy? Yes. Doesn't come here any more, anyway. LARGER PROBLEM is here to there: think this through. Write it out.
4. Where to from there? Got to go somewhere.
5. Money: yes, Saint will lend $$. Travel to larger city, find work and repay. Work? Cook, sew, music? Write!?! Test chances, short-term and long-term plans: cook and sew right away, keep eye out on

Richard Hood

writing. Saint says everything you see in print someone got paid to do. So it's possible. "ICE-COLD NU-
GRAPE?" ha

The great problem will be how to disappear from this area
unseen. I had been thinking that I would simply walk away, but
this is an illusion borne of the dreams of easy freedom. It can't
possibly happen. A lone woman walking along the highway
would cause immediate notice. Besides, I couldn't walk that far
in one stretch, so I would be forced to stop overnight in someone's home. That would be the end, right there. Talk runs up
these coves like the streams run down, and word of some sort
would be up this way by the next day. Worse, it wouldn't even
be unvarnished, it would be distorted word, the way all telling
warps and alters, not so much with time as with distance. If I
were a man, I could do this easily, concoct some sort of business
to explain my running down to town on foot. Or just behave in
a surly manner and everybody would be afraid to ask and worried about telling. But a woman. Everyone wants to look out for
her, the moment she seems out of place, like stray stock. And
so, in the same way, she becomes everybody's business: *Now
who do you suppose she belongs to? She ain't where she ought
to be, that's sure.*
So I can't go alone, or I can't go straight down the road. Or I
need to get a ride in from someone. But this must be someone
who won't tell it. That requires some thinking, and some more
writing, to see what will come down on the paper.
Because writing gets away from you and takes on some kind
of independence, the minute the pen moves toward the paper.
Nobody can sit and write down anything in a straight line, but
must let go of the cool slide of hand across paper, the *skitskitch*
of nib over and along the fibrous hollows and peaks, and watch
the long dips and turns of meaning as it unrolls. They say Flau-
bert would plan and select and painstakingly try each single
word and would spend hours at a time worrying about the de-

190

gree of precision reflected in that one, naked word. Well, no wonder. He may finally have completed *Madame Bovary*, but I never did. I guess she kills herself at the end. Well, no wonder.

Music is like that, too. If you find yourself wondering how you play that particular turn that sounds so supple, in *Fisher's Hornpipe*, what you discover is simply that you can't play it at all. Because the music is already in the tune, deep down in the thousands of playings that have drawn that tune along through the coves and ravines, the years and decades, until it got to you. So it doesn't belong to you so much as you belong to it, and you've got to take your hand off it, let it loose to be what it is going to be.

That's why an old regular preacher won't write out his sermon, or even think about it before he gets up there on Sunday. He'd be outraged to think that you thought he planned any of it. Because the truth he's trying to tell isn't his truth, and he can't make it come out, can't draw it up. He can only let it come through. So he has to clear himself out of all planning and scheming and empty himself out of his own speech so that the spirit, as he says, can come through. Same as the music. Then he can open up his heart and let that sermon tell you what's what. He's got to stay clear off on the side so the truth can get through.

So I write to find out what I don't already know and to see what that curving flow on the paper has been waiting to tell me. Then I can work out my plans. But not before.

I suppose everything you do is like that, really. You always have to let it get away from you, even yourself, or nothing can happen. Catching up with what you have just done. I don't so much move my hand as I find myself moving my hand. Even if I try consciously to decide something as simple as *I will now turn my head to the left*, even then there's a distance between the willing and the acting, somehow, so that the acting takes place and then I become aware: willing, acting, realizing. So, in fact, we are always catching up with our own decisions, never quite in time to control them absolutely. That distance, like the space between the ticks of a clock, or the moment when you have completed the first step and are about to lift your foot to take the next one. If we could freeze that moment, what would it look like?

So, now, how to get to town? I need to find someone who wants to stay as quiet about the going as I need to be. Someone for whom being quiet about comings and goings is second nature and who will be more worried about my telling on him than interested in telling on me. Who knows how to get into and out of town without anyone to bother about who or what he has with him.

Camp Ten. Camp Ten. I can get to Camp Ten. They drive into town twice a week. Running down their liquor. Both Saint and Noah have attested to that. And they are criminals, and so they can and must keep secrets. Of necessity they wouldn't want to tell anyone anything about driving a lone woman into town. They must travel under some sort of cover, because they want to get that liquor in and the money out without having to answer any sorts of questions about it. And so they are likely to impose silence upon me. So I will know that they have already done the planning and the learning how, and will be concerned with making sure that I stay quiet. Camp Ten is the answer. If I can get from here to Camp Ten, I know I can disappear as utterly as the alcohol they drive down out of these mountains, pull the stopper, pour myself into the city and become substanceless.

I have enough that I can pay them to take me, and that seals a transaction that implicates both of us further in secrecy. Then, when I get to town, I find Saint and he will put me up and lend me the money to move on and to get started. I know I can make my way. I've been rehearsing freedom for years and years, in my dreams, in my reading, when I gaze into the laurel. I am practiced. I can make my way, once I get free. But I will have to abide a few more days of asking and accepting: the money, the ride.

Wait. What about the walk along the ridge to Camp Ten? I don't know precisely where I'm going, or even who I'm looking for once I get there. I can't go blundering around asking, because that will draw in people that have nothing to lose by telling the world about me. And I need someone who can get me accepted by folks who are, no doubt, close-doored and suspicious of strangers. I need someone they know and don't fear, someone I know and can trust. I need a guide. And if I can't trust him, I need to establish a situation in which he stands to lose by telling. I don't know.

If I appear to give in to Noah Kersin, would I be able to get him to guide me there, introduce me and such? I wouldn't want to go the main trail along the side of the ridge, but to go up over White Oak Flats, for fear of seeing someone or dropping something along the main trail. And I know how to get to White Oak Flats. So, could I arrange to meet with Noah Kersin one night, on the pretense of leaving with him from Camp Ten? He appears to have grown into sufficient of an egotist to believe that he might have charmed me so far out of my mind as to actually agree to a rendezvous. He still appears to think that the earlier horror at Possy's Camp was a fulfilling consummation of some kind, and that I owe him a favor for outraging my youth and my body.

Can I trust him to be that benighted? If so, I can use his own version of the truth to guarantee an escort to Camp Ten. And if he believes so assuredly in his own abilities as a seducer and conqueror, all I need do is disparage him once he shows me to Camp Ten and he will find a way to explain to himself why I was unworthy of his attention. If I reject him with sufficient contempt, he will put the finish to the affair himself. And he will have to make a show of turning me loose, in order publicly to confirm his own opinion of his power. But because I have, in fact, spurned him, he will also walk away from my kin and neighbors, show them his disdain, his superiority, his power and immunity, as well. He will never return this way to take the risk of being gainsaid by myself or anyone who might know truth from mere blustering assertion.

So I can have the escort and the introduction in Noah Kersin and I can use his own deluded pride to ensure his silence and exaggerated apathy. From there, I can rely for transport upon the bootleggers of Camp Ten, their proven ability to move discreetly and their fear of discovery or betrayal, to erase any possibility that my presence in their company will ever be publicly remembered.

This is beginning to sound very possible. Certainly Noah will approach me again soon. But he won't bear stalling. He has risen back up out of the dark to become means as well as exigency. Because I cannot remain here to relive the very same struggle that has taken me thus far, only to get but this far again. And again. Because if you are bound to stay in the same place, the Noah Kersin's of your life will always return to you. You have doomed yourself by refusing to allow—or even to demand—change, growth, becoming. So his return is among those terrible graces afforded us so totally against our own inclinations, like pain itself. Pain, wounding always serves at least to direct all of our wayward impulses toward taking care of ourselves: avoiding that flame, nursing that aching limb. Lepers lose their fingers and toes not because the disease has rotted their flesh but because it has occluded their sense of pain. Because they cannot feel the throb of a wound or an infection, they fail to protect the lacerations or bruises that come along in the course of a day. Left without the pain, the leper ignores the abrasions and gashes, reinjures the same hand, fails to cover and protect the damaged tissue. And so the flesh tears and falls away, injured beyond redemption. The disease has stilled the terrible pain that would have protected that hand, the gracious torture.

Perhaps this explains our strange tendency to seek out our own aches and injuries, and work them, to bring on the ache. Who, with a bad tooth, hasn't found herself continually touching tongue against tormented nerve? Who doesn't stretch out that tender muscle to feel the ache, again and again? What is this but a celebration of the very pain from which we would flinch were it administered by another hand? It reassures us to feel that reflex *ouch* again and again, reassures us that the pain remains to thrust us away from damage. Gracious pain.

Noah Kersin has returned and my very soul shrieks in agony, and I take the inexorable actions to cover up, protect, seek surcease, escape. So he is, in fact, the medium of healing itself. And thus I will use him. Blessed horror.

JOURNAL OF HAZEL TAYLOR
January 15, 1998

This all makes it rather difficult to determine a point where it all came together: inclination, determination, application. Nothing was "concocted," exactly. There was no arranging and sorting of details, possibilities considered and rejected over a course of days, weeks. No.

Oh, I was aware of the impending action. At some point that summer it became a constant presence, an atmosphere in which I moved, worked, ate, slept. And the fact of my leaving—for it became fact before it became a reality, an event—transformed the place itself. You see, it was no longer just the mountain cove of my birth, the context of my life, *where I live*. The fact of my leaving had transformed it already, marked it anew as *where I once lived*. And this transformation was so total, so fundamental as to change forever the notion of *place*, itself.

You have experienced something of this if you have ever changed residence after a long period in one place. For awhile before you go your old home turns into something akin to a stage set. It has reorganized itself according to the terms of leaving, and, instead of being the place you are inhabiting, it becomes an element only of this one act: the leaving, itself. And so you have already become an outsider, observer. Your old place is no longer permanent and surrounding, but is suddenly temporary and enclosed. Because it no longer signifies the boundaries of your existence, the way it once did. Now, it is an arrangement, smaller than your existence, a provisional part rather than the determinate whole. A detail of the painting rather than the frame itself.

So you find yourself seeing it and hearing it in unaccustomed ways because you are now larger than it. And you're already recomposing the canvas, your movements now the frame within which this place becomes one of several details. And you're standing outside of it, looking at it. And it is changed utterly.

So the mountains, the creek, the cove had already begun to accommodate themselves to the change. But I was unaware of my own mind as composer. This all seemed more something that was happening to me—us—than anything I had made any sort of decision about.

I began menstruating that winter after Mamma died, and I recall the feeling of standing back and watching my own body beginning this strange, improbable routine. I hadn't willed it, certainly, hadn't even made it happen. Oh some version of me must have signaled the flow to begin, released some spring in the internal mechanism of self. But I had already rejected the possibility even while I recognized the inevitability, and I was frankly surprised to discover the actual soft blotted evidence of the event that seemed at once to be uniquely mine and so totally alienating that I seemed not to belong inside my own body any longer.

The actual moment remains: in the shed house, the dry cold wood on my skinny, bare buttocks and the sharp morning air tanging my nose. And looking down at the stretched cotton panel drawn down between my calves, and the haloed round spot that could have come from nowhere but myself. It must be the same sort of confusion, the same way, for the infant who discovers that she produces fluids and extrusions that are *hers*, alone, but are not *her*. And now, for the new woman, this paradox that will determine her life, and so must need repeating in such a striking way, the reiterative fluid each month. And it derives anew each time from my delicate, intimate center *but it is not myself*. And this is the secret reminder and rehearsal for the ultimate version: the actual being who slides and thrusts a way out through that same most private passage, only now too large, too brutal for this to have been very carefully considered by anyone who bothered to ask the woman herself about it, this labor of blood and pain and shrieking effort that has given life to each sentient being in the entire span of time, this birthing that slew my mother.

And so the lucent red spot came, to my complete surprise. Oh it wasn't ignorance—I had washed my own mother's menstrual cottons many a time. And it's odd how they seemed to me some ultimate evocation of her. I would dash the blooded cloths against the rim of the smoking kettle, and flop and roll them and push them along the slick ridges of the washboard, watching them gradually fade and whiten, thinking *Mamma, Mamma*, as though the sopping cloths were a part of some sacramental ritual, *this is my body, broken for you.* Mamma. Mamma.

But for me, my own blood carried no sense of my self, whatever. Those cottons partook of nothing of Hazel. Instead, they seemed some mocking evidence of some botched decision made by a remote deliberative body that had neither asked nor allowed my own opinion.

And I wonder if Mamma felt this way, too. These cloths not the precious transubstantiation of self handed mystically to her daughter, but the stigmatic mark of a betrayal so total that it had merely swept Mamma aside on its rush to completion. Not *ecce*, "behold," but *sabbacthani*, "forsaken."

Because this decision to leave was the same: not some determination on my part but an accommodation to that betrayal already pronounced, decided, someplace in some deep mountain time beyond my presence. And so I had been reacting, negotiating, coming to terms with that decision for as long as I had been. And had been responding for so long that I could no longer distinguish the inevitable consequences of the original decision—the working out of a fate already prescribed—from the improvisations attempted to avoid that same fate. I couldn't tell which actions were evidence and which were denials of that original betrayal.

And perhaps that explains why Noah Kersin became the pivot upon which it all turned. He stood as the ultimate incarnation of all the swindle I had ever sensed, and he stood at the turnstile of the gateway to escape. And whether my meetings with him, my concurrence in his control of events, and that kiss that sealed everything—whether these were machinations on my part to secure my freedom or indications of how closely I was bound within his—or some other's—trap. Well, I don't know.

Because I couldn't appear—either to Noah or myself—to be bargaining, gradually considering and consenting to the plan he had hatched. Because to him I had to be completely unaware that there was a plan. I had to be ardent rather than calculating, swept-away rather than persuaded. And to me his plan had to be irrelevant, no strategy of his at all, but rather sheer opportunity for me to work my own wiles at last. You see? He had to believe that I *wanted* to see him, that I sought him out as a means to satisfying a physical longing I could not ignore. And I had to believe that I had selected Noah Kersin as the counter-force, the perfect lever that could be driven between the closing jaws of the trap, to work and wedge the teeth apart, to effect that delicious drawing away of the flesh from the encircling steel.

And where was the difference, after all? Was I running to Noah Kersin, as he believed, out of an uncontrollable physical desire for release? Or was I doing so, as I believed, out of an uncontrollable physical desire for release? Which was mere trick, which sheer truth?

In the end, I found myself—we found ourselves (I cringe at writing this collective truth, even seventy years later)—sneaking around, scheduling and holding our surreptitious meetings in which I showed him each time only as much of desire as was needed—or was it he who attempted only as much of caress as he reckoned I would accept? And so, when I wrote, *We have* kissed, once, and then stopped, in a charade of chaste confusion. Terrible to pretend in this way, but it at least indicates that I have him still on the line. How much of this must go on before we make the final assignation? At the moment I wrote these lines, was Noah Kersin standing outside our house in the dark, and squinting at the lampshine from my windows, thinking, We have kissed, once, and then stopped, in a charade of chaste confusion. Ridiculous to pretend in this way, but it at least indicates that I have her still on the line. How much of this must go on before we make the final assignation?

JOURNAL OF HAZEL TAYLOR
August 9, 1927

I am ready. I have asked him. Actually tried to persuade him to do just what he wants to do in the first place. And it fills me with disgust, this communing with this Noah Kersin who has filled my life with fleeting images of disaster and with lasting memories of deep, lacerating shame. Why am I doing this at all? Why? Is there in fact some profound flaw, some base looseness inside that drives me to seek out contact with someone so wretched, because his character festers like mine? Was it all in fact my fault—the meeting and the lax pleasure that turned wrong because I wasn't paying attention but only responding, responding to the wrongness itself, until I was overpowered by my own willingness to bring this man down on top of me? Is this the proof of my own guilt?

But what else is there to do? He has returned, and his presence puts a seal upon my life as binding as doom. There is no escape from this lurking presence, none whatever. The trap has sprung and the steel teeth have closed and the only respite is to ease the body into the weight of the trap. Because the struggle sets the teeth deeper. But the relenting, the easing: perhaps the grip is relaxing a little and I can slip out from between the jaws. Perhaps.

Or is this wrong, too? Am I falling prey to his own lust for that sort of power? Letting him weigh back over me, pushing me down like he did on that day, when I was a girl? A girl! Dear God I hate this. I hate this.

Have you seen the photos of Mary Surratt, the woman who hanged along with the other conspirators? She was the house-keeper where the plot was hatched, and she dangles there from the gibbet with the others, a clotted lump of death. What must she have felt when she was arrested? *Was I wrong? I served them food, cleaned up after them, I was discrete and dutiful. Virtuous.* And so she wouldn't have worried, *Because surely they will distinguish duty from dereliction.* And through the trial, and the pronouncement of the knelled sentence: *Death. Death? For me? Is it that I am not only responsible for my husband's demands and desires—those that are directed at me—but am liable as well for those he directs outwards? My fault for the crime of being an embodied presence lashed to this house, this boarding house, where I not only cook and wash, but, doing so, earn our very keep?* But, even then, unbelieving, because it can't be, it can't make sense that she must be at once totally incapable and entirely culpa-ble. *I was invisible to them, don't you see? They took no more note of my presence than of the coffee pot, as they plotted and played at murder. Furniture cannot conspire and I was furni-ture. More valid to hang the horse he rode to the scene than the woman. The woman.*

And what must she have felt as the hood was tossed over her head and the pitch darkness holding the after image of rope and noose, the last sight she will ever have, changing color and floating within her darkened, collapsed sense, the suck of her breath, her wet mouth on the heavy cloth, and the rough bruise of the knot against her neck—*he once kissed my neck with a tender, sighing, passion, whimpering like a boy*—and the swooping snap of red death? Mary Surratt.

And we stare fascinated at her gray form, with tiny, hanging feet and the small, clumped hood, the bellowed sides of her hanging body. And we say *Abraham Lincoln*, or *John Wilkes Booth* or read the caption on the brittle newsprint: *the conspirators hanged*. And we see her, thrown on the pyre with the others. And what should she have done? And do we celebrate this faithfulness even unto death? Of course not. It is not honor, but horror that swings, heavy, at the end of that hemp.

And this Noah Kersin cannot be wished away. He is here, and he can only be led away, and I alone can do that. Or perhaps this is not the only way. Probably not. But it is a way and it will work. It will serve to carry me to Camp Ten and to introduce me to the people there, and it will offer me the chance to exact something of revenge when I spurn him as he so deserves.

No, there is nothing good about any of this. Only so much loss, so much. I looked at George this morning and I couldn't bear it. He is such a good man, and I love him so. He was bent over, wiring up a harrow tooth, and I watched his hands, so knowledgeable, so beautiful. His hands are hardened with work, but they still touch and curve around things with a curious grace, shaping the wire, or the fence post, or even the live animal—horse or cow or shoat—so that it all blends together, the man and his farm, his place. And in the evening, with his music, those same hands look as though the music is moving them, not as though they are striking and touching the strings, but the other way around, so that although he is making the music, it looks as though he has tapped the wellspring within instrument and place and is letting it run up his arms through him. And when we love, it is the same, those hands. They seem to find a shape to my body that it has never had before he touches, and makes of me a place, too, with hills and coves, flower and stream and stone. O what a pleasure to see him. I can hardly turn away.

But the more I love him, the more I have to leave.

And I have no choice, do I? Turn or stay, I will leave, disappear. Either into the mountain woman's world of care and pain and hardening that I have seen again and again, without exception—the gradual thickening and dulling of every woman I have ever known, here—or into a new world, across and over the narrow scope of these knobs and ridges and into a new-fashioned Hazel, who must of necessity become another one, someone besides the heavy swaying bulk that awaits me here. No choice.

And so, if I go, I leave George with the Hazel who knows and loves, and who still quickens with passion at his touch, not the inexorable lurching from one child or chore to another, the worn mind and body who is a denial of every vow I still hold dear. For she can neither love nor cherish, and there is no honor in insensibility, while I, leaving, can continue to sense, care, and love. At least there is that.

And must betray him with Noah Kersin in order to remain true to the vows I intend to keep? Oh what kind of a cruel paradox is this? To remain true to our true intimacy, our own selves, who have held and offered and explored and found each other with daring, wondering hands, lips, bodies? Remain true by playing him false? Because I will never offer anything to Kersin, never open either body or sense to him. Use him as vehicle and spurn him as he deserves.

So I found him today. Or rather put myself where I knew he would find me, out back, beyond the tobacco shed, near the trail. And he arrived, as ardent and deluded as usual. And I told him, yes, yes, I wanted to go, to head across the mountain, toward Camp Ten. And this much is true: I never told him I would go further with him. In fact, I told him the precise truth, that I was leaving and that I wanted him to meet me and escort me to Camp Ten. That I wished he would take me there, where folks could drive me further, into town. Even that I expected him to behave as escort only, that I insisted upon honorable behavior—I said something to the effect that he might *redeem the former crime*. I never said I would be going further with him, that I surrendered, that I was his. I let him draw those conclusions, as, of course he would. And as I needed, for without that he would not leave, himself, after Camp Ten. He had to expect and be crushed, so that he would absent himself, as well. But that was the easy part. I could see that he believed all the words he told himself, and that he never even heard the truths I told him.

And so tonight he has agreed to be on the mountain, at White Oak Flats.

ANDREW KAYER

"So you left," I said.

I dropped the packet onto her writing table, next to the water glass, half-full, stagnant and bubbled. *She's been writing more feverishly than usual*: her paper was strewn across the desk, and there was a brush-shaped crescent of wet ink on her inner-wrist. The skin there was isinglass-thin and the black arch gleamed and pulsed where it covered the soft cable of her vein. *She's in a hurry. Why the hell is she in a hurry?*

"So I left," she said. She went back to her writing, turning her wrist and leaving a diffuse smear on the tabletop. She saw it, stopped, and, looking for a moment confused, she pulled a red handkerchief out of a pocket and scrubbed at the mark, softening, but not erasing it. She sighed. "Oh my. Oh my."

"It's okay, Hazel," I said. "I'll get it up. Don't worry."

"Don't worry?" she said, distracted. "I'm not worried." Then she stopped. The red rag was in mid-air, the pen in her left hand poised to write. She held herself still, as though she were posing artificially, for an "action shot" of some sort: the photograph would look as though she'd been captured in the middle of that furious writing, rather than in this suspension, this lapsed inattention, confusion. The frictionless, still-spinning of an aging mind.

"So you left," I said again, trying to jog her back into the correct groove. She turned slightly and looked at me. *Not at me, through me. She's looking beyond, behind me.*

"I've never written, never written it," she said. "Not that, not the having left." Her right hand shook in a slow, steady tremor. I was beginning to worry: *Is she okay? Is something about to happen? Something is about to happen.* But I tried to calm my voice, remind, reassure her.

"Yes, you have," I said. I touched her shoulder as gently as I could. "Yes. That first packet. The flint-lighter and the trail up the mountain? In the dark?"

"No. That was the leaving. But not the having left." Her eyes snapped into focus, no longer looking beyond mine. The pen came up off the paper. She pulled the cap off the end and snapped it over the nib, set it down on the table. Reached out and straightened the sheaves of paper. She was back.

"The leaving was later. On the mountain. When all the planning and the thinking and the regret and hope and worry and fear—the wondering *how will it be?...how will I act?*—had rushed aside. You know how that is?" she asked. "How you try to know what you will do? You come to a stream and you decide, *I can jump to that rock and then to the next, without having to stop and teeter on that first point of granite, one motion, this rock that rock and across,* but you don't know. You don't even know that you will make that first try, leave the ground for that first leap, where you hope you will place your foot down on the dry spot of that curved, pointed rock. But will you?

"And you're in the air and your foot grazes that rock and slides off and now what? Will you fall, drop into the rushing wet, thrashing, hearing the sick snap of bone as your arm breaks? Or will you rebound, feeling the slight cold wet on the one foot, already bounding across to the next rock and on from there? Oh, the leaving is one thing. The having left, standing on the other side, already moving onward, breathing a little harder, but supple, strong, swift, saying *now, now, now now*? Or standing on that far bank, shivering, broken and wet, hurt and afraid, saying *now, now, now now*? Oh no. I haven't written that yet. I am writing," she said, and brushed her hand across the gathered sheets.

"Yes," I said." And…"

"And I'm still on the side of that stream. The *nigh* side. I'm writing, and it's only pacing back and forth on the nigh side of that stream, back and forth. I see the rock, I know it's there. I even know the awful, sliding slip, like the turning, tilting, of a whole world, the moment when *I'm falling, I missed* and the reflexive cast back, flinging back to seek the counter-balance. I know it's all there, and it's all to be done, crossed over, again. And I'm trying to take that step, so I can actually write it, put it down and hand it on."

"Hand it on to me?" I asked.

"To you," she said. "I need only take one step. Not across a stream, not really. Out of the thicket, up one step and around a curve to the top. Opening out. On top of the mountain."

"White Oak…"

"Yes," she said. "White Oak Flats."

"And Noah Kersin?" I said.

"Oh yes," she said. "He was there."

She turned back. Uncapped the pen and began writing, as though I wasn't there. As though I'd never been there.

"Hazel," I said.

"No," she whispered, writing.

VII.

Atop the mountain where the growth cleared out it looked bright with the moon shining so and it gave everything a casting of yellow-blue. It seemed to make the air into a different element, as though I walked in some new atmosphere, full and strange. As though it took a bit more effort to move and breathe, as though I were in the process of becoming a new organism, a fish feeling my fins turned round and solid, and making that unimaginable move up out of the water and into the air. It must have felt so outlandish for whatever poor animal—alone of all its kind—that found itself crawling up, slouching into that air and discovering she could breathe it. Discovering what breathing was. And here was this new world, that she had sensed all along was there, but forever forbidden—not so much inviting as enclosing and rejecting. And now here you were, not just in it, but filled with it, breathing it into your body, feeling it touch and enter and fill out places so deep inside you that it has become you, the air infusing your lungs and then percolating through blood and membranes and becoming more than the element you live in. With that first breath, it has become the element that defines you, fills out your blood and cells, is you. And it's only now that you realize how the water, before you walked out of it, was you too, filled you, in the same way. And you know what longing is.

And now you know you can turn back and resubmerge yourself, but you must stop up your passages against the old element, not let it into yourself, or it will drag you under. But, instead, you must gulp and hold this new thing and return to the new place quickly to nourish yourself again on the thing that becomes you. And so you realize you no longer belong to the place that bore you and raised you and filled you; you can never go back and swim, and fill yourself, even once, with the old element, but will forever walk, walk in the new place, and even your children will walk, forever forbidden from return. And now and again you will walk back to the edge of that water, and one of those dwellers will float up out of the depths, and you will peer at each other through that separating membrane that you both call *surface*.

And you will recognize each other. Like a prisoner and his relative who has come to visit, sitting decorously and a little bashful and gazing across at each other, through the intervening glass. And they know each other, and can even see themselves in the other and read the chronicles of family and love and death in each other's faces. *He favors his daddy. His daddy and mine was like as a doubletree team.* But all the while they are peering through the glass, and not looking at one another so much as watching each other, and with some unease because they are both aware of the hostile element on the other side, the element that has seeped and blended and suffused the other so that he is forever unreachable.

Just so, you look down at that fish. And he at you. Only this time you are both prisoners. And both of you have come to visit.

And so it was on top, when I walked out of the cover and into the moonlight on White Oak Flats. I remember that moment in its detail, as if I'd stood there for years, when, really, I didn't hardly stop, but drew one deep, aching breath and walked on out into the open. And I can come back to that long moment that never really existed, and I can dwell there for awhile. Because what happened next goes too fast for memory, or longing or regret, until that other elapsed moment that I can see and feel in stillness: his hand clawing at me, clawing as it slides off, and my foot slipping horribly once, then finding purchase again, and the fabric of my shirt tearing, torn by that clawing hand that is disappearing but feels forever to be making that one last grasp and emplanting its touch forever on my body, even in death, at the moment itself of death.

Oh, he was there. I came to the top and the trail curved upward suddenly and spilled itself out on the Flats. Except they aren't flat, but curved, arched, like a breath, upward and over toward the ridge. The entire sweep of the arch had a strange bluegray graininess in the moonglow, everything fadey and pebbled, and the air felt full and new. Across the curve of the bald, I could make out the apple tree, a twist of yellowgray with a puff of blue around it, and its moonshadow, black as a pit in the ground. The surrounding trees and brush along the rim of the bald looked like deep blackstrap, glazed over, like molasses does when it gets old, with a light sheen of moongray. And all the grasses up there made the entire reach of the bald appear wavy and uncertain—as insubstantial as a pool of mist, with the deep darkness of the trail in front of me, not like it crossed the slow curve of the bald so much as it seemed to *enter* it and carve its way gradually deeper into the heart of the mountain.

I saw him in the moonlight, and it is the seeing that starts everything to moving again in memory, too fast. Because I now find myself standing by him and he talking, low and steady and everything seems to be in a hurry to get it on over with, the thing that was about to happen. And I watch this part like I'm in the audience at a theatre that's playing the same show we saw last week, and we know just what's about to transpire. But the characters in the film don't know. They are forever living these events for the first time, and we watch them struggle and rage and see them trying to make the movie come out a different way. But it never does. And so, at this next showing, the events on the screen seem to take place faster, or are more concentrated, because we know what they are and we're looking ahead to that final catastrophe. But the characters don't know. They just don't know.

So he was there, and I must have walked on up to him, in the clear, and along the trail. But I don't know what we said. I can't see us standing there in the moonglow. But then I can see us walking along the little trail that passes across the middle of the bald, along to the left of the apple tree. And I suffered him to take my arm, as wary and scared as I was. And it was sometime in here that I started to feel better, because I told myself, *It'll work out. He'll get you there and you'll get to town and it's just this little bit that you have to get through and it'll be fine,* and I could feel a warm pulse of relaxing flow through my body, and I actually leaned against his arm and we picked our way on down the trail.

So we were at the far end, where the Flats narrows down and the trail cuts to the left, and down the edge of the mountain. The bald ended there and you saw the bushes looming higher, like a witch's wall. And his hand was tugging at my sleeve.

"Come along here, Hazel," he said, and I felt a hot flow of fear. But I think it was the fear itself that silenced me, that made me comply, abide by, his request. Because I moved in that flow of fear. It took away my will and my sense even of who and where I was. And I found myself resisting, not his voice, but my own—that voice inside me imploring *Don't go there, Hazie! Just stop here*—my own fear fought away the warning voice inside me, and I was afraid to do anything but just what he said.

"Set your things down a minute, and come here," he said, and let go of my sleeve, while I set down the flour sack full of all I wished to carry out of there. Just let it down to the ground, where it glowed in the moonlight, a bright yellow with, next to it, the yawning black pit of its moonshadow. And found myself nudged along, actually in front of him, into the darkness of the mountainside, all the while struggling against my own voice saying, *Don't go there, Hazie! Just stop here. Just stop!*

We walked on into it, but it feels as though we stood still, in some grotesque hiatus, while the darkness of the scrub flowed back around us. And it was darker than before, because we'd been up in the light on the Flats, and the trail narrows down because the ridge falls away on the left and rises up on your right, and he was behind me. I could feel him. I could smell the earth and the vegetation on the slope rising up past my shoulder. But I could see nothing. And so this part is in memory an entirely different way. Not a movie show, oh no. More like waking up in your bed and the clothes are all thrown around and you're covered in slick, wet cold. You know something about a dream *I was struggling with something, fighting it off but it was a dark liquid pouring on me and trying to smother me, and the harder I fought, the heavier it poured on me. It was hot and dark and filthy and it was pouring down and I wanted to keep it from going in my mouth and eyes, but it was starting to gel as it soaked me and my arms and legs were getting heavier. And I fought. I don't know.* Because you don't know any more beyond the feeling, and the cold sweat prickling your brow, and you know that you won't ever find out what was happening while you slept. But you keep going back to that feeling and looking into it, because somehow you wish you could solve the puzzle. Because somehow that dream has changed you. Your day is entirely different because of something from the dream that keeps reaching up to pull you back. And if you could only get back there and find out. But you never will.

A banjo has a skin head stretched on it that has been scraped down as thin as it can be. The old folks made them out of cat skin, if they could get it, because a cat's skin is translucently thin and stretches easily over the ring. The head is soaked in water overnight, then stretched out over the banjo while it's still wet, so that when it dries it will tighten up and span that circle as taut as can be. *Listen to that ole cat scrawtch!* they'd say when the banjo was up and playing just right. Because the least change in weather, humidity, would affect the head and soften it up. If it did, they'd say the banjo was *a'sounding tubby* and they'd tighten up the head until it was right again. But it could dry out, too, and this was even worse, because the head would get brittle and split. So they'd have to walk a thin line between having the head stretched up too taut or letting it loosen up too much. And, of course, you couldn't ever find what that point was, because it depended on so many things you didn't know. George would say, *you tauten her up until just before she breaks.* And that was pretty much it. You didn't know, couldn't know—but you needed to know. *Just until she's ready to bust.* Can you see?

It's just like tobacco at grading time. You have to wait for a damp day, so the leaves will be in case, before you grade and tie them. You pack them in corn fodder to keep them damp, because if they dry out while you're working them, they'll break up and you'll have nothing. But you can keep them too wet and they'll start to rot. So you're always looking at your leaves and looking at the sky and figuring time and weather and trying to figure when they'll be in case and you'll start grading so you can get it done before Thanksgiving without ruining a whole thirteen month's crop.

Sometimes if it was a dark, rainy night, the kind that makes the mountains loom over you and *lonely thangs up*, so you feel like you're the only ones left down in this cove, I would hold George's banjo up to the lamp and gaze at the head. It's a fine, delicate skin, not cold to the touch and smooth, like paper, but with just the least nap to it, so it feels soft and warm to the touch, even as tight as it's been pulled over that hard ring. And it has a web of lines and figures running all over it, membranes and vessels and pores. I once said to George, "It looks like it's alive."

"Of course it's alive," he said.

* * *

JOURNAL OF HAZEL TAYLOR
February 11, 1998

So I was up on the edge of that mountain, feeling my way along as close to the cool damp earth and branches rising up alongside me and not seeing, but feeling the chasm dropping straight off into some absent deep hollow so that it seemed just like the shelf of the world itself. He was behind me, close.

"Hazel," he said, a strident, hissing command, through the dark, like a child, shaking with the fever will sometimes sound harsh and demanding. And I hear it now as though it is the voice that moves around my left side, the hissing tone of the word, my own name, that nudges my elbow aside and curves in along my side and closes over my left breast. Because it was only sound and touch, like one sense, the same thing, the shivered voice and the groping touch, and then it was pulling me back into the wall of his body,

"Hazel," he said. This time a pronouncement, a claim, and the rising inflection swept around to my right and, this time, outside my elbow, so as he felt for my right breast his arm clamped mine against my side. And so now it was no longer just touch and sound, but arms, intertwined: my left arm free, his cupping my breast and drawing me back, my right arm held against my side and I can remember feeling the curve of my own hip—while his reaching arm bore around to violate me again, not caressing, but gouging, hooking at my other breast. And I hear the name called and questioned and this the violation itself, his calling my name on this pitched mountainside the selfsame act as his grasping hands and fingers, the clutching sound of my own name on his lips as grotesque and overpowering as the wet touch of those same lips onto my neck, sucking and sliding along my neck.

He was pulling me back and suddenly I was again that new organism, creature, that has perhaps tried to turn away, resubmerge, but now finds itself gasping desperately after the new element, as though it was the wall of his body that was the surface dividing this darkness from the light on the hill, and I must, must break the surface and draw in that new, unfamiliar, sustaining light. And, as though I were drowning in the old darkness, I tried to move my free arm back through the surface toward that light on the hill. And I found the wall of his body.

It shames me to write this—shames me yet more to remember and to know that I will never quite uncurl my hand from along the beating length of him. No. Touch is indelible: it shapes our hands to the chronicle of their own histories, so that every touch, every gliding caress, every rough feel of the stubble on your Daddy's neck, or the piercing burn of that old sliver, remains, shaped and shaping each gesture, each searching quest for self as our fingers rub questioning across our own surfaces. And so whatever you have touched, ever, stays there in the memorial play of your own hands. But this touch, this seeking and finding, feeling him, is like a phantom presence welling up out of my own memory. Because it's not the touch of my curved hand, but the beating solidity I feel as I run my hand, twisted back behind my own body, and feeling down along the length of his sex in what he takes for a caress, for more than acquiescence, for the echo of his own lust.

But I am not caressing, not responding, no message of willingness or avidity. I am seeking, because, you see, I know. And I am unerring. When I reach the tender spot below, I spread my hand out in one last gesture that he will think is fondling desire.

Because he didn't know, couldn't know that *sexual* means *intimate*, and if you try to use command, you can never touch the intimate part of anybody. Because command closes up everything in its own mistaken selfness, and turns intimacy into incursion. Touch is where we trade all those various selves we've collected from each other—where I give you back the *you* I have constructed in all my experiences of you, and I receive from you, the *me* dwelling in your hands, your stroking and gestures. But if you confuse intimacy with invasion, you wind

213

up demanding that your lover pay attention only to the *you* you have made of yourself. And so you can't recognize the real *you* that she is trying to hand to you, caress into your skin. And you can't hand back to her the *she* you have made. Because you don't know either one of them is there, and so you take this dreary person that you think you are and you batter at her body to let you in. When you should be asking her to let you out, and offering to set her loose. This is what intimacy is.

But I think once you've confused incursion and intimacy, you will forever be unable to find what you really need. You think you want to impose yourself on another partner, but when you do you have merely overpowered another and your need is even more frustrated, and you find yourself, like those in Dante, forever boiling in a torrent of hot blood.

And that was Noah Kersin, who grappled and hooked at me. He wanted to use me to confirm his own version of himself. And he thought this was what he wanted, desired. He didn't want my body to tell him anything he didn't already know. Didn't even know that he didn't know it, and so he was doomed from the start. He had always thought that beauty was something to own, something to see your own reflection in. And so he never understood that beauty is the self you never knew, a gift from another, not to be owned, but to be handed back, transformed, again.

So he read my gesture, and, to him, it had to be lust, pushing back against him, the way he thought lust worked. And so he spread himself to push back against my spread hand. And that was when I grasped him in what I hoped was his tenderest part, and squeezed, and held, in a spastic, wrenching vigor of disgust.

He recoiled in reflex, breathing a sharp, loud *"hunh!"* and the hand that had been clapped tight around my right breast opened up and, in a moment, my right arm was free, too. He breathed again, *"hunh!,"* and reached back around to grab my shirt between my breasts, and pull, to turn me toward him.

I thought he would spin me around and hit me, and, without plan or anticipation, I swung my right arm back and felt my elbow dig into his soft fullness.

This time he made no sound, or I never heard, because he was grabbing and pulling at my clothing, pulling at me frantically, this time, and then I realized that he was falling, swaying over the edge and trying to hang on to his purchase on that narrow path by grabbing at me. He had turned me right around, and I had felt a burning slash across my brow. And now he was trying to pull himself back upward, to climb up me onto the trail.

I felt myself start to give in to his weight as he tottered over the edge. My foot made one terrible slip, sliding along the rolling pebbles by the edge, and, in what seemed to be a nightmare's swirling, blasted, heaving effort, I grabbed back for the bushes rising up the slope on my right. I grabbed and held onto a thick root, twisted, smooth, and cold. And I felt my shirt tear in a splitting ecstasy of release, like I'd broken free from some sucking mire. And he was gone.

There is no sound of his falling in my memory. There never was anything to see, and, now, no touch, no feeling whatever. And in memory it isn't even like an event that occurred so much as a sudden absence. A great, dreadful struggle of arms and voices and bodies and then a sickening slip and a rending release. And then just nothing. No struggle, no power, no other at all.

I dropped onto my knees in the black depths, drawing hard laboring gasps that were halfway between breath and sob. My body shuddered with the effort to breathe, while my hands lay curled and utterly useless, formless, on my curved thighs. And I never thought for a moment about Noah Kersin. He was gone totally, like when something heavy falls from your hand and you can't even reach to try and catch it, but just let it go, and brace yourself for a crashing shock that never comes. And you can feel the absence in your hand, the afterimage of the full jug's weight. But that's all. Gone totally.

I don't know how long I sat curled over my knees, like that, until I suddenly found my hands sprung alive and tearing at my clothing, ripping off the remaining shreds of shirt, and casting them out. And then the rest—standing up and pulling off clothes and hurling them into the darkness.

And here is the strange part, because I kept my shoes, my leather moccasins. I must have stood up and taken them off and placed them carefully down into the blackness at my feet, against the slope, on the trail. I don't remember doing this, or what part of me remained as scrupulous and careful, while my hands tore and pulled and wrenched the clothing from my body. As my shoes sat sedately on the rocky trail, waiting for the fury to pass.

And when it did, I bent down and found them and slipped them on, like I was going out to the springhouse in the morning and turned and edged back up the trail and out into the moonlight, naked and white and preposterous in my moccasins.

My glowing body suddenly felt the clasp of his hands, and I tore away and ran, stumbling and weaving, up the curve toward the apple tree. In the middle of the running, I realized that I was bleeding, hard, from somewhere above my eyes, and I ran, rhythmically wiping away the blood with one hand and then another, like a bizarre sort of swimmer. The briar and grasses whipped and snatched at my bare legs as I ran. And I was thinking just nothing. I was running from that feel of his hands, running toward the tree as though I might find some balm, some salve, to wipe away the touch of his hands. My naked body was cold and damp, but I only felt myself as if through a screen, a veil made by his clawing hands.

I reached the tree and threw myself down to my knees again, wrapping my arms about its trunk, drawing my body up against its rough, cold bark, rubbing and crushing and scraping my bare breasts against the harsh skin of the tree, as if to rasp away the feel of his hands, the memory of his hooking grasp, until my flesh was torn and bruised and I fell back, outstretched, into the pit of the tree's shadow, and lay there, breathing.

I lay there for some time. If I slept, I don't know it. But I awoke, at any rate. I awoke to a rim of dawning day and I blinked and sat up. I reached up to myself and weighed my breasts, sloped into each palm. I sat there, holding myself and breathing slowly and looking across the dawning arch of the Flats, and it was alright. It was over.

I cupped my wounded breasts and caressed, comforting a broken bird.

VIII.

GEORGE—It ain't easy to talk out about Hazel, but I suppose I
can tell you some things, an' T.R. will get in the remainder.
Well, now, let's see. I couldn't say when I met Hazel. I'd known
her all my life. We was a lot together when we was kids, kicking
around, you know. Hazel, she was a wanderer, and she'd drag
me around with her quite a lot. She liked to be alone, but I
guess she liked to have me with her once in awhile too. Weren't
nobody else she'd go walk with, until we growed up, some, and
she got to walking around with Noah Kersin.

She'd want to walk on down to the two-lane into town and
climb on down by the bank there, across from Possy's Camp. I'd
say, "Hazel, let's just set up here by the road." And she'd give me a
smile and say, "Come on, Georgie, the water's a'sparkle." And
down we'd go to the big branch. We'd just set there by the water.
Hazel would tell stories about made up places, or she'd tell me
about things she'd been reading. Said someday she was a'going
to see all them things, all them places. And I'd laugh and say,
"Long as you can get back in time to sucker them plants," the
way her father would say it.

Hazel always made me feel good. I believe I always did love

her, even when I was just a little one. Well...

That Noah Kersin, he was no good from the start, anybody could see it. Except Hazel. I don't know. I reckon she thought he knew a lot, the way he talked, and, you know, he was a man that'd have something to say to a young girl, make her feel right special. And he was a little older, and that'll turn a girl's head, some. But it was like watching somebody lay out bait for a deer, you know. It made you feel right bad to see Hazel drawn into that feller's trap. It wasn't right. He wasn't nothing close to her level...

T.R.—He was a salesman. He'd ramble up and down these mountains, all about here, selling farm equipment and arsenic of lead, tobacco seed, all that. Had a great big book he toted around, called it the "master catalog" and he'd act like that was the Holy Bible. He'd come into the store already talking about politics, or baseball, or some damn thing, and he'd set down right here, where we're sitting, right now—this old store ain't changed much since then, you know that? And he'd drag a barrel or a table over and flop out that great big old book, and he'd say, "Now, Aunt Badie, honey, what are you needing this trip?"

GEORGE—That's Aunt Badie Shelton—she run this very store on Lower Crick, right where we are, right now. T.R. is right: it didn't look all that much different in them days than it does now—I remember that she didn't like that "honey." No sir.

T.R.—Didn't like it anymore than a bite on the tail. She says, "Don't call me 'Honey,' young feller. I ain't nobody's honey. Leastways I ain't yours." Hah. She didn't take to old Noah the way some of the younger ones might have. But you would think old Noah didn't hear nothing she said, for he'd just keep on with the "Sweetie," and "Darlin'" and all that, until Aunt Badie, she'd ramble right out the back door, yonder. That old door would slap-to, saying "BANG"—make you jump out of your god damn skin. But old Noah, he'd just look around at all the boys and say something like, "You fellers think them New Yorkers going to wrap-up another championship?" Just happy as a smoked ham.

GEORGE—Aunt Badie, she'd make out a list.

T.R.—Yessir. He'd be setting there talking about how the "voters ain't going to let the wet legislators pass the damn bill," or some such hogwash, and BANG goes the back door again, and here comes Aunt Badie waving this here piece of paper. And Noah just going-on now about the constitutionality of the whatsoever. Badie she'd hand him the list, not saying a word, hand it to him with a snarl like he was a dead rat and that list was a shovel. And then she'd kindly swirl-round and march back out the BANG door, madder as hell.

GEORGE—T.R. don't mean no harm, the way he talks.

T.R.—Hell, George, it's just the way I talk. Most folks'll toss in a cuss every now and then, just to get through the goddam day. But George, here, he just ain't the cussing kind. Hazel neither. Course, she was a woman. But he don't make a fuss about it. Least most times.

GEORGE—So long come Noah Kersin, and by and by, he took to staying round here a little longer every time he come up, you know. At first, he'd just come on up and get Badie's list and leave next morning, or he'd set around for a day and go from farm to farm a'selling stuff to the women. But now he's staying three, four days. Well, it weren't long before I knew he was likely courting Hazel.

T.R.—He weren't courting nobody. He was sniffing-round to see what he might fetch-out for his own self, by way of seducing and leaving some poor gal. Courting, hell. He was no more courting than a one-eyed tomcat.

GEORGE—He was interested in Hazel, you know. I knew it right off, and I knew she liked it, too. He just turned her head, you know? Well, she was only fifteen or so when she met him, and, you know, she was always dreaming about the wide world and I reckon Noah Kersin might seem a lot more experienced in the world than most folks around here. So I reckon she saw him as a man with some fine airs about him, you know. She was always talking about ancient Greece and all that sort of thing, and Noah Kersin was the type that could pick up on something like that and just play a nice young girl along with it, you know? It weren't any of Hazel's fault.

T.R.—No, it weren't Hazel. She was just a kid. He just done took advantage of a gal's dreams. That's what it was. And that's the thing you didn't like about him in general. He'd just find out about you, like he'd get by you and listen to you and figure you out, you know? Then he'd up with something, make it sound like he'd known you all your goddam life. Get you so everything you did turned out to be something he owned. Like he'd be discussing your crop, say, and he'd pitch in and ask you how is your wife's health, just like he knew that you was worried about making enough on the crop to pay the doctor bills. Just like he knew, already. And then you'd realize he wasn't talking about your damn crop at all. He was talking about how much in-charge of a talk about your own damn crop he was. And when he left, you always felt like he'd took something from you. Or you felt like you'd kindly grassed on your own self, or your wife, or whatever it was he'd used to turn that conversation back to being about how in-charge he was and what a fool you was. I can't say I liked the son of a bitch.

I told George, here, that he was sniffing around Hazel. I knew George was close to her, like. Told him he might keep a eye out, because I knew he was meeting Hazel up by the Tighrow's after school. I thought maybe George ought to say something to Hazel. I knew they was kindly looking out for each other, Hazel and George, or I wouldn't have stuck my horn in it at all.

But we was up to the dance that weekend, George, and I saw you watching him around Hazel and I could tell you wasn't liking it a bit. And you having to set up there and pick the five-string while you're looking at that bastard just leading Hazel around like a duck on a string. I could see you could see. And that's why I told you my own mind when you was taking your break.

GEORGE—There really weren't nothing to be done about it, though. Hazel, you know, she was her own self, and that's sure. Always been her own self. Off by herself half the time. Now don't get me wrong, there's nothing wrong with Hazel. She's just thoughtful, you know? I said it to her more than once, "You sure do like to go out and walk around, Hazel. Looking at all the things that are out there, laurel and skies and stars and seems like just about everything." And she says, "I ain't looking outside, Georgie. I'm looking inside." Only she said it prettier than that.

Hazel could talk prettier than anybody I ever knew. Half the time I didn't understand what all she was talking about, but I liked just to hear her talk. She had a bubbly voice, you know, like running up and down a fiddle neck or something. Light and bubbling, especially when she wanted to tell you about something she'd worked out: "You know what, Georgie. I think I know how they figured hominy out." Now can you imagine that? Thinking about something like that? And I don't even recall what she said about the hominy or any of that. I listened to her all the time. But it was so much more like music than words. Well...

FIELD NOTES: INTERVIEW—T.R. BLANKENSHIP
May 13, 1998

T.R.—Well, dammit, he's right. It weren't none of her fault. That old Noah was one them snakey boys, you know? Tall and thin and thin-faced like. Snakey. Seems to me like folks down around here, men, anyways, come in two varieties. You got your roundish bear-like fellows, and your lean, snakey ones. Now it ain't always the case, you can find some right mean old fellows out there that favors the bears, and you can get right friends with a lean one or two. Ole George himself is kindly on the lean side. Though he ain't snakey. Don't got that skinny damn face. As I was saying, it ain't always the case, but nine out of ten times, I say, you can trust them bear-like fellers. And you ought not to turn your back on one of them snakey ones. And I'll tell you, Noah was mister goddam snake. I wouldn't trust him as far as I could throw this here store, hams and all. Especially not around no young gals. Nothing but a goddam rattler. You could see that right out. Hell, I wouldn't trust Noah Kersin around a guinea hen.

But I reckon George is right; there wasn't nothing he could do. I mean he had no claim on Hazel. No promises and not even the asking of anything, as far as I know. So he could just set there with that banjo, picking-away and looking sick, while Noah smart talked that poor gal. Besides, George wasn't the sort to start up nothing. He was just peaceful all the time.

And you know? I don't think there was nothing Noah Kersin could do about it, either. If he could have done anything, stopped himself, left that girl alone that thought he was fancier than creamed corn, well, he wouldn't have been Noah Kersin. He was just in there doing what he done told himself to do, down inside. So it's like George couldn't do nothing, and Hazel, she couldn't do nothing, and Noah couldn't do nothing, and Lord knows I weren't able to do nothing except tell George what he already knew. And couldn't do a goddam thing about anyhow. So I guess whatever the hell happened was just bound down to happen. Just in the cards.

Because I ain't got no idea what happened, at last. One minute, that snake was talking about Gay Paree and all that sluggamugga, and Hazel hanging onto his arm like a goddam fish on a line. Next thing, Noah Kersin is gone like the boy that took the turkey. And George and Hazel is walking around just like nothing happened.

And maybe it didn't. Maybe we'd not be talking about this at all if Noah had stayed gone. But then he come back. And then they both took off. And then I reckon he just upped and killed her. Well, I reckon that'd make you get thinking about what happened that first time around to make him leave and stay gone for years.

Because the next month old Noah didn't come to the store. There was another man in his place, toting the Holy Bible and calling Badie names. And nobody thought a thing about him after awhile. He just was gone, like he'd never been here at all. And that was that.

I don't know. George, he talks like something happened, like Hazel got into trouble somehow, or Noah got thrown out or something. He never said nothing to me, though. From all he ever said about it, even while Noah was waltzing around with Hazel, you wouldn't know he ever heard of Noah Kersin. Never said a goddam thing. I'd like to think that George sidetracked the son of a bitch and knocked him out of the country. But I know that ain't what happened. George would never have done nothing like that.

So it must've been Hazel either told him to lam or she done give-in to him. But we'll never know, now. It is a goddam shame to think of her lying dead in that ravine, all alone like that. And him off somewhere probably seducing some other poor little girl. If that's what he done.

And old George here to pick up all them pieces.

IX.

How I arose from the curve of the flats that morning, found my sack, dressed myself in my spare clothing—all of that—I just don't know. I have only a vague, watery picture of a young woman, torn and bruised, stumbling some. And a quick image or two—my bare arm extended, shaking out a crisp yellow shirt, a fumbling foot finally sliding into the leg of a pair of overalls. And that's all. Two or three isolated pictures. No thoughts.

I must have been terribly cold and I must have been in some pain. My forehead was cut—I bear the scar to this day—and most of my body would have ached and throbbed. But I recall nothing of this. No memory of bodily sensation at all, until I was being nursed by Hastie. I have one persistent image of a young woman, viewed from high above, walking off the flats that bright morning. She is dressed in a clean yellow shirt and overalls, and she is walking slowly, deliberately, to the trail that curves down along the side of the ridge. And that is all.

So Noah Kersin was dead. I had killed him, pushed him off the side of that shelf of a trail and sent him tumbling into the darkness. But, of course, I hadn't killed him. He was a victim, and a murder victim at that, sure enough. But I was killer only

225

in the self he had made of me, within his own body. Because he still didn't know. He reached out and grabbed at me, because he still thought that was what he wanted. He wanted sole control, wanted to be alone with his undifferentiated will. And so he made himself into a victim, and he created a murderer within him, this Hazel who only existed to be grabbed at,

Because it's hard to be a woman, to be looked upon as receptacle to the entire world, held up like a finely polished mirror by so many who only want to see themselves. Some group, the Sufis, I think, have a legend about the embodiment of Natural Beauty, and her lover could think of no gift worthy of her, but to bring her a mirror, so that she might gaze upon her own beauty. But as she held it up to look, the world of people flocked to its other side, and began preening and gazing at their own reflections, in the wrong side of the mirror. And even now this is what women are for. Even our skills and graces only become reflections of them: *did ya hear that woman pick the banjo?* or *Now there's a gal I could spend some time with*. And women, even looking upon a mirror themselves, aren't looking at themselves, but at everyone else, who insists upon looking from the wrong side. Because women look into mirrors to put on makeup, and fix their hair—to create whatever face it is that the world wants from them. Because the world wants to see them as surface, as highly polished surface, so that men can come and gaze at themselves.

Perhaps that's why, too, that Sufis see death as a mirror, believing that it is at the moment of death that we discover whether we are beautiful or ugly. I don't know.

I wonder what Noah Kersin saw, as he swooped into that giddying blackness. Because as hard as it is to be a woman, at least women know that they don't want this dragging and pulling and pounding. Most men don't even know that. And so they are the ultimate victims, hunting through their lives for something they believe that they want. I really think they do. They believe that they want to conquer you, to control and overpower you, to force you only to reflect themselves. They believe that pleasure is invasion and sensuality is conquest. And so they turn themselves into weapons and they turn you into enemy. And they have destroyed their own world. They have dragged themselves into a living perdition where they have to fear you, and hunt you and bring you down. And when they do, they think this is pleasure. So they do it again. And again. And they never know even what we know: that they're not getting what they want.

So Noah was the victim. Doomed by his own definitions of himself to create me as a murderer. Because I must bide my time and work my strategy and count on repulsing that attack on a dark ledge. Because he is not a person anymore, but a tactic in my pitiful need to escape this receptacle I've become. And Noah, who wants me, not as a person any more, but a resistance against which to push and shove, toward his own pathetic, sad, orgastic release. Oh I was hurt, back there at Possy's Camp, and scarred here on the mountainside. But I knew I hadn't gotten what I wanted. I knew that whatever sensuality and pleasure were, they weren't this. Noah thought that what happened on Possy's Camp was sex, because he thought sex was pushing and thrusting, instead of what it is: shaping. Shaping the way wind shapes water in the sea, and the way water shapes air in the fountains. Or the way the sky shapes the mountains. Nudging against that surface that separates us, rubbing up to it, curving it, curling it to fit us like the swell of the hillside fits the curve of the air.

Most men are doomed never to know that they have missed this. Most women at least know what it is not. A few lucky ones see and understand and find themselves in the hands of another, sculpting each other, stroking the damp clay, pressing back on the turning hand that feels the already turning surface.

George and I would shape each other that way, like merging that surface, one skin the same as the other. There's a place in your lungs where two membranes come together to form only one thin film, where the oxygen passes through into the blood. And so the blood is bounded by the same thing as bounds the oxygen. They aren't in two passageways any more. They're a part of each other: the skin of one is the skin of the other, and when the breath draws in, the skin arches itself against the blood, or the urge of the pulse pushes out, and everything moves to that throb. One skin.

But I grew to feel the other way, as well. Sharing that surface bound us both to the impulses of the other. And I saw that the woman George had shaped, and the woman the place had already made, and the woman I was becoming, couldn't all blend to the shape of that surface. No, it wasn't George I left. People won't understand this because they've already shaped me to the wrong side of the mirror. I believe I loved George with an abiding love, for as long and as hard as I could. I still do love George. But I couldn't stay there just because I needed him. The woman that the place had made would take up my side of the bed, and her thick and nubbed skin would cover my fingers, and George would reach out to find me in the night, and I'd be gone.

Well, and I guess that's exactly what did happen. But not as far gone. I still had my fingers and the curve of George's hands on my hips. Like Heloise, I can lie me down in my cell of a room and relive every moment, every beat of our heart.

But I didn't need a man. I needed a whole world.

PART THREE

I.

JOURNAL OF HAZEL TAYLOR
March 1, 1998

So I will continue to try and tell it, with as much of honesty as I can. There is no measure for truth except what you can find by balancing the voices within your own mind, finding a consensus of sorts among the many members of this self. Any conclusion you draw will be only provisional, and then you will have to begin the long process again, tracking that resolution backward to find its motivation, its intention. Because it all depends on its own cohesion to whatever impulse it thought it was following in the first place. And all of this prior to any act of judgment or even conscious will.

Do you see? Let us turn the corner on a bright, peaceful morning and come at once upon a house fire, a little girl hanging desperately from an upstairs window. Do you see? There are two nervous systems operating inside each of us, aptly enough named the *sympathetic* and the *parasympathetic.* The first takes charge when you find yourself in an intense situation: fear, excitement, anxiety. When the sympathetic chains are operating, the self that takes charge is wide-eyed, tense, flushed, circulating adrenaline. That self might be a hero, and spring into whatever action is necessary, fighting the fire or saving the child. But the same system may make you a coward, turning and fleeing from whatever danger caused all this excitement in the first place. And, of course, it's both, both the hero and the coward, possibilities tapping their ways along these wet threads, through this chain of rifling synapses, ascending and descending columns, tied together like stage weights by something called *you*.

Do you see? Your enemy confronts you. And there you are again, cowards and heroes debating instantly, constantly, each presenting her own case, and this *you*, this place in which all reside, only capable of discovering, after the fact, whether you've raised this hand to strike a blow or to cover a cringe, only then to know if these are tears of rage or retreat. No central self about it, no core of consciousness: there they are, inside you, operating in milliseconds, shifting around the juices—calcium ions, sodium channels, potassium pumps, action potentials, and the catch and pull of muscle fibers, like a billion tiny oarsmen—that make up you and your actions. And if there is a control center of some sort, it, too, is multifarious, with no center at all, except an absence of will. *I will*...the most fraudulent assertion of all. Better *I find*, like Henry Fleming, *who found himself running*, one day, only to discover that he is running the other way, a totally undeliberate hero, the next. An army himself: straggler and leader and recruit and veteran. Enemy, even. This swarm of decisions and desires, intuitions and instincts: it's all you. Second person plural.

Perhaps there is some genius in our mountain expression *you uns,* because it never speaks in the singular. We address one person as *you uns* just as readily as we address a group. Because this is accurate. You uns.

So what did I do, and what did I *find myself* doing? And for what do I owe explanation? And to whom? No central *me*, no integral *you*, these pulsing desires, tugging appetites, recoiling aversions, meeting behind a curtain that is only raised after the blocking, the action, the inflections have been learned, rehearsed, everything accomplished except the puzzling out of a title for the whole charade of *I will*.

But isn't this is all deflection, all dodging the issue of my own responsibility for my own history? Because if I am solely a warring mob of fibers, how is it that I can feel an overwhelming longing, as I did, and do? The very fact that I am submerged in yearning, or despair, or lust, is proof that there is a *being* who feels eclipsed by the emotion, even if we can know this being only in its total inundation. And although we probably cannot control the feelings or the impulses, of whatever sort, we can, at least, decide *not to*, like Tietgens and Valentine. Cannot restrain the desire—and what would be the victory in *that*?—can only choose to feel the urge and *not to* act. Turn away from every surging swell of the ocean within, even while it batters you. Hold still, even as the flood of feeling sweeps over you.

And I have failed so utterly in this regard that I seem to have thrown myself totally into this second-person pool of random action. When I thought I was planning, devising, reflecting, all I did was deflect the restraining possibility. I merely facilitated the discussion among the oarsmen within, never once calling for mere silence, mere emptiness. And I should have known. I had such a teacher.

For all the while, here was Saint—so aptly named—holding himself in absolute suspension, while the pounding hunger of...of what? Of love, lust, passion...appetite or spiritual longing? Sensuality or soulfulness? I don't know. Does it matter? The slippery ropes of nerve and muscle conspired to overcome him, offering him pleasure or self-fulfillment, or at least surcease. And he said no. He agreed to drown in the wanting rather than to become mere moral flotsam, like the rest of us. His was the hardest way.

Because he had nothing to show. Not even a self to whom he could offer the satisfaction at least of having resisted, since that one being who might accept the reward has never even been there for the struggle. So there was nothing: no pleasure, certainly. No moral high ground, since the onerous emotion itself was sufficiently disgraceful to censure him outright, that final tentative fumbling notwithstanding. And so he had to repudiate all he wanted in order to acquire absolutely nothing more than the wanting itself, growing ever more insistent the more he turned away. He was aptly named, Saint, indeed. Even Augustine only renounced the sins he had enjoyed for a time. Augustine at least had the experience of the dark grasping, the thirst of one body for the other's warm liquid, the submission, the swooping plunge, the groaning release, the holding and joining and sated sundering. And so his repentance was merely the choice of another motion, the turning, not away, but toward another desire.

But Dunstan only could say no. Oh, he announced his struggle, told me he loved me. But not as an attempt to persuade, seduce, whatever you might call it. The pronouncement of love was no joyful resolution of the suspense of secret loving. No. It was, instead, a caution to me, that could only have the effect of putting me on my guard. Had he suffered these pangs in silence, he at least might have stolen an intimacy or two that became available precisely because I was unaware of the intent or the significance of this caress or that furtive looking. But he denied himself even this by telling me beforehand, so that I might not allow him any, even the most impulsive, relief. And so even his hopeless final attempt to clasp me, enfold me, was a sort of renunciation, doomed even before he made the pitiably awkward attempt.

He never begged forgiveness, even, for desiring me. He simply informed me that he did, put me on guard, and then continued to want me, and withhold himself. He did not run away from me, so as never to suffer the pangs of my presence. On the contrary, he became a better friend than I could want: trustworthy, eager, always, always on my side, showing me a Hazel far better than any I contained within myself.

And so I suppose he was the finest lover, his the greatest love. I don't know.

But, still, the very act of loving someone is an imposition upon her, whether the love be outright caress or mere whisper, action or avowal. Because she has to receive it, has to assimilate it within and among all the constructions of *me* she has ever known. And now: Hazel, *beloved,* has to take a place. And it's a place not only among but coopting all the other versions of Hazel and Dunstan stored away in memory, and changing them, forever. Like an old photo, pulled out after decades: like that photograph of Lincoln's second inaugural and the pallid, thin face in the crowd, just below the dais. It is a face utterly meaningless to photographer, president and crowd alike, until a few weeks later, the same man, pointing a derringer, will utterly change the composition. And the photograph is only the chronicle, for he has changed everything—the crowd, the president, the event itself, into something extraordinary and ghastly. It is ever thus.

And, in my own puny sphere, Saint's declaration was just such a transformative moment. And I didn't want it, didn't want it at all. It is disgusting, says Clea, somewhere in that wondrous *Quartet,* to be loved without consent. And she is right. It is a violation, an invasion, not so brutal as a rape, but molestation nonetheless. Not forced sex, but forced love. It makes a claim on your innermost, secret parts, and worse even than a physical assault, it is an assertion you can do nothing to resist. "I love you." Oh my God, how disgusting.

So his confession of love, if confession it was, is not so noble, after all, is it? It isn't a gift, it's a theft; worse yet, a murder. A theft of my emanation, the self I want to put forth to him, and a slaying of the Saint Dunstan that I had nurtured and grown inside myself, and of the Hazel who accompanied him. And he had no right. None whatever.

He will come to me in a dream, beseeching, hands outstretched, the prayer of petition: *But I had no choice. I drank of the philtre and was overcome. And I have suffered utterly in silence, save the single cautionary caveat made so timidly, to you alone, with no expectation even of acknowledgment. And I have buried my love deep inside, where it sizzles and seethes, like an undersea volcano, and no one, no one, even to witness even its dormancy. Oh no; it is not I who have imposed upon you.*

But this is mendacity of the most self-serving sort. He is drawing himself to me, breathing my air, stealing my memory, my odor, and the sight of my body and doing with them what he will. He even told me he had done precisely this, in that final letter, read on the rocking train, with the last of Hastie throbbing in my deepest core. Hastie. I wonder if hers was the greatest love. Could she love me as I loved her? Hastie.

And in the fullest moment of my grief at having left everything, to steal that pathetic caress, like a dirty schoolboy? No, Saint is no hero. Is he? I went to him following my escape from Kersin, and dropping Hastie before him like a proud student trying to impress by her most recent accomplishment. And he took me in. And tried to love me.

I don't know.

II.

ANDREW KAYER

She had been confined to her bed for a week with a bronchitis, an irritant to most of us, life threatening to someone of Hazel's age, where pneumonia continually lurked beneath the surface, ready to suffocate her from the inside. Still, she was restless, even at the worst of the infection. She seemed to be struggling for space as well as air, continually treading the covers as though trying to stay afloat, now and again thrusting a swimming hand above the surface of the blanket.

"All right," I said. "But what about George?"

"George."

"Yes. You write about your 'lovers,' and who was the greatest lover. Goodness, Hazel. What about George?"

"This bronchitis makes you want to break out of your own body," she said. "Odd to feel like you're drowning in a sea you can't escape because its shores are the walls of your own body. You have to lie here, and feel your lungs filling with water pooling out of some interior seepage, pouring out of the blood and across that single worn and wasted membrane to fill alveolus and sac, then duct and bronchiole. Lord, the body becomes a terrible thing."

"Yes," I said. "But Hazel. Lovers. What about George?"

"George," she said, again.

"I read this," I said, waving the sheaf of pages at her, "And here are these people, one of whom I know nothing about. And you measure and place them within your life, and I see nothing about George." She narrowed her eyes into the distance. Regret? Guilt? Memory?

"Oh he was a lover," she said. "But not of the character or quality of the others. Because he never had to make an attempt. He just put out his hand. And he never comprehended. George, whom I had known all of my life, who had walked beside me, seen me grow up. Who talked to me and watched me for all those years, and never understood. Never. Until when I most needed someone to recognize *me*, he offered himself. He would be the solution to my problem. And he never saw that I had no problem that needed solving."

"He was your husband," I said.

"Husband. Husband? Yes. That's the solution he offered. 'Marry me and the horror, the insult, the wound will go away. I will expunge your character.' But what is that? Yes, he was a lover, too. They were all lovers.

"But a husband? You can't keep the others away with a name like *married*. It's a sham and a pretense. Impossible to be alone with a solitary spouse. Impossible to be faithful, when you can't even identify, much less ensure, the chastity of all these beings running around inside. The so-called faithful—those who cling frantically to one lover for life—are the greatest betrayers of all. They deny the very lusts that have moved them, shaped them, arranged them, without anyone around upon whom even to pin the label, *virtuous*. I have had myriad lovers: four of great significance to that part of my life, not all of them of my choosing. They came to me as much as I to them. Maybe five," she said.

"Five," I said.

"You know when I dream of love, I dream of Hastie. I dream that she has returned and is standing in the door. The door is always at the house on the Creek. Our house, George's and mine. And Hastie has come to that door. And she holds out her hand and beckons me closer. She takes my hand and leads me out the doorway. But we are not outdoors; we're in another room, her room, in Camp Ten. And I'm lying there beside her."

"I don't know who Hastie is," I said. "Hazel..."

"Here." She held out another packet. And a smile, washed with regret. "Meet Hastie." We stood suspended for a moment, each of us holding a sheaf of Hazel's journal in front of us, handing it toward the other, like a baton through which each tried to conduct the conversation. Or scripts, and we were at the earliest rehearsal, blocking out a sword fight.

"You said five," I said.

"Yes. George, yes," she said. "And no, I was wrong just now. About George. I try and try to put him in the wrong and he just won't fit. No. He was the love of my life. He had no choice but to love me the way he did, to offer marriage as a kind of solution. What else could he do? He had no more choice than I. And we were never allowed to be the lovers we could have been. Because I was always threatened with the woman that marriage would make out of me. And he? He was trapped into that domestic role of his own. If only we could have run off together, been somehow joyfully illicit. But that could never be. Impossible.

"So, yes. Five. George. And Dunstan loved me. Hastie, I loved. Noah Kersin." She was looking directly at me, now. "The fifth is yet..."

"Noah Kersin!" I was very nearly shouting, spitting in outrage, as though he had wronged and wounded me, not Hazel. "Kersin!"

"Hush," she said. She smiled again, that same tinge of grief. "Noah Kersin."

"How can you call him a lover? Hazel? Sometimes I don't understand a thing you say. He raped you Hazel. *Raped* you. Even you said he was incapable of love, didn't know what it was, something to that effect. Your lover? Hazel, he was your enemy!"

"Love thine enemy," she whispered.

* * *

"No, Hazel," I said next morning. "You're wrong." I had just swung into her room and dropped the packet on her bed. I was, strangely, spoiling for a fight, furious with her. *She has taken me too far. There is no end to this, unless I call a stop. Does she think she can cast a line and draw the entire world into a circle with her hand at the center? No. I won't have it.* I woke up with these thoughts, out of some strange, disturbing dream of flesh and darkness and water, I couldn't remember. Just this insistent struggle against her, this Hazel Taylor who could walk out of and into so many lives so easily. *What is it that makes her think her story ought to be so important to me?* And I had ridden the train to work with the flashing windows and bricks going by, tearing at my eyes, but all the while shouting at Hazel: *Yes, okay, you were violated. But is that license for you to select and snatch out whoever you might want to have, to surround with your words and your demands, your circular, self-verified justifications?* So that by the time I had reached the home, I was drenched to the skin in the liquid of that dream; its atmosphere had replaced the normal one, and I was struggling, pushing away this embrace that felt so dark and enticing and wrong. *Wrong. That's the thing: she's wrong.*

"Wrong?" she said. She looked at me, placidly, pen in hand.

"All of this," I said, picking up the packet, again. "All of it. And lovers. These weren't lovers, these men. You wouldn't let them be lovers. And what about five?"

"What about what? Wait…"

"Five. You said yesterday, five. That it might be five, but you'd have to wait and see."

"I meant…"

"I know what you meant. Well, you can't have me." I was startled by my own outburst, but the recognition of anger within me served to generate more passion, the way paying attention to thirst compounds thirst. "You've chewed up and spit out every man you've known. You say you loved them, when you used them."

"Loved. Used. What else are we to do with those we love, Andrew?" she said, mildly.

"Oh no. Don't try it on me. I'm proof against it, Hazel. I've read all of this and I've been a part of this, and I don't want it anymore."

"All right," she said.

"But don't you see? I can't let you have it this way. I can't be complicit in this reinvention of your own life. Wait: not your life, their lives."

"Andrew, I did what I had to do." She was angry, too, now. "And what right do you have to come in here out of your own privileged life and tell me I've used anybody? I had no choice."

"No choice!" I felt the anger burn a little hotter, and I found myself wanting to wound her, to enter into some of this terrible pain-giving, wrenching and tearing. "Read these again. Everyone you encountered offered you choice. Let's see, you could have accepted Kersin's version. Who knows? He might have been right. You might have come to like it."

"Now just..."

"Okay, okay. He was your enemy and he did you a terrible wrong. But he certainly paid for it, didn't he? Paid because you used him as an accomplice to your own bid for control, just as you now accuse him of doing. And arranged a meeting, just as he had. And ended his life. Right? And then George. George, who you say never understood you. George took you in and married you and all right, all right, he was wrong to offer you an escape from a shame you hadn't created. But he hadn't invented the rules, now, had he? And you created a house and a home for both of you and then you walked off. Left him the shame he had taken from you."

She looked at me. Her hand shook a little, and she, aware of it, laid down her pen and dropped her hand to her lap. Her eyes were bright, hard. No surrender.

241

"And Saint Dunstan. Wow. He told you he loved you because he didn't want to tarnish even his own image of you by hiding anything, how did he say it *like a dirty habit?* And never let his desire determine his actions. Always let his love for you rule him. Always. And offered to help you. And so you planned to go to him, take his money, demand his silence and then walk out on him, too. Isn't that right? And here you are, so I imagine you did that, too."

"Worse, Andrew. I did worse than you could ever expect. But you live in a world where nobody really does harm, don't you? Where everyone is safe and immune within themselves. Oh I remember your precious individuality, yes. And that's why it's so precious to you. It saves you from the terrible necessity of involving yourself with others—bruising one another—what you would call using them. No. You don't want to use anybody for anything. You want to *have* everybody, the way you might have a lamp. No interaction. No chance of *using* anyone. Everybody happy and empty…Well?"

"Shut up, Hazel," I said. She recoiled, startled. Offended. I felt a brief flush of something like victory or shame. "Don't use my flaws to cover your own. As I said, I'm not interested in being number five."

"No. You shut up. Shut up!" She held both hands out, as though she were pushing me away. "I have handed you my life, without asking anything of you. I have offered you my secrets, and you tell me I am trying to hold you, to trap you. Now you listen to me. I am a woman. I have been around folks all of my life who believe that I have but one choice and that is to find some man whose life I will suit, and that if I do anything, anything, otherwise, that I am somehow cruelly injuring whatever series of men has lined up to make me the stupendous offer of their control. Do you understand? Of course you don't. But you don't have to remember watching your mother die young from too much love and too many dead children. To watch the betrayal and destruction of all the young women who only want to stay free and happy, not to have to grow into drudges or schemers, calculating the odds, wary of trust, certain of either dullness or pain. And you! You have been able to choose not to take reading and thinking and the preservation of your mind as serious things, as parts of your self that might be threatened, and so you've been able cavalierly to toss your learning aside, because you know you can pick it up whenever you wish. When for me merely remaining in the place of my birth, in the mountains that I have loved, with the man I have loved—the man I loved—merely remaining there meant that my reading, my learning, my very mind were not just threatened, but doomed. And under the weight of this impending ruin, I had to learn to be a woman— to have a body sought after by others. By some as a tassel, a prize, and by others as a ground for intimacy and love. And how was I to learn the difference? How was I to determine my behavior, my withholdings and surrenders, when the only thing I had for certain—the power of my mind—was the item that I must surrender in order just to remain where I already was? Can't you see that Andrew? Andrew?"

"Oh I see it, Hazel. But isn't this the defeat we all have to face, sooner or later? That we will never be the wonderfully fulfilled people that we had imagined ourselves capable of becoming once? That we are trapped in some pitifully smaller version of life than we think we deserve? Isn't that it? And does that give us all license to walk away from those people—especially those people—who have sworn to love us in spite of the trivial selves we have turned into? Isn't that what you tried to walk out of? And did you get what you wanted out of all of this? And was it worth the sacrifice of all these others?"

We were at impasse, glaring across the bedsheets at each other, and then sliding our eyes away, searching the empty air for the next barb to throw. Because we had said what there was to say, and now we were only pushing and shoving, looking for some sort of advantage that might allow one of us to walk away with some satisfaction beyond what we were both beginning to see would be mostly embarrassment and sadness.

And Hazel gave it up. She lifted her hand, with the pen shaking in its grasp, and she made some sweeping gesture of either rejection or encompassment. I don't know what she meant by it. But that was all. Then she let fall the hand again, into the rumpled sheets. And looked toward the window, speaking not so much to me—her adversary—as to all of the living and struggling and loving that had led her to this point: this nasty little argument in an old folks' home in Chicago, so far away from home.

"Do you wonder that I have failed?"

And so she gave it up. And the fury, the rage just drained out of me. And I saw that what had probably infuriated me in the first place, as I guess I'd known at the very moment I began trying to hurt her, trying to win a victory over her very presence in my life, was the fact that she was irreplaceable. She had entered my life and she had become indispensable to my own construction of myself, of everything. That she was this sort of a woman, whatever you may wish to the contrary. When you came across Hazel, or ran up against her, she spread out around you, like enveloping light, and recreated you in a richer, truer tone. And you will resent this, or you will fear it, or you will try to disparage it. But in the end, you will have to live with it, somehow. And that it was Hazel's tragedy that she had become indispensable to so many people. And it wasn't her fault that we all had to have her. She had asked for no such burden. And yet perhaps we were all trying to blame her for having included herself among those who had a claim on her.

"Failed?" I said.

"Of course I have failed. Of course. What else have we been talking about?"

And so there was no answer to give her when she turned her softened, argued-out, eyes to mine and asked—not as a defense, I could see, but as a genuine question—for my own retroactive advice.

"But what other course should I have taken? What would you have had me do, Andrew? Andrew?"

III.

JOURNAL OF HAZEL TAYLOR
August 10, 1927

I have come through. But I am unable to write any of last night's terrible happenings: his wet lips, the holding, the struggling and the falling. The running naked across the bending arch of a mountain top. I know of nothing to say. Perhaps someday I will. Just now I can only think of this morning and, well, just now. Last night is too baffling and horrid and such a sad confusion of liberty and burden that I can only let it rise slowly, of its own accord. It will not submit to being put onto paper until it rises as a thing, an event, something that I can say has taken place. We say *taken place*, because that's what has to happen for an occurrence to become a thing: it must be given time to fill itself into reality, to urge itself into arrangement, to take form, solidity.

And last night's elapsed hours are nothing, yet. They have not even been, because they have no shape whatever, or they are still becoming, still happening. I don't know. Perhaps last night will never find its spot in memory, and so will never continue to be, will not solidify into anything lasting. I wish I could hope for such. But it will be in the cycle of memory, soon, and it will drop off and come back, drop off and return, just as certain as laurel.

But this morning is another turn for me, and I can and will

write of now. Because now is not an event and never will be. Only a state: sitting here on an ancient, bagged-out cane chair, in an upstairs room that must once have been a storage space, or a file room of some kind. Across one wall, from floor to ceiling, is a huge built-in oak case, filled with small drawers. A few still have tags slipped into the dulled copper frames that adorn each one. The one nearest me says, *SEG XXVI-HAC,* in a florid hand, in faded tan ink. The rest of the room is empty, save for a plain iron bed, with a split pine box at its end, a fat yellow candle waxed directly to it. Burned and broken match ends appear to have been mashed into the pooled swelling of paraffin at the candle's base while it was still warm. Now they obtrude crazily upward, like jumbled black twigs jutting from the frozen shallows of a stream. The bed has a shuck tick and a worn deep-blue blanket, rumpled like a series of heaving swells. There is one saucer-sized hole fringed with the dark residue of a burn. Through the hole, the tick peers grayly. The small window just above the bedstead is glared raw with sunlight.

And here am I. In Hastie's room, at Camp Ten. And I have come through.

Hastie I met yesterday, on the mountain. The trail comes out of the Flats and dips along the west slope, skirting a small knob. Then it rises to the knife-edge of the ridge itself, and runs along for a mile or more. And then it edges down the ridge, dropping hard through tangled second-growth, with a dead stream bed carving the way on the left. On the right, an impassable snarl, locust and sassafras interspersed among eerie stump sprouts: what should have been towering oaks have turned into thicketed bushes, with curved, multiple trunks. I have seen stump sprouts like this back home, five or six thin stems growing up out of the chopped base of what had been a vigorous oak. These sad not-trees, straining their numerous puny stems upward in a vain effort to achieve the sky, are the sign that a piece of land has been cleared and subsequently abandoned, death or hard times having swallowed whatever ambition once motivated the cutting. But here, across the deep slope of the ridge, the thicketing was on a huge scale. The entire side of the mountain had been turned into scrub and brushwood, a profusion of growth producing nothing, only an impenetrable riot of useless increase. This is literal *destruction*, the absence of structure, a deformation, and here what had once been a forested mountainside, with the layered sanity of trees, spindlings, ferns, fungi, and a floor upon which you walked in your own place, had become a profuse lunacy through which no one could ever pass.

At the base of this frenzied descent, the trail came out onto the leveled bed of what had been a kind of dwarf railroad, carved out of the contour along the side of the ridge. Spiked ties now grow heavy green moss and the distorted rails curve off into the brush. Braided steel ropes snarl and tangle in a grotesque parody of the crazed woodland above. It is the rail line of Saint's telling, where once teams of sweating men and groaning oxen had drawn huge carts of wood out of the flank of this ravished hillside, the track now strangely silent and congealed, like a plate of leftovers lying forgotten on the ground of yesterday's brush arbor dinner.

I could feel my bruises and the wound on my brow was throbbing inside with each step, stinging outside from my perspiration. But this ruin of a railway was welcome.

"Well, at least I'm heading the right way," I said aloud.

"What're you doin' here?" said a voice almost at my elbow. I started, and turned, throwing up a defensive arm. *O my Lord, he's come back!*

But it was a short woman, thin as a tobacco stick, with hair and skin the color of the drying leaves on the ground. She has that look, either child-like or too old for account, but you can't quite determine which it is. And I think this is what makes her so compellingly beautiful: the indeterminacy of her face and figure. She is a woman you would walk by, just as I had, without noticing at all. But begin to search that expression and that thin strand of a body, begin to wonder about those large eyes that seem to have no color at all, and suddenly they begin to contain all colors, all ages. And you are caught. It has taken me all of a half a day, and I feel as though I have become connected to a singularly important person. Hastie.

In any event, I raised my arm to fend him off, and there she was. My defensive reflex set off a mirror-like reaction in her: she jumped backward, lifting her hands in front of her face, and grimacing in surprise and fear.

"Unnhh! Get you behind me," she cried. We must have seemed an odd pair, each fending off a non-attack from the other, arms upraised and palms out, like strange dancers involved in some ritual.

She was the first to move again. She slanted her head and peered around the screen of her own hands. Then she let the hands down and leaned forward to investigate, her eyes all of a uniform creamy gold. She straightened herself and put her hands to her hips. Now, suddenly, she addressed me as though she'd known me for years.

"My goodness, sweet thing, what happened to you?" Her voice had the indefinite quality of a child or an archaic crone. She leaned forward again, and, looking at her, I began to realize what a shambles I must be in. "You run into a she-bear?"

Now it was my turn to assume a pose, and to explore this appearance that I couldn't yet quite credit. I was actually suspicious of her tangible reality. She seemed so thoroughly blended with the color of the ground leaves, and so definitively *not here* that the implication of any presence at all came more from the voice I heard than from any bodily weight or displacement of air. She just didn't seem possible.

"My name is Hazel," I said, in a tone too measured, as though talking to a slow child, or a deaf person. "I came across White Oak Flats last night and I'm looking for Camp Ten. Are you from Camp Ten?"

"It looks more like White Oak Flats done come across you, sweet thing." she said. "You're all tore up. You got some trouble?" Her eyes gleamed colors, then, and the entire mountainside lit up. What a look she has! Out of that apparition of a face, and in spite of her filthy hair and terrible teeth, she flashes that look your way and you instantly surrender to her. She is unlike anyone I have ever met. She appears to be entirely without guile. She seems incapable of performing the least task and her entire physiognomy seems to cry out for protection. And about the time you decide you can help her, can attend to her aimless inability, you find her taking care of you, nursing you, handling you with hands as gentle as any mother's ever were.

And so, the next I knew, she was bathing my gashed forehead with springwater from the side of the path, and binding it with her own bandanna. Then she scrambled into the brush and emerged carrying a handful of bloodroot. She snatched a knife out of somewhere and sliced the wet roots into dripping strips.

"Daub these on them bruises," she said. "It'll take that ache out of them. I got two too many men myself," she went on, either on an odd tangent or because she knew, somehow, or suspected I suppose, that these wounds were caused by a man. "I'm fixing to get shed of one right soon. He ain't worth a nickel and he only gets up to see me one time and another." As she talked, she smoothed my clothing, and swept her fingers through my clotted hair. "You need to get all that muck out of yourself, sweet thing. We'll get you down to the station house and get you cleaned up."

I asked her again for Camp Ten and I told her I was looking for a place where they rode liquor into town.

"Yes indeed," she said. "We'll get you there, to the station house and get you fixed up and they'll be going to town in a day or so, don't you fret. Maybe I'll go in with you, if you need help, if that's what you're looking for. I got me a place in the town that Sammy puts me in, and I'm fixing to leave all this up here and just stay in the town. He's got enough of what I'm after and I oughtn't to be fooling around with any man back up in these mountains. Took me long enough to come down out of them. Let's get on."

The house was a mile down the hill, past one swooping switchback, and then I could see it below us. It was quite close, down a steep bank, so that you saw its roof first, and passed by it, down the contour to another shorter switchback, and then around and down and back to the house. Only this time on doorway level. The narrow trail made its final twist, and opened out into a wide, tilted field, at the far end of which stood the house, with *there it is*: a flatbed T-model truck out front, parked under two young spreading maples.

It is a big house, the biggest I've seen outside of town, and it doesn't look right: it isn't a house, properly speaking, at all, but more of an establishment, a business and office place, more like a small version of the tobacco warehouse than a large version of a house. It had been painted, once, long ago, and the red has flaked and faded to a hint, a whisper, of former color. We approached toward the long side, planked in thin clapboards, with a second level that had once borne a message, a sign, a name, long since faded and indecipherable. It all gave the impression of an immense sheet of lined pink paper, on which some dutiful giant of a writer had carefully drawn out her name and then furiously erased it, leaving a smudged hint of meaning, but no discernable script.

"I'm right glad to get down again," Hastie said, as we angled across the field toward the front of the house. The sun, that had been so warm on the ridge, was now occluded by the rise of mountain behind us, and the air had a sharp, still bite, like a second morning. "Let's see who's here." I could hear a touch of little girl excitement in her voice. Hastie already seemed to me the type that would thrive on entries, meetings, greetings.

"I don't know," I said. "Do I look too bad?" I felt at the makeshift bandage on my forehead. "I feel like Henry Fleming," I said.

"What?" said Hastie. "Who?"

"Nobody," I said. "Another runaway. Or Eliza. I'd rather be Eliza."

"It don't matter," she said. "You look fine. Just a mite be-draggledy. Hold on fer a minute." She reached up and patted my hair down, where it had worked free of the bandage. I could feel the thick rope of matted blood under her hand. "That's just fine. Nobody's going to care what you look like." She laughed. "Not here, sweet thing."

We passed around the corner and walked along the front of the house on our right, with the truck on the left. Two men were half-squatting, half-leaning against the running boards. One appeared to be about sixty years old. The other might have been his grandson, judging by their similarity of build and pose. They wore blue work overalls, not like farmers, but like you'd see on town workers or yard men. The younger man looked ex-pressionlessly at nothing. His eyes were clouded and vacant, his yellow hands draped limply over his bent knees. *He's drunk*, I thought. *Crazy drunk..*

"Where you been, gal?" the older said. His voice was blus-tery and forced. "You been yonder across that mountain again? What, again?"

"It ain't no part of your business where I been, old man," Hastie said. Then, oddly, she ran over to him, leaned down, and gave him a quick kiss on the cheek. "Don't you worry none," she said to him. "I ain't going to bring him here."

"I could give you more to thank about than any sonofabitch over to that creek, I tell you that right now," he spluttered. He lifted a finger and turned it in the air, obscenely. "Hey! Who's yer friend? She needing any of this?" The finger curved and beckoned rawly, an unmistakable gesture.

I turned away. Hastie came back and ushered me toward the house's large front door—too large for a house. I moved as quickly as possible.

"Who is that man?" I said. "Surely he isn't…"

"Hah. Not a chance," Hastie said. "Don't worry about him none. He's all right. He's actually a nice ole fella. He's just a'fooling around."

* * *

I'm lying in the small iron bed, writing by the light of the tallow candle. Hastie is curled in beside me, so slight in her thin cotton nightshirt that I would hardly feel her presence, were it not for the heat she gives off. So much warmth from such a tiny body. She feels comforting beside me, while the rain smatters down against the single pane. The sputter of rain cultivates your awareness of how trifling a margin the narrow glass provides, the way drops of pollen show you the thin film of surface on still water.

Hastie shifts a bit beside me, and I feel a tight breeze of warmth. I remember lying on my back, naked sometimes, beside George, and feeling the reassurance of his deep breathing as he slept within that cave of our commingled heat. He would turn, and his bare buttocks would shape my hip, and I would feel secured, in place. Then, later, he would roll back and throw his arm across my middle, pulling me to him. And I would feel so terribly alone, seized by this grasp and listening to the huge wind beat and roar around the dark mountains. And I would run my hand across my body, seeking out some uneven spot or blemish, or a sore place—a boil or a scab, or rub my feet together to feel the rough callous—and caress that spot, stroke across it tenderly to learn its shape. I would want to know its feel on the tips of my fingers at the same time as I felt my fingers' touch on my body. Or reach into some deep part of me and bring the odor to my nostrils, because that demonstrated that I was more than one self if I could smell my own scent. And here was some solace in this terrible seclusion, as the mountain winds tore about, just beyond the dreadfully thin shell of the house, blanket, skin.

And what is this? Here I lie, feeling Hastie's warmth but recalling that frightful loneliness. So what is it that's occurring right now, a warm comfort or a dread solitude? I don't know.

But here I am, lying in Hastie's bed, having been bathed and fed by Hastie's hand. All the while she rambles on about her own life, her man who meets her up on the mountain "when he gets around to it," and her town man, Sammy, who is chief of the bootlegging operation, and "has big money, and spreads it around like lard on a biscuit."

Already, she feels like a part of my life. And so now I will snuff this candle and turn toward her and settle into her heat, like some small animal, drawn to a fire.

It is some time into the night and I am writing again by the candle, after a series of upsets and alarms. We were awakened suddenly by a slamming noise in the house, and I jerked up in the bed, terrified, feeling hands on me again—not George's, this time—his. Unaware of time or place, just those grasping fingers, I crossed my arms over my breasts, and shrank back against Hastie, who appeared not to have wakened.

"S'nothin," she murmured. "S'okay." She rolled over toward the wall.

"What is it? Hastie, wake up," I said. I felt an unreasonable fear at the banging and thrashing noises that continued, from somewhere down below. "I don't know what to do."

For the first time I have realized that I am in a new place, entirely. Here, all my old manners and tactics must give way to an abiding ignorance. Everything is provisional, everything. There is no possibility of stepping aside from all of this to measure, or sum up, or pass some sort of judgment. There is no *aside* to stop-on. Everything is right in the middle of things.

I feel like a tobacco worm, my body too large and horrible to afford me any place to hide. This is the part of tobacco making that everyone hates, hunting down these worms as thick as your middle finger. But now I am the worm, so primitive as to have no awareness whatever of what is coming at each brush of the air, each swaying swing of the leaf I cling to. This time is it a vast being who will peel me off my leaf and slam me to the ground? Where the last awareness I have will only be the terrible clutch of those huge hands and the throwing down and the concussion, as I hit the ground, so splintering that the only sense remaining is the coppery taste of my own death?

I never liked it, the way we tore those worms off the plants and slammed them to the ground. It was horrible, the thick, green struggle of the body, trying to maintain hold on the leaf where it was, after all, *made* to be. I didn't feel sorry for them: you can't feel anything but disgust for a tobacco worm. But I felt some sort of shame at participating in this grotesque, atavistic grappling in the hot stick of the tobacco gum, this totally uneven struggle, not for life and death, since it was a foregone conclusion, the worm smashing fatly against the red ground, while we move along hating it for being where it was, after all *made* to be.

And here. Not *made* to be here, but at least feeling that there was no other choice. Not a worm, because I have made decisions, I have fought back. I have, in fact, vanquished. But my victory is crowned in a freedom so total that, like the worm, I am left with no safe place. Not even the leaf for whose protection I was colored, from whose nourishment I grew heavy, for which abode I have instinct and accoutrement. No. In fact, it is this very intimacy with the leaf that will spell my doom, since it is the leaf that the vast beings want, and not me. I am only an obstacle to be removed. And so I have no defense against my own instincts when this freedom reaches down its huge hand for my drooping, swaying, clinging form.

It was a drunken brawl, of sorts. Or no. Not so much a brawl as an execution of sentence. Hastie got up and ran down the stairs in her thin cotton shift, while I hung back, grasping at the rail on top of the stairway, and looked down into the depths of the front hallway, where two shadowed men appeared to be dancing in exaggerated, extravagant motions of push-and-pull. The crashing noises we had heard, that had awakened us, were only the slamming of their heavy brogans on the plank floor, *glump, glumple, thoom.* Because, otherwise, they made no sound at all, except for a low hum of breath like a thoughtful snore. Until one of the dark dancers swung the other in a terrific, slow arc, ending in a deep thunder, as he hit the wall, remained still for a suspended second, then slid into a crumple.

"Son of a bitch," the surviving dancer said, gulping air.

Hastie had reached him. She was imperious, for all her littleness. "What're you two doing, slamming each other around and tearing up the patch in the middle of a night?"

"Goddam canned heat," said Dancer. He was still breathing hard, and he gulped out the words rather than saying them. "He got all—god damn corn he can—drink up here—goes off into town, swills that shit so he ain't worth a wad of warm spit. Hell, he ain't worth a whole lot to nobody as it is, he got to go get full up on that canned heat. Son of a bitch. Son of a bitch."

"You want me to drag him upstairs, sweet thing?" Hastie called up to me. "We could light him up, keep warm tonight. Or cook us a mess of greens."

"It ain't so goddam funny," said Dancer. "Who the hell is going to drive the truck this load? He couldn't drive a damn nail betwixt his own goddam eyebrows. Who's going to drive truck? Son of a bitch." He spat in the direction of his crumpled partner.

"I'll drive," put in Hastie, quickly, as though she'd been waiting for the question. "I'm a'going in anyways. I'll drive the truck. You know I can do it."

"I don't know, Hastie. Sammy…"

"It'll be fine with Sammy. You know he don't mind nothing I do. It'll be kindly like a surprise for him to see me. And I got me a place of my own, now, don't I?"

"Place to sweeten up Sammy, you mean. You wouldn't have no place if you didn't spend all your damn time in it on your back with your goddam feet up in the air."

"Shut up," Hastie said. "Don't you go…"

"Shut up, yourself. Help me get this sonofabitch out of here."

Hastie called up for me to come down and help. Walking down those stairs was like walking into a dark pool, knees, thighs, belly, until I found myself holding my breath for a moment, as though I'd submerged entirely. At the bottom, I felt Hastie's tug on the sleeve of my shift.

"You take a leg and I'll take a leg," she said.

"Well, good evening, there. You fixing to stay with us?" said Dancer. The politeness was laced with a thick mixture of soiled sexuality. I said nothing, but moved with Hastie to the feet of the crumpled form. I looked along his wrinkled body to his mottled, dead face and recognized the young inebriate of this morning—yesterday morning, I guess, now.

"He looks like hell, don't he?" said Hastie, bending and hefting a leg. I did the same, lifting a handful of trousers and curving a hand under his calf. I was surprised at his thinness.

"God damn canned heat," said Dancer. "I bet you don't mess with that slop do you, honey." He was talking to me. He didn't sound quite like us. He had a tanned, unshaven face, with a deeply cleft chin. His skin was quite dark. He looked twisted, somehow, not from evil so much as from hard work. And his eyes were set just a bit too far apart, so that you found yourself looking from one eye to the other, unsettled and uneasy. "What's your name, honey?" he said, hooking the drunkard's armpits and hauling him upward.

"Hazel," I said. "Hazel Tighrow." Now why did I say that? I didn't think to say it. I hadn't tried it out back and forth within myself. It was as though I heard the sound before I spoke the word. And here was Hazel Tighrow, whom I hadn't seen in quite some time, announcing herself to this shadowy shell of a place. And I felt like her, too, like all those years with George had just peeled off to expose the young, raw layer of me, as though I was naked, never having been clothed in marriage or householding or even womanhood. I felt as in a dream, naked in front of a room of strangers who hadn't yet noticed my nudity, and the longer their indifference lasted, the more uncovered I felt.

My entire body flushed and my bowels loosened.

"Well now, Miss Hazel. I'm quite extumerated to know you. Me, I'm Nigger John, but don't you believe it. I'm a god damn Injun." said Dancer. "Let's get this sack of…" and he pulled Drunkard toward the doorway, nearly yanking him from our grasp. "Let's put him in the yard."

"You just say it, and we'll all just do it," said Hastie, securing her grip on the leg. She tossed out a short laugh. "Chief."

"Shut up and let's get this bastard…"

"I need to use the shed house," I whispered to Hastie, as we lugged the dead, stick-like legs. The brogans were huge and warped, and the cold, hard leather knocked against my hip at each stumble of the way. We hefted him out to the front porch. The air had that warm, leafy smell that comes when a night rain has just passed. A humped-looking model-A sat slewed oddly in the yard, just visible out of the deep shadow that I knew was truck and tree.

"Shed house would be a right fitting place to shove this son-ofabitch," said Dancer. "But since you're fixing to use it, we'll just let him snarf…" He snatched the body out of our arms and, in two long motions, flung it over the edge of the porch. It land-ed with a dull *wrop-p* and lay completely inert. "Shed house is off that way," Dancer said, and disappeared suddenly back into the house, his brogans beating hollowly on the planks.

"We're headed for town for sure," said Hastie. "If I'm driving, I can take you wherever you want to be. Or you can stay with me. Except Sammy might not want you there. No. You better find somewhere else. Sammy might want you there, too. Neither way you want to be there."

"I've got to go."

"Don't worry, sweet thing. You'll go. Tomorrow morning, we're on our way. I got a load of money, too."

"No," I said. "I've got to go. To the shed house."

Back to bed, sitting together, backs against the barred iron head, with Hastie talking excitedly and clapping her hand on my knee. She fell asleep in mid-sentence, and she is lying still, now, her left hand still drawn down between us and drooped over my knee. There is something inexpressibly beautiful in her sleeping face, some compilation of all our hopeful dreams about death and peace. Or perhaps because she looks so brand new, *trailing clouds of glory,* a reminder of past anticipation more than future nothingness.

She came here when she was about sixteen years old, she says. The same age as I was when he brutally took what he thought was pleasure. And Hastie hasn't had it wrested from her, torn out like a barb through a lip. No. She has embraced it thoroughly and lustily and so she never could have been violated, since she never felt there was anything to violate: just passion and rutting, the joy of animal rutting, on the mountainside, or in a cheap room in town, with this man or that. What matter? She has been a participant, not a passive victim, never a victim. No, it isn't love, or intimacy, at least not the kind we sing about. But it's more than mere appetite. More, because it informs her, body and soul, makes her Hastie, the way she is, so that the lust grows out of the character that the lust shapes. Completely integrated. All she asks is that the man be the same: not power, but lust. Not conquest, but co-mingling, even if only of cries and breaths and liquidity.

We have talked of all this, in language I never imagined using: short, explosive words full of consonants. I wonder why there are so many hard Cs in this language of lust: *fuck, suck, cock, cunt, clit, come.* Hastie speaking them is the first time I have heard them when they weren't a form of brutality. She sounds more like a child, enjoying dropping thick rocks into a soft pool, and she can say things that make you envious, rather than embarrassed.

"First man I took for real I was twelve or thirteen years old and I thought he was a hundred. I didn't look no different than I do right now. I kindly hit a point around then where I got whatever I was going to get by way of woman's shape and all. Then I reckon God got busy with some other gal. Maybe they was a princess or somebody over to France caught His eye and He forgot me and left. So here I am just like I was six years ago. I ain't got much, sweet thing, but I knows how to use every bit of it, don't you worry about that." She laughed. "That first feller, he had hair on him like a damn whistle pig and a dick like a snath. He'd get on you and you felt like you was a'fucking a hay rake. But I liked it fine. Ain't quit, have I, sweet thing? No, I don't believe there's nothing in the world like having a man a'whimpering in your ear like a baby whilst you're a'pouring out like thick sorghum. Lord, lord.

"Hell, we didn't have nothing when I was a kid. Lived in an old shack away up yonder on the mountain with no windows and a mud chimney. Dirt floor. Cold nights we'd snuffle all together in front of that little fire, like a litter of puppies.

"My Daddy wasn't much account. Once in a blue moon you might catch him trying to work. But he never did learn how. Died up the ridge one day for no reason. Like as much to have choked to death on his own spit while he was trying to decide which way to let it sling. So we was pretty high and dry all the time. Wasn't much else to do but get a man inside you. Didn't cost nothing and felt a hell of a lot better than jumping in a thorn patch." She laughed. "I reckon I'm too backward to get a baby on me. Ain't never happened, anyway. I don't know. It mightn't be too bad a thing to do, neither."

"No," I said. "I don't think I'm able to have one either." It's the first time I've ever said this aloud. But I wanted to tell her. I don't know.

"No?" she said. "Now that's a mite strange. You ain't all tiny and grangly like me, you got some good flesh on you, sweet thing. I wonder how come."

"I don't know," I said. "I just can't." I thought of Noah Kersin and the terrible wound. I never really thought this had anything to do with it, but I've never quite put it out of my mind, either. I was sick and hurt, bleeding, for a good while after he laughed and walked away. It lasted off and on for a week or so, and, of course, I never told anyone. I suppose that could be a reason. *It doesn't matter*, I thought, just as Hastie answered.

"Well, it don't matter none, sweet thing." She put her hand on top of mine, on my stomach, and patted me, and I can't remember ever feeling so welcome, so comforted. Cared for. "So this old boy, the feller I was laying with? He got his likker down here to Camp Ten and he taken to bringing me down here with him. I reckon I could carry whatever was left back up the hill without busting the jug whilst he drug himself home. But I never drank the damn stuff, myself. Can't see it. You get plenty a chance to watch what happens when folks ties into the stuff, you'd think folks could see that once and say, 'Hell.' But I guess nobody can hardly leave well enough alone but he's got to fix up something to try to kill himself with.

"Well, now, he brung me down here one time too often and I just plumb stayed put. They was a woman running the operation then. She was a good old gal, tougher'n a sow hog. I tell you, they weren't no canned heat drunks flopping around here when she was around. Anyway, she kindly took me in, and I reckon she told old hay rake to bundle himself off. And I been here ever since."

How old is she now? All of this talk made her seem ageless, like the words she was using. Then she jumped up and giggled like a child. She snatched up the candle and moved over to the drawers on the wall.

"Look at this here," she said, like a girl showing me a secret. She carefully counted drawers, seven up from the floor and seven across, and jerked a drawer open. She pulled a handful of something out, returned to me, and showered it over the bed.

It was money.

Hastie laughed and returned to the huge cabinet. She counted again, yanked a drawer, and pulled out another wad of cash, to flutter down all around me. Then turned and performed the same routine again. And again. And yet again.

"We got all the money we can handle, sweet thing," she said.

"Hastie!" I said. "Where did you get all this?"

"I got it from Sammy," she said. "Over the years."

"Goodness," I said. "Sammy gave you all this?"

"Didn't give it," she said. "I got it from him."

"Got it? You mean you took it?"

"Little bit at a time," she said. She plopped her little body into the pile of bills, laughing. "There's a heap of it, ain't there?"

"Hastie, you can't just steal…"

"It don't matter. Sammy don't care about nothing. He got more money than a dog has ticks. He don't care. We're going to town, sweet thing. Going to town."

IV.

I'm not certain I realized until Hastie appeared just how collab-
orative this effort of mine—to run, to hide—had been. Virtually
everyone had contributed something important to the decision
or the actual execution of the act itself. All rehearsed, perfectly
on cue. Change one person's place or moment in the narrative
and the entire direction of the plot changes utterly. Oh, but not
random chance. Not iron-bound fate. Because I lifted my voice
more than once, turned my head, teased a little? Well, perhaps.
Seductress? No, that is too strong, I think. Although I tried very
hard to be seduced that second time, with Noah Kersin,

  Oh yes, Noah kissed me. The day before I left. Yes. We kissed. I
kissed him. Yes. Broke through every impulse and inclination on
the one hand, every form of denial and repugnance on the other.
Yes. More than "let him kiss me," because, you see, it had to be
more: he had to feel me kiss him, had to see the desire in my eyes.
His own version of what this all meant had to be confirmed. And
that vision led all the way back to what he believed had happened
between himself and an innocent, romantic sixteen-year-old on
Possy's Camp, six years before. Because he still believed that with
the springing of his seed, marking his conquest of that day, he had
implanted a hunger in me that would grow within me and would

ultimately overwhelm any restraining impulses of morality or of innocence or even of intervening loves—never mind the vows of marriage. He thought the years would see that seed burst forth, spread and grow in a kind of natural succession of desire: the desire, compulsion to be taken (that's a word he would like, *taken*) again and then again by this lusty (that, too) and strong-willed man.

Never mind that the moralities had nothing to do with the case. He would never see this, who was so hot to uncover some unmediated desire that I was surely nursing along beneath all the outward display of propriety, uxoriousness. So he couldn't allow himself to see that the morality of all this had been on his side all along. Because there's not a young woman anywhere in this country—mountain or city or shore—who doesn't feel that she is entirely responsible for the behavior of the young men who stand along the storefronts or the fields or the docks, and smirk, and leer, and talk about her body as something to have: *Man, I'd like to get some of that.* And so, whether the stirrings of desire, sexual wants, lusts—whether she discovers these welling up inside of her, from her deep heart's core, or whether she first greets them in the incursions of his eyes, or hands, or the weight of his body—either way, the task of making any decision, the *what should I do,* will remain entirely hers. Such are the codes of morality that pretend to protect her *innocence* when in fact they are demanding that she be defined entirely within the *normal* scope of his leering, his grasping, his demand for possession. She can decide either to give herself to that demand or to say no to that demand. But that is all. The demand remains the stage upon which she must act. Never can she decide to *take.* Never can she act to free the selfish male from his own trap by saying not *take me* but *shape me, as I shape you.*

No, she cannot *take,* certainly. But neither can she take herself out of the game, refuse to roll the dice, reject the sought-after objective because it is nothing she particularly wants to *win* in the first place. No. She is predestined to play, to make her choices within the bounds of this game board and these rules designed by someone else. Never allowed to pick up her marker, or to sweep the board clean with one bitter, triumphant brush of her woman's hand. Never. Not even when she sees that the prize for which everyone is so cheerfully playing is her own life, her own future self.

No. Noah Kersin could not have seen all of this, any of this, really. Because he thought he was a maverick, a flouter of propriety, a brave rogue who took what he desired in spite of appearance and courtesy. He thought this rogueishness was precisely what would cause women like me always to yearn secretly for his control: he would succeed with me because he was an individual so compelling that I would cast aside all of the niceties, all of the comforts, just to feel the force of his own will. He was Black Jack Davy, renegade and outlaw. And it would not do for anyone to see that he was the very model and mold of the same moral codes he thought he was haughtily rejecting. Black Jack Davy? Hah. If only there could have been a Black Jack Davy, beside whom I might freely lay my body, no encumbering sword in between us, both of us reveling in the embrace of our outlaw bodies upon the hard, cold ground that served only to enhance the hot liquid touch of each other's deepest selves.

But there never is any Black Jack Davy in this story. George? Well, George could have lain on that ground, but he couldn't have gone away. Couldn't have taken me up out of my spot in the first place. George's eyes colored the mountains as much as the mountains colored his eyes. George.

No Black Jack Davy except perhaps one. Or nearly so. And she was cast aside like a gamepiece that has been squandered and so can no longer choose even *to play* or *not to play*, on any terms at all. Hastie, who nevertheless found herself a bit of a world in which she could roll and take her pleasure (and give her pleasure) in whatever of joyous, naked, four-lettered pointlessness she wished. Whose sole desire and sole prize would have been to open to you your own vibrant, heated freedom.

265

So I kissed Noah Kersin. Even, perversely enough, attempted to respond to him, like an actress trying to "get into character." Tried to inhabit the Hazel he saw, the one who must assuredly arouse herself at the mere memory of having been thrown to the ground and overpowered by him. And who would fasten deliciously, twice-over, to the wet clutch of his mouth.

JOURNAL OF HAZEL TAYLOR
August 12, 1927

I'm sitting in Hastie's room in Asheville, where we spent last night, while she's out attempting to locate Saint's place for me. "You just set and relax, sweet thing," she says. "I know this town like a bear knows a bee hive. I'll find the place." So she took my little slip of paper and went off. She assures me that no one will come here while she's gone, but the prospect still frightens me. I don't want to meet Sammy—or any of them—without Hastie around to navigate.

We got up at Camp Ten early yesterday morning and helped load up the truck. I never did see any of the house except Hastie's room and the front hall. There wasn't anyone around except the old man and Dancer. The young man was still heaped out front like a pile of crumpled tin. He was covered with streaky tan dirt like rust.

"Little Boy don't look much better by daylight, does he?" Hastie said. She led me around the corner of the house to where a gray plank barrow leaned. "Let's get that corn loaded and we can head on down." I could hear the excitement in her voice.

She headed us up the trail the way we had come down, yesterday. It's difficult to accept the fact that it's only been a day. First, I'm in such a new world that the old measures, like time, sunrise, the elapse of *yesterday, last night, today* seem to have no meaning whatever. Because time is just another measure of place: how long it takes to walk from Upper Creek to Maddy

Creek, the interval between plowing one row and turning to start the next. And if your place has changed so utterly, then time has lost hold, because you literally *haven't got time* to repeat anything. You would need to have walked out to that shed house enough to have measured the intervening space, and you can't, because you've just turned a corner of the house and seen an entirely new ground on which to begin counting steps.

Besides, Hastie is so timeless, seems so permanent, eternal, a part of who I now find myself to be. I am sitting in this bare room—there's nothing here at all but a small table and a metal bed that's been painted exactly the color of Hastie herself, so that it seems to anticipate her body, to await her just as I am. So I now time myself by Hastie, Hastie's return. And since I don't know where she is going, I have no span to cover here, either. So I drift.

Dropped into this floating world is the strange abstraction called *Hastie meets Saint*, where these two parts of myself will meet and merge somewhere entirely beyond my own sight, hearing, somewhere apart. As though a conference has taken place, a consultation between two experts who have gathered in congress to discuss their specialty: *Hazel Taylor*. And, like a patient in quarantine, I await the outcome.

It is all so strange. Here a woman I have known for two days, but feel as though she has been with me all my life, is going to find a man I have known all my life. But the life that included this man seems to have disappeared entirely, two days ago, and he won't have known that I'm here—never would imagine it—until Hastie turns up and announces my presence to him. And only now do I have an inkling of the degree of trust that I've just sent floating off, like a message in a bottle: that Hastie will find him and tell him the right way; that Saint will respond with alacrity and welcome; that each will have my own interests foremost. But, then, it isn't sheer faith. It is knowledge. I know that each will do precisely these things, the way I know that I will drop a dot of ink at the end of this sentence.

Anyway, this morning, we went up the trail to the second switchback, where Hastie wrestled the barrel through a screen of laurel, out of which we emerged to find a narrow, well-worn pathway. We skirted the contour for several rods, then emerged on the front of what seemed a flat, oval plain.

It was, in fact, a huge canvas tarp, laid as a roof over a pit that had been excavated out of the side of the ridge. Hastie rolled the barrow down a ramp and we stood inside, under the tarpaulin, in a cave-like enclosure with a spring running freely along a sluice to one side. The room smelled of earth, wood-smoke and sicky-sweet cooking. The still took up most of the space in front of us, its worm looking like an exotic ritual totem, tipped mysteriously into the enormous font of the thumper keg. Along the wall of the cave, where the ridge had been dug out deepest, were stacks of silvery jars that looked as though they held only the purest of air.

A man emerged from a clutter of cans and debris behind the still. I had not seen him before. Thin and grizzled, he wore torn overalls and a wide-brimmed, preposterously official-looking felt hat with a braided band and a brass shield on the front. *He took that off a dead* man, I realized. He was carrying a paint can filled with a deep brown liquid that smelled sharp and strong, like hot sunshine. A huge pistol hung awkwardly in a cloth holster at his hip.

"Humm up a mite," he said. He pulled a tin funnel from the notch of his overalls and shuffled over to the wall of jars. "W'umms needs to sote a mite, umm."

He set five jars in a row on the ground and unscrewed each, carefully laying the lids aside, as though they were explosive. Into each jar he poured a dose of the dark liquid, dipping his head in time with the tipping of the paint can, as though his movement measured the pouring. When he finished these five, he rescrewed them, set them on the side, and lined up another row of jars. Again the dipping and pouring.

"Creosote," said Hastie. "He's got an order for Scotch." She laughed and shook her head. "Lord, lord," she said, in a voice half scorning, half pitying the poor fools who would consume these jars and laugh and curse, fight and vomit, in a night of what they took to be pleasure. Meanwhile, she began loading jars of the colorless corn liquor into the barrow. "Grab up that straw, sweet thing."

A broken bale shredded straw to one side of the jars. I scooped an armful and brought it to the barrow, where Hastie had just finished laying an even rank of jars. I knew my job, and I smoothed out a bed atop the jars on which Hastie began clinking the next row.

"Where's Water Boy, Filem?" Hastie asked.

"Humm up leep. W'uns up making hmm run all nought." Filem said.

"How much we got?" Hastie said.

"Humm mot tray score so," Filem said.

"Lord. Let's get to working.'" Hastie said.

So we loaded and packed jars through the cool morning in the wet damp of the cellared-out hillside. Hastie talked throughout the operation, and I thought, *For once I'm not rambling on about something, but listening, listening.*

"These ole fellers will keep a sharp eye on their stills. Got to, I reckon, or the law would get in there, shut you down. Take all your likker. Ha. We kicked up a still way up the mountain once, when I was a kid. Me and my sisters. We knowed it was one of Lonnie Hinkle's. Most of them was, anyway. He had it tucked back into a cut in the big ole rock face. Flume of water running down, where he had done built a little wood trough. And he had a big barrel buried in the ground, probably sixty gallons, where he was keeping his mash. And you could smell it was pretty ripe, about ready for him to run it, you know? Well, we got us some long little stems and punched the pith out of them, hollowed them out, you know?. Stuck them down in through all that canvas and netting and all, down into that beer that was a'working in that drum. And we'd suck up a drink of it. And get to giggling and suck up another little bit. Made us higher than a jaybird, I tell you what." She laughed. "And sicker than old Pharoah.

"Well I done told Lonnie the story a few years later. I said, 'Lonnie, you never knowed it, but you got three little girls right drunk one afternoon up on the mountain.' And told him about drinking up that beer like we done. And he says, 'I know it, Hastie. I was a'setting there watching you.'"

We'd get a barrel loaded and then we'd wheel and wrestle and lunge the barrow down to the house, where Dancer—the one called Nigger John—and a very old man in farm overalls put jars into crates and loaded them into the bed of the truck. Each time the old man hefted a crate, he made a *heezing* noise and thrust the tip of a white tongue between teeth and whiskers of a uniform tobacco-juice amber. He would drop the case the last few inches onto the bed and his entire body would recoil from the sudden absence of weight, throwing him back a step, his arms rising upward and his head tipped back as though he were preaching, or singing. Then he'd turn, spit, and bend for the next case. *Hallelujah.*

"Big load," Hastie said, pulling a handkerchief out of nowhere. She tugged me toward her and wiped my brow, around the bandage, with that harsh tenderness like you'd wipe the run off a baby's nose. "How's that head of yours holding up, sweet thing?" she asked. Then mopped her own brow. "One thing we got to learn you is how to hold your own head up, ain't it?" She laughed at her own word play. "Let's git one more bucketful of this here rat poison…"

"Whatchew a'callin' rot piyehzzin?" said Hallelujah. He was bent over, ready to *heez* another case upward. He stopped, looked at Hastie, and drew a jar out of the case.

"Waterboy been making this here swill for so long he done decided it's good for you," said Hastie. Hallelujah—Waterboy—was tipping the jar and shaking it vigorously. He didn't look angry; I have the feeling this is a practiced routine, rather than a real disagreement.

"No bead like that on no sweeyil," he said. "Won't hurtch-ew a beeyit. That er's good white likker, I'd say. Ain't no fauwt a mine if them city folks lacks eet red. 'Ey wants piyehzzin in thar likker, don't blame me, I'd say. I weren't drank eet no way but clar." He spat.

"Tell the truth, sweet thing, Waterboy knows better than to drink it at all. He's been down the mountain once, ain't you Waterboy? You seen yourself it causes bullet holes, ain't you?"

"Cayint 'ford to just drank eet," he said and laughed a rough, phlemmy cough. He slewed his arm across his mouth. "Lez git to it." He spat, bent again, replaced the jar, and hefted.

"Waterboy done figured out a long time back yonder that you could get five cents a bushel for corn on the cob, but you can get five dollar a quart if you put it up in the air. Ain't that the truth Waterboy?"

But he was doing his epiphanic stagger step, and said nothing.

JOURNAL OF HAZEL TAYLOR
August 12, 1927

And here I am, at Saint's house. I feel like a special guest, as though I've come halfway around the world for a visit. Of course, he treats me with that combination of intimate friend-ship and nervous restraint, because, I suppose, he loves me still and feels awkward, as happy as he is to see me.

I waited most of the day for Hastie's return. Late this after-noon, she came clonging back up her stairway. You step out her door onto a porch-like landing with a harsh yellow lightbulb burning, day and night. The porch gives onto a long, steep iron staircase, roofed, but not enclosed, so that ringing footsteps seem to carry direct through the window into the room. She threw open the door and gave an exaggerated curtsy.

271

"Found him, sweet thing," she said. "Didn't take a minute. He's easy enough to find: you just asks around for a feller looks like a ole black bear. And there he is"

"You know him?" I asked, surprised that she'd never mentioned this to me.

"Course I knows him. Saint's about the only man I ever found myself buying things from. Only man never tried to give me things until I choked on them. Of course I knows him. Everybody knows Saint Dunstan, lived in these mountains any time in the last five years. He's the peddler, ain't he? Ain't that how you knows him? Don't tell me—"

"No," I said, perhaps a bit too quickly. He doesn't deserve that rapid a denial, who has never been anything but gracious and kind, does he? "No, he's a dear friend. He was my schoolteacher. Where've you been until evening?"

"Schoolteacher? Well I be durned. He didn't say nothing about that. And you're right, he didn't sound like he'd ever seen you out of your shift. But I been sitting at Saint's listenin to him talk about you all this time. I wouldn't say he's sweet on you. I'd say he's raving mad about you. I'd say he ain't had a whole night's sleep since the day he met you, sweet thing."

"Oh stop it, Hastie. He didn't tell you that," I said. It wouldn't be like Saint to go talking about those feelings. At least I hope not. If he can tell someone about his own deep secret, how can I trust him not to tell about my running off? But no. I can. There are only a few certain things, but this is one of them. At least as certain as anything can be.

"Oh no, sweet thing, he didn't say nothing in the least about it. But I ain't been a'crawling around under men all this time for nothing. I can tell. Honey, I can smell it on them. And don't tell me..."

"That's enough, Hastie. You're doing him a disservice, and me, too. He has never, would never..."

"Lord, you sweet on him, too?"

* * *

So this all made for a rather clumsy entrance to Saint's house, because I could feel Hastie watching both of us, and I could feel Saint trying to be tender and loving and completely unthreatening at the same time, and I watched all of these characters inside myself arguing over what any move, gesture, accidental flicker I made might mean, until I felt like Hastie was inside me trying to find out, while I stood inside her wondering what to do next.

Saint gave us a glass of tea and he was careful to put a little more in her glass than in mine, so that I wouldn't think he was taking advantage of me. You see? I really must say I like being here, now that Hastie has gone, but we're both acting according to the most tedious, formal kind of manners, so that the warm glow of friendship (it is assuredly here, and understanding, too—we could call it *intimacy* if we weren't so afraid to) seems like an old coat hanging in the parlor. You know it's there, and you can put it on if it gets chilly, but you don't want to look so relaxed: someone might find it shabby.

Hastie did leave fairly soon, though her final warbling imperative to *have fun* didn't help much. She headed out in search of Sammy.

Sammy had been one topic of conversation as she drove us down the mountain, her jounced voice melding with the clinkling of the jars—they had been covered over with corn fodder and all of it tarped down with canvas, so that you wouldn't think *liquor*, but *farmer*, as the truck drove by. From inside, though, you smelled and heard *liquor*, with every jolt. Meanwhile, Hastie cursed the road, the alcohol and the loose brake band on the truck, all in a cheery, holiday voice, shouting over the noise of engine and cargo. She seemed in constant danger of being thrown out of the door by the jerking of the steering wheel, which literally slewed her body back and forth on the seat.

"Goddamit, they ought to have tightened her down a mite, this morning. You know that, sweet thing? It's like trying to stop Little Boy from drinking that damn canned heat, you know that?" She would tighten both hands on the wheel and push down so hard on the brake that her buttocks rose clear off the seat. "Leastways, if we drop off the side of this mountain, you won't need to worry about how they'll git us in no embalming fluid, for we'll be covered with about a hundred quarts of it the minute we hit the rock."

We had left Camp Ten at about ten o'clock climbing into the T-model truck that was weighted down with liquor. Hastie set the spark and Waterboy jacked-up the back end, then went around front and cranked the truck over, handling the crank like it was dynamite.

"He won't crank her flat no more. He had that crank wind back on him once and put a crease in his knee." Hastie said. "Split it open wide, and he lay right there and bled. Didn't say a thing nor make a noise. So we had to put one boy to set on one end of him and set another one on the other and sew him up with a fish hook and a line. I tell you what, he bellowed some then. So now he won't crank her unless he jacks her up first." Then she hollered out to Waterboy, "Let her down, old feller, and we're going. Oh, hey," she said. "If my mountain boy turns up here you tell him for me that I'm through with all that bri-arpatching. Tell him I'm a city girl now and he can just skeedaddle on back where he come from."

And off we went, around and down the steep slope, past a few log houses and into the woods, on down the mountain. On any long uphill grade, Hastie had to stop, turn the truck around, and back up the hill. She said with the load on the back, the gas would cut out if we went uphill front-first. She half-stood to push down the reverse pedal. Then on top, she'd turn the truck around and drop it down the next long grade, twisting and turning in the seat, as though the wheel was turning her, and not the other way around. Talking all the while.

"This here driving is like wrassling with a drunk man, and I guess I done that a few times. Sammy, he don't drink, not to speak of, and he's got high toned manners about him. He ain't one of these covites just as like to try and kiss you with a wad in his goddam cheek, not Sammy. I'm through with lying out on a hillside with some homegrown sourwood a'bucking away at you, stopping ever twenty second to spit right out over your head. I don't care how big and tough he is, I'm through with him. Give me Sammy who's got piles of jack and wouldn't wear a pair of overhauls if you done sewed him to them. Sammy's a lot of fun and he's a big time bootlegger, too. He done took me once to one of these high-class parties where we provided all the likker, all poured out into fancy looking bottles, so the folks would think it come all the way from China, instead of just down the damn mountain. Bought me a red dress and a white rose pinned on the front. I tell you, sweet thing, I looked at myself in Sammy's mirror and I like to break down and cried I looked so pretty."

"I bet you did, Hastie." I can imagine her, standing there in scarlet, with the clear blooming blossom on her breast. She has an unearthly beauty about her, standing there, shimmered in the glass, shaken by her own splendor, radiating heat.

"What'd you say, sweet thing? Never mind. Sammy he took me to this great big stone place looked like a damn castle and it was just full of smart looking people and a real orchestra, not your low down string band. Sammy wouldn't drink any of the likker there, because these quality folks don't want no regular corn. They wants red likker, like that Scotch or what they call Canadian Rye. That ain't creosote in it, that's iodine. And they'll drink that stuff and their eyes'll bug out like a gigged bullfrog, because it burns so, you know that? And they'll say, 'Now that's some real Canadian likker, there. It's got that genuine bonded bite to it. Count on old Sammy to deliver the goods,' they'll say. And drinking down that iodine. Sweet thing, you wouldn't believe it, now would you? The high class. Watch out, now," and she'd step up on that brake, while the wheel tried to jump out of her hands. "I bet I can get a mite more money from Sammy, we get down the mountain."

I'm not very comfortable with Sammy's money, but Hastie

continually reassures me that he won't care. I don't know how much is there, but it is an astonishing amount of money. It must be enough for two to live on for quite a long time, even without *scratching*, as T.R. would say. And I think she has that it mind, the two of us, escaping together. And it sounds very good to me, too. I believe I could do anything with Hastie around. I would have to convince her to go far beyond Asheville, though. But, again, Hastie appears to care not where she goes—or rather, she appears to leap at the opportunity to *go*, where matters not a jot. I've been wondering about that sister of hers, who fled to Chicago. I'll have to ask her.

Still, the money is worrisome. I know Saint would give me enough to get somewhere and get set up. But that would mean using his affection instead of Hastie's, and I'd do it only to escape the onus of using Hastie's. So what's the point? I suppose Hastie ought to know whether a man is likely to resent being robbed or not, she's *crawled around under enough of them*, as she says.

I just remembered that she has increased our stock already. We pulled into town around six o'clock and Hastie drove straight down what she called the *main drag*. A quick turn into a narrow alleyway, lined with the brick backs of buildings, already deepening with the late afternoon.

"Be back in a shake," she said, and dropped out of the truck. She went quickly to a metal doorway, painted in a dull red, without any external handle, and banged with her fist. "Sammy's!" she shouted. She turned instantly and came back to the truck, clambered up into the seat and sat.

"What..." I said.

"Shhh. Just set still," she said. "There ain't no point in looking about or nothing."

I heard a screaking of metal and a moment later, the chinkle of jars. There must have been quite a few men, because the bed of the truck lightened considerably very rapidly. In just a moment, a man appeared at my window and reached out an envelope.

"Take it," Hastie said. The man said nothing. I held up my hand and he thrust the envelope between my thumb and finger. "Let's go, sweet thing," Hastie said, and the truck wrenched forward.

"We'll just keep that money until Sammy asks for it," she said. "He don't always remember to collect it."

So we have even more. How much, I don't know. Hastie had it all in a cardboard suitcase beside her bed, where we spent last night. But now it's in my flour sack, in Saint's room.

"Sammy ain't going to hunt me up, tonight. He don't even know I'm here," she said. "You might just as well sleep here, and we'll find your friend in the morning. Ain't much room on the bed, but if Sammy can flop around on it the way he does with me, I reckon you and me'll fit without so much as a squeeze."

I was happy to spend another night next to her, this Hastie, who found me on the mountain, bleeding and lost. And who took me in. And who let me take her on my own journey. She has found a way to become my own journey, herself, and she lay last night with her head tucked into my side, my arm around her small shoulders, hers around my waist. And when it became too much, too much warmth, and I uncurled from her and tried to nudge her away, she turned and stretched like a child, and mumbled, "It's all right. Ain't nothing, sweet thing."

JOURNAL OF HAZEL TAYLOR
August 14, 1927

It's two days later. I didn't write last night, because of this business with Saint. He's gone, now, and perhaps I can sort some of this out, a little bit. I don't know.

I guess it began with Hastie and Sammy. He dropped her off here, yesterday afternoon, and she insisted that he come in to meet me. I don't think I like him. He reminds me of Noah Kersin, in a way, although this one isn't a coward. And he's no fool. But he's harsh under that slick city exterior, like a silky stallion that you know is just biding his time until he can kick you, and who knows without even having tried it just how hard, and where, to kick in order to kill you the quickest. I don't know.

He appears to care for Hasty, though, in a mannish sort of way. He holds his arm around her like someone carrying a precious vase. She belongs to him, but he's quite pleased to have her, and I think he knows that she's worth a good deal more than he, all things considered. He is quite a bit older than her, graying on the temples, very slim, but quick and hard looking. He's one of those small-statured males that can freeze a much larger man with a single glance.

Anyway, he came and he handed Saint a quart jar of white liquor, not so much as a gift, Saint said later, than a business card. And that may be how it all began.

Sammy left and Hastie sat at the table with Saint and myself and insisted that we have a toast "to everything." She was happy as I've seen her, and we all caught her enthusiasm. So Saint said, "I'll take a sup if Hazel will join us."

"Just a mite, now," Hastie said. "You know I don't drink this stuff but once in a blue moon, and there ain't no point in changing that just because I'm happy to be here, you know that sweet thing? But we need to mark the occasion, as Sammy always says."

So we did. I've never had more than a few sips of beer or a little *noodled* wedding punch, as George calls it. But I took a little glass. It was like swallowing hot air, and it streamed down into the core of my belly and then rose up and out, not burning so much as glowing, a spreading, hot flow. *It tastes like drinking Hastie must be.* And then I felt it reach my skin, and I didn't like the flushing itchiness, like wet clothes too close to the fire.

So we had a couple of toasts on Sammy's corn liquor and I imagine that's what began the thing. Sammy came back and honked his horn for Hastie. He didn't come in this time, and she jumped up with her usual alacrity and left us—and there we were, on our own. And I think we'd have remained perfectly polite and amiable and completely impersonal until one of us had to leap up and run out the door. It was that strange. Taut.

And that's such a sad thing. You'd think if any two people could manage a way to communicate frankly and meaningfully about something concerning both of us, it would be Saint Dunstan and Hazel Taylor. After all, we were both adept with words; we had both read deeply all those stories of complicated passions and avowals, surrenders and withholdings. We had talked of all these wordless intimate things—Romeo and Juliet's night of love, John Donne's doubled-up longings of the divan and the divine, the harsh sweetness of Heathcliff and the sweet lust of Hester—at times, in the most personal ways. We should have been masters at opening up those feelings and urges and denials, seeing them for what they were, and telling each other what we saw.

But we were tongue-tied. Each so aware of the other's presence that we could not give voice to the two of us inside the other, the Saint/Hazel I owned and the Hazel/Saint of his. If only we could have done so, I think we would have fallen into each other's arms. Not sexually—because we would be talking all the while—or at least probably not. No. But certainly as lovers: two minds who loved the embodiment of each other, each other's selves. And, after all, the great lovers are always teachers and students in some way. At any rate, we ought to have been better than this tongue-tied courtesy and the awful subsequent rejection.

Because I should not have pushed him away. The Hazel who removed his hand, and herself, in such a peremptory fashion, this Hazel was not the Hazel he had sought when he reached out tentatively, awkwardly, not even hopefully, with that caress and the whisper of my name, "Hazel?"

I was, after all, in his bed, the bed he had insisted I ought to use in place of him. And I'm certain that this was not a ruse. I'm certain that he had not had a thought in the world of reentering that room an hour or so later, in the complete darkness, and placing his body softly next to mine. And then the whispered question—perhaps he was, in fact, wondering if this was indeed the Hazel he sought—and then the timid, warm hand, also a question.

I should not have done as I did. I should have put my hand over his, pressed it closer, where he touched me, held us both in my hand and whispered the same question to him: Saint? Had I done so, we would have found another chance to meet again as the lovers and friends that we already were.

But, instead of covering him, I removed him, like peeling a worm off the leaf, and threw him off. And said, "No." Firmly, reprovingly. And so, instead of meeting each other's selves, we will forever be caught in this horrible, polite amity, the real Saints and Hazels running off and hiding themselves in these clouds of stars, a million miles from each other's hands.

JOURNAL OF HAZEL TAYLOR
August 15, 1927

Oh I wonder if there will ever come a time when this has all settled out, and I don't feel filled to burst and drained to wilting with each passing incident. Each day seems to use up more of me than I began with in the morning. I came out of home so eager for experience, but experience needs at least enough of time and dignity to allow it to be experienced, doesn't it? Or is this what growing is about? I don't know. I only can say that this has already been a week's worth of a day, as George says.

Hastie and I have talked together about Chicago, where she has a sister, or a cousin—she uses the terms interchangeably. I walked to her place—how quickly we absorb the lines, pathways, from one "home" to another—this morning. I awoke quite early after last night's late writing, the struggle with and over Saint. He was nowhere to be seen this morning. But I believe that is good. I believe he is doing us both a tremendous courtesy by moving out of our embarrassment for a day. He's a

wise man, as much as I resent him for showing me what an ob-
tuse brute I can be. Anyway, his absence allows me to move all
of that to a side track (I'm talking like Hastie, aren't I!). To
move that aside and try to consolidate all of today. Will there
ever be time to arrange, review, compose any part of these days
into something I can have and understand? Or is that all the
fatuous hope of anyone who thinks her life is some sort of
book, as though this writing I'm doing has any reality outside
its own pretense of sensibility? The order, the pattern, the significance is really in the writing, isn't it? Not in the living.
That's one thing that seems for sure, these days, anyway.

So here, at least, I will close the chapter on Saint and talk
about Chicago, and Hastie's near relation, whatever she is.

I walked to Hastie's by way of the back alley and around the
side, the way we drove out of there yesterday. She heard me
clonging up the outside stairs and half-shouted half-sang some
wordless cheery greeting, *HAAAAYoooo!* Inside, I found her in
her usual beautiful liveliness. She was wearing only a man's blue
linen shirt, that fit her little body almost like a dress, and she
was already talking about how she knew a place I could go and
get myself "started off."

"If you really has got to clear away on out of this country,"
she said, "You might ought to go see Myrt."

"Your sister?" I said.

"Yes, like I done told you. Cousin Myrt, she come down
through Camp Ten, all on her own, a year so back. She had her
some money, Lord knows how. Maybe she done seen Sammy,
too." She laughed. "And she's heading north, she says, *where I
don't have to look off another mountain long as I live,* she says.
So off she goes, and I thought never to see or hear from her
again? Well, not too far back, I got me a letter all the way from
Chicago. Waterboy, he read it to me and says she's a'doing fine.
Working and everything and getting on. And she sent an address and a number—she has a dern phone. Says when I gets
tired of flopping round here, I ought to come on up to Chicago.

So there you go, sweet thing. You been hunting a place to head to, here's one a'waiting on you. I reckon Chicago's a far enough piece for anybody to want to go, and Myrt, she'd be happy to start you up once she knows I done sent you. So here you go."

She dove into her suitcase and shuffled around, her tiny body like a child rummaging through a box of play-pretties and humming a tune like she was doing the wash. In a minute, she surfaced, the bulging sack of money in one hand and a folded blue slip of paper in the other.

"We're going to need you to mind the money," she said. "Take it on over with you to Saint's. Wouldn't want to have it here, where Sammy might get too reminded about it. It's a plenty for ten of us, but that ain't no call to be waving it around under his nose, is it?" She held the blue paper out to me. "That's Myrt's place in Chicago, ain't it?"

I unfolded the blue slip and read aloud, "Myrtle Carter, 25 West Heath Street, Chicago 32, Illinois," and a number.

"That's it, that be it," Hastie said, hopping up from the suitcase. "Sail away ladies!" She did a quick little backstep.

She danced a little explosion of sheer pleasure. And I saw Rosie rise up before my eyes. And I know, now, that I've been seeing Rosie shadowing Hastie's every gesture, every bright flare of delight, every childlike enchantment.

"I love you, Hastie." I said.

That stopped her.

I can feel the emotion fill up my eyes again as I write this. Rosie. Hastie. I realize now that until I met Hastie, I've been surrounded by men since Rosie's death. And it was the terrible loss of my life, Rosie's death, greater than my mother's, my father's, my own decision to erase everything—husband, home, everything. The loss of Rosie had cut me loose from any possibility of shaping my emerging self to and with another female self, making a Hazel/Rosie, Rosie/Hazel to sustain us both, against the women that the place, the men, the times would try to make us into. Rosie, the great grief of my life. And yet, I hadn't known it at all, hadn't considered this until today, looking across at my strange, dancing, beautiful Hastie.

Because I couldn't know it when Rosie died, literally stabbed in the back by this mountain place that could never suffer her exuberance to continue into womanhood—because mountain womanhood is not marked out for gladness or delight. And so it found a way to kill her with her own overflowing merriment: Rosie, that day in the barn, laughing and dancing and leaping, out of her own excess of joy, from loft to death, because she believed that the world was a fine and beautiful place. No. When Rosie died I was not woman enough myself to understand. I thought I still had T.R. and George, as though I had only lost one of three equivalent friends. I was too young yet—George and T.R. as well—to see. But, almost as soon as she was gone, I found myself awash in the first swells of womanhood, whence George and T.R. would forevermore be seen only as through a smoky, distorting surface, growing to be men, where we could only try to offer each other some refracted version of adulthood, difference, or longing. There was no Rosie to show me another young girlwoman, to hold out to me my, her, own fearfully curving body, self. And so, sitting here in this dark room—Saint's room, but it breathes only of his absence, today—I see for the first time how much I lost.

But grief is superfluous for a runaway, who has willfully forsaken all. And I can tell Rosie nothing.

But I tell Hastie. "I love you, Hastie," I have said. And it certainly stopped her little clog dance for a moment. She was startled and looked the closest thing to suspicion I've seen in her eyes since our first jumpy confrontation on the flank of Lynco Ridge. But not for long. A flicker.

Because she is as true as she seems. She is. And so she brightened and sat herself down on the bed next to me, hugged me to her and laughed.

"Love you too, sweet thing," she laughed. And a peck on the cheek. Then she stopped, again, and eyed me appraisingly. "Where in hell did you ever come from? I surely don't know." And she laughed again. "Sweet."

"Hastie," I said. "I." And I felt tears coming. "Please." I dropped my face into her burning, moist neck.

"What do you need, sweet?"

"Come with me," I said. "Come with me to Chicago?" The first tears dropped onto her throat.

"What the hell you crying about, sweet thing? Of course I'm coming to Chicago with you. We un's is heading for town, sweet."

"Oh Hastie, things are so hard."

"Of course they are," she said. She began to rock slowly, holding me in her arms. "You know that tune, *Jane's Alley Blues*? You know that one? Now that's a tune we ought to sing to every man we ever done seen."

And she sang it, as if it were a lullaby, this tough gal's song about men and trouble, her arms around me, while I wept for my friend, Rosie.

The times ain't now nothing like they used to be,
No, the times ain't now nothing like they used to be,
And I'm telling y'all the truth, take it from me.

Well I seen better days, but I'm puttin' up with these,
I seen better days, but I'm puttin' up with these,
Have a much better time now, ain't got these men to please.

Because I'm born in the country, he thinks I'm easy to rule,
Because I'm born in the country, he thinks I'm easy to rule,
He wants to hitch me to a wagon, drive me like a mule.

I give you sugar for sugar, let you get salt for salt,
Give you sugar for sugar, let you get salt for salt,
He can't get along with me, well it's his own fault.

I say if you don't want me, why don't you tell me so?
Now if you don't want me, why don't you tell me so?
Because I ain't like a woman got no place to go.
Tell you I ain't like a woman got no place to go.

V.

I am at Saint's, in his bed, trying not to cower beneath the wool blanket, trying to get this down, out of the world and out my sight, onto the page. I'm not certain that I can think, will ever think, think, again. I am seething and raging with voices and battles inside me: You've got to go! Get out! then Wait! Wait! And a third: Rosie Dad Haines Gran'! I don't know, can't tell which to listen to or how to think, think! Think!

I must write it down. I must uncurl my legs and calm my breath and write. I can write it down and it will be on the paper and then I can know what has happened in one voice only and I can sort it out and know what to do. Write.

All right. I left Hastie's late this afternoon and went to the station to find about tickets to Chicago and to send Hastie's letter. I held the money curled into a tight roll and squeezed into my hand, all the way there. I was so afraid I would lose it if I put it into my pocket, or even if I loosened my grip in the slightest. I could feel the straight ache in the backs of my fingers as I grasped the wad that meant *away*. I was enthused about it all, the train and the travel, the glowing city, the three magic syllables, each dropping a little further back into the throat—Chi-ca-go—like a newly discovered nostrum, a rubric, a sacred sum-

286

ming, Chi-ca-go. The weariness, the ache of parting and the struggling with choices, all dissolving into the bright ease of promise.

"The door is opened," I said out loud, and I felt myself relax into enthusiasm. You see? I had done it again. I had seen the ease and the thrill, *like a Christmas gift, that will be there for you to open and take out.* I had let slip the clasp tied around hope and confused it, again, with comfort. *But it isn't. Once again, a crucifixion: forfeit, not gift.* And this time no mere violation, no simple shame. Oh my sweet Lord, I've got to get away, got to go. No. Think. Think. Write.

So I bought two tickets to Chicago. A welter of place names and stops and changes, but Chicago stood out at the end of the list, the ultimate destination, the new beginning. And I hurried out the frosted glass double doors and back into the street. Came here and had a bite with Saint. Then back out. The afternoon had switched off into a close, hot night. A sack of a dog dragged itself into a doorway and dropped into a curl, as I went on by, still caught up by the evanescent dream.

All right. I turned up the hill and started for Hastie's. Coming from the north, I cut back through the side alley and around to the back steps. I wondered vaguely what we would do for the rest of tonight, to make tomorrow come without the restless discomfort of waiting.

And now tomorrow will never come for us.

I heard a slapping of footsteps, running. As I came around the corner, into the alleyway, I saw a flash of pale blue workclothes, the severe line of dark hair, cut close and straight across the back of his neck. His arm was pumping, his hand moving up and down with his steps, but I saw distinctly, as though in a still photo, the dull curve of the tobacco knife. And I knew him instantly.

Yes. I knew him immediately, but I couldn't think, couldn't put it together. I called his name, but too weakly. I stood still in the abject confusion that tries to reject, redirect true meanings.

Was he bringing Hastie some things she'd forgotten? Was he playing a joke? Was he going somewhere to cut tobacco? Oh my Lord.

The fear rushed past these puny denials and overwhelmed every sense but the need to hurry. I was suddenly flung into motion, as though I needed to run fast enough to roll back the day, make it not be now yet, undo the terrible deeds of time and never have left this morning. Run! Maybe it all hadn't happened! Find out that it isn't hot dark night. Everything—everything—is still too early.

I rang up the narrow steps, trying to control a groaning I heard coming from my chest, trying to hold some breath back from this grueling push against time, and save some for the running. The deep yellow bulb on the open landing was swirled with insects, and the doorway was gaping, the wooden door flung wide, with an air of having been torn open, like a flimsy shirt.

As I turned into the little room, my foot hit a drinking glass that was lying in the doorway and it rolled unevenly across the floor, with a hollow, wobbling roar *unhunh, unhunh, unhunh*. It stopped with a metallic *clacque* against the leg of the end table, on which stood a bottle and another glass, clouded on one curve with a foggy brown smear.

In the corner was a pile of clothing and things, covered with the torn, opened suitcase. A little makeup purse slashed open and yawning.

There was nothing else. Hastie lay with her arms outstretched. She was nude. The feather tick beneath her was sodden with her deep blood, thickened and waved like wet paper. Her throat gaped darkly where he had sawed it open.

JOURNAL OF HAZEL TAYLOR
April 3, 1998

I ran to Saint. Ran to him and threw myself into his protecting arms. And what must he have thought? We hadn't seen each other since that night in his bed when I had tossed his hand aside and sent him reeling. And now here was this same beloved woman, cast into his arms, holding on to him, passionate, if only out of horror and grief. It must have seemed—must seem—a terrible, bitter joke on him. There is nothing he couldn't have done to me at that moment. Kissed me or killed me: I would have welcomed anything, anything that would have been *something else.* Not this. *Not this.*

Well, what could I have done? I was alone and terrified. Where else to go but to Saint? Yes. I'm certain that this night added to his pain. And the next morning, the offer refused. Oh my heavens how I must have injured that man.

I was very nearly hysterical, and it took him a good while to shake me down into some kind of calm, at least enough that I could tell him. And I was so frightened. Because *He saw me! He looked straight at me!* So terrified of him that I couldn't speak his name. I was afraid, you see, that even the telling would conjure him up out of the steaming evening. To leave me naked, sprawled and mutilated, floating on a sea of my own deep blood.

So I said *Hastie. Hastie.* Letting her name and my state create the story for Saint to read.

"Something's happened to Hastie," he said.

"Oh my God. Hastie."

"Hastie. Has she been hurt?" he asked.

And I collapsed onto his body, leaning into him, breathing harsh sobs.

He held me back away and looked at me. "Hazel. Tell me. Is Hastie okay?"

I shook my head, sobbing and sweating into his embrace.

"What can I do, Hazel? Tell me what to do."

And this quieted me. And tore the response up out of my broken heart. Not shouted, not screamed. A quiet, exhausted murmur: "She's dead, Saint. She's dead. He killed her."

It took some time for Saint to assemble the patches of the story and to arrange them in some pattern that made sense. Each piece a scrap of some larger fabric, hinting at what was not there to be held and placed: the room, the terrible blood, the roaring wobble of the drinking glass across the floor. And my own terror: *He saw me! He looked right into my eyes! I've got to go! Got to get away!*

And he knew exactly what to do. To hold me just that way and to usher me into his bed. To make me drink more than a swallow of that white liquor that tasted of Hastie. Hastie. To speak sternly when he must, and to soothe when I most needed soothing. As though all of the game of love and desire and caress and rejection had all flown away when I burst through his door, in trouble. And then, some time later, to knock at the door and enter with my journal and pen in his hand. Without a word, handing me my book and turning again to go. How could he have known this? When I didn't know myself? And today I think of Daddy, making me sarcle the garden on the day of Rosie's death. And how, both times, I didn't understand. *How can he suggest that I do something so trivial—routine—in the midst of this terrible grief?* Because I didn't understand that this is the soul of grieving: to move about and sweep, cook—think, write, work—in the chromatic wash of all this pain. To include grief in everything, in the things you do. To incorporate Hastie's absence in the curve of my wrist as I move this pen along the paper, telling it, arranging it, putting it down—*here lies Hastie.*

So I wrote, and I told it. I still couldn't bear to breathe the name, even as a scratching on paper. But I vowed that I would tell, that I would get along, out of here, then I would say it. I felt as though I had to backpedal from a fire that had blazed up and become too hot for me to bear. So I must escape that immediate threat, first. And then I would send back word. I would throw that wretched man's name back into the pit, where they could burn it.

I dreamed of Hastie that night. Terrible joyous dreams of her arriving at Saint's, laughing that it was all a mistake. Or rising up off that dripping bed, saying *Who made this mess, sweet thing? Let's get this cleaned up and get on out of here.* I awoke crying softly, calm.

Saint fetched me coffee and pulled a chair up by the bed. Took my hand in both of his. And asked again.

"Hazel," he said. "Hazel, I can't let you be alone like this. I want to help you…No. Stop. Let me speak. I don't expect anything, any recompense. Nothing. But listen. There are two tickets to Chicago. Let me have one of them. Let me go with you. I can help you. I can…" His eyes were wet.

"Saint," I said. "Dear Saint. Dear Mr. Dunstan." And he knew that, saying this, I had said *no*.

"I only want…"

"I know," I said. "I know. But it isn't going to happen. It can't. I can't. You can't."

"But…"

"The world just isn't made that way," I said. "And I'm so sorry that it isn't. So sorry. Dear Saint." And I drew his hand to my left breast, over my heart, and held him against me. So he could feel my pulsed breathing.

"I have to leave," I said.

JOURNAL OF HAZEL TAYLOR
August 17, 1927

And this all tells me nothing about anything. Only memory, only reflection: the long, drawing of time across the slow patterns of place, and the meanings that accumulate to tell us just nothing. Hastie lies on a flat pallet somewhere just out of sight, as though she is on the page just beneath this one, and when I fill this sheet and turn the page she will be there, on the blank surface, neither time nor place, but only loss. And the worst of it is the certainty that she won't remain beneath. No. I will continually n this page. I will walk out of here with Hastie living and breathing in my body and bubbling forth without my bidding, whenever she decides to turn the corner of my mind. And I can't kill that Hastie. She just won't die, but insists on inhabiting this flesh of mine, for as long as I continue. And this is not solace, but grief—a presence that continually calls forth the absence: Hastie, herself, informing me, whenever she wishes, that Hastie is dead. And she reorganizes and reinvigorates an entire chorus of voices: Mamma and Rosie and Daddy, all singing about loss and being gone forever, and here forever. The horror of death is love. And the horror of love is grief. And loss is the natural order of things.

This is how we know God: in His absence. He is the great void that is always present within the world, our bodies, our selves. His is an absence so powerful that we organize all love, all loss, all grief around our hunger to attend to this unspeakable nothing. In fact, the act of our creation is the genesis of desire itself, that irrepressible ache to reconnect with what is already lost. Who is it that looked for God in a "cloud of unknowing?" That is the secret. You will feel Him most deeply when you realize that He isn't there. And we are all made in this image.

And this is why we long for each other so hard. We are commanded to love God with all our heart, and we do with a pulsing pain directed at nothing. And then He says, *Love thy neighbor as thyself.* Yes. Two negations desperately seeking contact with each other. And so I need so much to touch you, to confirm something that I know not to be true: your presence. And to feel you touch me. Oh, please.

The only medium of love, contact, is loss. All we have to give.

And so, George. George: I would make the attempt to say something, explain something that would assuage your grief. Because I know you, and I know that you're grieving, still grieving. And grief is so hard. And grief is such pain.

But grief is all there is, isn't it? Grief is the surest and truest expression of love, isn't it? When my Mamma died, my Daddy told me that all love was sadness, and I didn't know what he meant by that. But I do know, now. All love is the anticipation of leaving, the leaving itself, and the grief after. In our secret hearts, we long for grief, because we long for a person we can love deeply enough to grieve, a person whose loss will cause us inexpressible grief. And whose loss we will feel all along, with every caress. That is the secret of desire. The passion to touch one more time. To say goodbye.

And we long for someone who will say to us, "I will grieve for you." Because we all wish for a tragic death. To be an important loss. And all it takes is one fierce lover to guarantee that tragedy, that elevation. Because if I know you will grieve for me, then I know that my life has been tragically ennobled and your love has spared me the horror of dying unmourned.

Perhaps this is where I betray you, finally. Because I think I always depended on that knowledge to give me the strength to leave. Oh the sordid irony of this: that I used your love as a springboard for leaving you. And left you without the seal of my grief, my side of the covenant. I tried to leave you with that look in my eyes, that look that said, *If only I could leave you; but you will be with me forever.* And I tried to give you my promise then. But I know I didn't. Not really.

And so here lies Hastie. Here, within me. Not the clay on the pallet, but the living significance that is Hastie. Because the world would see a sad, pointless life, followed by a pathetic attempt to become something else. But I cup a tragic loss within my body, like we cup the upsurge of fire from a match. And I agree to let it burn me. And that is love.

VI.

JOURNAL OF HAZEL TAYLOR
August 17, 1927

I am riding the train, my first train ride, and it has come at the wrong time. I'm beginning to learn that the key to everything might lie in timing. If we could only discover a way to bend or warp time to suit our needs, so that we could arrange a distinctive place for each experience, then we might have reasonable, understandable lives. But it never works that way. Here is my first train ride, an experience that calls for apprehension, timidity, then wonder and exhilaration, maybe. And there is simply no place for any of it. The time is so filled up with Hastie, and my own flight, and Saint Dunstan's forlorn hope and such a terrible evening and day of outrage and surprise, grief and fear, that I no longer know what it is I am feeling. And the train has become only a conveyance for rushing all of this through a blur of cut-and-brush, warehouses, and the backsteps of dingy, yellow-lit boarding houses. Nothing experienced, because snatched up and away before you can even see, recognize, what it is. The recognition, the naming *that was a boarding house* coming along only after the thing itself has fled violently into the darkness, so that the perception and the consciousness are forever displacing each other, forever out of time, themselves. And then a spell of several minutes, or an hour, when *Hastie, Hastie, Hastie* is the inarticulate exclamation that takes the place of the flash of yellow light awaiting a meaning and the realization that she, too, has been snatched away into the flowing darkness that is running you all through the deep turns of these mountains too fast for thought or knowing or even time for guessing, wondering. Just a flash of something and then a sad, slow series of recollections: *that was Hastie*, no more instructive than *that was a boarding house.*

So I am rocking through a bizarre picture show on a darkening mountain night, unable even to distinguish the visual flicker of forlorn buildings and scrabbled sheds from the emotional flares of regret and rage. All of them don't even exist except as snatched glimpses of memory, always absence, always gone, and never presence, never here.

So, too, I will again write my way out of this welter. I will arrange all of this into a single line of words, where, perforce, one thing must follow another, and each will have at least a place of its own on this surface, this paper. And I will find some sort of way, even if the way is only a trace—not a trace like a remnant, but a trace like a cutting, a swath, itself an absence. Like the Natchez Trace, that we know because it is nothing, a perforation in the surrounding jungle, an eradication rather than a feature. Our writing becomes linear by leaving out, selecting, excising, so that it becomes a line and not a plane.

And so, first, I can begin to chop a pathway that leads away from Hastie. It will not be forgetting her, a cessation of grief or ardor. I wouldn't want that. I would reject any intimation that either love or loss can be set aside, even for a breath. No. But she remains, now, in the surrounding jungle through which this particular pathway opens its way, curving around hollows and up switchbacks from one point to another on this particular way. She is there, defining the trail the same way all the laurel and rhododendron and sassafras do: by their sudden dearth where the trail has scythed itself.

And perhaps this helps to explain us all. Each of us as a

clearing, a negation of the surrounding woods and briars and streams, a trace, chopped out of all the possibilities of self, embodiment, character, being. Where we know our surroundings because they are not us, because we are the vacancy cleared in the midst of this jumble, this riot of presence.

I had always puzzled over the meaning of God's knelling pronouncement to Catherine of Sienna—that thunderous assertion that altered her forever: *I am the one who is; you are the one who is not.* Now I think I understand.

And so this track of writing will lead from point to point toward the story of Saint Dunstan. Only a small part of the way, but a new vista along one bend of the trail. Saint Dunstan and that first night: was it only two days ago? That night, that diffident attempt at embrace that we perhaps both had seen coming and that had been guaranteed some discomfited form of emergence by our sheer wariness and circumvention. And so the moment, that night, when it had waited so long for expression that its ultimate coming was too exigent to be denied, but denied so long that the moment of opportunity was too sudden, too hurried, to afford grace or dignity. How to say this? I'm grasping at words as they slip by *do I mean 'exigent,' really?* just as he must have arrived at the moment itself with nothing to hold on to but a thin, slick handle lodged between impulse and denial. *Do I extend or inhibit? Is this a new moment in which all the self-possession of years past will tumble into action? Or will this be only another fleeting impulse, to be buried away among all the other urges, arousals, compulsions that will serve to measure out my life in a string of redundant repressions?*

And did he act nobly, thinking *she is alone, she needs comfort and warmth?* Or was this naked opportunism, realizing *she is distracted and vulnerable, she can be overcome?* I will never know. Perhaps he will never know.

And today. I arose this morning to an empty house, a new suitcase set out open on the table, with, beside it, an envelope, carefully inscribed *Hazel / Saint.* And I used the toilet, washed and dressed—all the mundane little things we do throughout dull, seamless days or the imperatives of crisis and alarm— normalcy or warfare, business or death—packed what little I have of things, delayed as long as possible, awaiting his return. And that was all. He held himself away as the time ticked down to the last possible moment, the inexorable steam engine rounding the last bend, when I would have to hurry to the station to make this departure I had planned so deliberately for so long.

So, yesterday, he asserted himself one time more, asked me to allow him to accompany me, and was repulsed—and this time I did so as tenderly, coaxingly, as I could, like I was moving a child away from an attractive danger, not to scold or chastise, only, gently, to avert the burn or the sting, *no no no, you don't want that*. And with that, he removed himself. And I will not see him again. Ever.

ANDREW KAYER

"Lovers? Oh yes, I've had lovers. I've had quite a life, Andrew. I've known, loved many people, many places. I've worked and I've shirked, lusted and cooled."

"You don't strike me as the lustful sort," I said. "Desire, yes. But..."

"Yes. Lusted," she said. "You're disappointed because you want me to be the Hazel Taylor who is focused in that one moment, my left hand reaching up and grasping the bedclothes, turning them back. Swinging my bare thighs over the side of that shuck mattress, the touch of naked feet to cold, chalky, bleached floorboard. You want the tense and expectant Hazel who took that step and disappeared, and you want all the rest, all of it, to be the extrapolation of that one moment in the dark of a deep mountain cabin, smelling of cedar and love."

"How do you know..."

"But that Hazel is only a character in a story. Or, at best, two stories. Because a story exists according to what it doesn't tell. All of the doings and beings of this Hazel Tighrow Taylor that surround the story, enclose it, become the medium through which this particular story cuts its particular swath. And this is only one scything cut out of all this field that is "Hazel." Or perhaps two: the one swath, swept open seventy or more years ago. And then another, starting at the other end of the field, not even remembering that the first one is even there. But cutting out a new, clear line of air in the surrounding wheat, harvesting the relatively miniscule amount of grain necessary to this story, following itself into the depths of this field, where, lo and behold, it transects the older single swath. And, in crossing it, stops for a moment, feeling the muscles in the shoulders slacken and draw up against the still weight of the scythe, a tool that only has palpable weight when it is not being raised and swung, raised and swung, but hangs, heavy and idle. And, stopped, you gaze along the trace of that earlier cut. And you wonder: *Why did I do that? Did I cut where I needed? What yield could I have expected out of that narrow stretch? Did I receive even that?* And so, in asking, you tell another version of the earlier story, not only in order to revisit that old swath, but in order to try and see why and where the new one is going."

"But no," I said, feeling something like despair, disappointment, the student catching the beloved teacher in a gross misstatement. "You're wrong. You've said so yourself. God knows you've said it enough times. Not one swath…"

"Two."

"Okay, two. But listen: not two, either. Because you've said it a thousand times: *you'uns.* George's cut, and Saint's, and your father's, mother's, even Noah Kersin's."

"Hastie's," she said.

"What?" I said.

"Never mind," she said. And reached that shaky, thin, age-blasted hand across the table to close over the mottled-blue fountain pen.

"Not two swaths, ever," I insisted. "Ten. And ten times ten every time one of yours crossed one of theirs. Or one of your versions of them, or them of you, you've said this a thousand times, Hazel. God knows…"

"A thousand swaths. Yes," she said. "But…"

"But what?"

"Different fields," she said. "Different crop."

August 13, 1927

My Dearest Hazel:

You will be reading this as you undertake your voyage away from everything you've ever known. And that means you will be going away from me, as well. I had always imagined you out in the world, on your own. But I realize, now, that I'd always thought, somehow, that I could be there with you. Or at least that I would be watching you. Now I see that only your independence is true and I am left behind like everything else.

Please indulge me in this bit of self-pity. It is very hard to be old and to love young. I hope you never find how hard. But you need to realize that you have left us, and that everyone you have left will grow old loving the young Hazel, because the young Hazel will be all we know of you. And so we all will suffer this anguish of watching our own years separate us from this terribly young and lovely person that you remain. It is as though you have not actually left us. Instead, we are on a boat pulling inexorably away from a shore where you stand, unmoving. My only solace will be that I will die sooner than most of your compeers and loved ones, and will suffer from gazing at your youth and beauty for a relatively shorter time.

However, I came not to bury myself, but to praise you. And I see that our entire history has consisted of a series of attempts on my part to draw the boat back onto the shore, by sheer willing, if nothing else. But the current is too strong and the attempt too feeble. Onward I go, away from you. You, whom I have come upon in my middle age, like a fever out of some unknown tropical place, invading me, infusing me with your fluid grace. And so, like an infected man, I could no longer imagine a reality unmediated by this burning thirst. I breathed, smelled, tasted this fever in all I did. I took you to bed with me each night—no, not that way, not exactly. But each night, I have turned in my bed to embrace your absence. You are everything to me.

Is it some bitter joke that the fates have played on us, separating us by this breadth of years? Or is the butt of the joke only me? Were we the same age, would you then ever love me? Would I even love you? Oh yes. That is certain, certain. But whether you and I might have become a life, had our chronologies matched more acceptably—this is the kind of foolish question I conjure up in order to rub salt more deeply into these wounds.

And so I am jealous of your life, jealous of my own desire for your happiness. Because, of course, that happiness will depend upon your having found more suitable lovers and a more suitable life.

Oh, this is terrible, this wretched sniveling. I hadn't intended this sort of letter at all. I hadn't intended any such fumbling commonplaces, such dreary words and dull endearments. It has all been such a failure.

And so I suppose this letter is a plea for a reordering of memory. This recent night has put a seal upon our relations through which all your memories of me will be forever filtered. This is the problem with memory: say we can return, in memory, to a childhood time. Say we can relive that distant time completely. Still, we can't expunge the memory of the times that will subsequently come. I can remember hunting with my father in such detail that I can smell the tangy air, feel the slickness of wool mittens on the cold hard gun barrel. But I can never remember these moments without remembering, as well, the later truth that my father has died. And it is impossible for memory to take me back and make me into the child who doesn't know his father is dying.

And so now you will remember distinctly the afternoons up on White Oak Flats, but you will never escape remembering them as they relate to that night. The man climbing into your bed to try and touch, hold you. You will never again remember me as a man you might, in fact, have already loved, even if unconsciously. And that I have forced this single focal point upon all the years of remembering, this is what I cannot bear to live with.

You see, I do love you.

There is some consolation in the midst of this whining. Since my love never had a chance from the start, I have stolen one shameful consolation: my hands now contain a fleeting memory of your body. Disinclined, resentful, affronted though you were, you nevertheless were unable to avoid giving away that one unwilling touch. And so, if my rashness led to failure, it only led to a failure that we both already knew to be preordained. So I lost nothing. And I gained at least this momentary curve and weight of your own real, breathing flesh.

Believe me, I know how dishonorable this all is. It doesn't matter. All love is dishonorable.

Forever,

Saint

VII.

JOURNAL OF HAZEL TAYLOR
March 15, 1998

Oh yes: being loved without wishing that love is a terrible thing. Saint's declaration, completely unasked for, unnecessary to the Hazel-and-Saint we had been, even had become, the expression *love* a complicating corruption of a *friendship* so much more precious. Why did he have to test the bounds of the friendship by inserting the terrible shoddiness of *love*? What an imposition on us both, on all four of us: the Saint-Hazel in each of us. The imposition of unwanted intimacy dragging an obligation out of you that you have no wish to own.

And what of God? Is this the problem we all seem to have with God? Is God's love another version of a demand we don't, won't acknowledge, a vast, eternal version of my dismay at hearing Saint's *I love you*? God, hovering around and over us, continually bothering us with His declarations, assertions of love? When it would be so much easier if the world, life, were just a *friendly*, a pleasant place? Not this hard, aching, grieving struggle to reach through, open out, touch and show the nakednesses we would be happier retaining within ourselves?

Perhaps this is why so many people, today, turn God Himself into a congenial personality, an advisor or a consultant. Certainly not a fierce, passionate, suffering lover. Not the God of

302

the medieval mystics—Julian and Catherine and Hildegard—whose recognition of the demands of a love so abiding drove them to starvation, the self-infliction of real wounds, literal madness. Catherine of Siena, seeking out the most terribly afflicted human beings of her time—lepers and plague victims—and discovering herself licking their bursting sores, their suppurating buboes, in the ecstasy of a disgust so transcendent that it could only have come from the recognition of this love she had neither wanted nor even imagined.

Is this why we can understand God only as a parent, *God the Father*? Because, perhaps. only parents can impose such unquestioning, abiding love, a love given always and forever without the consent of the loved-one. And it is certainly parents who discover the unimaginable sorrows of a loving that is so fervent, so unwanted. And I believe that is why all children discover themselves flailing and striking out against the terrible burden of this love, resenting the terrible demands of *being loved*. It is so hard to have someone around insisting that you are so precious, so significant, such a gift as you. No wonder I recoil at the love of this Dunstan, this Saint. What a burdensome paradise! And hell? A longed-for fantasy land, where God will leave us alone to our own sordid, filthy selves, the way we know we really are. Oh the vertiginous joy of escaping from the demands of this love, to be rejected and thrust out into such a gloriously *selfish* place.

George's family were "no-hellers," members of that small sect that rejected the prevailing obsession with a flaming perdition prepared by God for unregenerate sinners. Around the Creek, the no-hellers were treated with a sort of tolerant condescension, as though they were people too childish or fragile to deal with the full face of reality. Nice, good folks that couldn't bring themselves to see the burning pit in store for most of their neighbors and kin. In truth, I think they saw horror aplenty and saw that hell was a thing invented by people themselves, for their own satisfaction, an ultimate escape from the eternal demands of love.

They saw that, in fact, a loving God had no need of a hell. Or if there is anything like hell, it resides in the act of loving, itself. Nothing burns so deeply or so eternally. And God, who loves without cease, suffers the pains of the damned without cease, like the parent of a brutal murderer, forced to watch that child with eyes of deep and tender love, as he turns away, readying the flashing knife for another fatal plunge.

This is the most terrible love of all, love incarnate, the love of the parents for the beings they have created, brought into the world to suffer and die. And must watch as the children repay concern with scorn, counsel with carelessness, anxiety with abandon. And, in the end, nothing to do but love as fiercely as possible, knowing that all children are useless, wasted, doomed flesh. Oh, it is not God who forsook Jesus.

And, you know, Saint catechized me in two versions of love-suffering—Tristan and Iseult, Abelard and Heloise—both of which I see now were background to our own stories. At the time, I saw them as romances, sensual fairy tales, suffused with undying passions.

And of course they are that, these sad stories of erotic longing, to be peeled slowly and bitten into deliciously, the sprayed juice running down your chin and neck.

But they could never be this without the bitter pith of rind, the sharp pain when the juice trickles downward into some wounded part. Or the appetite that drives you to rip off the skin, the terrible tearing sound your own teeth make as they slit open the flesh of the bared fruit. Love, death, loss, joy, suffering, cries of ecstatic pain, painful explosion and release, cries of grief, the desperate pulsing, the pitiful press of one empty mouth upon another.

Saint told the stories with deliberation and care. Under the tree on the Flats, one spring day. One of those bright days of vernal sunshine that are too cool and breezy for lolling on a mountain. But there we were. He had given me the books on his last visit, saying something lighthearted about *romantic appeal.* And it was so clear that he wanted to talk about these books, that windy day under the budding tree. And so I should have listened more closely. But I didn't let him lead me through these tales; I had read them and they were mine. I rejected his direction, perhaps for the first time. And, in doing so, I proved his thesis. Because I didn't know, then, that he was talking about himself.

"The entire story of the philtre is an explanation for love itself, isn't it? These two young people, both sworn and obligated to King Mark, and, purely by chance, they drink of the potion intended not for Tristan and Iseult, but for Mark and Iseult. And they fall into suffering and passion. This is what love is: it's something that happens to you. You suddenly discover that this other person is everything, that you are willing to break any laws of morality, honor, even self-esteem, for this love that you neither wanted nor deserved. *We have imbibed of the philtre. We are in love. We suffer.*

"And what if only one had swallowed that potion? What if Tristan had opened eyes to a world in which only Iseult mattered? Iseult, awaiting her betrothed, looking in anticipation at her coming life as queen of the realm. And here is this smitten knight, imploring her with his love. Does it really make any difference? Don't we all love alone, gazing in rapturous, intoxicated desire at this infinitely desirable other?"

"But no," I said, oddly offended by his words. "We don't, can't love alone. Or we would only be looking at ourselves. And there is a name for that, but it is not *love*. No no. Love is a meeting of selves, I think."

"But Tristan loves and Iseult remains at best ignorant, at worst, contemptuous. What of that? And his only defense is that he is not responsible: *I drank the magic and I suffer.* But the very excuse sounds like a denial. *Then you don't love me, if your own will is not involved.* Oh, but she doesn't see, can't understand, since the potion passed her by. *My will? My very being is suffused in you. Of course, my will. I will love you whether I want to or not. Can't you see?*"

"Besides, Saint, it didn't happen that way, and you can't re-write the allegory to have it suit your theory. They both drank the potion."

"Both of them. And suffered doubly."

"Oh, but they found rapturous pleasure in each other's arms," I said, half mockingly, the way the young do, who can't quite admit to being moved, or aroused.

"Oh yes," he said. "Of course. That was the potion in the first place. And they drank it, drink it, again, each time. And it instills unquenchable thirst for another sip, another droplet on the tongue."

"Then you were wrong, they don't love alone," I said. But he refused me the empty logic of victory.

"Oh, yes they do. This potion creates desire, not satisfaction. Each sip of that liquid fires the blood to want more liquid. And, as I said, that was the potion in the first place."

FIELD NOTES: INTERVIEW—T.R. BLANKENSHIP
May 13, 1998

Course there is a God. Damn silly to even get riled up about it, because there ain't nothing you're going to do to get him out of the way on the one hand and there ain't no way to turn your own damn mistakes onto his plate on the other. So, either way, whether you'uns is running around trying to pin everything on God's wrath or whether you're busy trying to show how there ain't no God, no how, you're pretty much pissing down your own leg, now, ain't you?

Well, I guess I used to worry about such things, my own self, but you get a few real situations happening you recognize who that God is and what he's all about. Because God done spoke to me once.

Because I once went to the preacher, old Zack, for spiritual assistance. Cousin Zacky folks called him, from the time he was too little to unbutton his pants. Now ain't that a hell of a name for a preacher, Cousin Zacky? I believe that'd make your job about fifteen times rougher, trying to sermonize about some damn thing and everybody setting there, saying, *What's Cousin Zacky got on his mind this Sunday?* I don't imagine there are too many folks who would say, *Well it must be the truth if Cousin Zacky done said so.* Ain't no grown man folks calls Cousin Zacky going to have too much say-so amongst the folks, now, is he? Sounds like a damn cowboy fiddler, or what have you.

But I went and saw him, because I had this problem troubling me and I didn't know what in the world I was going to do about it, you know? Because after Hazel took off, George, he didn't mind the place too much, you know. He kindly give up on everything. Just did what he had to do and not a lick more. Now that ain't like George, but that's just the way it took him, Hazel running out like that. So he'd spend about half the day setting on the porch and picking mournful tunes on the five-string. Make you want to jump off a cliff just to hear him. Anyways, with him not keeping no kind of an eye on the place, some of these moonshine boys, Camber mostly, they took to stealing chickens off George every once in awhile.

Now you know damn well they was just doing it for sport, just to be mean like. Go out there and snatch a chicken and run off with him. And they'd sing that song about how them chickens can't hide behind the moon. What's it, "You can't roost too high for me," some damn thing. Just a'making fun at poor George's expense. Stealing his chickens for God's sake.

Now I hated to see that. So I got me all snarled up on it for a couple weeks, wonderin what I ought to do about it. Because, you see, if I told George them boys was stealing his chickens, well, he'd feel even worse than he already felt. Because, as it was, he didn't have the least idea that anyone was stealing chickens nor cows nor grandma's teeth, for all the attention he was paying round the place. So if they was trying to hurt his feelings, well, they wasn't, because you got to know someone's dealing you dirty before you can feel done dirty to, now ain't that right? But if I didn't tell him, well they'd just keep on picking up them chickens and singing that song and what not. Make a fool of him behind his back. Or then I thought I'd go up to old Camber myself and tell him to stop grabbing them yard birds. Or else. Ha. Or else what? Or else I wouldn't let him bust my head open with an axe? Which is just exactly what he'd do if I tried to tell him anything. Or I could go to the law so Camber would just have to shoot me dead and that would put an end to the chickens and everything else, far as I was concerned, anyway. Or Camber, for that matter.

So you can see I had a problem. And my wife—I'd got married by then, rest her sweet soul—she says "Why not go talk to Cousin Zacky about it? You're tossing all night long worrying about what to do, why not go ask the preacher what you ought to do? He's put there to help folks understand what's right and what's wrong. Go see him."

So I did it. I went on over to the church, that's the old regular church down the crick, next day and found Zacky and I told him I didn't want to use no names but some folks was stealing chickens to make some other folks feel like a fool but them other folks didn't know nothing about it and so wasn't feeling foolish yet, and what should I do?

"Ask God," says Cousin Zacky. "Come into the sanctuary and pray to God to tell you which way He's wanting you to go. And brother T.R., he'll tell you what he wants you to do. He may not tell you today nor tomorrow, but you keep coming here and you keep on praying, saying, *Lord, tell this here servant what you was a'wanting me to do*, and you keep on asking that and God will speak to you."

"God will tell me what he wants me to do?" I says.

"Yessir," says the reverend Cousin Zacky. "You pray to God to tell you and he'll out and tell you just what he wants you to do."

Well, so I done it. I went into that church every day for a

week and I prayed just like he told me—*Lord, tell this here servant what you are a'wanting me to do*—and I explained the situation about the chicken stealing, and Camber, and all. And I went every day. Now that ain't just as easy as it sounds. Man working a place, he ain't got all kinds of time to wander over to the church every day, waiting on God to talk to him. And them churches, they get a right funny smell to them, too, you know? Like there ain't enough air, like everybody done breathed all through it last Sunday. But I done kept at it, every day, praying to God and waiting on him to answer me. And I stayed with it for most of a week, when, by God, the Lord did...he done spoke right to me.

I told the preacher, Cousin Zacky, that I had prayed to God and he had answered me direct, just like Zacky said he would. And Couzin Zacky, well he was just tickled pink.

"And the Lord done spoke to you," he says, kindly struck with awe.

"He done spoke to me," I says.

"And he done answered your questions. He done told you what he wants you to do."

"He done told me," I says.

"And what does he say he wants you to do, brother T.R.?" Cousin Zacky says.

"He says he wants me to make up my goddam mind, Cousin Zacky," I says.

JOURNAL OF HAZEL TAYLOR
March 17, 1998

Heloise, another case, entirely, though Saint thought it was about him, too. Abelard, the teacher, who seduced a girl half his age, and it wasn't merely the tired old story, intellect as aphrodisiac. At least not the teacher's brains that attracted, but, this time, the student's. Imagine the aging man, who may never have met anyone to whom he could speak, write, at anything approximating his own level of thinking. Imagine the bitterness, the loneliness, the terrible disgust at his own arrogance, to find himself the intellectual superior of all around him. And into this outrageous solitude steps a young woman, seeking learning. And as she speaks to him, he gradually begins to notice, to pay attention, to wonder, and to thrill at the realization that this voice belongs to a compeer, a mind! A mind! And that mind shapes a body so extraordinarily desirable, because it is hers! And they both drank the potion, because every word of the correspondence confirms love—passionate, insatiable, aching love.

That first consummation was not much more than a rape. And yet, one senses that the woman took charge immediately thereafter, turning him from a conqueror into a lover, shaping him with her hands and her mind.

And then the discovery, the separation, the terrible mutilation. And she does his bidding, driving herself into sexual exile and ravening with unquenched desire for the rest of her life. *I love you more than God and I would gladly go to hell for your sake.* The horror she must have felt as she walked into that cloister, allowed it to swallow her, mind, body, inclination, love.

Abelard, responding to her yet-burning desire, renounces himself, denies his own deepest memories, rejects any notion of the work of their love. *It was sin, and I was only wallowing in appetite.* And this seems to us such a betrayal of the woman.

"But," Saint said, "After all, he was trying to save her soul. He was rejecting himself as a worthy claimant, in the face of God. Delivering her to salvation by denying her solace in the flesh. We may not believe this, but he did, and the belief makes his sacrifice of what *must* have been an ardent love into a heroic act. Not a rejection, but a gift. A recompense."

"But he no longer desires, has no further thirst for the potion," I said. "His restraint is imposed upon him, isn't it? By the mutilation? I mean, isn't it rather a convenient renunciation, to renounce the flesh he no longer even has?" I laughed a little, again with that inordinate shyness of adolescence. This talk is so wonderful, but it is dizzying, as well, and I feel an insistent need to appear nonchalant.

"Besides," I said, "It is she who has buried herself away in a totally inappropriate life—body even, since she must act the virgin—and done so for no other reason than that she believed in this passion. A passion inspired by her own brilliance, not his. And yet she must pay the price of a lifetime's imprisonment within the walls of her own yearning body."

"All right," he said. "All right. Now, tell me. Does this make her a noble martyr to love, or a foolish sexual suicide? Which is it for her: admiration or scorn?"

"She should have taken him away. But there was no world for him, other than the academy. And she could find none for herself. Still, I think she should have left, not buried herself alive."

"So, Heloise the fool? Or the coward? Certainly not to be esteemed, hmmm?"

"I don't know," I said. "I don't know. I only know what she felt when those doors closed behind her. And don't ask me: there is no word for it."

VIII.

Chicago is not to be believed! I feel as though the entire universe has transformed itself. The sky is blue, yes. And I can recognize some of the trees and flowers—although here they grow out of concrete circles and brick beds. Squirrels in the park, although these aren't red. Nothing else is remotely like anything I've ever seen or imagined. Photographs of cities have made them look uniform, solid, and still, but this is nothing of the sort. It is throbbing and thrumming and it smells and sounds a thousand different ways. Chicago.

The train came in, right into the middle of the station. And from that moment on I've been swept and tumbled around like a leaf running on the creek. I was carried through the enormous station and out onto the street before I had time to arrange, or to place, everything—anything—out of the explosion of glimpses among the flashing movement: an enormous, round man, sweating in a curved, velvet hat, a newspaper rolled under his arm, stops suddenly, right in the middle of the streaming crowd, bends his head thoughtfully to flaring cupped palms, and lights a fuming, blueblack cigar. A child of about ten, greasy with soot, sits all alone on the floor, his back against the yellow-tiled wall, a huge snap-front cap pouring over his ears and a cigarette hanging

312

from his mouth, sitting silent and unmoving, a snag in the swirling stream. Such a lonely sight. A huge brass clock with a white moon of a face, illuminated from within, black roman numerals on its face, and the whole thing appears far too large ever to swing its two hands around the circle of a puny half-day.

And somehow I have found my way. I am at Myrtle's apartment on a dripping, narrow street—she says she is neither cousin nor sister to Hastie, but I have found no way to tell her of Hastie's death. I am trying not to tell myself again and again. I am sitting on a creaking, slatted, slant-back chair, quite unlike any chair I've sat on before, and sweating with the heat. This is a heat unlike any I've experienced at home, though Myrtle says I'll get used to it. She blames *humidity*. It feels as though I never left the crowd at the train station.

As crowded as I still feel, I feel intensely alone as well, and I wonder about George, especially, and home. It requires an effort to realize that he is there right now, and when I see him, I see the house, the trail, creek, school, Badie's. So many places in this one man's life. Impossible. And all around me here, at this moment, a press of people, living, loving, fighting, struggling, dying, all at once. So many lives in this one place.

I must make myself think about future, because this is my key, my cure, to throw myself completely into constructing a life worthy of those I have had to leave. George. Hastie.

I have the great wad of Sammy's money—I must write Saint, tomorrow, and send a message to Sammy about Hastie's death, and the killer—and these funds will stake me, as Myrtle says, while I find a place and a job and get used to this strange city. The catalogue houses hire people quite often, Myrtle says— writers and editors! Though I would have to start lower. Or I might talk to the newspapers, although Myrtle says only men are hired to write news, except for what she calls "society items," and I couldn't do these because I have no knowledge of society. Well, she's right, there.

So I'll try the catalogues. What a thought! I do know something about them, and they seem to me to draw a comforting line between this new place and home. It fascinates me to think that this taut thread has always been extended from Chicago into our own home on the Creek, this catalogue that has always been such a part of our lives, taking this incredible journey twice a year from one universe to the other. I would feel right attaching myself to this end of that thread.

JOURNAL OF HAZEL TAYLOR
September 1, 1927

I suppose the desire for revenge is a terrible thing. So I tell myself, *This is not vengeance, it's justice.* But I know that I lie. I want to hurt him. I want him to feel terror and pain. I know this is wrong, but how can it be moved aside, when it suffuses my mind. I awake with a lingering thirst from the night's dreams of cutting, sawing, burning. I want to hear his scream, see the pain wash over his eyes as he looks at me and remembers.

Oh Lord, and then I don't want any of this. I want peace. That's all. Peace for me and peace for my beautiful Hastie. So she can dance again, inside my body. My mind.

And I struggle with these longings. Violence. Peace. And am I using him as effigy, a symbol for all of these men who have injured me, placed me, put me into their lives so thoroughly without any of my consent? Have I become an embittered old woman, already? Have I become the very woman I ran from? The insensitive, burdened drudge who lurches from one day to the next, bearing pains so deep that she has ceased even to feel those? Am I now incapable of love, intimacy? Because I have been turned into the kind of grasping, pushing, murderous wretch I see in each of them? Have they finally conquered this place—this *self*—and begun to reconstruct me as one of them?

I found a bookstore yesterday, downtown. I was walking

through the city with Myrt, after a day spent turning in employment applications. And there was a store: *STATIONERY and BOOKS*. Gold lettered on a flat black sign. Immensely satisfying. And I went inside and I thought, *This is the grail at the end of my quest*, looking at, even smelling, the crisp, new volumes. So many.

And a young man who worked there who wanted to talk with me about these books, the new ones and the "major writers," Thomas Hardy and Theodore Dreiser. He wore spectacles and he had beautiful, curved hands. He was quietly attractive and he liked me. I could see that. And I know that I could walk back there today, and he would want to talk to me again. To pick up books together, and run our hands along the smooth, cool covers, feel the suspended weight on our palms. I know that.

And I feel soiled, tainted. As though I would damage him utterly were I to bring him into my life, force upon him a Hazel that he must forever have, working away inside him to bring us both to some terrible destruction. How could I ever have imagined that I could arrange a meeting at White Oak Flats with Noah Kersin? What ever led me to believe that this would be a means of *escape*? And it's not even tragic: it's foolish. Not even the consolation of knowing that there is some knelling significance in that night on the Flats. Only a clown's game, a sleight-of-hand, and Noah disappears, leaving the fool alone in the arena. His death a stupid accident, a slip on the peel.

But what greater tragedy than to discover that you are a fool?

And then, in the midst of all this, I see another face rise up before me, the blue work clothes, the wet tobacco knife. And I must resolve this. I will never move beyond this without putting his name to paper and condemning him. His is the lurking figure that walks beside the lurching woman. He is the haint who needs to be buried. His the name that must be re-painted on the wall, for himself to see: accused, known.

The slayer of my beautiful Hastie.

And so today, I will stop this writing and I will pen a note to Sammy, who, I imagine, can stand this one further imposition on his grief and loss. And I will point to the murderer and I will say *Him.* And Sammy will kill him. I know that. I've looked into Sammy's eyes and I know he will do this for me. For Hastie. And maybe then we can all rest.

FIELD NOTES: INTERVIEW—SHELTON BLANKENSHIP
May 12, 1998

You'd say on the whole that these are quiet parts around here, just folks farming and trying to get by. Most folks is too busy to get into much trouble I reckon, and mountain folks don't go around looking for trouble, believe me. *Just leave me alone to do as I always done,* most of them would say. But then a man like you comes on down and he's always looking for something happened back here sometime, like you're looking for folks that got lost. And we get to telling these stories and you'd think there was ten murders round every switchback, now, wouldn't you? I reckon that's one reason folks think we run around with knives and shotguns fixing to make the first feller we see pull his pants down and squeal pig. Ain't no truth about it even in the least ways, but folks will get to believing such things and they'll get to be scared of you, you know? Ain't that funny?

No, most folks ain't got no more excitement up here than getting up to see if the pig done littered. That's about the shape of it. And these are good folks, all back into these hollows, what's left of them. Hell, someone was to get lost in here, I reckon just everybody'd turn out to try and help. That's the truth.

There was a stir up when Odge got found killed there in Asheville. That weren't too long after Hazel left, sometime around then, anyways. That same year I reckon. Never was any doubt in my mind who killed him, it was that feller who mashed his tooth-pick into the banana pie Odge was eating that day. The law said it was a gangster feller from Knoxville name Tony Serlin. And everybody around here said he was working for Sammy Baker, ran a big bootlegging operation all over this here country. But didn't anybody ever get caught.

And ain't no doubt in my mind that Odge Shelton got con-fused with his brother, Camber. That's the worst goddam thing, you know? Got himself killed for nothing he ever done himself except to get born looking just like his brother. As alike as two sides of a knife blade. So when Sammy Baker sent that Tony Serlin feller out looking for Camber, well he got hold of Odge and thought he done caught the right one. Killed him. Killed him ugly: slit his throat and left him there in an alley, under one of them old covered stairways. Now old Odge didn't deserve any such an end.

But Sammy, he had something on Camber, something Camber had done to him. Nobody knew what it was. Camber, he'd got to messing round over there toward Camp Ten. Got so he was up that mountain most ever week. I don't know but what he got mixed up in that moonshining and bootlegging operation of Sammy's or what. There was plenty of it going on over there back around that time, and it seems like everybody knew about Sammy Baker. Or got to know of him, by and by. After he be-came the big shot around here, ran everything in Asheville or Johnson City. Well, he started as a bootlegger, running that white liquor out from Camp Ten. And I hear he pulled down a powerful lot of money. And he weren't the kind to put up with no nonsense from some overgrown farm boy like Camber Shelton. And Cam-ber was just the kind to get his nose stuck up into Sammy Baker's business, going over there and horsing-around, getting in fights, screwing them moonshine gals. Had him a gal for awhile that he'd meet up on the mountain middle of the night, like two damn bobcats. Said she was sneaking up from Camp Ten. Who knows? Well, he done something to get his brother killed.

Later, he got caught with a load of moonshine in his truck and got sent up to federal prison in Kentucky. Well you hate to see a feller get snatched up just for running a little white liquor, but if anyone ever deserved it, I reckon it was Camber Shelton.

But old Odge, he was always back home on the farm, before he got killed, doing the work for both of them and just as steady and square as Camber was crooked and wild. And then not only had he done all his brother's work, but he died his brother's death for him, in a city he didn't never even like to be and was there for no important reason at all, just bringing in a load of tanbark, as far as we ever could see.

And Camber, why you'd think he'd get mad about his brother's death, go looking to set things straight with this Serlin, or at least swagger around here some and say he was going to fix that feller. That was Camber's way. But he didn't do any of that sort of thing. Just kept to himself and stayed home for the better part of a year. Ain't that odd the way folks will do just like you expect them to do when you ain't really thinking about it, ain't really watching them? But let them get involved in a thing and you think you know just how they'll act, because you've known them all your life. And you look up and they're going off the other direction. Ain't that just the damn way of it?

JOURNAL OF HAZEL TAYLOR
April 5, 1998

So I found work at the catalogue houses, work out of which I built a life and career. I began in an office they called "catalog audit" (they always insisted you spell it like that: c-a-t-a-l-o-g), where I sat in an enormous bank of desks, all aligned by a long strip of tape on the floor, and checked the words of the catalogue against the rules of style and accuracy set by the company. But gradually I became a copywriter, and I learned my picas and points and layout and paste-up. Because we did far more than write the page: we set it up and planned it—doping the page—they called it. We typed multiple carbon copies of our writing and we cut up proofs and pasted copy blocks in place with rubber cement. And we traced headlines, and pasted the shiny graphite tracing to the doped page to show what it all would look like, because back then you had to order display type special. And over the years I worked with hot leaded type and then phototype and the first of the compugraphic typesetters. And all the while, I felt a distinct link between the catalogue and home. I felt the tug on that thin line I'd imagined my first day in town, when I first heard of work at the catalogues.

Early in our marriage we had piled together a blanket full of coins surrounding an open catalogue and had ordered a smoker for hunting beehives. And when the package came, we opened it as if it was a gift from some ethereal being, and I said to George, "Imagine. This piece of merchandise has traveled from somewhere so far away that we can't even imagine the place, let alone the journey." And I told him about the Great Lakes, Lake Michigan, the size of an entire state. "I can't even begin to think what that must look like, can you?" I said.

And George said something that will always stay with me. He said, "It's a mite like Gray Eagle."

"What are you talking about?" I laughed, and leaned into his chest. We were sitting on the floor, on our knees, with the cardboard and packing strewn around us, smelling of far away. Here. Chicago.

"Gray Eagle. You know? When I play that tune it feels like it has done come to me over a long, long way, you know? Because it goes so far back. Because folk is been a'playing it for so long, from grandpaw to paw to sonny and on beyond. And if a time came when nobody had done learned it, why it'd just be gone. Just disappeared. And I think about that whenever I play that tune. It's gone such a long ways. Don't know why it's Gray Eagle makes me think that way. They all of them's come from so far back. But there's something in that tune makes you notice how it's carried with it all the playings that was ever made of that tune, you know? Change one of them playings, way back, and you'll change the way that tune gets played whenever it winds up here, now. You see?"

And I laughed and poked him and we rolled around in the packing and cardboard for a long while. So that the first time we used that smoker—we went out behind the house with T.R.—we got to laughing about how we'd unwrapped it. It gave us a thrill to have that little joke in front of T.R. And for awhile we'd talk about love-making as *unwrapping a smoker*. But what I remember most is what George had said about that tune.

The first time I saw Lake Michigan, I believe I felt the worst homesickness I have ever had, standing in front of this immensity of water that I'd never seen before, that bore no relation to anything anyone had ever seen, or even imagined, back home. But all I could think of was showing it to George, and I began to think of Gray Eagle and the deep years of mountain time built into that tune, and I watched the huge, gray water, rocking and foaming alongside this city, and I felt an unimaginable grief.

And for all my years in this city, I would look out across that expanse of gray rolling and pulsing, and I would see George, a small figure in faded overalls and brogans, standing infinitesimal in the vast swellings and hollows of the lake, and I would try to hear that tune. But it would not come. And I would try to let it flow into me, that lovely old tune, the way George would play it, and it just would not come. And it never did.

And I felt there was nothing in the world as empty as my heart.

IX.

ANDREW KAYER

One day I found myself scheming and planning, in a strange reversal of Hazel's story, to run away to Shelton's Trace and the Creek, driven, like her, by some impulse I couldn't quite reconcile. And so, like her, too, I began examining my motivations and desires in what, to be truthful, was a trivial shadow of Hazel's real process. But my feelings were as strong as I had any room for, and they were certainly enough to drive me to behaviors I'd never expected of myself. The first shock came when I realized that I was in love with Hazel Taylor.

I am aware of how ridiculous this sounds. I had just reached thirty and here I was profoundly enamored, captivated, enchanted by a ninety-year-old woman. *Come on, Drew, what's the matter with you? This is laughable. It's positively impossible.* All of which was, of course, true. But the mere fact that I had to think thus was proof that I was struggling with a real issue. How many young men have to insist that they're not in love with someone sixty-plus years older? *Hah. This makes you the opposite of a cradle-robber. What? A grave-robber? Hey, if you pick her up and take her to a hotel, she can get a discount!* But the adolescent attempt at humor didn't work. I thought of her every night as I drifted into sleep; I awoke in a hurry to get to work, where she was awaiting. I saw her name printed everywhere. I even (honestly) began to drink hazelnut coffee. She became the absolute pole of my existence. Hazel Taylor.

There is no explanation for this sort of thing. There also appears to be no defense against it. I knew that falling in love with Hazel was as unrealistic as falling for a movie star. And a stage or two more perverse. Because I loved her passionately. I discovered, to my annoyance, that I desired her, as well.

Not her, of course. Not Hazel, the stooped, dwindling old woman who inhabited that writing chair by the window of the conservatorium. Of course not. But that is not the Hazel I had come to know. She never appeared really to inhabit that body, or that chair, room, city. Never. She was created of and by her own journal, those writings that she passed along my way for no given reason whatever. Those same writings that had gradually brought me around to this point: where the writing and the character—for she had certainly become a character in a narrative—had become the sole reality of any value. I had come to measure everything in my daily life in the terms of the life of this Hazel, a young woman driven by some sort of inner necessity to turn her back on all she had known and loved in order to avoid becoming the woman she would be if she remained. This woman, violated and hurt in her youth, only to be redeemed by the true growing love of a marriage. And then to turn her back on that, too, in order to make herself disappear.

This was the woman I loved. *More ridiculous than even the movie star: you've fallen in love with a character in a book.* Yes. And not just love, but a deep, corporeal longing. A desire to share, somehow, in her passion. Oh yes, I was pretty far gone.

She would appear to me at night, in those tossing melodramatic dreams of flesh and contact that we pretend disappeared with our teens. She rose up, a long-haired, curving willow of grace and fever, driving me to distraction not by her presence, but by her very insubstantiality.

The ninety year old Hazel was my medium of access to this abstraction of a beloved young woman. In a quirky sort of way, talking to Hazel was like talking to the mother—great-grandmother—of my lover, asking for her hand, so to speak. But, also like a parent, Hazel barred the way to my full access, chaperoning every meeting. I began to resent this obstruction. I even determined that Hazel had arranged the journal entries—splicing the observations of the aged Hazel alongside those of my young lover—in order to scrutinize vigilantly the growth of our affair. As a result, I found myself wanting to experience my Hazel without the encumbrance of this dying shell of what once was the woman I loved. Oh yes, far gone, indeed.

So I plotted and planned, looking for a way to run off with my Hazel. At night, in that fervent quarter hour that just precedes sleep, I would concoct schemes. I could steal the journals and keep them all to myself. Or, I cold-bloodedly thought, simply wait for Hazel to die, which she would soon enough, and collect the journals, never telling a soul. Living my life hidden away in a positive orgy of reading and being. I would be a skulking, ravished man, like some character out of a Russian novel, living only for and by my secret ardor.

In the saner daylight, I developed the idea that actually became the event. I resolved that, rather than attempt to bring Hazel to me, I would go to her. I would travel into the mountains to find what I could of the Hazel I desired. Like some driven archaeologist, I would sift through the rubble, looking for evidence of her passage. Or like the religious fanatic, I would undertake a pilgrimage in search of some holy relic or other that would bind me physically to the essential verity of her presence. Could I find people who knew her, witnesses to her young spirit and beauty? What of George Taylor? Was he still living? Could he confirm, attest to, the presence of my beloved, still walking those hills filled with grace?

Yes, it was insanity, but, in the end, it was right. Because it cured me of the world of these ravenous fevers, and yet it did bring Hazel to me as a real person in a real place. And this place was peopled by real individuals who had suffered and borne

Hazel's disappearance as well. Before my trip, the mountains out of which her story had drifted seemed only a dark and hazy backdrop to her person, like the deep woods of Hansel and Gretel, more Black Forest than Blue Ridge. Going there, I saw the place—or what was left of it—and I began to understand all of Hazel's words about *place, taking place, stepping out time in distances.* I saw that she was right about her own memories: that she remembered the details of a place and a way of being that, except in the soft tang of the wrinkled, worn voices, no longer existed. That Hazel herself was the artifact among the ruins, the fragment of a black-figure calyx showing the slaying of Sidero, as she hides in Hera's temple. Or a half-ruined, pitted marble figure of Nerea, the goddess of the fair knees, her young body curved like a shell. Yes, I still loved her. Still do.

So I told Hazel I was taking a vacation, in May—the end of the semester, by my as yet academically-delineated calendar. I could not tell Hazel my plans. She assuredly would object to turning me loose in those mountains with her younger self. At the same time, I determined that I would have to lie to anyone I found on the Creek. It was not for me to upset whatever historical balance had been found concerning Hazel and her disappearance. Her secret must remain safe; I could reveal to no one the living Hazel Taylor. It might, in fact, be that I would meet no one having any recollection of her at all. It was likely that George was dead, certain that Saint Dunstan was. Hastie was gone, Noah Kersin was gone, both, to hear her tell it, by Hazel's hand.

But it wasn't so much people I was looking for. It was place. I was confident that I could find the Creek. From there, Possy's Camp, if it remained, would be easy. White Oak Flats would be up the Creek to its source and a bit beyond. From there, I might be able to find Camp Ten, and come down the mountain to Asheville via Hazel's own route. Making that circle, I could travel with Hazel, and I would try to see through her eyes.

The topographical map for that area had Shelton's Trace

marked on it as a small village at the intersection of the Creek and the larger stream, Laurel Creek. The Creek itself bore the name "Middle Fork," though a search for the left and right forks was in vain. Except for the land along the highway, and either side of Middle Fork, shown in white, the entire area bore the wash of green ink that designated U.S. Forest Service land. The only place name along the Creek, itself, was "Maddy." By reading the contour, I could approximate the site of High and Lower Creek. There was no White Oak Flats on the map, but, again, the contour showed where it must be: a wide ellipse of very slow rise on the south end of the ridge. Nor was there a Camp Ten, though there was a rather straight trail along the contour on the west slope of Lynco Ridge (that name was there, as was the town of Lynco, at the northernmost base of the ridge) that might once have been the logging railroad, and a small cluster of houses shown at the very end of a finger of white that curled up another creek on that side. This could be the remains of Camp Ten.

I was transported even by this cold, green and white representation of the place of Hazel's writing. This meant that there was, in fact, a reality to match the narrative, and this meant a vindication of my mania: if there was a place, and that place remains, then there surely was a Hazel to occupy that place, and she, too, remains. I could run my finger along the Creek, trace the lines she had walked, turning where she had turned, stopping where she had stopped. If I could actually be there, I could breathe the scents she breathed, feel the stones she walked upon. I could reconstitute Hazel Taylor out of pure mountain air.

By way of explanation to any people I encountered, and particularly if I were to find anyone who remembered anything of Hazel, I concocted the pose of folklorist researcher. I would tell it around that I was studying tales of disappearance, missing persons, that sort of thing, in these mountains. This would not only explain my presence, it might generate the very responses I was actually looking for. I could certainly play the role well enough. *Just be yourself, you nerd*, I told myself. I would take along a recorder both to affirm the disguise and to capture anything that might, in fact, be said about Hazel.

So I told Hazel I was going camping in the Smokies. Close enough to the truth to pass the eye test. She didn't question or waver. No problem.

"Watch out for them bears," she joked. "They'll muss with you. They've been up out of the den long enough to know a city boy when they see one. You know, you ought to wait until June and see the laurel when it's out."

"Sorry," I said. "I want the springtime."

"It can still be winter yet up the mountain," she said. "Even in May. Blackberry winter. You dress plenty warm."

"Yes, Mom," I said, pushing the door into the dark.

And that was that. I headed south the next morning, an unseasonably cold day, with a "mackerel sky," Hazel called it, the clouds scaled like the side of a fish, the wind blowing cold with that dry taste of the frigid north.

It's a long drive, down through Indiana and across the Ohio at Louisville, then through the bluegrass country. The road cuts tell you where you are by the color: a deep burnt sienna along the cornfields, a lighter brown or soft waves of turf in the bluegrass country, then gray shale and the first deep purple-black seams of coal appearing, as you rise into the Cumberlands. There, the road cuts are glossy black with coal and the farms disappear. You find yourself driving through industrial slum neighborhoods tucked into the middle of these steep and brooding mountains. There is no trace of farming and no trace of any production not associated with coal. Place and people are tenebrously blasted. Wasteland.

You come out of the coal fields at Pennington gap, and the road cuts gradually turn from black to bright rust-red, the hard, impervious clay of the South. Agriculture returns, in the tiny family farms tucked into the base of the hills, sowing their hopes into the narrow strip of good land along the valley.

Pale concrete and pale asphalt, ringed by garish signs through Kingsport and Johnson City, where you could be anywhere in America, but nowhere else in the world: the utterly homogenized interstate non-scape, bounded by McDonald's and Arby's, BP and Speedway. Then out and up again, and the roadcuts are hard, mauve stone, the oldest rocks in the world, studded with quartz and stained with malachite. Bedrock. Hazel's place.

All that's left of the old mountain ways is what you can see in the eyes of the old people and hear in their soft accents. Perhaps that's all we should ever hope for. Perhaps that's enough.

I spent that first night at a Red Roof Inn in Johnson City, where I lay in the bed sipping beer and watching a soccer game from Argentina. I awoke in the morning groping through the *poiking* of empty cans to find the singing radio alarm. Sitting up, I discovered a fuzzy headache, with a sock on each tooth.

"What's the matter with you?" I said aloud. "Jesus Christ." This was not the spirit with which I had imagined entering Hazel's domain. But here I was, and I would do what I could by way of coffee and orange juice to restore the sober, brooding Byron who had begun this quest. I realized that such a beginning to my journey exposed the shallowness of my will, my desires, and the feelings themselves upon which I had based this trip. But I couldn't much help being shallow, and, besides, emotions seek their own level. So the paltry feelings for me were as intense as the grand ones for her. You see, if, while we were sleeping, everything in the universe doubled in size, we'd never know it. We'd wake to the same impressions, the same measurements, the same truths. What pained us yesterday would hurt equally today. Nothing would change. Who was it, Poincaré, who realized that?

The highway leaves Johnson City and curls widely through Erwin, on the Nolichucky River. At a diner there, where I stopped for more coffee, I engaged in conversation with an elderly tobacco farmer, feeling already a closer connection to Hazel's world in the sharp, narrow eyes that looked at me, and the soft whisper of inflection that spoke to me, the essential sound of the place. He informed me, with a perfectly straight face, that Erwin has the questionable distinction of being the only town in the United States that has arrested, tried, and convicted an elephant for murder. And brought in a railroad crane to commit the subsequent execution. I didn't even begin to believe him until we were standing at the cash register, where he pointed out an ancient newspaper photo. And there it was. An elephant, suspended from the improbably thin gibbet of the crane. I left the diner shaking my head at this grotesquerie, not knowing whether to laugh at this story, cringe at its brutality, or weep for its victims.

As the road wound up into the mountains, a gelatinous fog set in, as thick and liquid as any seashore. It obliterated the view, the road itself, until I felt as though I was driving a mass of gray fabric, bunched and folded and wisped in tatters around me. Isolated within the rounded clear space of the car's interior, I felt as though I were entering a new place, where the old certainties would disappear and leave me floundering, aimless. As compelling and beautiful as they can be, the mountains conjure a deep, visceral unease as well. Their primordial age seems to scorn all measure, to deny any reckoning of time or place. To say that they are phantom-ridden is wild understatement. As the car wound back and forth through this colorless obscurity, I found myself remembering lines from Dickinson about horrors unrolling in my face, and *one need not be a chamber to be haunted.*

The road swung around another bend and descended in a series of sharp switchbacks until, at a relative straightaway, I barely made out a long thin green sign with watery white letters that appeared smudged by the billowing and drifting fog. SHELTON'S TRACE. I had arrived.

Around a slow curve and there was a flashing yellow light, diffused and grainy in the fog, with, to the right, the wash of red and blue neon, like ink drops spreading on wet paper. A gas station-store, no different from the ones I'd passed at every inter-change, all the way down from Chicago. Except here the station was backed up to a dense, rocky slope, and there was nothing else around except what had once been a pay phone secured to a line pole, its wire dangling uselessly down, its headset long gone. Papers and bottles littered the edges of road and parking lot.

Inside, everything was a bit shabbier, a bit more tentative than in its generic peers along the way. Behind the counter, a heavy, middle-aged woman in overalls grasped a can of Dr. Pepper in a determined hand, as if her drink might attempt to run away from her at any moment. She shifted her gaze toward me and said, "Morning."

This was my introduction to Hazel's world, and it turned out to be a fortuitous one. The woman was apparently named "Little Bessie," as that was embroidered on the bulging bib of her over-alls, and she was friendly and loquacious. She offered no sign of the suspicion or resentment I'd feared, and when she found out I was a "researcher," planning to camp up in the National Forest, and looking for folks who could tell me old stories and legends about people disappearing, she brightened up even more.

"They's a heap of folks gets lost up in these hills every year," she said. "You might get to have that experience yourself, if you get too far off the main drag in this here fog. Two years ago, a couple of college kids come up this way and went camping up the crick and got lost. Now how anybody could get lost going up a crick, I don't know. Seems like all you'd have to do is head down the crick to get yourself unlost. But they managed it. Parked their car right here at the store and said they'd be gone two nights. Come back about four days later and Lord if they didn't look like they'd been in a mud wallow every minute of them four days. Nice kids, though. They said they loved it up this way and they was coming back. Never saw them again, though."

"What creek was it they camped on?" I asked. I was beginning to doubt it could be this easy, at the same time that I hoped it was, in fact, Hazel's creek.

"Creek runs out the cove yonder. Comes down from Lynco Ridge. Crosses under the road right yonder, where you was headed."

This was so quick, so easy, I figured that I might just as well keep pushing. Sometimes, I suppose, there really are things that just fall into your lap. By grace, I guess Hazel would say. *The Lord's good grace. Just to remind you what it is you're hoping for.* So I barged on.

"Wasn't there some woman who disappeared out of this area years ago? Without a trace?"

"Well now," Little Bessie said. She crumpled the empty Dr. Pepper can with one hand and tossed it into a huge green trash barrel, all in one motion. On the side of the barrel, stained with running droplets of spilled soda, was a sticker that said, "Tennessee—Home Sweet Home to Me," and, underneath that, "Y'All Keep it Clean." A grinning, bearded, cartoon hillbilly pointed a shotgun out of the sticker directly at me. Next to him stood a jug with XXX scrawled on its side. "Well let's see," Little Bessie said.

"Say back in the twenties, early thirties? It would be well before your time, of course," I said hopefully. "But I wonder if..."

"We ought to ask some of the old folks," she said. I liked hearing that "we." She was in on the expedition, And whatever reason she had to be interested in my pseudo "research," I was glad to have her as a guide. How easy was this going to be?

"Do you know anybody who's lived around here a long, long time? Anybody old enough to...say, ninety or more?"

"No, I reckon not." *Damn!* "Not too many old folks still living up in here. They're all on down the mountain in the rest homes, or into town where their kids can kindly take care of them. You know."

"Well, I wonder..."

"There's T.R. Blankenship, now. He's way on up the crick yet. And I reckon there's George. Even further up, clear into the Government land, almost. George Taylor. Them two."

Bingo.

FIELD NOTES: INTERVIEW—T.R. BLANKENSHIP
May 7, 1998

Oh there's been a few folks got lost and weren't heard of no more. And this fella even now, whatsisname, threw a bomb at them folks or whatever he done, run off from the law and he's hiding around up in there somewhere, right now. So I reckon it's a pretty good place to get disappeared in. But most are just folks who got confused and got lost and died. Likely shock from the cold, you know. They's still campers and tourists get up here ever year and one of them dies of the hyperthermia they call it. Nice warm spring day and he's fixing to have a nice outdoors campout, what have you. Next thing he knows it's colder'n the bottom of a rock, and its dark out and he ain't got nowhere to go and he's in trouble. Makes it worst these here kids that come down here with five hundred dollars worth of tents and bags and these fancy little stoves that you always see them fooling with, trying to fix. Them kids don't know what trouble is. Never seen trouble. And that's a dangerous lack, I'd say.

So they get up in here and something goes wrong, they're like to do just the wrong thing. Or not do nothing when they could. Just panicked or foolish or just not had enough trouble to know how to take care of it when it comes. They was a feller up here a mite back who died right on the trail. Hypothermia. Now he weren't two miles from where we're standing, right here. And he had a friend along with him, and George saw them both, up yonder heading for the trail. Said they was loaded down like pack mules with all this fancy outfits and stoves and all. Next morning that kid was dead.

Well, they went up where they had no business going. And toted all that stuff up there and got wore out and sweaty. And then the rain came and the cold snapped that night. Regular blackberry winter. And they got snarled up they was so tired and couldn't get their ten-thousand-dollar tent set up right and couldn't get dry and crawled into these goose down sleeping bags that ain't worth a handful of lugs if they's wet. And lay there and died. The one kid. The other found him in the morning, just as dead as a corn biscuit.

Now that's an awful thing to think about, young kid like that, just trying to have some fun, go camping on the mountain and next you know he's lying there dead. But the worst of it was when we got up there to fetch him down, we found all that gear lying around like. That poor kid was laying two feet from the fancy stove and he had a goddam canteen full of water strapped right onto his hip. Ain't that a awful thing? Didn't even consider using that stuff for nothing but fixing up some of them freeze-dried filet on the half shell, what have you. Here's a kid freezing to death. Freezing to death, now. And neither one of them even thinks maybe they can fire up that stove and boil up that water, pour it in the canteen, and make a hot water bottle, stuff it down their pants. Hell. Damn shame, but these kids they want to have these adventures, strap a goddam cargo cord round your ankle jump off a bridge. Pay somebody to push you over. Bungee jumpers, some damn thing. Now there's a feller ain't got enough to do, I'll tell you that.

But that's all just playing, because there ain't no trouble in it. Maybe a mite of risk, sure, but no trouble. And there's a right smart of difference between just risk and real trouble, ain't it? And if you ain't never learnt to work your way out of some troubles, you ain't going to be worth a cow eating buckeyes. Them kids hopping off the roof, and thinking that makes them brave, I wouldn't take one of them on a goddam turtle hunt.

Well, now, but you ain't fixing to look up that sort of thing, somebody kindly gets lost or something, are you? You're a looking for something' from right round here, some kind of mystery. Now I'd take a look at Hazel Taylor if it was me. Or maybe Odge, Odge Shelton. Course he didn't exactly disappear so much as he got found. Got found in Asheville with his throat cut, damn near took his head clean off. Of course I ain't too sure how much of a mystery you're going to find in neither one of them. Because I know who killed Odge, and I reckon most folks can figure what done happened to Hazel. You ain't fixing to camp up here, are you?

But Hazel, even so, that's still a strange one. Because don't matter what happened to her so much as what made her go off at all. Getting up out of a married bed where she'd been right happy, working that farm yonder with George, to go up to White Oak Flats, meet some slick-handled no-good...No, I reckon George is right, it just don't make no sense. We decided for a spell that snake had done kidnapped her and drug her up there himself. But that can't be, for George was right there in that bed with her. Any kidnapper would have had to nap George too, ain't that so?

You're out hunting vanishing stories, well that's a right smart of a story. And George, he's up on the crick to this day. He'll tell you all about it. Happened to him. And he's trying to work it all out yet.

George and me, we been pretty good friends all our lives. He and me and Hazie, we was kindly a group when we was little kids. And my sister, Rosie. We was always running around together, playing at this and that, you know. Rosie, she died back in nineteen and eighteen, we was all just little kids then. Jumped out the loft and catched herself on a fork. It was awful enough, I see it to this day. But Rosie, I miss her yet. She was the spark. Seems like there's a time in your life, something happens and you ain't just a bright-eyed kid no more. Well, I reckon that was Rosie for me. Rosie dying. Put an empty spot inside me that never got filled back up. Nothing was quite so pretty after. That's what done happened to George when Hazel left, too. Just emptied out all the pretty from his life.

I don't know, I think maybe Hazel felt that too, losing Rosie. We was about all the friends, playmates, that Hazel had, since she didn't have much family—two brothers and both of them a sight older than her. Hell, most of us had more friends than we ever wanted, what with folks having youngsters like they was pop corn. Hazel, though, she was just all on her own after Rosie died. Her Mamma passed on somewhere in there, about that time, and so there was just her and George and me. All her brothers—well, now, they was only two of them still alive by then—they was all grown, so she didn't even have no family to speak of. Her and her dad. And Hazel, she'd be sort of lonely at a church supper, anyway. She was her own self and that's for sure. Well, Rosie I think was an important friend to Hazel and when she died I reckon Hazel might have got a little more backward than she already was.

But now George and Hazel, they always had something, some closeness that I couldn't never figure into. They'd spend a right smart of time on their own, just a walking around or sitting by the crick watching their toenails grow. So George, he can tell you about Hazel in some ways I couldn't. But I was there for most all of it. Mostly. But old George, he's still living that first morning, I reckon, every time he gets up out of the bed. The poor son of a bitch.

But of course you ain't got a notion what all I'm talking about. But I reckon you want to hear about disappearances, you ought to study Hazel. And you all are going to need to hear the complete story. Well I can do that. But we ought to climb on up and see George. He'll be pleased to find somebody besides himself that gives a damn about Hazel anymore.

ANDREW KAYER

George's place was precisely where it should be: on Upper Creek, on the Timb's Hill side. It was Hazel's place, too, the very house she had walked away from, and it gave me a feeling of walking through the glass case of a museum diorama, inhabiting something that people were only supposed to look at. The house and outbuildings were not in good shape: they appeared not to have been painted in decades, the traces of paint looking like some final oozing of fluid working its way out through a wound, an indication of an ache that hasn't quite been sealed away. The middle front step was loose, and there was no door at all at the home's entrance. Just the gaping door frame.

Inside, though, there were things that could have been—must have been, in fact—Hazel's. A bookcase, obviously homemade, but made with care and skill, out of chestnut wood that could fetch several hundred dollars itself, today. And the case was piled deep with books. *Hazel's*, I realized with a thrill. *Hazel's books, given her by Saint Dustan. I'll bet George built her that case.* I scanned the spines, looking for *Wuthering Heights*. Found it. I was loose in the museum case.

T.R. had become my guide. We had stopped at his place: a pre-fab doublewide on a small bluff above the middle creek, and he had responded to my semi-false interest with enthusiasm. I was to find out that this wasn't the first time for T.R. to lead an inquisitive interloper through the story of Hazel. But he did everything with eagerness and good humor, in spite of his years and an obvious bronchial problem that came awfully close to being emphysema. Still, he led us quickly and tirelessly up the steep trail from the road to George's place. I could almost point directly at bends in the trail where *Hazel must have met Noah here*, or some other conjunction of place and narrative. I felt that I was getting the experience I had set out to get.

The pose of college researcher worked so well that it was almost unnecessary. The two zeroed right in on the Hazel story, one out of a surplus of querulous regret, the other simply because he was a natural storyteller and this was the best disappearance story he knew. It was quite clear to me that nobody had the remotest suspicion that I might have heard anything of Hazel's own self before.

And so T.R. and George clarified my feelings by further complicating them. For, as true as it was that Hazel had been driven from her own home by what in today's jargon would be called "the patriarchy," it was equally true that she had left a victim behind. George had loved Hazel and, whatever the injustice of the social taint she carried through no fault of her own, George, at least, did not exercise that particular prejudice. And no matter how blindly vicious it may be to consider a woman "ruined," who has lost her "virtue," most of Hazel's world believed that such ostracism was the "moral" thing to do. So it was no small thing that George did: the concept of a woman's "virtue" may have been an outrageous fiction, but its consequences, and the moral opprobrium that attached itself to whoever ignored it, were real enough. Perhaps Hazel didn't owe George gratitude for flouting this moral power, but she certainly didn't owe him the degree of suffering and solitude that she dealt him. And he did not deserve to live the life of loneliness and despair that he had assuredly led in order to pay for this masculine world's sins. Or for Hazel's freedom, either. My impression of George from the moment I first saw him was that of a man who has survived some terrible ordeal, who has watched himself through years of experiencing some searing horror, and who is, nevertheless, still surprised, even startled, by that first terrible moment, and by the ongoing rediscovery of the vehemence of his own pain. If there had been a crucifixion in this story, the figure on the cross was George, not Hazel. She had traded a true, generous, intimacy for a selfish "fulfillment" that she had never really found anyway. And he never once blamed her, when perhaps he could have purchased something of relief by redefining her as the villain, the loose woman, some character that would reflect worth onto himself. He never did.

But then, George was, in fact, the agent of that patriarchy that had fixed Hazel inexorably to a future she could not bear. And by marrying her, George had attempted to fasten Hazel forever to this role, to direct her on her predestined pathway: wife, mother of a swarm of children, worn and tired laborer. When she was certainly more than that. And, if he had the power, being the man, wasn't it incumbent upon him to realize the oppression he wielded, even if he intended nothing but good?

Is it forgivable in a man to be so blind to his own wife's discontent? Because it was clear, as I talked to George, that he had no idea of the deep, burning, frustration that walked about Shelton's Trace with Hazel. He simply could not understand what had driven her from their home. In fact, he insisted that she had no sense for adventure whatever, when, in fact, trial and hazard seem so obviously the central modes of Hazel's existence. And can we make Hazel responsible for George's lonely life? If it isn't George's job to pay for the injustice of the world he lived in, why should she pay for the patriarchy either? And her flight was certainly not without personal loss. She felt forced to leave the place she loved, a place to which she belonged and a man she loved, as well, because she could not remain the very person who loved and was loved here.

So perhaps they both have been called upon to pay for our sins. Both victims; both criminals.

Or perhaps this is all the only possible outcome of any combination of people whose lives are bounded by moral laws of any sort. Isn't it the moral constraint that is at fault, here? Isn't there some deep culpability in the framing of these moral codes themselves? Or is it really only morality that holds us back from a submersion into the wild waters of appetite and bestiality? Is there any way to know?

So with George and Hazel. Those who enforced the codes that bound Hazel to a suffocating life did so because they believed in the goodness of that life. They followed a moral code by which men and women were judged according to what we could find out about "how they live their lives." If only we could remove this morality, Hazel and George would be free to care for each other and to live in the ways they wish, together. Isn't that right? With the moral code, they have been violated, sundered, and turned, one on the other, into the agent of the other's pain and terrible regret.

I don't know. Because they are all so warm, so caring, so deserving of at least a little peace. And yet here is George forever asking *why*, forever struggling with the impossibility of conceding that, yes, Hazel walked away from him and went to White Oak Flats. And here is Hazel, a thousand miles away, sitting at a cheap table writing, in a room full of people waiting to die, writing her interminable explanations, justifications, confessions, never to find any more peace on her side than George will find here.

If Dante had saved a space for these mountain people—all of them—he would have placed them in a circle, holding each other's ankles in small, tight, steel-toothed traps. Each of them, like a caught bobcat, gnawing away on its own clenched leg bone.

FIELD NOTES: INTERVIEW—GEORGE TAYLOR May 7, 1998

I reckon there's some reason for you to come all the way down here to go searching for stories about lost folks. I reckon information of that sort is important to somebody. It's got now so you read about everybody's life like it was in a play, or on the television, these folks a'getting up and telling you whatever have you about their own selves. It don't set right, though. You know, there are some folks that can just get you a'talking about yourself, even if you know at that very time that you ain't interested in telling them nothing. And it seems like exactly them folks that can make you feel most ashamed about talking to them, those are the same folks you find yourself telling things you didn't want to tell nobody. You ever notice that?

I'm sorry, mister, I didn't mean no offence by that. I ain't trying to make you feel unwelcome. It ain't that I mind talking about this thing. T.R. knows me about as well as anybody and he'd not have brought you up here if it was something I ain't ready to talk about. Sometimes I want to talk about Hazel all day and night. Then, other times, I'd sooner tear my tongue out of my head. So I don't mean nothing by that. It's some folks can get you talking and you're running beyond your own sense, saying things that you can't really believe you're hearing yourself say. And you get done and you feel like you done uncovered too much. I wonder if folks on them television shows doesn't feel kindly like that. *How in the world did I ever say all that to all them people?* That's all.

I can tell you all I know, and what I figure from what I know. The biggest part, though, that's the part I don't know: why she picked up and walked off in the first place. It'll get you gnawing at yourself until you can't hardly stand it. Gnawing at your mind, your memory, trying to find something, some reason for what happened. And the harder you look the more you don't know and so it's like you're back inside this here cave and you got to find out what's at the end, the deepest part, because you got to get home and tell your folks what you found. But the further down into that cave you go, the longer out below you the passageway opens and the further you are getting from being able to go home and tell nobody nothing. Make you feel sick and crazy with sorrow and wondering.

Like that phantom pain they talk about with folks that's lost a leg can still feel their toes a cramping up something terrible and ain't nothing they can do because them toes is gone. Only the feeling of them is left behind and it won't leave, no matter what. That's it, you know. Hazel done gone seventy year ago but that phantom pain in my heart, where she used to be and it still feels like she's there and there's nothing to do about that kind of pain.

So what is it you want to know? Hazel was my wife, Hazel Taylor. She was born a Tighrow, down the crick. And I knew her for my whole life. And we was married in June of nineteen and twenty four. And lived fine, raising a good crop and making a home and talking now and again about having children. And then, one night three years later she got up out of the bed and walked off. And that's what there is to it.

And there was quite a stir about it for awhile. Folks worried and trying to help out, you know. But then, two years later, they found her bones and her shawl up on the edge of White Oak Flats and that finished it for everybody. She just became a saying around here, but nobody remembered much of anything about her, and nowadays it's just as if she weren't never here. Except down here in this heart, where I'm still paining and wondering every single day. So I reckon I could tell you what you want to know because she ain't never left, not down in here, inside. Poor Hazel. I loved her so.

And so if you want to hear about Hazel, well, I'll tell you what I can. I don't know if that's going to be the sort of thing you're after or not, but it's worth it to me to hear myself say her name.

X.

ANDREW KAYER

This won't be any too easy. Just drive back into Chicago and take up as though nothing had happened? Not a chance. You found George. Her husband. George. You can't just let that little detail go, just leave Hazel at sea about all these connections. So now you've got to tell her you went. And what you found.

These are the dues you hadn't counted on when you took it into your mind to go down there—in disguise, for chrissake—in the first place. Because you've got to tell her, now. Now that you've found out these things she needs to know, deserves to know. Because you compromised everything. you surrendered anything you might have had of dignity, honor even, when you ran down there like a horny schoolboy to find your lost love and found...we'll, and found the husband. And admit it, up until then, you hadn't even believed in his existence. A character in a story made up by an old woman who didn't exist, either, to explain the one person who really existed: the blooming, brilliant young woman, the lover for whom you made this unlikeliest of trips in the first place.

"She's going to kill me," I said, aloud. Appropriately enough, because I felt like a child who'd been caught in some ultimate felony. One of those illicit enterprises of childhood, doomed from the start to be discovered, and carrying with the discovery an unthinkable degree of punishment. *I'm in more trouble than I've ever imagined there could be.* The crime—surreptitiously opening the presents when the folks are out, or the snatched cigarette on the schoolground—laughably trivial in this world of mayhem and hard-edged advantage-mongering, but hiding by its very paltriness the gross overstatement of outrage that will accompany discovery, or the extent of sheer worry, guilt, shame that you are about to suffer. Perhaps that was Hazel's trouble. She never had those trials, rehearsals, by which to measure the possible extent of complications we will endure for involvement in the most trivial of transgressions. Hazel went straight from innocence to assault, rape, grand theft, murder. She is a true fugitive, and she's still blinking away the tears of shock and surprise at the pain necessary to the daily coexistence with violence and death. But I, I was only a naughty little boy, caught by the husband as I rummaged through the young wife's things.

"She's going to kill me," I said, again. And I actually began the exercises in avoidance—the *maybe it didn't happen* that is the sure mark of immaturity and irresponsibility.

But, of course, I would tell her. And, in imagining the telling, I, in fact, began the process of shifting the material responsibility back onto her shoulders. *Well, what the hell? It wouldn't be news if she hadn't left him, walked out on him, in the first place. I didn't make this mess; I'm just making an unselfish attempt to pick up some of the pieces she left behind. What did she expect would be there? Nothing? That she could run away from that place and by so doing could erase the place itself? Place and people? She said so enough times herself to at least begin to believe her own weird philosophy of multiple selves. That there isn't one Hazel within her own control, and so she can't possibly remove all the Hazel's there are. She can't ever—no one can ever—run away. Because our selves are too sloppy: we get left around all over the place, and it's simply impossible to collect any of that back together. When we run away, we don't take that, we leave it. And that's what Hazel has to face. All the Hazel's she left there, that she thought maybe she'd taken away from the place. But that are still there, today, left there by her and so existing and appearing and being in the people who are left and in the place itself. That's why I went there in the first place, isn't it? To find the Hazels she left behind, among them the Hazel I love. Love?*

When I arrived at the home, I went straight back into the kitchen. I suppose I needed to stand for a few moments and breathe in the air of institutional cooking, the sicky wet smell of over-boiled vegetables and pasty potatoes. Like some inversion of a diver, resurfaced, who must lie in the chamber for a little time in order to effect the transition back into the vapid, wispy, insubstantial air, I had gradually to put back on the thick weight of this element of *nursing home* to which I had returned, before I could engage in naked encounter with Hazel. So I stood there, in the middle of the glaucous pressings of taste and texture, squeezed out of all these ingredients into the supersaturated atmosphere, where eating had somehow switched places with breathing, the eating now a tasteless, rhythmic, semi-conscious behavior, while the breathing had become suffused with taste and effort, glut and queasiness. And I waited, quite deliberately, until I no longer stifled instinctively at this invasion of odor and weight, but began to forget its presence and to ingest it as though normal.

Then I swung around and drove myself through the door into the blazing explosion of conservatorium. Groping toward Hazel.

And at once all the imagined meetings flew away and I was left standing uncertain in all that light, with no possibility for a facile explanation. Because I hadn't expected this: Hazel was not alone. She was sitting and talking with another woman, a stranger to me, and I had no idea even how to drop in my line under these circumstances. I felt an immediate tug of jealousy: *What's she doing talking with someone in my place? Just what does she think she's up to?*

So the roles reversed: Hazel grabbed the line and took over the play—the snatch and pull and the release *let him run a little*, then the tension, setting the drag, drawing him in to you, letting him go again, two fingers lying on the line itself and feeling his tension, his gathering despair, the dawning recognition that would lead to the final understanding that it is easier to go along with the tugging line than to attempt escape.

"Andrew," she greeted. "Come meet Opal. Opal is from Jackson County. What do you think of that? She's the first person I've seen in fifty years who knows what *lugs* are. What do you think of that?" She looked me over. I felt as though she already knew everything, as though she were merely sizing me up to see how much sport she might get out of me.

"Hazel," I said. Then recognizing my own rudeness, "Hello Opal," I said in the direction of the faceless shape sitting next to her. "I'm pleased to meet you. It's wonderful that Hazel has found someone like you."

Hazel smiled at me, savoring some sort of humor she'd discovered in my discomfort. "Opal's never been to Shelton's Trace, though. So we still have our own secrets, don't we?"

"What?" I said. "Did you..."

"Write any more? Oh no. I stopped writing after you left. I don't believe I ever looked around this room before then. And lo and behold, here's Opal. It makes you wonder, doesn't it, how many Opals have just walked through here and out the door while I've been sitting here writing."

She looks older. Something more has happened. She's gotten old. She's dying. She's dying. I found myself in a state of absolute tongue-tied despair. At that moment, I realized that I'd never quite found the young Hazel, the lover, on my journey south. And now I had returned to find even the old Hazel gone. And this garrulous dying old woman in her place. And this Opal. *She's already executing her punishment upon me. I thought I'd be in trouble with her after I told her about my trip, about George. But she's ahead of me, already exacting revenge. And running away again. This time from me. From me.*

"Did you have something you wanted to tell me?" she asked. "Excuse me, Opal. I'm being rude. But Andrew and I may have *some private business to settle. You see, we've both been to Shelton's Trace, haven't we?"*

Was she speaking in figures here, or did she somehow know—using that unerring sense with which she seemed equipped—that I had been up that cove? I never had the nerve to ask her outright and her answers in our subsequent conversations never quite settled the question. Now that she's gone, I suppose I'll never know what she knew of the frenzied infatuation that drove me down there the first time. I suppose it doesn't matter anymore.

At any rate, Opal excused herself, having already been excused by Hazel, and left us to our usual selves. Except, still, I had that manifest sensation that nothing was any longer as usual, that Hazel was fading, folding-up, going from me. That she had aged in a way beyond years in that short time that I had been down there trying to rediscover—by sheer force of some kind of reiterative presence—her youth. Irony enough.

"How are you Hazel? You okay?" I asked, hoping that perhaps I might hear of a touch of the flu or a cold that had temporarily sapped her strength. Some explanation at least so that my graver worries, premonitions, whatever they were, could surface and dissipate. "You look as though you haven't been feeling too well. You okay?"

"I've seen better days, and that's certain," she said. "But I'm puttin' up with these." What a relief to see the old smile. Was she back? "It's nice to see you Andrew," she said, reaching out the familiar, crooked fingers. "Did you have a nice trip?"

"I went to Shelton's Trace, Hazel," I said in a rush, taking her hand, not so much to comfort her as to have hold of some buoyant object to hold me up as I swam along. Talking in a flurry. May just as well get it said and start picking up the pieces. "I went down there. I wanted to see your..."

"Yes," she said. "Shelton's Trace. You went on down there, and..."

"Yes," I said. And now the difficult part. Like you'd planned that day's journey down to the last step, the final inch. But you knew, too, that there was that one stream to cross, right in the middle, that couldn't be planned for. But only had to be gotten to and encountered in a rush, swept aside in a spate of action until, on the far side, you could get back to planning and measuring again. "Hazel, I found George. I saw him. George. I talked to him. Hazel, he's alive. He's well. He..."

"Yes," she said, almost dreamily. "Course he is." *Then her eyes locked back on to here and now and sparked for a moment.* "George? Andrew. You didn't..."

I put my other hand atop our two, a gesture of earnestness. "No. No, Hazel. No, I didn't tell anyone. No one knew that I know. You, them, anything at all about..."

"You didn't say anything," *she said. She wasn't asking anymore. She was confirming, as though this fact needed her own pronouncement before it could become certain, true.* "You told them nothing," *she said.*

"Nothing, Hazel. I know..."

"But George," *she said.* "You saw George."

"And T.R.," I said. "T.R. is there, too."

"T.R.," *she said.*

And she began to cry. She pulled her hand away from mine, turned her bent body away, toward the window, and wept, steadily and quietly, leaning her head to one side and letting fall a lifetime of tears.

FIELD NOTES: INTERVIEW—GEORGE TAYLOR
May 14, 1998

Why will I just keep on asking myself about Hazel? Well. Well, I don't know. It ain't worth thinking much about, is it? She's gone and she ain't never going to hear my voice. Even if she could from where she is right now, heaven, or wherever, she most surely would have answered by now if she was fixing to. It's been a right

346

smart of time that I been asking her *why*. Ain't it?

So I don't reckon there's any answer to a question like that. Oh there's times yet I wake up in the night and find myself reaching my arm over to put around her, you know. Like she never did leave. Like maybe she done got up to check on something out in the front, and when I woke and found her gone I went back into a dream that she'd gone for good. But not really. Really she'd just checked on that thing, whatever it was, and had come back into the bed. And so, this time, all I need to do is throw out my arm about her like always, and she'll be there. It seems that real, you know? But she ain't, of course. And so instead of swinging my arm around her body and drawing her to me, I'm just swinging that arm through the empty air. Just waving goodbye.

But some of those nights you'll wake up and before you can get a grip on yourself, you find yourself saying it right out loud. Whispering, just to see. *Hazel?* Not to see if she did come back, because you know she ain't never really left. Just to see whether or not she's yet awake: *Hazel? Hazel?* That's all.

JOURNAL OF HAZEL TAYLOR
July 24, 1998

And has it all been a failure, nothing but loss? Was Andrew right that day? that I'd used everyone? I was the monomaniac, bent on acquiring more of life than any of us has a right to demand? I don't know.

It is certainly true that I cherish those days in the hills more than any other time of my life. I look upon them as I suppose all old folks look on their youth, through a thin veil of golden gauze. But it is true enough, yet. I see us all sitting in the room and cracking walnuts by the firelight, and Daddy making us feel that this is the cleverest activity in the whole world. Or a very early time, with Rosie, when we lay on our bellies and craned our heads downward into the little stream that ran out back of her place and looked for the water nymphs. I told her they were there and if you were still enough and let the stream rush by your eyes without moving them, the nymphs would rise to the top and sing. And, of course, Rosie saw them. But of that day mostly I remember the cold damp breath of the ground on my belly, through the thin cotton, and the smell of close water on the wings of your nose.

And later, George and I coming in from suckering and he trying to kiss me and I said to be careful not to get the gum on each other, even though each of us was covered over already with gum. So he just grabbed me and said he was 'agoing to rub his gum all over me and he wanted my gum on him, and I said let's trade gum and we started in. But it felt just awful and George said, "Are you enjoying this as much as I am?" And later, "I reckon tromping-up a slew of yaller jackets ain't as much fun as you think it's going to be neither."

And I do believe that I would have lost all of this if I had stayed. I would have come to resent and disparage the young woman who could play like that. Or set her work aside and pick up a book. The only remembrance of that Hazel I would allow might be a slight silence, before I came out with a bitter dismissal, *Well them times is sure enough changed.*

But I left, and we are all still there in the gauzy glow.

And is this gain or is this loss? And what might I have done otherwise? Look at Noah Kersin, a young and foolish man who behaved exactly as he must have thought he was supposed to behave, for he certainly watched himself in order to make certain he lived up to his model. And was this evil in him, or was it foolishness, youth? And did I do right in fighting him off, sending him reeling and dying off the mountain that day? I could have submitted. It would have saved his life.

Oh you will say that actions never succeed if the act itself is an abetting of sin. Or that in saving him, I would only have confirmed his distorted behavior, and so I would have saved him only into further degradations. Perhaps. But he died at my hands because I refused a stupidly clutching caress. Shouldn't I have been willing to trade a moment of shame and pain for a life? How many other women have done just that? How many?

Or Hastie. Oh, Hastie, who opened up a warm nook in my side and left it burning with grief and loss. Should I have seen that she was too susceptible to me? That I should have treated myself as a carrier of some disease, a disease she had never been exposed to and so never built up any of the hard immunity most of us simply take for granted? And took her into town and left her spread out naked and butchered by a man—a world—a God who had become jealous of her and simply flung her away.

Or Saint or George or the entire curve and range of mountain and hollow that grew me into a young woman of remarkable intelligence and sensitivity—oh yes, I know that much—and deserved to be paid back for the gracious gift? Ought I not have stayed there simply as recompense to the place that bore me?

And I asked Andrew about all of this, today, and the questions seemed to sadden him. And I asked him what was wrong. And he said, "Hazel, I think they have all lost. Everyone in the story, including the young woman in the photograph, Hazel Tighrow, who wanted to be who she could be. Because they were all looking for something they didn't get, or couldn't hang onto. No one got what they wanted. And here we are, a thousand miles away, looking at all of this as though we'd just seen it on a screen and we've come out dissatisfied with the ending. How absurd."

"Because, Andrew, it ended seventy years ago," I said. And I felt stronger. I felt that I had been right, or at least that I had known something of the truth, all along. "And of course we are losers. Life is loss. That's the problem today, isn't it? Everyone wants to be a winner. And there aren't any. If we realized that each of us is doomed to lose, the world would go better—because we'd become so precious to one another, soothing the wounds that lead to the inevitable loss. Defeat is our best mode."

"What are you saying? That…"

"That if we'd recognized ourselves, recognized the inexorable truth of loss, I never would have had to leave in the first place. Because we would all be so much more ready to see and to understand, to nurture those aches and passions so that they wouldn't die so soon, but might stand a chance against the pain and the drudgery. Had we recognized loss, we could have slain that Hazel I was destined to become. But we didn't, we couldn't. Perhaps no one ever can."

ANDREW KAYER

But it wasn't enough, not yet. Because I had been there and had seen George and T.R. and had drunk in some of their own memory and regret. And I had told them nothing. Nothing of the Hazel who remained, alive, in my own place, this Chicago that had bundled her away, out of their sight, for so long. And I felt an obligation, now, to George, as well. As though my very faithfulness to Hazel's secret had implicated me in the original betrayal, so that my own hand had been accomplice in seventy years of pain.

So I concocted another plan, that I saw might provide the final resolution of both narratives as well as a way for me to take a direct hand in the story and simultaneously to release myself from it. End it.

"I think it's time for you to go back," I said.

"No," she said. And, "No," again.

It was late afternoon, late winter, late snow falling. And it was getting late for Hazel. She knew she was sinking, and I could see the knowing in her eyes. Knowing and wanting, but then a fierce resistance to her own expression. That repetition of *No* set in those same eyes, like bars, through whose interstices the longing reached through. *Like hands on prison bars,* I thought, and then *Oh Christ, you're starting to talk just like her*, though, in truth, I hadn't said any of this aloud.

"You won't have to go alone," I said. "I'll take you." I reached out what I hoped was an encouraging hand and laid it on hers.

"I don't need you to help me," she said, softly, at the same time pulling her hand out from under mine. She pointed her long, index finger, crooked and bent with arthritis, at me, and her voice seemed to run along its wavering length. "Because I could go, would go, myself, if I was to go. But I'm not, Andrew. Haven't you been listening to me? Haven't you looked at them papers?"

Them papers, I thought. The mountains were creeping back into her voice, as her body faded, weakened. She pronounced *papers* a little more like *pipers* than she had before. *She's going home in spite of herself,* I thought. *She really wants to go. She just don't know it*—this time, hearing George's voice in my mind, and trying to shake it off.

"Don't you see, Hazel, that you can go back, that you can make it right, return and bring everything you've been thinking and feeling, and the conclusions you've come to, even the reasons you left in the first place, back to him? That he's waiting for you?"

"He's got the most of me he could ever have, now. You read them papers? You can't..." and I heard the *cain't* like an evocation of the place, and I thought again, *you aren't even going to be here in a few days, you're going back home, like it or not,* and then, *damn you, Hazel.* So I didn't hear the rest of what she was saying, and I had to ask, "What'd you say?"

"I've spent these years trying to tell it, trying to get it down so that it can be seen, so it won't just go away," she said. "Like I did. Like I will. Can't you see that?" (*Cain't,* again, and I found myself willing her to stop these soft, tanging accents so I could listen. Because I was hearing George, again, too: *Oh, she's alive as you or me. Maybe more.*)

"the writing and the placing, putting it out of me and on paper where it can be in its own place, not just here, in me, where it will only disappear, like I already done. And you want me to go back. Go back, now? When there's nobody left to be me? Nothing left to bring back there at all but an old woman who has decided at the last that she'll receive some balm or solace from returning to the place she spurned? To the man she walked away from, young and strong? And bring back to him an old woman who we all know will have come there just to go away again?"

"What?" I said. It wasn't a question, but a demand, ultimatum. I could feel the frustration building. *She isn't going to go. She's going to say all kinds of things that don't mean anything except that she isn't going to go, isn't going. She'll die here, and she won't listen to the obvious fact that she wants to go home. Hell, she is going—listen to her talk—whether she wills or not. Damn her.* And then, again, "What! Leave again! What are you talking about, Hazel?"

"I'm dying, Andrew" she said. "You know that. I know that. If I go back now, it will be only to bring to George a woman he lost seventy years ago. And he'll take her in—I know George, yet—and he'll forgive and open up himself and take her in. And then she'll die. And she'll have left again. He'll have lost her again. Don't you see?"

"How do you know?" I said. "How is it you know everything, Hazel? Maybe, just maybe, you ain't—aren't—going to die, damn it." She looked at me reprovingly, but I chose to ignore her. I was destroying her argument, debating soundly, putting a good analytical mind to work on her hardheadedness. "You might get down there and feel much better, and get along fine and have years and years with George. How the hell do you know?"

"Don't lie to me just to win the point..." she said, smiling. "You...(*And now she's back. She's the Hazel who has walked away and left all that mountain talking back in the past somewhere. She has escaped the encroaching of the old Hazel, the old mountain, George. She has gotten away. And she's not going back.*) "...just what you think ought to happen, but you're thinking out of some movie you once saw, with the parted lovers falling into each other's arms at the last..." (*Oh yes, she's back*) "...the way it really is, not like the movies, or even all the books I built my life on. The books that made me into a runaway. Not at all. Because it was the laurel, too, and you don't understand laurel."

"Now you're talking non..."

"Because laurel ought only to blossom and fall once. It shouldn't come back the way it does, only to leave again, and again. Because if it left once, the leaving would be another kind of presence, the absence always calling up those cups of laurel every time you look and they're not there. You can't..." (*"Can't"* this time) "...leave it, because you never left anything, never lost anything. You don't know that life strips away everything you ever had in order to make you feel it even more. Oh, I don't need to return to George. He's already got more of me than he wants, every time he looks up that hill and finds me gone. And you want me to return so I can die and leave him again? I didn't think you thought I could be so cruel."

"But you said—no, listen to me!—you said you had to write it down so it wouldn't just be you. You said that. And so if you need to put it somewhere, why don't you take it back home, put it there, so someone who cares can see that it's something else, not you? Take it back and have it written on your damn gravestone so that everybody, anybody you want, can walk by and say, 'Yonder's ole Hazel. She ain't here no more. And so we don't have to suffer her presence because she's absent. Instead we can celebrate her absence because now this here tombstone is present, and we may not know what it is, but we know for certain that it ain't her.' Okay?"

She was silent. She tucked her finger, that had pointed waveringly at me all along, into the bedclothes, where she seemed to stretch herself, like a child waking or getting ready for sleep. She looked away from me, turning those longing, dying, fiercely resistant eyes away from me. There was a fly buzzing against the window sill, and she turned her head to look at it. A fly.

"What's a fly doing out this time of year?" she said.

"Damn it, Hazel," I said.

She turned her eyes back on mine. They were different, now. She stretched herself again, languidly, almost sensuously.

"You're right," she said. There was a note of quiet surprise in her voice. "You're right." Her voice was soft. Not mountain-soft, but close-soft, the way you'd soothe a child, or a mourner. "I believe you're beginning to understand. And this time, you're right. You know that?"

"You're damn right I'm right," I said, too loud, too harsh, against her supple tones, thinking *What did I do, say? She's going? I did it?* And now I pointed at her. My finger looked pink and fat, like an infant's in the air that still held the aura of her long, crooked chronicle of a hand. "We can start down in a few days. We'll just…"

"No," She said, peremptory now. Scolding. "No. Not 'we.' Just you."

"Me? What?"

"Just you. You and my book. Because you're right. It needs to be down there where it can announce my passing. They need an artifact, a tomb, with something written on it to end that awful presence. Because you're right: not me, you see. Not me."

"Hazel…"

"Just take it. Take the book. I have a letter too. Take them and give them to George. I must have wrote them all for him anyway. To try and explain to him. So they need to be down there. So he can look at something besides me, besides my memory always there whenever he looks up that hill. You're right. And now you've got to do it."

"Hazel," I said, sighed. "Please. Go home. Go back where you belong. Take the book, if you want. Take anything you want. We can buy a goddam tombstone and take it down there with us, if that'll make you feel better, make you feel like you've erased yourself sufficiently to satisfy whatever weird…"

"No. The book. And the letter. I don't need to go home. I need to leave home. And George don't need me there. He needs me gone."

So I went. Went back to Hazel with my acquiescence, like a basket of flowers to the dying woman, thinking bitterly, *I feel like the goddam make-a-wish foundation*, the bitterness and sarcasm covering the realization that *this is really going to be the end. You will never see her again after you leave to fill that wish.*

She was composed and pretty, in her usual way, but with something of a glint in her eye. Victory? Success? Or relief, at having made this decision, whatever it really was, and having come to some sort of peace with this life, this death. She was gradually failing, and I thought of the useless cliché of the dying ember, brightening up in final throbs of life, this look in her eyes more the announcement of the end than a return to energy and life. She started in as though she'd read my thoughts, not even saying hello, but already telling it, like she'd drawn breath to speak before I even came into the room.

"I recall when our old dog, Tanner, died, up on the Creek. He'd had a hard time, suddenly, caught up with some kind of seizure, *tossing a fit*, Daddy said. And it laid him low, so that he couldn't walk or eat, or even turn over. He just lay there, for days. And I lay by him, whenever I could. I slept next to his warm, breathing body, and I spoke to him. And he gradually seemed to come out of it. One morning he'd lift his head just a bit, and I'd pet him and praise him. And the next, maybe, he'd lay his head flat out on my body. And I knew he was going to be okay when he rolled over on his back for me to scratch his belly. Because that was a gesture, you know, selfish. It was for him, not just for me. So I knew he'd be up in a day or two.

"And, sure enough, he got better. Not just better, but all of a sudden, now, he was like a puppy, romping and playing, pouncing around on sticks, snatching them up and waving his head in the air, so proud, as if to say *look what I've got*, like a puppy again. And it was a new chance for us both, both to see and touch each other again, only this time knowing that it was all evanescent, all bright love blowing out like a candle, doomed, all of us, from the start. And so we rolled and wallowed and scratched and played in this gift of time, me and Tanner, knowing that death is the mother of beauty, as the poet says. We loved out another lifetime in those days, me and Tanner, romping against that tick of time that won't never stop, both of us so happy that he was all well again.

"And then he died, a week after. Just lay down, again, just like last time. And this time, I was holding him, and he pulled back away from me, he stretched back his head and curved in his back, like a swimmer diving into a deep pool, drawing himself out and away, and he died. And was gone.

"But I told Daddy about that past week, how Tanner was like a young puppy, so happy and playing and how we just had such a good week with each other. And how I had thought that Tanner was happy because he was all better. But then he died.

"'It was the knowing that done it,' Daddy said. 'I seen it before, with all kinds of critters. It's like the Indian summer comes in the Fall, like the whole world knows that the year is a'dyin' and so it turns on the warmth for a week to give itself one more chance to be nice and to watch you all out a running around in your bare feet. 'Cause it's a'going, and it knows so. Just like that with ole Tanner knowing he was a'going and so givin' you 'uns both a Indian summer for a week. So you all kindly got that to have and think on when the dyin' comes. I seen it before, Hazie. It's all right. You understand?'"

She looked at me with that smile and that light, and she reached out a pale yellowish parcel. This time it was an ancient flour sack, its letters so faded as to look unfocused, like they were covered by a depth of water. I felt the journal inside.

"You said a letter, too?"

"It's in there. I wrote it and sealed it and never sent it. I've had it for years. Now I guess you're right. It's time to send it on down, and get rid of myself." She actually laughed. "Get me done with."

"Don't talk like that, Hazel. You make me feel like an undertaker," I said.

She reached out and lay her old hand on my arm. Her skin felt cool and dry, like paper.

"Not an undertaker. Call it a messenger. From the lost and found." She smiled again. "Now git," she said. "I got things to do, places to get to. You get that on down yonder." She rolled over, away from me, her back a white curve of sheet and gown, with the long stretch of bare back, where the gown gaped open, her shoulder blade showing its curved edge, like a young girl's.

"Git," she said, into the wall.

XI.

ANDREW KAYER

And so I found myself again following the changing roadcuts south, moving through the blueblack slough of the coal belt—this time at night—with the heavy shadows of decayed tipples and loaders appearing as cavernous maws rather than solid bulks, distended jaws swung open at the mouths of the narrow serpentine hollows you knew were there but could only sense as a grayed absence in the grainy dark.

But no overnight personal limbo of alcohol and that routine fury at discovering the morning's raw consequences, the recursive accusations—*You idiot, why did you do that?*—as much a habit, addiction, as the drinking itself. None of that this time, because the presence of the journal making its final journey added a kind of desperate haste to the driving. It was as though there were a coffin in the back seat. And in this case, it contained not just a corpse, but a body already cut up, autopsied, and crudely stitched back together. A journal no longer in its binding, its solid integument of glue and signature and end pages but reconstructed into loose fascicles tied with fragile wisps of ribbon. Like a body that has been too long held back from its rest, violated the way only an inquest can violate, acquiring this need for haste out of the very deliberateness that has held it forth.

"Only here the medical examiner was the deceased herself," I said aloud, speaking, perhaps, to the package lying at arm's reach. "Victim, murderer, detective, coroner, prosecutor, defense, judge, and jury." I snatched a look at my own tired eyes in the rear-view. "Busy woman," I said.

And, mid-morning, a reunion with Bessie, shared coffee and a litany of sicknesses and deaths afflicting people who, for me, never existed in the first place: *Old John Dilton, he passed on last week, he'd been sick a right smart, it's a blessing that is, and his girl had that tumor removed ten year back, that cancer that's a awful way, my Daddy died must be fifteen year now, he got so bad he couldn't swaller his own spit, I tell my kids that ever happens to me you just brew up a pot of this coffee with about a half cup of arsenic a' lead, put me out of my misery, you sure y'all don't want a sweet roll with that coffee, them sweet rolls is homemade.* The talk, as gruesome as it might seem, serving instead to soothe and relax us both. Not to humanize these people—John Dilton and his poor daughter and Bessie's dad, Bessie's kids—but somehow to characterize yourself, draw you in to a circle of community where all these people cared about you, whether or not you gave a damn at all about them. And where, within that circle, you and Bessie could share something of warmth and life. Because there is something oddly comforting in the shared assumption that all life is gruesome, because the suffering and death is no tragedy fit for the mythic stage, but is everyday life, fit for coffee and sweetrolls. *It don't much matter where you bury me*—can you hear T.R.'s voice?— *Hell, you can just spatch me anywhere you got room. Prop me up in the corner if you want. Long as I can get to the frigidaire.*

And Bessie has greeted me like a dear friend, and what could be warmer, nearer, more comfortable than to share these everyday tales of sickness and death? "Because," Hazel said once, "You need to ask yourself, *Why are sickness and death so grotesque to me? Why do I insist that they belong among the hushed, extraordinary things, when they are the most common*

359

of events, shared, ultimately by every last one of us. Doesn't the grotesqueness lie in this pretense that they are tragic, awesome events? We only wish that were true.

And then on up the hill in the bright high sun, to George's house, and up the soggy wooden steps (that loose step, though, nailed tight this time) to the narrow porch and wide open entry, completely without screen or even sill, and into the close center of the parlor, George sitting in a chair, facing me, as though he'd been waiting this entire fortnight for my reappearance. And, in front of him, back to the door, another, empty, cane-seated chair seeming to be similarly expectant, waiting for me. *I wonder if Hazel caned that seat,* I thought, absurdly, because *Of course not. That would have been sixty-five years ago. No cane seat would last so long. So who did it? George, himself? Certainly not.* And then a rushing, almost shameful realization, *He bought it that way, bought it already caned.* And I realized that Hazel had been right. She was the expert observer and commentator for a place that no longer existed, a place tinged with the romantic hazed regret we reserve for places that may never have been there in the first place. *So what is it? Is it that maybe Hazel has been lying to me all along, and so I'm standing before this man, about to give him a chronicle of a time and a place and people—Hazel, and himself, even—who never existed at all? And he will read her excruciatingly selected and rearranged text and he will pause and look off toward Asheville, along the stream bottom to the highway and down to the broadening fields, now choked with kudzu—a plant Hazel has neither seen nor even dreamed of—and he will say, "What in the heavenly days?"*

But there is nothing for it; I must go on through with this delivery, if not for George's enlightenment then in recognition and endorsement of Hazel's bid for understanding. And peace. "If that's what she wants," I heard myself say.

"What's that?" George said.

Have you ever looked at something for so long, so fixedly

that you have ceased to see it? Not because you lost interest or your attention wandered, no. Because, in fact, you remained rapt, fascinated by this thing, wanting to know it fully, to incorporate it as fully as possible into your own life, your world. This is love and this can be the terrible, startling ending of love. Because the man sees the woman and he finds her more than attractive, compelling. And he looks and he experiences and he discovers that he wants to be with her always, always to have this woman within his sight. And this is love. But love tumbles, not because the gazer becomes inured to the object, not at all. This love ends precisely because he can't stop looking, can't govern that desire to see, and so from being the sight he loves best, she begins to elude him. You know this: because it is common experience to discover that you can't conjure up the image of a person you love passionately. You try to summon that picture of her into your mind and it won't come, won't compose itself into her. And so perhaps we all disappear from one another at the moment that we truly begin to love, to desire. We're gone like Hazel.

I had told him, as best I could, in the best of a measured, gentle, deliberate voice as I could muster. About Hazel, her life, her being. My own connection to this painfully personal story. Because I felt I owed an apology to this man, who had borne so much, without any possibility for any hope that he might be able to do the least thing about it. And myself, who had bumped into him as antecedent to some fulfilling, pleasant acquaintance, this wonderful old woman I met. As though I had cynically profited from his pain and grief. And then, perhaps the most difficult, to put an end to the story, to Hazel, herself.

"And now she's dying, and she wants you to know some of this. She wants to give you some writing that will explain," and I stopped short.

"Explain," he said, as though he'd never heard such a word,

was trying out the feel and sound of its syllables against his tongue. And me: Explain? How ever to explain all of this? And to a man who had spent his entire life—seventy years…seventy—trying to settle upon just one word of satisfactory explanation. That you now tell him you've brought him, arranged and tied in bowed pastel ribbons? How dare you? How dare she? Or is this what she meant by cruelty?

"She's dying," I tried again, dogged. "She's gone this time, anyway, for good. And she wants you to know about…"

He held it with both hands in front of his body, raising it slightly as though it were a communion wafer, or a tray with a visiting card on it, or as though he were trying to present it, give it, to someone else. It quivered minutely in his unsteady hand. I thought for a moment he would drop it and I made a peremptory start forward to help him, as though the journal was glass and might shatter if he turned it loose. He let it down into his lap and waved me off with one hand.

"Well," he said, sighed. "Well," again.

He raised himself painfully from his chair, turned his back to me, and crossed toward the dresser with the excruciating slowness that comes with extreme age, pain, or wisdom, the journal again held out in front, like a presentation. When he arrived at the bureau, he set it on top and pulled open the upper left drawer. He fumbled a moment, and then drew out a folded cotton fabric that I knew instantly was a feed sack that had been laundered over and over until it had attained a softness and a kind of patina, a compounding of quietude and wear. As threadbare as it was, it was a thing of significance, for something lay hidden, a secret, in its pliant folds.

He delicately removed some hand-sized object from the cotton and placed it into the drawer. Then he held one corner and let the weight of the cloth itself release it from its folds in a soft unfurling, aided and completed by the quiver of his hand. He squared it up and carefully let it drape over the journal. Methodically, patiently, he folded the journal within—lifting it to wrap beneath it, like you would swaddle an infant. He smoothed down its surfaces, folded up the ends, smoothed these, then reached down and slid out the bureau's center drawer. It made a sound like a sharp, harsh intake of air. He settled the package into the drawer, half caressing and half pushing on it, the way you would tamp down soil around a seedling or a grave. Then the drawer exhaled as he slid it closed. He straightened himself, and rubbed his left hand along the seam of his overall leg as a shadow— something partly blocking the light from the doorway—dropped a deep reddish blue across most of his back, and rippled the mirror above the dresser.

He turned around toward me and groped a hand out for the back of his chair.

"Well," he said.

The shadow shifted again, suffusing his face, closing off the bright sunlight. And only now I know that I hadn't understood what Hazel had tried to tell me, that last day, about Tanner, the dying dog and the last week of loving and being together. But now, the shadow, covering George, drew his eyes slowly upwards, away from my seated form and, suddenly intensely, squinting, seeking focus, rapt, looking up over my left shoulder, squinting and questioning, then, suddenly sure, recognizing her, he sighed the two, lost syllables of her lost, lovely name.

"Hazel?" he said.

And from the shadowed doorway, behind me, came the liquid, whispered response.

"George," she said.

Richard Hood is a musician, photographer, and writer, living in Greene County, Tennessee.

HoodsBooks.com

BOOKS

On the following pages are a few
more great titles from the
Down & Out Books publishing family.

For a complete list of books and to
sign up for our newsletter,
go to DownAndOutBooks.com.

Avenging Angelenos
A Sisters in Crime/Los Angeles Anthology
Sarah M. Chen, Wrona Gall, and
Pamela Samuels Young, editors

Down & Out Books
June 2021
978-1-64396-204-7

With an introduction by Frankie Y. Bailey and eleven original stories by Avril Adams, Paula Bernstein, Hal Bodner, Jenny Carless, LH Dillman, Gay Toltl Kinman, Melinda Loomis, Kathy Norris, Peggy Rothschild, Meredith Taylor, and Laurel Wetzork.

NEW YORK TIMES BESTSELLING AUTHOR

Moonlight Sonata
A Dick Moonlight PI Thriller
Vincent Zandri

Down & Out Books
July 2021
978-1-64396-220-7

When a savvy and sexy literary agent by the name of Suzanne Bonchance lures Dick Moonlight into searching for her missing star client—the boozing, poet laureate, Roger Walls—the PI with the piece of bullet in his brain finds himself waist-deep in a whole lot of trouble.

But when a hot MFA in Writing student who claims to know Walls personally comes to his rescue, Moonlight not only becomes smitten with her charm, he falls head over heels with a young woman he barely knows.

Stalker Stalked
Lee Matthew Goldberg

All Due Respect, an imprint of
Down & Out Books
September 2021
978-1-64396-229-0

What happens when the stalker gets stalked?

A fan stalks a reality show personality only to discover that she's being stalked as well, and learns the only way to beat her stalker is to use her own prowess to outsmart them at their own game.

S-10 to Valhalla
Ken Teutsch

Shotgun Honey, an imprint of
Down & Out Books
July 2021
978-1-64396-113-2

It's Saturday, and Nashville lowlife Jake Croom needs money for the beer joints. But his seemingly straightforward plan to steal some sends him ricocheting through the lives of everyone from bat-wielding grandmothers to down-and-out typesetters to inadvertent Robert E. Lee impersonators, violently knocking them all into various unexpected pockets in life's pool table.

Meanwhile Jake, fortified by tequila, unidentified pharmaceuticals and a thirty-five-dollar pistol, caroms toward his own final collision with a counterfeit Valkyrie and a bona fide hail of bullets.

Made in the USA
Coppell, TX
14 October 2021